L.A. Rex

L.A. Rex

WILL BEALL

RIVERHEAD BOOKS

a member of

Penguin Group (USA) Inc.

New York

2006

RIVERHEAD BOOKS
Published by the Penguin Group
Penguin Group (USA) Inc., 375 Hudson Street, New York, New York 10014, USA •
Penguin Group (Canada), 90 Eglinton Avenue East, Suite 700, Toronto, Ontario M4P 2Y3,
Canada (a division of Pearson Penguin Canada Inc.) • Penguin Books Ltd, 80 Strand,
London WC2R 0RL, England • Penguin Ireland, 25 St Stephen's Green, Dublin 2, Ireland
(a division of Penguin Books Ltd) • Penguin Group (Australia), 250 Camberwell Road,
Camberwell, Victoria 3124, Australia (a division of Pearson Australia Group Pty Ltd) •
Penguin Books India Pvt Ltd, 11 Community Centre, Panchsheel Park, New Delhi–110 017,
India • Penguin Group (NZ), Cnr Airborne and Rosedale Roads, Albany, Auckland 1310,
New Zealand (a division of Pearson New Zealand Ltd) • Penguin Books (South Africa)
(Pty) Ltd, 24 Sturdee Avenue, Rosebank, Johannesburg 2196, South Africa

Penguin Books Ltd, Registered Offices:
80 Strand, London WC2R 0RL, England

Library of Congress Cataloging-in-Publication Data

Beall, Will.
L.A. rex / Will Beall.
p.   cm.
ISBN 1-59448-926-2
1. Police—Fiction.   2. Criminals—Fiction.   3. Los Angeles (Calif.) Police Dept.—Fiction.
4. Los Angeles (Calif.)—Fiction.   I. Title.
PS3602.E243L   2006   2006023264
813'.6—dc22

Printed in the United States of America
1   3   5   7   9   10   8   6   4   2

Book design by Stephanie Huntwork

This is a work of fiction. Names, characters, places, and incidents either are the product of the
author's imagination or are used fictitiously, and any resemblance to actual persons, living or
dead, businesses, companies, events, or locales is entirely coincidental.

While the author has made every effort to provide accurate telephone numbers and Internet ad-
dresses at the time of publication, neither the publisher nor the author assumes any responsibility
for errors, or for changes that occur after publication. Further, the publisher does not have any
control over and does not assume any responsibility for author or third-party websites or their
content.

This book is dedicated to my adoptive family,

the men and women of 77th,

who ride to the sound of the guns.

L.A. Rex

PROLOGUE

A gang of fools wanted Wizard tits up. Those creepy-ass headhunters from Mara Salvatrucha had buried a statue of the Blessed Virgin upside down and sworn to drink his blood. And shermed-up *mayate* gunners in every mudfucked hood from here to East Oak Town drove around with Wizard's picture tucked into the sun visor. Even the Nazi Saddle Tramps, those shit-stinking bikers from the high desert, would have skinned him alive—he'd heard stories of caves outside Lancaster with human hides stretched like Japanese screens. Over the years, Wizard had spilled enough blood on the street and in the yard to give them all kinds of reasons, but none of that mattered anymore. All his would-be *asesinos* were officially assed out. Wizard was protected. Only God could kill him now and even God wanted no part of the Mexican Mafia.

Cesar Salcido (nom de guerre: Wizard) had been just another *sureño* pistolero from Florencia Trece, serving out his time in Tehachapi for armed robbery, when his destiny arrived on the bus from County. El Viejo, the gray-whiskered *Eme* cat who ran the whole enchilada inside, sent a kite down the bloc about a snitch on the transfer from county lockup. Wizard wasn't doing anything special that afternoon, so he melted a container of deodorant, melted and rolled it, melted and rolled it, until he had a weapon resembling a plastic icicle.

The secret shame of the California Penal System: most cons didn't know how to really stick somebody. They'd just bum-rush you at chow

and shank you the way a teenage boy fucks—with that same furtive pis-
ton motion—punch a dozen leaking holes in you while you're waiting for
your scoop of powdered mashed potatoes. Sure, it was messy. A lot of
guys lost kidneys, and some wound up wearing bags, but most of them
survived. Stupid, Wizard thought. Why bother sticking some fool if
you're not going to put him down for keeps?

Wizard lay for the snitch in the showers, waited for the guy to tilt his
head back to rinse that delousing crap out of his hair, and drove his shank
into the guy's eye. No official witnesses (this was prison, after all), but
there was a shitload of Polaroids—photos of the dead snitch with Wizard's shank buried to the hilt in his ruined left eye, blood running like
tears down his cheek, and his scalp weirdly tented where the tip of the
shank had poked clean through the back of his skull. The pictures traded
around the prison like baseball cards. Screws and cons alike were relieved
to see the snitch taken out before his presence threw the whole place out
of whack and touched off a riot. And just for restoring the prison eco-
system's delicate equilibrium, they gave Wizard a year in the hole. Wizard
figured that injustice put him in the company of Gandhi and Mandela,
but he couldn't get those faggots at Amnesty International excited about
his case.

Wizard was still raw about the whole thing when he paroled four years
later. Then he found a limo waiting for him outside the prison gate and all
was forgiven. Joe Carcosa rolled down a tinted window and beckoned
Wizard, patting the leather seat next to him. Wizard slid into the limo
next to *Jose Fucking Carcosa,* the Dude himself, *Eme*'s Hombre Número
Uno in the City of Angels. Wizard leaned down to kiss the ring, but Carcosa stopped him, pouring Wizard a shot of Patrón. The two men drank
to their families and to Aztlán, Wizard already thinking this was worth a
year in the hole. Then Carcosa made Wizard the offer of a lifetime.

Carcosa said they needed a South Central tax collector and Wizard
was their man. "It's your hood," Carcosa said. "You know the players. You
know the street." Carcosa held up one of the snitch's death Polaroids ad-
miringly. "And you're good with people."

The *Eme*'s monthly taste was a straight ten off the top of all dope, chop shops, extortion, whores, and numbers, but they made it clear they wanted no part of punk-ass chickenshit liquor-store holdups. "Leave that shit to the niggers," Wizard told all his payers. "Just do your thing out here like gentlemen, render unto Cesar what is Cesar's, and we'll all get along just fine."

Carcosa's setup was pure genius: Wizard's front was a Gang Intervention and Outreach Program called Calle Respeto. Wizard spoke to school kids about the evils of gang life, the horrors of prison, and all his dead homies. He made obligatory weekly appearances at some half-assed midnight basketball gig. Once or twice a year, he posed with celebrities at charity events. Wizard was a reformed gangster now, a force for change in his community. Calle Respeto allowed him to move through the hood without suspicion when he called on his payers, and with the *Eme*'s heavy mojo orbiting him like a force field, Wizard walked without fear of man or beast.

His job's other perquisites included clean guns when he needed them and clean whores when he wanted them. Still, what Wizard loved best about working for the *Eme* wasn't his neighborhood juice or his on-call harem, but his *cosas*—his things. He'd filled his modest home to the point of clutter with earthly possessions. Throughout his stint in prison, unattainable *things* had haunted Wizard from dog-eared mail-order catalogues. Studying those glossy pages, Wizard came to want things, to hunger for things the way a man hungers for a beautiful woman. (On one occasion he'd actually jerked off to a picture of an air-hockey game from the Sharper Image catalogue.) And now, at long last, Wizard possessed the *cosas* that had so long dogged his dreams.

Wizard had his air-hockey game, a snooker table, a jukebox with bubbles in it, and a high-def TV. Wizard had a macaw that talked and a huge framed picture of Elvis and Marilyn at some heavenly diner. The picture had a real neon light built right into it, the diner's OPEN sign flashing and sizzling. These were things few men could expect to attain and no man could expect to keep in South Central, but Wizard's pad was painted with lamb's blood, an invisible 13, the *Eme*'s special blessing, and a warning to every burglar and home invader in the hood: find another spot.

On the last day of his life, Wizard collected a little over seven hundred thousand from his payers. The crew from Barrio Mojado was a little light this time around, either underperforming or holding out. Wizard made a mental note to find out which and deal with them accordingly. Otherwise, his collections went like clockwork. The bills were bundled with rubber bands per Wizard's instructions and they rustled like dry leaves in the Calle Respeto duffel as Wizard dropped the monogrammed bag on the couch. Wizard cracked a Budweiser, poured a little into the macaw's water dish, and flopped down next to the duffel to watch an old rerun of *Adam 12* on Nickelodeon.

The macaw's ears were keener than Wizard's. The bird squawked a warning before Wizard heard the first boot land heavily on his front porch. Wizard saw the shadows shifting under the door and reached between the couch cushions for the Sigma pistol he kept there. He took a deep breath, reminding himself that he wasn't some punk who needed to sleep with his eyes open anymore. No one would dare come for him at his home, but old habits die bloody. Wizard still ate like a con, hunching over to shovel it in with his elbows pressed against his sides for protection. He still came like a con, lips pursed with silent intensity, so that the whores had no idea he was finished until he told them to hit the bricks. Old habits, Wizard thought, caressing the Sigma's textured grip.

Wizard hit the remote, activating the television's PIP (picture in picture) feature. His peace-of-mind security cams fed right into the TV's auxiliary port and the PIP window popped lower right in the screen—a little box under Reed and Malloy displaying Wizard's own front porch. The surveillance camera stashed under his eaves showed two real uniforms at Wizard's front door. At the sight of them, the macaw squawked, "Five-Oh! Five-Oh!" Wizard ignored the bird, narrowing his eyes at the two figures on the screen.

He had counterparts in town who would have shit at the sight of blue suits on the front porch, but Wizard didn't trip. He was, after all, a reformed gangster and cops dropped by all the time asking him to lecture a wayward kid, scare some little *pendejo* into leaving this gang shit alone and finishing school. He'd just invite them in. No big thing. Still, something about these two made him hesitate.

The big guy was a hulking monster, roughly the dimensions of Wizard's Wurlitzer jukebox. He had hands like wet catcher's mitts and a Cro-Magnon brow, like rolls of quarters had been sewn right into his forehead. In profile the guy resembled a black Ben Grimm, The Thing from *The Fantastic Four*. His mouth hung open and even in the grainy resolution, Wizard could see shiny spit pooling in the guy's huge bottom lip. His eyes were flat, lifeless.

But it wasn't the big one that worried Wizard. It was his partner. This guy was a light-skinned black, might have had some PR in him. He was lean, muscular, and pretty enough in his Billy Dee Williams mustache to make some bull con a fine prison wife, but he didn't look like a bitch. This dude had the eyes of a hunter and he radiated real street cunning. In fact, the guy didn't look like a cop at all.

Crack! Crack! Crack! The big one's meaty fist hammered his front door, a cop's knock, the kind that rattles hinges. They actually taught them that shit in the academy. Establish your authority the moment you arrive. Let them know you mean business.

Wizard hesitated a moment, racking slide on the Sigma to chamber the first hollow point, and weighed his options. These weren't rookies, no fucking way, but they seemed mellow enough. They didn't stand offset from the doorway the way he'd seen cops do when they were half expecting the occupant to shoot them right through the front door. Their gun hands dangled absently at their thighs, never rising to caress the holstered Berettas on their hips. Wizard had never met a street cop who could resist the urge to touch his burner every few seconds. So, these guys were either taking it easy or they were aware of the camera and wanted to appear casual. Wizard leaned in close to the screen, trying to read the hunter's eyes through the pixels. Fuck it. He tucked the Sigma back between the cushions and opened the door.

"Cesar." The hunter smiled at Wizard, baring teeth too white and straight for Wizard's taste. His nameplate said RISLEY. The big one was MAPES. Risley offered his hand and Wizard took it. His grip was right, Wizard observed, dry and not too tight. "I'm Officer Risley." He spoke in a slow-jammin' bedroom voice—Don Cornelius on Quaaludes. "This is Officer Mapes." Mapes nodded, noisily sucking the spit out of his bottom lip. "We need to ask you a favor." Sure, Wizard thought. Scare a little act-right into some delinquent. No problem. "May we come in for a moment?"

Wizard moved aside and the two cops stepped across the threshold. Risley closed the door behind them and Wizard somehow knew he'd made a mistake, an odd bit of Creature Feature wisdom coming back to him: once you invite Dracula in, you're fucked.

"Five-Oh!" the macaw squawked, bobbing on its perch.

"*Cáyate!*" Wizard hissed at the bird more forcefully than he'd intended. All his prison survival instinct, all his street time, was pumping him full of spooky juice. These dudes were bad juju, but there was no shaking them now. He'd just have to ride this out.

"Cool." Risley tapped the flat television screen. *Mierda*, Wizard had forgotten to hit the remote again and the screen still displayed his front porch. "Can't be too careful in this neighborhood, right, partner? Right?"

"Huh?" Mapes, who had been studying the skittish macaw with a look of childlike wonder that was somehow obscene from a man of his size, turned reluctantly to face Wizard. "Yeah," Mapes said, sucking spit. "Right."

"Not with the kind of cash you keep around, Wizard." Risley nodded to his partner and Mapes drew his side-handle baton with samurai quickness. Wizard lunged for the couch, but he wasn't fast enough. Mapes caught him on the side of the head with a backhanded stroke. The solid aluminum baton connected with superhuman force, crushing his right cheekbone to powder and smearing his nose across the left side of his face on the follow-through. The room spun and he went down hard, blood bubbling from the torn nostrils of his crushed nose.

"Goddamn, nigga!" Risley scolded, his silky DJ voice replaced with a vicious ghetto bark. "The fuck I tell you? Damn near kilt his ass with that Sosa shit!" Mapes hunched his immense shoulders as though he expected Risley to hit him. Risley grabbed Mapes's ear and twisted it, forcing Mapes's head down the way you'd hold a dog's nose in shit. "You see blood fillin' that eye, nigga?" He pointed down at Wizard. "If you fucked up his brain, homeboy can't tell us shit." Mapes nodded shamefully. Risley rolled his eyes to Wizard, one professional to another, his exasperated sigh saying: you see what I have to work with here.

"Goddamn nigga!" the bird squawked.

Wizard knew this game well enough to know he was dead. Badge or no badge, no one with the *ganas* to steal from Carcosa would leave a witness alive. Wizard clawed his fingers into the carpet as the room spun further out of control, tilted his head to the right, and vomited a froth of blood-tinged Budweiser.

"Concussion," Risley pronounced, shaking his head. "Get him up. Don't let him pass out." Risley stepped over Wizard, heading for the kitchen. He paused at the Wurlitzer, and leaned over the menu, tapping his chin with his index finger. He pushed some buttons on the juke and his selection plopped on to the turntable: The Fleetwoods crooning "Come Softly." Risley stepped into the kitchen, bobbing his head to the music.

Mapes yanked Wizard up by a huge fistful of his blood-soaked guayabera shirt, twisted Wizard's arm behind his back. Mapes half carried, half marched Wizard into the kitchen and rammed Wizard into the big stainless-steel sink. Wizard bent double over the sink, coughing blood into the basin. Mapes still had his left arm twisted behind him at an impossible angle. Risley hopped up on to counter next to the sink, banging his heels against the low cabinets like a kid. "We're not here to arrest you, Wizard," Risley said.

"I kind of figured," Wizard mumbled.

"So," Risley said, absently scratching the ingrown hairs along his jawline. "Where is it?"

It seemed crazy to Wizard that they didn't already know. Either they hadn't noticed the bag on the couch or they'd just figured he'd never leave

Carcosa's cash lying around like that. They were expecting a loose floorboard, a false bookcase.

"Tear the place apart," he whispered. He was dead anyway.

Risley nodded to Mapes. Mapes hooked a massive arm around Wizard's neck, nearly lifting him off his feet. Risley grabbed Wizard's right forearm with both hands and shoved his hand down into the garbage disposal. Wizard felt the dormant teeth of the disposal, slick with greasy offal. He tried to yank his hand out, but with Mapes on his back, he had no leverage. Risley jammed the heel of his palm against Wizard's elbow, forcing his hand down against the teeth. Then Risley reached across the sink for the switch. His fingertip touched the toggle. "Where's the money?"

"Fuck you," Wizard spat.

Risley turned on the disposal. The motor hummed. Wizard's vision blurred, but he would not scream. The machine was eating him. Skin peeled. Tendons tore. Masticated nerves sent wild currents up his arms, commanding him to pull away, but the disposal had him now. Even without Risley jamming his hand into it, Wizard couldn't have pulled free. He heard the wet crunch of those spinning teeth as they chewed his bones and cartilage to bloody paste. The gears ground to a halt, choking on what must have been his splintered wrist. The sink backed up. Transfixed, Wizard watched thick blood bubble up from the drain. His fingers floated among the corn and carrots.

Risley leaned in close to Wizard. "This is only the beginning, *amigo*," he said, "It doesn't stop until you tell us where the money is."

"Then I guess we're in for a long night," Wizard said.

1

PRESENT
(1998)

Crude letters burned into a wooden plaque over the 77th Division roll-call room read, ABANDON ALL HOPE YE WHO ENTER HERE. Ben arrived early and took his seat in the first row with the rest of the street candy—pimply probationers fresh out of the academy sporting buzz haircuts, neatly pressed uniforms, spit-shined shoes, Sam Browne belts and holsters so new that the stiff leather creaked with even the slightest movement. The old-timers braced their scuffed boots against their desks to rock back in their chairs, called "fresh fish," and pelted Ben with wadded Winchell's napkins and paper airplanes fashioned from domestic violence pamphlets, but he knew better than to turn around.

The watch commander, Lieutenant Vintner, made an elaborate show of plucking his half-glasses from his breast pocket, like he still couldn't get used to the damned things. Vintner's family had come out here from Louisiana in the postwar black migration, some Caddo Parish still left in his voice. At sixty, Vintner's hair had turned to steel shavings. He was thickening through the middle and he had the beginnings of a stoop, but there was still some hardwood in him. He'd walked a beat in the projects and never lost his feet, not in twenty years of knock-down, drag-out, donnybrooks. The guy still had women all over the division.

"I've got a parolee at large." Vintner peered down through his glasses to read from the hot sheet. "Keith Wallace, male black, six-one, two hundred and some change. He's an Avenue Piru Blood out of Inglewood.

They call him Little Quiet. As some of you may remember, Little Quiet was shooting dice with a few of his homeboys and got the notion he was being cheated. He jammed his knife into a guy's ribs and broke the blade off inside him. He liked to dip his knives in rat poison, an old con's trick. Strychnine prevents the blood from coagulating, but they transfused this guy and he survived. Wallace was popped for attempted One-Eighty-seven, but our beloved district attorney, in his infinite wisdom, let him plea to ADW. Little Quiet did a fast nickel in Chino at Her Majesty's pleasure. He's been out for three weeks and his parole officer says he hasn't checked in for two. CDC thinks he may have cliqued up with some Brims and gone to ground somewhere in the division."

Vintner passed around the wanted with a mug shot of Little Quiet. He was light skinned, the camera's flash turning his face the jaundiced color of eggnog. His square chin upturned over his magnetized booking numbers, staring into the camera with a smirk of defiance that was almost childish. Wallace had the words PIRU and BLOOD tattooed in crude prison style under his dark eyes. Hard-core, Ben thought, dude willing to jab his own face with a hot sewing needle dipped in a black concoction of burned newsprint from a communal toilet with only a few swigs of *pruno* to dull the pain. According to his sheet, the Bloods called him Little Quiet because you didn't hear him coming.

"We have a brand-new probationer with us tonight," Vintner announced, motioning to Ben. "Son, why don't you stand up and tell us a little about yourself."

Ben stood and turned to face the watch. "There isn't much to tell, sir," he said. "I feel lucky to be here and I'm eager to learn." Appropriately humble, Ben thought, and moved to take his seat.

"How about telling us your name, boy?" Vintner asked. The watch chuckled.

"Oh, sorry," Ben said. "My name is Ben Halloran." That name still tasted strange.

"You'll be working with Officer Marquez, Halloran," Vintner said. The watch roared, their laughter telling Ben he'd drawn an old-school hardass, but he knew that already. Before roll call, he'd ducked his head into the watch commander's office to read the lineup.

Marquez was both loved and feared as one of the toughest officers in the city. If you didn't count bloody skirmishes during the riots, and no one did, then Marquez had dropped the hammer three times in his career, sending three free-range assholes to the Happy Hunting Ground. In two of those shootouts, Marquez had saved the lives of brother officers. Every street cop in the city knew those actions should have earned Marquez the Medal of Valor, but these days the kinder, gentler LAPD was loathe to bestow its highest honor on relics like Marquez, a species all but extinct. There were even rumors he'd dumped a dirty cop in Rampart, gone into the maze and killed himself a minotaur.

Marquez and a few others like him were all that remained of Chief Darryl Gates's legacy. These men had been too stubborn, too prideful, or just too damn stupid to lay down their swords after Rodney King, the LAPD's Appomattox. The war on drugs was all but over. Nancy Reagan, their Hecuba, was up in Bel-Air, feeding her husband through a tube. After retiring in disgrace, Gates now lent his name to a series of cop-themed video games. His famous white chariot, the armored assault vehicle Gates once used to demolish crack houses on national television, moldered under a musty tarpaulin up at Piper Tech.

Vintner dismissed roll call. Ben ran to the kit room and signed out a Remington 870 Shotgun, an Ithaca Bean Bag Shotgun, a taser, and three radios. Marquez grabbed the AR-15 they call the Urban Police Rifle. They loaded up their black-and-white.

"If you need to go to the can, go now," Marquez told Ben. "Always crap before you leave the barn. You never know when you'll get another chance. Less bacteria down there in case you happen to take a bullet in the gut. If a round makes it under your vest, it bounces around, tears everything open. Your own shit poisons your blood, so even if you somehow survive the initial wound, you'll die of septicemia."

"I don't have to go, sir," Ben said, figuring the guy was fucking with him anyway.

"Suit yourself." Marquez shrugged. He took Ben through the station workout room, where the big brutes clanged rusty dumbbells in front of cracked mirrors and a printed sign asked: WILL YOU TRAIN AS HARD FOR GOOD AS THEY WILL FOR EVIL? Metallica blasted from a boom box in the corner. Creatine, carnatine, and glutamine, oh my. Judging from the size of them, a few of these Masters of the Universe must have been skin-popping cocktails from south of the border, but steroids remained outside the spectrum of the department's supposedly random piss-tests.

Marquez rushed Ben through the rest of the new station, but he seemed embarrassed by it. The city had razed his dear old rat-infested brick station house and replaced it with this modern architectural marvel that looked grotesquely dated by the ribbon cutting.

The Jesse A. Brewer 77th Street Regional Facility (named for a beloved black assistant chief) seemed to have been designed for an era of community openness that never materialized—a misguided attempt to bring Athenian aesthetics to a Spartan culture—and the station's piazza design was a security nightmare. "They get baseheads wandering through Bureau all the time," Marquez said. "People just think they're CPAB until they start helping themselves to staplers and shit."

"CPAB, sir?"

"The Community Police Advisory Board," Marquez said. "Don't get me started."

In the basement were locker rooms, the roll-call room, kit room, and a subterranean entrance to the jail facility—breeding ground for staph and TB. The officer cot rooms, Marquez called them the Fuck Huts, had been closed indefinitely following an outbreak of scabies. All the mattresses had to be burned, but the city refused to replace them.

Marquez brought him upstairs into the station's crowded atrium lobby, where a cavalcade of dejected nonemergencies, 911 transfers, and long stories waited for counter service from two young cops at the front desk. Two lines snaked through the lobby and out the big glass doors. Sex offenders who'd shown up to register and DA rejects fresh out of County lockup, looking to track down their property. Day laborers hoping to talk their truck out of impound. Nappy nymphs in Tupac T-shirts and fearsome, three-hundred-pound fertility goddesses in TJ Maxx pajamas, demanding to talk to someone about their son's or grandson's case. And kids, Ben hadn't expected so many kids. Kids in strollers, kids napping on the benches, kids hanging on their moms, chasing each other back and forth across the lobby. Above them, the two-story walls of the atrium were decorated with cartoonish Aztecs and Zulu warriors marching on the great citadel to conquer the conquerors.

Marquez showed him the watch commander's office, report-writing rooms, and arrestee holding tanks—bona fide miracles of low-bid city construction. "They're just plain drywall," Marquez said. To demonstrate, he used his fingernail to scrape a flaky chunk out of wall. "Not reinforced or anything and you know half the assholes in there are pissing all over the tank, so the walls are about half rotted. Few weeks back this Four-Fifty-nine suspect just punched his way out." He pointed to a man-sized section of the corridor patched with plyboard. "Fucking Hey Kool-Aid! Escaped out the emergency exit door, which was broken, by the way. We'd have never caught the guy, but I guess he went on and on to his homies about how no jail could hold him until they got so sick of his mouth and stiffed in a call."

Marquez took him up to the Detectives' Bureau on the second floor and showed him the helipad on the roof. Everywhere Ben saw framed pictures of 77th officers killed in the line.

"They must have invited the rats back here for the ribbon cutting," Marquez said. "Roof leaks worse than the old station did."

Marquez drove them up to the top floor of the parking garage. "Get out," he ordered. "We need to get some things straight before we hit the street." Ben stepped out of the car. From only four stories up, he had an unobstructed view of downtown and the San Gabriel Mountains. South

Central clung tightly to the basin, mostly low buildings clustered from Imperial Highway to the Staples Center. Nothing up here but bowed palms and a few power lines. Ben heard the constant conch-shell rush of the Harbor Freeway, the hot wind sizzling through the palms. Laughter and screams, the kids at Seventy-sixth Street School careening around on the warm blacktop. The faint pop of gunfire from blocks away, somewhere east of them. Sirens. A red-tailed hawk circled overhead.

Marquez came around the car to loom over him and Ben had the vertiginous feeling that he'd seen Officer Miguel Marquez somewhere before, but he couldn't place him. Maybe it was just his type that was familiar. He looked like a piece of cover art from those ridiculous Mack Bolan books Ben had devoured as a kid.

He had the kind of chest and shoulders that you can't get in a gym. He wore a coarse black pompadour brushed back from a face like an unfinished Rodin sculpture. His nose had been broken into a kind of sierra that ran from his heavy eyebrows to his Tom Selleck mustache. Beneath that frowning mustache, his chin jutted like a fist. A jagged archipelago of putty-colored scar tissue knotted along his neck under the left side of his jaw. Ben caught himself staring at it, wondering what kind of survivable wound forges such a brutal scar.

As for Ben, he tended to run thin. He had pumped iron and quaffed protein shakes all through the academy, but the uniform still hung on him. He had the kind of boyish face that inspired trust rather than fear and his Ralph Lauren spectacles didn't raise the badass quotient any. It wasn't easy to look foppish in a police uniform, but he managed. Ben was most self-conscious of his hands. He had played the piano growing up and every recital showed in his thin, almost feminine hands with gracile, tapered fingers. They weren't cop hands at all.

"When you get some money together, you get yourself a man's gun," Marquez said, sneering at the department-issued Beretta 92F in Ben's holster. Marquez had long since turned in his own blue-steel Beretta nine and he now carried a big stainless-steel Smith & Wesson .45 caliber with a mother-of-pearl handle. He wore the gun low on his hip in a swivel holster. "You carry a backup?"

"Yes, sir," Ben said, lifting his left pant leg to show Marquez the little five-shot .38 caliber revolver that he wore in an ankle holster.

"Good. It's better to carry a wheel as backup," Marquez said. "Contact-wound some asshole if you have to, press the muzzle right into his sternum and pull the trigger. You can't do that with an automatic because the slide will foul your shot."

Marquez reached across his chest and there was a static sound as he pulled open a hidden Velcro slit that ran down the left seam of his uniform. Ben saw that Marquez didn't have a Kevlar vest under there. "They always aim for your head anyway," Marquez said. "Those guards up in Pelican Bay that put on stab-resistant suits and they still end up getting shanked through the fucking eye."

Marquez wore only his scapular, white cotton T-shirt stretched to translucence by his broad chest, and a shoulder holster. Marquez reached inside the slit and drew a snub-nosed .357 Magnum revolver from the shoulder holster. The .357 looked like an angry totem sprouting from his meaty fist. Ben could have fit his whole thumb into the bore.

"I didn't know the department had approved that weapon, sir," Ben said, knowing damn well they didn't.

"Don't get your chonies in a bunch," Marquez said, sliding it back into the shoulder holster and sealing up the slit in his uniform. "It's not a throwdown piece. It's a weapon of last resort. I've never had to use it, but you never know out here. I'd much rather go home alive and apologize for this cannon later than play nice and go home in a box." He pulled a bag of Red Man from his back pocket and jammed a load of tobacco into his cheek. "Better to be judged by twelve than carried by six." He spat. "Now get in the fucking car.

"Oh, yeah, and a lot of us in patrol smash our dome lights to deter snipers," Marquez said. "I use a flathead screwdriver to dig airbags out of my car. Thing is, you never know when you might have to ram the shit out of something, or someone, and believe me you don't want that damn bag blowing up in your face in a gunfight."

Marquez hated this white boy on sight. The sweet stink of privilege was all over him. He smelled like a Brentwood baby out here playing Adam Fucking 12. Welcome to the New LAPD, Marquez thought. More of these faggoty new boots were showing up in roll call every month, products of Burns's kinder gentler academy, not one of them worth a pinch of dry shit.

"Do me a favor, forget all that shit they teach you in the academy," Marquez told the kid as he drove them up Florence with his baton resting in his lap. "Forget verbal judo and lose all those bullshit grappling moves." He spat a brown comet of chaw out the open window of the black-and-white. "Nothing will get you killed on this job faster than all that academy patty-cake."

"Yes, sir." The kid spoke with a snappy eagerness that made Marquez want to dunk the little bastard's head in a stopped-up toilet. Toilet training, Rourke used to call it, a porcelain attitude adjustment.

"You catch some producer gobbling cock in a public shithouse out in West L.A., maybe you can talk him into the handcuffs, but not down here," Marquez said. "These assholes make you work for it. Arresting hard-core felons is an ugly business. They don't much want to go back to prison. They'll run from you. If you catch them, they'll fight you and if you let them, they'll kill you."

"Yes, sir." That square diction made Marquez's teeth itch. Last stall in the locker room, he thought. Hold this kid's face under until those little brown bubbles slow to about two or three seconds apart.

Miguel Marquez had grown up in MacArthur Park, right in the heart of the Eighteenth Street Hood. Gangsters would roll past nine-year-old Miguelito on his way home from school, four-deep in slammed El Caminos, handing the boy their big-yard stares as they orbited his block like sharks nosing the water for blood. He grew up seeing XVIII *placas* painted like lamb's blood on every garage door, street sign, stop sign, panel truck, and garbage can. In a hood like that, you claim Eighteenth Street or you get the fuck out, but Miguel never claimed, never backed down, never ran from a fight.

Marquez grew up hating gangsters because his father had told him their big secret: shine a light on any one of those fuckers and you'll find a coward. *You're not a coward, are you, mijo? No, Papa. Never.*

He never claimed. Not once. When he was old enough to meet their big-yard stare with his own, they hopped out of their rides and beat his punk ass down. They jumped him in the schoolyard, jumped him on the way home from school. They once put the boots to him in front of Catechism, for Christ's sake. By the time he was fourteen, Miguel had a nose like Rocky Marciano, but he never claimed. He would have made one hell of a gangster, but Miguel had no taste for tyranny and the idea of hiding behind your homies every time you left your house had a pussy-assness that Miguel could not abide.

The summer after his fifteenth birthday, something miraculous happened. Miguel grew and grew and grew. It was the kind of spurt that people have in science-fiction movies after being exposed to radiation. One autumn afternoon, Sleepy and Shyboy, two of Eighteenth Street's finest, waylaid Miguel on his way home from football practice. It was like these chuckleheads hadn't noticed that Miguel now had an extra foot and a good forty pounds on them. Miguel walked away brushing bloody bits of Shyboy's teeth out of his knuckles. His hands hurt like hell, but he had never felt so good in his life.

When his father came home and saw Miguel pouring peroxide over his knuckles with a shit-eating grin on his face, he was furious. He slapped the grin off Miguel's face and packed Miguel's mother and sister off to stay with his aunt in the valley. *This is no joke, mijo. Next time they come for you, you'll understand why I'm angry.*

That night, the front windows of their house blew inward. Plaster and

Sheetrock flew. Cushions burst open and spit their stuffing. Miguel lay on the floor of his bedroom until the shooting stopped. He found his father clutching his leg in the living room and called 911.

The responding officers smirked at Miguel after the ambulance had taken his father away. Be straight with us, they said. We can't help you if you won't cooperate. They refused to believe Miguel wasn't a gang member. The report died on somebody's desk, just another gang-related shooting. His family moved to the valley after that and Miguel's father walked with a cane for the rest of his life.

Six years later, Miguel graduated from the academy and went straight to Rampart Division, his old barrio. Four months into his probation, he got up the courage to tell his training officer about the shooting. His training officer, an old-timer named Rourke, told Miguel he knew where to find Shyboy if Miguel was interested. Miguel said fuckin'-A I'm interested, sir.

By then, Shyboy was an old-timer in his own right, a *veterano* by Eighteenth Street standards. Nineteen is middle age for a gangster and Shyboy was twenty-five. One night, Rourke hauled Shyboy's *borracho* ass out of a bar called El Toro and brought him spitting and cursing into the alley behind the bar. His teeth still looked like busted china. It took Shyboy maybe twenty seconds to recognize Miguel. He sobered up fast. Miguel put his revolver into Shyboy's face, listened to him beg for a few seconds before pulling the trigger six times. Those six blanks went off loud and fast. They left Shyboy curled up and bawling like a baby in the alley with a half-pound of his own shit cooling in his razor-creased counties.

"What you learned in the academy will kill you," Marquez told the kid. "Want to know how to stay alive?"

"Yes, sir."

"When you have to fight, fight dirty," Marquez said. "Hit early and often. Go for his balls. If you can't get his balls, go for his eyes. Take him down any way you can and forget all that schoolyard crap about not hitting a man when he's down. Your suspect's on the ground, don't be afraid to put the boots to his ass until he's soft enough to hook up. You remember that, you'll be okay."

"Yes, sir." Toilet training was too good for this kid, Marquez decided. No, he'd take the kid up to Central Avenue and let Teirasias work him over.

"You have any prior military?" Marquez asked him.

"No, sir." Here it comes, Ben thought.

"What did you do before you came on the job?"

"I was in the Peace Corps, sir." He fed Marquez the practiced lie.

"The Peace Corps?" Marquez shouted. "There's a fucking pinko in my police car, probably a fag too."

"No, sir."

"What the fuck is some pinko college boy doing on my job?"

"I want to help people," Ben said. That sounded about right, better than the truth anyway. He had beaten the department's polygraph examination with two Valiums and a little concentration. Their background investigation of him had been negligently shallow, but that shouldn't have surprised him. This was the LAPD knee-deep in the nasty nineties, officers jumping ship left and right, swimming like hell for other agencies. It was the reign of the Dark Lord Chief Benson Burns and the department felt like the Soviet Union just before its collapse, long on parades and short on penicillin. The city was desperate for warm bodies to fill blue uniforms.

"The only thing that'll kill you faster than the academy is that bleeding-heart crap," Marquez spat again. "You'll kill us both with that shit."

"I won't get us killed, sir," Ben said, meaning it.

"Oh, you're right about that, boy." Marquez said. "That's the first right answer you've had. You're not going to get us killed because I'm going to get your mind right. Your heart may belong to Maxine Waters, but your ass belongs to me."

Marquez parked their black-and-white in front of the little Korean liquor store at the corner of Sixty-seventh Street and Central Avenue—the East Side, the Bottoms. Once L.A.'s Jazz Quarter, Central Avenue had become a kind of KOA campground for crackheads. An old wino slumped in a battered wheelchair on the sidewalk at the entrance to the liquor store. Ben figured the wino for about fifty, but the man also might have been pushing seventy. The wino's hair and beard had clumped into long dreadlocks and months of uninterrupted outdoor wear had turned his clothes the color of tar. He cradled a bottle of something cheap and corrosive in a crumpled brown paper bag on his lap.

"Frick him for drinking in public," Marquez ordered. *Frick:* the bastardized LAPD acronym for a Field Release From Custody, a simple ticket for bullshit misdemeanors like drinking in public, or smoking a jay. Starting me off slow, Ben thought, Fair enough. "And hurry the fuck up, Professor."

Ben got out of the car, approaching the semiconscious wino the cautious way they had taught him to move in the academy, hands up and gun leg back. He could smell the guy from ten feet away, sour urine and fortified wine, clothes rotting right off his body like some kind of cave lichen.

"I'm going to have to ask you to put down that bottle." Ben mustered his best take-charge voice. The wino bared his teeth, or what was left of them, and leaned over to set his bottle on the sidewalk next to his wheelchair. "Let's see some ID?"

"Don't got none."

"Okay." Ben flipped open his brand-new leather ticket book and clicked his pen. "How about we start with your last name—"

The wino launched out of his wheelchair and onto his feet the instant Ben took his eyes off him. Before Ben had time to react, the wino dipped his shoulder and expertly drove a quick uppercut deep into Ben's solar plexus, the punch sinking deep into that breadbasket right between his Sam Browne belt and Kevlar vest. Ben's vision blurred from the pain and he dropped his pen and ticket book onto the sidewalk. *Christ, he can't be that fast!*

Ben was reaching for his baton when the wino landed another fast punch that he felt in his bowels. Ben's knees buckled and he went down sucking wind. Gasping, he scrambled onto his hands and knees, trying to regain his feet. The filthy sidewalk blurred in and out of focus, littered with butts, gum, broken glass, a condom, and a purple press-on finger-nail. A shadow fell across the sidewalk. The wino stood over him, grinning with his fist raised like a hammer.

"Not his face." Marquez said calmly. For a second, Ben actually thought Marquez was talking to him.

"You better send this boy on back, Marquez." The wino cackled, lowering his fist. "He ain't ready for—"

Still gasping, Ben jammed his hand up into the piss-stained crotch of the wino's pants, took hold of something soft, and clamped down on the guy's balls the way you crush a beer can. The wino stopped cackling, made a ragged wheezing sound, and fell to his knees. Ben rolled the guy over and cuffed him up. Then Ben staggered over to the black-and-white and leaned against it to steady himself while he caught his breath. Ben wiped the back of his hand across his nose and stared at Marquez, letting his watery eyes tell Marquez to go fuck himself.

2

1972–1985

His given name was Benjamin Kahn, Jr., son of Big Ben Kahn, so everyone called him Little Benji—Big Ben being one of Century City's celebrated Semitic power-elites, West L.A.'s mouthiest millionaire mouthpiece, and the rumored drafter of the infamous "Adolf Fuhrman" speech delivered by Mr. Johnnie to close the O.J. trial. Benji actually suspected his father of starting that rumor. Having placed himself on the short list of L.A.'s courtroom conjurers, the man's ego suffered minor contusions when Mr. Johnnie didn't choose him for his Dream Team in the first place.

Benji grew up in the People's Republic of Santa Monica, the sun-dappled neighborhood north of Montana Avenue, just seven blocks from the rolling expanse of the Pacific Ocean. There wasn't a family picture in the whole house, just head shots, movie posters, and album covers—all framed and autographed by clients who had beaten the rap.

His earliest childhood recollections of his father were purely kinetic, Big Ben in constant motion, palsied with restlessness. He was heavy, but not rudely fat as he would later become. His dolphin shorts and gray Harvard Law T-shirt soaked from his weekly handball game, a sweatband around his bean-shaped head cinching his thick brown hair into a frizzy hourglass. Lacking anything that could be called athleticism, Big Ben was still a handball demon because, as he said, "Handball is all about angles."

Benji never knew his mother, who'd supposedly run off to Italy with a viscount she met on one of her annual trips to the Golden Door—this would have been when Ben was about three. Years later, he'd gotten his hands on a vintage *Playboy* just to get a look at her. Pure California blonde, a golden go-go hourglass wearing only creamy tan lines and staged expression, palm flat against the side of her face, her delicate mouth an O of surprise, like the last thing she ever expected was for you to walk in and catch her there buck naked. She'd listed, among her turnoffs, smelly cigars and big talkers, which called into question either the journalistic precision of the magazine or the purity of her intentions when she'd hooked up with Big Ben.

They'd actually met at the mansion. That was Big Ben's story, anyway. The way Big Ben told it, he was in the Grotto, water up to his furry chest, deep in cosmic conversation with Debbie Harry, when his future bride backstroked past them. Big Ben excused himself to give chase, his feeble YMCA sidestroke severely impeded by the half-finished mai tai in his left hand. This long-limbed California cutie who'd probably spent her every summer at the beach slipped away like a greased porpoise, but she let him catch her under the waterfall. Big Ben was, after all, a lawyer on the come, defending television stars from drunk driving and possession raps, and she was a Playmate of the Month who couldn't act her way out of a paper bag, a trophy wife waiting to happen.

They eloped to Maui, but by the time Benji made the scene two years later, their marriage was already terminal. With Big Ben waddling after every young piece of ass that crossed Sunset Boulevard, she'd taken up diet pills. "Your mom's favorite breakfast was black beauties and Tab." Big Ben smirked when he caught his son pillaging his sock drawer for old pictures, any hard evidence of her existence, and finding only an empty pill bottle. "You'd think a pill hound and a pussy hound could have reached some kind of understanding, for your sake," Big Ben said, a trace of genuine regret in his voice. "But she met another meal ticket on that goddamned spa trip I paid for and that was the last I saw of her, kid."

She called Benji on his fifth birthday. He remembered jamming his

hand over his other ear, desperate to hear her voice over the hired magician and all the kids, but the connection was terrible, like talking to a
ghost.

Benji attended the Road Less Traveled School, crown jewel of Santa
Monica's ultraprogressive K-through-twelves, where west-side elites shelled
out thirty large a year for a faculty of would-be Ph.D.s who wore Tevas to
class, let students call them by their first names, and assigned Jack Ker-
ouac to their fifth-graders. The diverse student body consisted of cutters,
huffers, baggers, bulimics, the casualties of divorce and nonintervention-
ist parenting. Two of Benji's classmates turned sweet sixteen in rehab. Another kid died of autoerotic asphyxia. Guy's mom came home from a
broker's open and found him in the bathroom with his shorts around his
ankles and a plastic bag over his head.

Benji didn't have any friends at school, which is not to say he was un-
popular. Benji was on the RLT surf team and girls vied for his attention,
scrawled his name on their folders, giggled, and mooned when he passed
them in the quad.

Benji told himself he had no real friends because there were no friend-
ships to be had at the RLT. And while it may have been true that RLT
offered only mutually advantageous associations, mergers, arranged
marriages—the Ivy League mafia slotting their highborn offspring into a
sink-or-swim caste system that was supposed carry them to Stanford or
Yale—the reason Benji kept his classmates at arm's length was Big Ben's
veering, incontinent rage.

Benji's grandparents flew in from Scarsdale for his bar mitzvah, which
they pronounced an appalling spectacle of meretricious exhibitionism.
Tom Petty played a set at the party, and Steven Seagal, who Big Ben knew
through one of his PI friends, actually took the stage for a duet with
Petty—a bluesy rendition of "Sunrise, Sunset." Later that evening, Anna
Nicole Smith stumbled onto the dance floor and kissed Benji full on the
mouth, but Big Ben swore he hadn't put her up to it.

After the party, Benji's grandparents, Big Ben, and his shiksa du jour

(Mindy or Cindy, Benji always got them confused) bellied up to kitchen table for coffee. Drink had taken hold of his father. Every time Big Ben whispered a naughty aside to his date, Mindy or Cindy snorted laughter, causing her breasts to bounce against the table. With each blast of laughter, Grandmother fixed her husband with a hemlock stare and Benji's grandfather, who must have felt her stare but contrived to ignore it, focused instead on his own cup. When his grandfather tilted his wrist to sip his coffee, Benji could see the neat blue numbers tattooed there.

Big Ben had ignored Benji for most of the party, but slumped here in the kitchen, Benji found that he was suddenly and inexplicably the center of his father's attention. "Look at him, Pop," Big Ben said, jabbing his spoon in Benji's direction, his heavy-lidded eyes glowing, as though they held some hazy intimation of the regicidal events still years away. "Spitting image of his mother, kid's about as Jewish as Tab Hunter."

Benji stared down at his coffee cup, shrinking in his chair. Big Ben's golfing buddies and revolving mistresses always teased that he was a frustrated borscht-belt comedian, but Benji wasn't fooled. Under all that congenial obesity, the son of a bitch had a mean streak to land a plane. His pernicious insecurity was like anemia that left Big Ben bloodthirsty.

"You know he was damn near kicked out of preschool for biting," Big Ben said. "Those fucking goyim call me impudent, but they'll probably call this cheeky little bastard *brash*."

"Benjamin, that's enough," Grandfather said, dropping his napkin on to the table. He was shaking and Grandmother placed a steadying hand on his shoulder.

"No, I mean it." Big Ben belched. "He's a poster boy for the Hitler Youth."

Grandfather's hand flashed over the table faster than Benji's eyes could track, slapping his father hard across his face. Everything just froze, like that *Twilight Zone* where Burgess Meredith finds the magic watch. Benji watched the palm-shaped mark coming up on his father's face. Grandfather had slapped thirty years off Big Ben, down to the gaping child. Big Ben's mouth moved in a kind of slow-motion tremble, his eyes wide and glistening, suspending his tears by sheer force of will. He levered a smile onto his face, lifted his napkin from his lap, and dropped it on the table. Then he got up from the table and walked out. Mindy or Cindy hurried after him, her heels clicking on the hardwood.

That night, emboldened by his bar mitzvah or maybe just desperate, Benji padded into his father's room, something he'd never done before in his life. "Can I talk to you?"

Big Ben sat up on his elbow to squint blearily at the kid. "The fuck do I care, sure." He shrugged. "I mean, yeah. *Of course*, yeah, take a pew." Big Ben rolled toward the small shape in the sheets next to him, spanked the girl once, smartly.

"Knock it off, asshole," Mindy or Cindy hissed into the pillow.

"Got to do my daddy thing here, babe." Big Ben hooked his thumb toward the hallway. "Hit the couch or hit the bricks." Mindy or Cindy slid out of bed, hastily wrapping herself in the top sheet as she slipped out into the hallway. "What gives?"

Benji didn't answer right away, taking in his father's familiar scent, the babyish tang of Big Ben's sleep-sweat and just a hint of Dewar's. He stared up at the dancing patterns the pool reflected on the bedroom ceiling.

"I think I need you to be nicer to me," Benji whispered.

"Oh, Benji," he said thickly. "I got a little juiced tonight, that's all. Doesn't mean a thing. It's still you and me against the world, pal." He fumbled in the darkness, brushed Benji's shoulder. "Me and you and a dog named Boo."

"Only without the dog," Benji said, smiling a little in spite of himself. His father had been making that lame joke for as long as he could remember.

"Look, I'm lousy with kids," Big Ben sighed, scratching his belly. "You *know* this. Just never had the knack, I guess, but anyway, you're a mensch now, right? Rabbi Sherman said so. And things are going to be different from here on out, that I promise you. Your old man's finally going to get his fucking shit together, Benji. That'll be my gift to you on your bar mitz-vah, okay?"

"Okay."

"You want a Valium or something?" Big Ben said. "Help you sleep?"

"No, thanks."

PRESENT

Marquez whistled as he walked into the liquor store and came out with a bag of ice. He uncuffed Tony and helped him back to his feet. Tony slumped back into his wheelchair and Marquez set the bag of ice in his lap. The wino held it there, moaning softly. "You okay, champ?" Marquez asked him. Tony nodded. Marquez handed him a twenty. Tony reached for it without looking, crumpled the bill in his fist, and slid it into his pocket.

"Well, you coming, Professor?" Marquez asked the kid as he slipped back into the driver's side of their black-and-white. The kid walked to the passenger side and slid in next to him, wincing as he moved. Definitely hurting, Marquez thought. Good.

"What the hell was that?" the kid asked him as the black-and-white pulled away from the liquor store.

"Sir," Marquez said.

"Well, what was that, sir?"

"Survival lesson *número uno*, grasshopper," Marquez said, handing the kid his patented Tony T. Speech, but having to edit a little because this kid had gotten lucky. Marquez had never seen a boot get the better of Tony before. So either the booze had finally soaked the pepper out of Tony's punches or this faggoty white boy actually had some *cojones* on him.

"What you don't know can kill you," Marquez told the kid. "You let your guard down because you assumed that Tony T. there was just some crippled old juicer. Back in the day, before he became chief engineer on the Red Nose Express, Tony Teirasias was a heavyweight contender, went the distance with Mike Weaver. So, next time you think you can handle some guy in your sleep, remember Tony would have spoiled your face back there if I hadn't called him off. You'll be sore for a while, but if you learned something, maybe the next guy won't snatch your gun and kill you."

"You pay that guy to pummel all your new probationers," the kid said.

"Not all." Marquez cocked an eyebrow, letting the kid chew on that. "Look, you want to beef me, Professor? I'll drive us back to the barn and you can cry to Patty Cream Cheese. She's had a rhino clit for me ever since she got transferred to this fucking division." Rhino clit was a new one. Marquez was trying it out, not sure if he liked it.

"Who's Patty Cream Cheese, sir?"

Marquez cruised the hood, giving the kid his nickel tour as they worked their way west toward Crenshaw Boulevard. In the gut of South Central L.A., 77th Division encompassed less than twelve square miles of fucked America with the highest murder rate of any blighted patch of real estate west of the Mississippi. Every night brought automatic-weapons fire, screams, and shattering glass. In the hottest months of L.A.'s killing season, the poor black and Hispanic families in 77th had their kids sleep huddled on the floor in the room farthest from the street, where they'd be less likely to catch a stray bullet. Gangs warred to control the flow of crack, warred out of boredom, warred to ward off depression. People killed each other in petty arguments, guys coming up dead over dominoes games or borrowed lawn mowers. Slow-motion massacre or mass suicide, Marquez thought maybe it was both. Chuin called them Starbellied-Sneech Murders.

"After Rodney King the Christopher Commission said the department had to be at least a quarter female," Marquez said. "The recruiters ran out and snatched up every split-tail with a pulse and pushed them through the academy. Eight months later, I get assigned a brand-new *chingada* butterball fresh out of the academy. Girl had an ass on her like a forty-dollar cow. Patty Pendergast. I didn't have her a week before we jacked some yoked-out parolee and I'm patting the guy down and he turns on me. Guy had about fifty rocks in his pocket and he was looking at some tall time. Fight's on. I'm rolling around in the street with this asshole, huffing and puffing for five fucking minutes, and what does my partner do? Patty runs back to the car, locks herself in there, just sits there biting her nails until backup arrives. I got winded and had to split the dude's head open against the curb. He's a fucking turnip now, dying of bedsores up in Mule Creek."

Big billboards hocked cheap booze, bargain funerals, cigarettes, and the latest albums from rappers like D.J. Post-Mortem and Certain Death. Yellowed posters stapled to telephone poles advertised bus charters out to visit prisoners at Corcoran and Chino.

Discount liquor markets stood shoulder to shoulder with storefront *iglesias* where ecstatic Spanish garbled out of screechy megaphones. Out in front, compact women with papooses slapped together *gorditas hechas a mano* at sidewalk grills. The preachers inside were going like auctioneers, carnival barkers, red-faced from hours of breathless rambling. Time was, every brown brother in this barrio was a crucifix-kissing Catholic, but Marquez had watched screaming evangelicals take root here over the years. He was a Catholic boy himself, but he took secret solace in their doomed fervor. Like the devil was South Central's cattle baron and these wild-eyed Christian Soldiers were calling him out into the street.

In the days of restrictive housing covenants, the West Side had been whites-only. Now it was South Central's Strivers Row. Single professionals and dual-income families, union electricians, nurses, postal workers, city and county employees paying down mortgages on their spotless Spanish bungalows along the Avenues. Easy to forget about them altogether because—other than the odd 459 investigation—you didn't run into these folks on radio calls.

Always on their way to some church function, they appeared to live their whole lives with this furious rectitude, as though God fearing would make them bulletproof. They raised their kids hard, kept them indoors, in school, and during the summers, packed them off on Bible-study bus trips to youth conferences in Atlanta or D.C.

And still every year valedictorians and salutatorians somehow managed to die bloody down here. Poor kid gets sick of waiting on his city bus and hoofs it and some hoodstas hunt him halfway home on a long block after dark, and he hears the slow approach of an engine and he knows they're sizing him up, wanting to turn his head to look, not daring to until one of them's shouting "Fuck Naps!" or some shit out the open passenger window—not so much for the kid's benefit as for the rest of the neighborhood—and by the time the kid sprints for it the first rounds have pierced his caramel skin. Or shots ring out at some house party where he had no business being in the first goddamned place—dragged there by his wayward play-cousin or a wild girl—wrong-place-wrong-timed right into Inglewood Park Cemetery.

As they rolled north on Crenshaw from Florence, Marquez leaned his elbow out the open window and slid back in his seat. He cranked the A/C against the undulating, primordial heat, but he kept his window open. That way he could spit tobacco juice into the street or shoot out his open window, come to that. Telling Ben the Patty Cream Cheese story, Marquez looked relaxed, almost sleepy, but his hooded eyes scanned the boulevard for prey. He rested his Smith .45 across his lap.

"So, I march into the captain's office," Marquez said. "Pretty banged up and bloody. Uniform's torn all to shit. I tell the captain he better fire that fat little bitch before she gets somebody killed. Captain tells me he'll take care of it, but he just transfers her ass over to West L.A. Department didn't want to lose any precious females.

"Patty spent a few years in West L.A. writing speeding tickets to rich Jews and blowing a few very married lieutenants." Marquez spat. "They call her Patty Cream Cheese because she's soft, white, and easy to spread. Somebody actually made her a sergeant and that bitch would like nothing more than to see this border brother back selling oranges on Pico Boulevard. You want to dime me out, Patty'll probably suck you off for it."

"I'm not a rat, sir," the kid said quietly.

"Right answer," Marquez said. "You're two for two, Professor."

Traffic on Crenshaw heaved with salvaged junkers, rusty trucks packed with *jornaleros,* lowriders bouncing and rearing up on their hydraulics, a few tricked-out SUVs, and fuzzy pimpmobiles. Fruit of Islam stood on the concrete median in their dark suits and bow ties, selling bean pies and copies of *The Final Call.* Zacatecas street vendors, wearing filmy T-shirts drenched in sweat, dashed in and out of traffic, hocking heavy bags of fresh oranges, pistachios, and boxes of ripe strawberries. Baseheads prowled the gutters for aluminum cans and packs of mongrel dogs nosed through garbage-strewn alleys. Mexican kids in hand-me-down Catholic-school uniforms skipped past a wino pissing against a wall. A group of middle-aged black women, wearing church hats and corsages, stepped out of a cinder-block funeral home dabbing their eyes.

Marquez spotted a G-ride. Two gangsters hunkered in a puke-green, pig-iron Bonneville with a busted draft window, the driver trying to look casual with his bug eyes glued to his rearview mirror. Marquez called out the numbers on the license plate and Ben ran it on the MDT. Code Six Charles indicated. The vehicle had just been snatched off Venice Boulevard in an armed carjacking. Ben reached for the radio.

"Keep the mike below the dash, dipshit," Marquez said, jabbing Ben with his elbow. "Don't let them see you broadcast." Ben held the mike low and tried to keep his voice even as he requested backup and an airship.

The Bonneville picked up some speed, putting a little distance between them. "He's testing me," Marquez said. "Doesn't know if the car's hot just yet." Marquez gently accelerated with the flow of traffic, keeping the Bonneville in sight, working the gas pedal the way an angler works a reel.

The driver spooked and the Bonneville lurched into the intersection of Slauson and Crenshaw. The Bonneville leaped the southeast curb in front of the Arco station and obliterated a wobbly card table some poor vendor had set up to sell bootlegged Laker T-shirts. The vendor dove clear as his table shattered against the Bonneville's grill, spitting cotton T-shirts in every direction. The T-shirts wafted into the street and baseheads dashed out in front of traffic to gather them up. They scurried away with armfuls of crewneck cotton before the vendor could react and Marquez had to swerve to avoid hitting them.

"*Okay,* he knows." Marquez grinned, cranking the wheel. He hit the siren and floored it up Slauson after them, hoping this white boy's guts were still loose from Tony's sucker punch. Marquez wouldn't count the shift a total loss if he could make this wiseass kid puke on himself.

The Bonneville was pouring it on now, weaving in and out of traffic. As the gangsters passed Tenth Avenue, the passenger tossed an AK-47 out his window. The rifle sailed over a tall iron security fence and landed in the courtyard of the Dorset Village Apartments. As Marquez gunned the black-and-white past Dorset Village, the homies were already racing across the lawn to claim the discarded weapon. Marquez continued after the G-ride.

The Bonneville punched the light hard at Western Avenue. Cross traffic screeched and spun. Marquez followed them through the intersection without slowing. "Look for them to bail in the next block or so, before we have a chance to put the airship in play." Even these poobutt assholes had to know they'd be as good as booked once the ghetto bird got over them, Marquez thought, nowhere to hide from the chopper.

Traffic backed up around Halldale for the Slauson Swap Meet, blocking eastbound lanes. The Bonneville swerved to the left, careened across westbound traffic, and jumped the curb. The car continued over the gravel toward the train tracks that ran along the north side of Slauson Avenue.

As Marquez closed on the Bonneville, he saw the driver's-side door swing open and the driver tumbled out of the moving car. The gangster went down hard, rolled in the gravel and scrambled to his feet. He'd twisted his ankle, maybe even broken it. Marquez clocked him loping north with an awkward, desperate limp and watched him disappear over the fence.

The passenger wasn't fast enough getting his door open. The driverless car drifted and fishtailed, spitting loose gravel from its tires. The car clipped a transformer box, pitched up on two wheels, and flipped over. The passenger was thrown out his open window, flopping heavily onto the train tracks. He was crawling across the tracks when the hood of the Bonneville crashed down on him, pinning his legs.

Marquez and Ben jumped out of their car and ran to the guy. Marquez had his gun out until he saw this kid's hands were empty. He had the tentative beginnings of a teenaged mustache and he was sobbing like a little bitch. "Oh God, it hurts." The Bonneville had pinned his legs to the tracks just below his knees. There was no blood that Marquez could see, but he knew the weight of that car had pulverized the kid's bones. The only things holding those legs together were the kid's FUBU jeans.

Marquez keyed his microphone: "Twelve-A-Forty-five, I'm going to need an RA unit for a male black, approximately sixteen years—"

"I'm seventeen," the kid whispered, slipping right into shock.

"Correction, seventeen years, conscious and breathing, suffering from two broken legs," Marquez said. "Advise the fire department. He's pinned under a vehicle. We're also requesting a t-unit and additional units for a perimeter. We have an outstanding GTA suspect—male black, five-ten, one sixty-five—running northbound through the industrial park at Slauson and Halldale."

Ben squatted next to the gangster and placed his hand on the steel track. There was no mistaking the vibration thrumming up through his palm and growing stronger. Ben looked at Marquez, wanting to get his attention without alerting the gangster, but the train's air horn sounded in the distance. "Oh, Jesus," the gangster whined. "Please."

"Twelve-A-forty-five, notify Union Pacific," Marquez said. "Tell them to stop the train." Marquez turned and shoved his shoulder against the Bonneville, trying to tilt the car enough for Ben to slide the kid out from under it. Then they both tried to tilt the car, bracing their boots against the ties for leverage, but the car wouldn't budge. "Get the jack out of our trunk," Marquez told Ben. "Hurry the fuck up." Ben ran back to the car and returned with the jack. The vibration in the track had intensified.

The freight train bore down on them. It looked like a skyscraper turned on its side, easily half a mile long and moving at a good clip as it rounded a bend up around Normandie. Marquez keyed his mike. "Twelve-A-Forty-five, I need you to stop that goddamned train now," he said, but the train showed no sign of slowing.

Ben slid the jack under the car next to the boy's legs and cranked it. Metal groaned. The jack began to lift, buckling the hood of the car, but the work was maddeningly slow and Ben could feel the vibrations of the train closing in. The ground shook. Loose gravel popped and jumped around him. His fingers slipped and he cursed. Sweat stung his eyes. Ben tried to concentrate, but he could feel the kid's eyes on him, wide and pleading. "I've almost got it," he whispered, wanting it to be true. "Just a little more time."

Marquez ran ahead to meet the oncoming train, waving his Streamlight to get the conductor's attention. The air horn blew a long, plaintive blast. Its message was unmistakable: the engineer couldn't possibly halt the momentum of this half-mile locomotive in time. Ben cranked the jack harder, wondering if the kid could feel any pressure letting up on his legs. He extended the jack to its full height, tenting the hood of the car.

"Get clear, Professor!" Marquez shouted. Ben looked up and saw the train's engine rushing at him, peppered with black diesel exhaust and dead bugs. He grabbed the kid under his arms and pulled hard. The gangster screamed in pain, but he wouldn't budge. His legs were still caught.

"Officer," the kid pleaded, gripping Ben's hand. "Please, don't let me die."

Marquez tackled Ben out of the way just as the train filled the world with the sound of grinding steel. The Bonneville crumpled as the train plowed into it. Grinding yellow sparks caught the Bonneville's gas tank and a bright orange fireball spun the car, lifting it off the track. Hunks of flaming wreck cartwheeled across the gravel and settled in smoking heaps as the train groaned to a stop. A single hubcap fell out of the sky and rattled on the ground in front of Ben like a dropped coin.

Ben stood up, lifted his arm to wipe the smoke and dust out of his eyes, and blinked dreamily at the bloody, twitching thing that clung to his palm. He tried to shake it loose, but the dead kid's severed hand still gripped his, desperate fingers digging little half-moons into the heel of Ben's palm.

"Welcome to Seventy-seventh," Marquez said.

The sirens overlapped, units pouring in from all over South Bureau to close up the perimeter before the driver could slip away. Marquez figured the driver was now good for 187. If somebody goes tits up while you're committing a felony, you go down for felony murder even if the death was an accident.

Air 18, orbiting the scene at about five hundred feet, directed the responding units to optimal street corners until a tight perimeter took shape. Within minutes, officers had taken line-of-sight positions at Dauber Avenue and Fifty-sixth Street, Normandie and Fifty-sixth, Dauber and Fifty-seventh, Normandie and Fifty-seventh, Dauber and Fifty-eighth, Normandie and Fifty-eighth, boxing the suspect within a tight four-block radius. Once the perimeter was locked down, Marquez heard the airship send additional units to block the alleys. It wouldn't be long now, Marquez thought. A K-9 unit was on its way from Metro Division in Elysian Park.

"This guy's gone to ground somewhere close," Marquez told the kid, who looked a little green, but had confounded Marquez by failing to blow chunks. "But he can't hide from the dog."

Gangsters swore by all kinds of ghetto remedies for throwing off a K-9, but none of them worked. They'd hide out at a homie's crib, burn their clothes, and bathe in vinegar and cayenne pepper. If no safe houses were within reach, he'd seen them ditch their clothes and smear dog turd all over their bodies. Marquez had even found one knucklehead crouched down in the bottom of an Andy Gump, up to his eyeballs in a stinking reservoir of human waste, but no matter what kind of disgusting-ass ploy these assholes tried, the dog always found them.

The homicide scene itself stretched for half a block and the TV news helicopters were already hovering over the smoking wreck before the traffic cops could get the carnage sealed off with yellow tape. The train had been forced to stop, blocking the street and backing up traffic for miles in every direction. Horns blared and cars would begin overheating soon.

The officer in charge of the investigation was that fat fuck Keyes. Detective Keyes was that obscene kind of fat where he had actually developed another ass on the front of his body and he cinched an oversized belt around his middle to suggest a waist. Years of booze and sun had left Keyes with a face the texture of chewed bubble gum.

Marquez watched Keyes interview the train engineer. The engineer looked badly shaken and Marquez felt for the guy, wringing his cap in his fists as he answered Keyes's terse questions. No way to stop her in time, the engineer said. Keyes didn't argue with him, but he didn't console him much either. By the time Keyes finished with the engineer, dark sweat stains had spread from Keyes's armpits and threatened to meet under his tie. He was eating an orange Popsicle and most of it had melted, turning his pudgy hand safety orange to match the traffic cones out on Slauson.

Keyes waddled toward Marquez, pausing along the track at a bloody Nike basketball shoe with most of the kid's right foot still in it, already covered in flies. Keyes shrugged and dropped a little numbered pylon next to the shoe so the SID techs would know to photograph and bag the thing.

"So let me get this straight," Keyes told Marquez. "You're following Amos and Andy in a Code Six Chuck vehicle." He paused to wave the flies off his Popsicle before shoving the rest of it into his mouth. "Driver takes off like a striped-ass ape, and does a jigaboo jackknife over the fence, but his homie doesn't make it out in time. Car rolls, trapping the passenger under it. Train comes along and grinds him into Hershey's syrup.

"Going to need a goddamned cherry picker to recover that fucking mess." Keyes pointed up at the kid's torso hanging in the telephone lines like a broken kite. The fiery blast had reduced him to charred flesh and bone from which the remnants of his clothing hung in blackened tatters. The lines sagged under the kid's weight. "Explosion probably punted this dude's head clear into Inglewood," Keyes said. "Fuck it, NHI, right?" He clapped Marquez on the shoulder. No Human Involved.

"Aw, *shit*," one of the uniforms guarding the perimeter groaned. "Here he comes. Somebody call a fucking supervisor."

Marquez and Keyes both turned to watch the Miracle Mobile gliding down Slauson like a galleon. Beyond the yellow tape, the familiar gold-rimmed Cadillac pulled to the gravel shoulder, custom horn blasting "Go Tell It on the Mountain." The Caddy's doors bore a gold crucifix superimposed on a map of Africa. The Reverend Malachi Silas stepped out of the Caddy wearing a long dashiki and traditional wooden necklace draped over a chest like a fifty-gallon drum.

"King Kong himself," Keyes snorted.

The press had dubbed Mal Silas the Lion of Judah, which Marquez knew pleased the cat to no end. His huge head was wreathed in an Afro-mane like steel wool, his jaw covered by a thick beard. His shelflike brow shadowed blazing hazel eyes and broad nostrils that flared with righteous indignation. Mal stood at the edge of the tape, his massive arms akimbo, and nodded across the tape to Marquez. Marquez smiled, and spat a brown gob of chaw onto Keyes's shoes.

"Cocksucker," Keyes hissed.

News crews that were encamped along the crime scene tape hustled over to Silas, shoving their mikes up at him, poised for a juicy, racially charged sound bite in time to make the six-o'clock news. Mal stroked his beard and cleared his throat for dramatic affect, threw a little wink at Marquez. Fucking Mal, Marquez stifled a grin.

Mal Silas was the celebrated founder of the First Church of the First Continent, a "multidenominational ministry of activism," which Mal ran out of a derelict movie theater in Inglewood. Mal was also a founding member of the Four-Six Neighborhood Crips, and Marquez knew Mal from way back when he was still pulling 211s and running whores up and down Western. A thousand years ago, when they were both young and dumb, Marquez had happily chased Mal all over South Central, and had personally kicked the living shit out of him on more than one occasion.

Mal could take a punch, and for that reason alone Marquez just couldn't bring himself to hate the guy.

Before cuddling up to Jesus in Chino, Mal had hacked up a Six-Deuce Brim with a machete back in '92 and served ten years. He'd beaten a guy from Bloodline to death in Chino, but he'd walked on that one after two hung juries. After reinventing himself as a community activist, Mal had beaten a RICO indictment. He'd sired six illegitimate kids from five different mothers. His oldest, Mal Jr., was himself doing a stint up in Wasco. behind a video-store robbery. Marquez had sent Mal Jr. a care package of Nutter Butters and a *Penthouse* last Christmas and the kid had sent Marquez back a handmade thank-you card, all done up in a con's careful calligraphy.

"I'm glad y'all here to see this prime example of the Gestapo tactics employed by the LAPD," Mal's tenor boomed. "What you got here is a occupyin' army, a jackbooted invasion force. See, they don't ask no questions, don't make no apologies. They just be shuttin' down our streets, blockin' our intersections, keepin' our hardworkin' daddies from gettin' home to their families and our hardworkin' mammas from gettin' to market. They ain't tryin' to keep gangs *out*. They ain't tryin' to keep drugs *out*. They tryin' to keep us *down*." Silas folded his arms over his broad chest. "Well, I for one am sickened by this invasion, but I must tell you I am not surprised by it."

"That makes two of us," Marquez muttered.

The radio crackled, the air unit barely audible over Mal's performance. "Air Eighteen to units on the perimeter, be advised: we have a male black matching the suspect's description moving northbound through the houses with a pronounced limp. Suspect is midblock on Fifty-eighth between Normandie and Dauber. Units on the perimeter, hold your positions."

4

1972–1985

He was born Darius James Washington, but never had much use for slave names. The homies called him Darius, and later Crazy D. Darius came up in the Boot Hill Mafia Crip hood and the BHMCs jumped him in at nine. It wasn't like he had any choice. Anywhere west of Raymond, you got jumped in or you got jumped on. Four of the homies, all sinewy, dead-eyed teenagers with rolls of quarters in their fists, descended on him like jackals. Blow after punishing blow, Darius managed to keep his feet until a wild right caught him behind the ear, the impact splitting open both Darius's head and the roll of quarters in the guy's fist. His blood and the shimmering coins spilled into the alley and one of the big dogs finally signaled this boy had had enough.

His father could have been any number of Boot Hill homeboys who visited his unconscious mother after she passed out, bombed on skunk weed and Boone's wine, splayed on a roach-infested couch at an album-scratchin' Boot Hill house party when she was thirteen. Marie, Darius's sainted mother, sampled freebase cocaine at nineteen and decided everything her teachers had told her about drugs was a lie. She was posted out on Figueroa by her twenty-third birthday.

Now, Figueroa isn't the fishnet-and-feather-boa stroll of the Sunset Strip, isn't even the drive-thru head factory of Santa Monica Boulevard, and the johns seeking their pleasures down on Fig are never gentle. Early on, some rough trade spoiled Marie's face and she found herself working harder for less. They used Marie up in a few months, just about devoured her until all that remained was a haggard zombie in a Naugahyde skirt and broken heels, a piteous creature that had once dreamed she was a pretty girl.

Darius, now ten, had eschewed elementary school for more practical instruction, working as a lookout and runner for the Boot Hill Mafia because everyone knew a kid that young wouldn't do any tall time for packing a strap. When the BHMCs put him to work as a courier, Darius skimmed a few bucks whenever he could get away with it and brought the cash straight to his momma, taking his life in his hands in the hope that he could treat Marie to a night off.

By then, a kind of post-traumatic dementia had set in and Marie could not, or would not, distinguish her son from her other johns. If the boy brought her money, that meant the boy wanted sex. So, she gave it to him. Darius, who knew nothing of sex and had thus far received little in the way of motherly affection, was thankful for any attention his momma would give him. He liked being so close to her. She made him feel good and he liked holding on to her. He wanted to stay with his momma, but she always sent him away as soon as his money ran out.

With the money he skimmed from the Boot Hill Mafia, Darius became one of Marie's regulars, visiting her whenever his funds allowed. If she were busy with another john in an alley or a car, Darius would watch her from a distance, waiting his turn. It always made him feel strange and anxious to watch her with these other men and Darius often imagined getting his hands on enough money to take his momma somewhere, away from all the rough hands, just the two of them.

One night, Darius crept along the shadows of an alley and saw his momma with a white man in a dark blue uniform. Crouching in the dark among the shattered crack pipes, beer bottles, condoms, and plastic lighters, Darius watched the wolf-eyed cop take Marie from behind with his trousers pulled down to his knees and his gun belt slung over his shoulder. He pulled her tangled hair and called her filthy names. Darius watched the cop's face change and knew he was finished with her.

Now another night creature that had been prowling Fig spied ten-year-old Darius as Darius ducked into the alley. The boy was just what he had been hunting for. The creature followed Darius into the alley, but he too kept to the shadows and made no sound. Fixated on his prey, he evidently didn't realize the whore at the far end of the alley was servicing a cop.

Watching the cop zip up and put on his gun belt, Darius didn't see the other man sneak up behind him until the man had knocked him to the ground. Darius tried to get up, but the man on top of him was too heavy. Yanking the boy's pants down around his ankles, he told Darius he would kill him if he screamed. Darius felt like he was being torn open and his stomach was suddenly on fire.

Marie, who for months had seemed oblivious to everything but her next hit, experienced a moment of maternal clarity. She ran to Darius and tried to protect her son. Marie screamed, clawed the man's face, and somehow forced him off Darius, fighting like a cornered polecat while Darius pulled up his pants.

Darius struggled to his feet, turned to the cop standing at the far end of the alley, looked into the cop's pale eyes, and said please don't let that man hurt my momma. The cop, who had just taken a little break from his patrol to bust a nut on some crack whore, evidently decided whatever the fuck was going down at the other end of the alley wasn't really any of his concern and he would much rather protect and serve elsewhere, thank you very much. He frowned back at Darius behind his Marlboro Man mustache, turned, and beat feet back down the alley to his black-and-white.

Darius heard his momma scream and turned back to her in time to see there was now a knife in the man's fist. Darius watched the man plunge that knife into her stomach again and again until she stopped fighting him, watched her collapse, vomiting black blood. The man stepped over Marie, his face a lattice of bloody scratches, and came at Darius with the knife raised. Darius ran like hell.

Jax, one of the hard-core Boot Hill Mafia Crips for whom Darius couriered, had taken an avuncular interest in Darius, allowing him to crash out on an old mattress in his garage. Perhaps, Jax saw a bit of himself in the boy. When Jax was Darius's age, they had called him Apache, on account of his heritage, but the Boot Hill Mafia changed his moniker to Ajax after he blinded an enemy in prison by grinding cleanser into the man's eyes.

When Jax saw the blood soaking through Darius's pants that morning, he shook Darius awake. "The fuck happened to you, bwoy?" Darius told Jax about the man who had hurt him down there and how the man had stabbed his mother when she had tried to protect him. When Darius started to cry, Jax slapped him, hard. "Don't you ever let me see you cry like a bitch," Jax told him and slapped Darius again. "Get mad," he said and slapped him a third time. "Get mad, bwoy!"

Jax went to the alley and saw Marie curled up in large dark puddle of her own blood, blowflies crawling over her open eyes. "Dumbass ho," he whispered, shaking his head. "You used to be fine." He thought this poor bitch had actually been dead for months. She just hadn't had the sense to lie down until last night, but he didn't share this opinion with Darius.

On his way home, Jax went to the market and bought some antiseptic ointment and a box of Maxi pads for Darius. Jax had done some time in Chino for aggravated burglary and another nasty stint in Folsom for ADW. He knew more than he cared to about prison pussy, knew dudes like Daddy Python who had a genuine taste for Pelican Bay poonanny. He showed Darius how to apply the ointment and pads and told the boy he would stop leaking in a few days.

"How do you know?" Darius asked.

"Trust me," Jax said. "I know." Jax, lifelong gangbanger and stone killer, by all accounts a poor role model and a poorer child psychologist, knew only one remedy for Darius's trauma. No need for anatomically correct dolls or regressive hypnotherapy. When somebody fucked you, you made that somebody all kinds of dead. "What'd this motherfucker look like?"

"He was white," Darius said.

"Course he was," Jax said.

"He was big," Darius said. "His face was bloody where Momma scratched him."

Jax reasoned this chickenhawk would need boys the way Marie had needed her rock, but he would need other things too, like underground magazines and fuck flicks that featured small children. Jax asked around, heard tell of an albino who ran a wig shop on Hollywood Boulevard, the wigs just a front. The albino, who called himself Strange, used his little shop to sell kiddy porn to dudes with short eyes. Jax left Darius on the couch to heal while he drove over the hill. Eighteenth Street controlled that part of Hollywood, so Jax got with the man out there, an OG he knew from the pen, told him he was just in the neighborhood to kill a white man who fucked little boys. The OG said cool beans and Eighteenth Street left Jax alone.

Jax left his beat-to-shit Buick parked on Whitley, just off Hollywood Boulevard. He sat on the sidewalk in front of the wig shop with an empty Big Gulp and spare-changed it. No one paid Jax any mind. He was just another free-range basehead on the dirty boulevard. He even made a few bucks in change. He hung there every day for almost two weeks, watching furtive guys in baseball caps and dark glasses hurry in and out of Strange's wig shop. After ten days, Jax was about to pull up stakes and try something else.

That's when he saw that big white motherfucker with the bandaged face come out of the wig shop. Jax sidled up next to him, jammed his nine into the chickenhawk's ribs and told the guy to walk with him to his ride. Jax figured the guy didn't have much of a choice. What fuck was he going to do, holler for the cops? Not with the latest issue of *Little Boyfriends* hot off the presses and burning a hole in that wig box under his meaty arm. Jax bound the guy's wrists and ankles with duct tape, placed a strip of tape across his eyes, another across his mouth, and tossed his fat ass in the trunk of the Buick.

As Jax drove him back to the hood, it must have dawned on Old Short Eyes this wasn't just some carjacking, and keeping his filthy secrets was suddenly the least of his worries. The guy screamed through the tape and pounded the inside of the trunk. So Jax cranked the tunes the rest of the way home to drown out all that whining and blubbering.

Jax opened the trunk and hauled the thrashing chickenhawk out into the dirt, told him everything would be cool so long as he didn't act the fool. "Stay loose and you live, dig?" The guy would have smelled unpleasant things, would have heard the dogs. He would have sensed he was indoors, but he couldn't have known where. Of course, this guy never heard of the Spook House, the Ghetto Golgotha, the place the Boot Hill Mafia's rivals prayed did not exist. Every hard-core baller accepts the inevitability of a bullet or shank, but jailhouse yarns about that place, whispered stories of the diabolical shit that went on there, shook even the baddest hope-to-die Crip Killas to their core.

Jax shook Darius awake, told him to get dressed. Darius rubbed his eyes and followed Jax out to his Buick. When he climbed into the passenger seat, Jax handed Darius a pillowcase and told him to put the thing over his head. "It's for your own good," Jax said. Darius thought he had an idea where Jax was taking him. He draped the pillowcase over his head and didn't peek, didn't speak for the entire ride. When Santa offers you a ride to his workshop, you don't question the man's security measures, and damn you sure don't ask him are we there yet.

After a few twists and turns, Jax stopped the car, came around and opened his door. Darius heard monstrous growling and baying, and the stench scared him. He felt like he couldn't breathe at first, and he said wanted to stay in the car.

"Just take my hand now, Boo," Jax said. "After tonight you won't have to be scared of the dark." Darius let Jax lead him through the darkness. The ground felt uneven, but he knew they were indoors. "Now, when I take that hood off, you don't have to look around too much you don't want to," Jax told him. "What you need to see be right there in front of you."

Jax removed the pillowcase. He held a moth-battered Coleman lantern, and by its dim light Darius saw the chickenhawk there on the dirt floor, naked and hogtied with strips of duct tape over his mouth. Jax reached down and tore the bandage off the guy's eyes, taking his eyebrows with it. Darius could see the bandage where Marie had scratched him.

"That's him," Darius said, his voice full of childish wonder, thinking Jax had worked a kind of ghetto magic here, conjuring his attacker from Darius's bare description of him. The man didn't look scary lying there buck naked, skin pale and pulpy in the lantern light. Darius reached out and pinched the guy's nostrils shut, telling himself he was just curious to see what would happen. With the tape already over his mouth, Darius was cutting off all his air. The guy's body jiggled, his eyes bulged pleadingly, and he shit himself. Then Darius let go of his nose and the chickenhawk sucked air noisily through his nostrils. The dogs howled.

"This is payback, D," Jax told him, handing Darius a pair of rubber gloves and a box cutter. Darius went straight to work, cutting the man's ears off while the man screamed through the duct tape. Darius wanted to carve his mother's name in the man's chest, but he didn't know how to spell Marie, so Jax helped him with that. Then Darius sawed off the man's penis. The chickenhawk passed out, but he came around again when they rolled him into the pit and he was awake when the dogs tore into him.

"Feel better?" Jax asked.

"I don't feel nothin'," Darius said.

"Hell, ain't that better?"

5

PRESENT

"Come on, Professor." Marquez turned his back on the Mal Silas Show and Ben followed him to the black-and-white. Marquez drove them into the perimeter, jumping a curb and tearing a muddy swath across some-one's lawn to avoid hitting the other units blocking Dauber Avenue. He continued north on Dauber and east on Fifty-eighth. Marquez keyed his mike. "Twelve-A-Forty-five to Air Eighteen, we're primary on this and we'll take him."

"Roger that, Marquez," the Air unit responded. "Your suspect's to the rear of that white house coming up on your left. I've lost visual on him, but I think he's under the eaves on the back porch."

Marquez halted the black-and-white two houses west of the target lo-cation. "Get the beanbag," he said. Ben fetched the beanbag shotgun out of the trunk, performed a quick safety check, and jacked a round into the chamber. The beanbag shotgun was a standard Ithaca 12-gauge pump, retrofitted with a threaded barrel to fire a heavy nylon square about the size of a tea bag and filled with an ounce of lead birdshot, designed to de-liver enough blunt trauma to knock the wind out of a suspect without killing him, but the rounds had been known to penetrate, causing inter-nal injuries and death.

The K-9 unit arrived about four seconds after they did, pulling up to the curb behind Marquez. The K-9 officer was a tall black man with green eyes and a permanent smile. The name tag printed on his black fatigues read GRANT. "Miguel," he said, slapping Marquez's outstretched palm.

Marquez dug his battered bag of Red Man out of his back pocket and held it open. Grant plucked out a wad of tobacco and slipped it under his bottom lip. He eyed Ben and spat on to the sidewalk.

"Fresh fish?" Grant asked.

"They don't come any fresher," Marquez said. "First day out."

"You introduced him to Tony T. yet?"

Marquez nodded and spat.

"No bullshit." Grant lifted his eyebrows at Ben. "And you're still standing. Man, he got through with me, I couldn't walk." He smiled and held out his hand. "Bobby Grant." Ben shouldered the shotgun to shake hands with Grant, feeling a little thrill of pride. So, Tony was the *Kobiyashi Maru* and Ben had come out more or less even.

"Ben Halloran," he said. "Pleasure to meet you, sir."

"You'll piss blood tonight," Grant whispered to Ben. "It'll be gone in a week or so."

"Not too chummy, Bobby," Marquez said. "I don't expect him to last a week in Indian Country."

Grant rolled his eyes at Ben and opened the rear door of his car. A Belgian Malinois leaped out onto the grass. The dog resembled some morphological distillation of a German shepherd, with smaller triangular ears and a tighter bone structure. He circled them once and sat at Grant's feet like a sphinx.

"This is Snake," Grant said. "Don't try to pet him unless you want stitches. I'll take point. Ben, you cover me with the beanbag. Marquez calls the shots."

Marquez keyed his mike. "Units on the perimeter stand by," he said. "We're beginning our search."

The house was a swaybacked postwar craftsman, one of hundreds built in those heady Truman years when this neighborhood still held promise for young families starting out. The house had weathered the white flight, two riots, and four recessions, and it had the scars to prove it. Dry rot. Termites. Flaking paint and split shingles. Windows long painted shut. The rosebushes had been tended in the not-too-distant past. The lawn was slightly scorched and salted with dandelions, but hadn't quite run to riot. Whoever lived in this house had made some effort at upkeep.

The gate was open. Snake nosed along the side yard and they followed him single file. The dog moved over the grass with agility uncommon in an animal of his size. He sniffed the air and his mouth hung open, displaying bright teeth in what Ben would have sworn was an expectant smile. They rounded the corner at the back of the house and found the driver on the back porch.

You had to hand it to the guy, Ben thought. He was resourceful. Trapped inside an LAPD perimeter with his left ankle swollen like a grapefruit, he'd picked up a crowbar somewhere in the neighborhood. Ben was pretty sure he didn't have it with him when he jumped out of the Bonneville.

At first, he was too busy prying at the doorjamb to notice them. The guy braced the screen door open with his hip while he hooked the crowbar into the narrow space between the back door and its frame. He yanked on the crowbar with both hands, splitting the doorjamb into long splinters. The door groaned and shifted on its hinges.

Snake didn't bark a warning as he bounded across the grass and launched his body over the porch. His jaws clamped down on the driver's right thigh. The driver screamed and lifted the crowbar high over his shoulder, poised to bring the weapon down on the dog.

"Drop it!" Ben shouted, raising the beanbag shotgun to target his abdomen. Snake snapped his head from side to side, tearing through denim and flesh. The guy swung the crowbar at the dog's head and Ben squeezed the trigger.

The shotgun coughed smoke and sparks. The wadding tore a hole through the screen door, but the beanbag round caught the driver square in his solar plexus. His crowbar clattered on the porch and the guy doubled over, gasping and clutching his gut. Ben felt for the guy, remembering the impact of Tony's fist in his gut.

"Revere!" Grant snapped and Snake reluctantly disengaged from the guy's thigh, circling back around the porch to await his next command. Thick blood dripped from the dog's teeth.

"Hit him again, Professor," Marquez ordered. The guy heard him and immediately raised his trembling hands in surrender. Still doubled over, the guy looked like some bug-eyed biblical supplicant, gulping air, unable to speak.

"I think he's had enough, sir," Ben said.

Marquez snatched the shotgun out of Ben hands and roughly shoved Ben aside as he jacked another round into the chamber. Marquez blasted a second beanbag into the driver's gut, knocking the guy off his feet. The impact slammed the driver backward against the door, splitting what remained of the frame. The door fell open, dangling from a single hinge. The driver lay curled in the doorway. His eyes protruding, mouth opened wide as if to scream, but only small, rasping sounds came out.

"Now he's had enough," Marquez said, shouldering the weapon. Ben wrenched the guy's arms behind his back and cuffed him.

Snake noticed it first. He was too disciplined to growl, but his ears flattened and the fur bristled around his neck and shoulders. "Something in the house," Grant said and raised his pistol to cover the open doorway.

Ben heard it now—a thin buzzing, like a mild electrical field, coming from inside the house. Marquez kicked the door off its remaining hinge and peered into the small kitchen. When he saw the cloud of blowflies whirling through the squalid air, Marquez sighed heavily. "Get another crime scene going," he said. "We're gonna be overtime."

"Keep your mouth closed," Marquez said, stepping through the doorway. Ben followed him into the kitchen. It was like walking through a storm of raisins. Fat blowflies lighted on his eyelashes, under his nose, and at the corners of his mouth.

Flies covered the bloated thing slumped over the sink, the same way bees cover those Guinness freaks. The effect distorted the size and shape of the body so that it didn't look like a man at all. It looked like a dead bear.

Marquez stepped closer and the flies scattered, blinding them for a second. The crouching smell of rot, fetid and sweet, hit Ben with almost physical force, and he had to steady himself on the linoleum counter. Marquez cupped his hand over his mouth and nose. Ben noticed Marquez eyeing him expectantly, as though waiting for him to vomit.

After weeks of decomposition, the techs would have some trouble determining the actual cause of death. The guy's right hand looked like something had gnawed it off at the wrist. Ben saw the desiccated fingers in the blood-caked sink and figured they'd shoved the guy's hand into the disposal. *They,* he thought, because this kind of torture would have taken two or three guys at least.

Shock and blood loss alone would have killed him, but they hadn't stopped with the disposal. They'd also jammed a tin funnel into the man's right ear and poured drain cleaner down his ear canal. The open bottle of Drano stood on the counter next to the sink. Blood and yellowish matter had leaked from that ear down the side of his face. Packed into the guy's eye sockets, nose, and slack mouth, thousands of pale maggots, each no larger than a grain of rice, wriggled and moiled. The dry, delicate sound of all those tiny bodies twisting against each other was like the ragged, unceasing whisper of radio static.

He'd probably been in his forties, but Ben couldn't tell for sure. The guy's flesh had darkened to the blue color of a bad bruise where his stagnant blood had settled and the expanding gases trapped inside him had stretched his abdomen as tight as a drum. His bloody guayabera shirt had ridden up to accommodate the swelling of his belly, which had bloated thin and translucent, like the bulging throat of a bullfrog.

Ben turned away from the body. His eyes followed a thin ant trail that ran into the living room, up the leg of an air-hockey table, swarming over two plates of what had probably been sandwiches. The ant trail continued over the air-hockey table and into a standing birdcage. Ants covered the body of a dead macaw, hurrying into its open beak. The bird had probably starved to death sometime after the murder. The only other movement in the house came from the flat-screen television tuned to a George Foreman infomercial.

6

1985

For all intents and purposes, Benji lived alone the rest of that summer after his bar mitzvah. Once a week or so he'd find a hundred-dollar bill stuck to the fridge with a magnet, his only evidence his father was still alive. He supposed this was the old man's way of making good on his promise, sparing Benji his unpredictable rages by avoiding the kid altogether. Or maybe, in his secret heart, Big Ben was just hoping his son would take the hint and disappear. Benji lived on Domino's and takeout Chinese, just let the boxes pile up until the cleaning woman cleared them away. He was still young enough to hatch vague plans to locate his mother, to find her in a bustling marketplace. She'd know his face.

A shriek woke him late one night. Benji jumped out of bed and went to the window. A great horned owl had a possum pinned to the diving board, its talons buried deep in the creature's spine. The trapped possum craned its head at an impossible angle, snapping and snarling soundlessly. Its tail whipped and coiled on the board as the owl leisurely plucked the meat from the creature's body. No, Benji realized; the owl wasn't gobbling morsels of the possum's own body. It was eating her pups. Benji watched the owl gulp down the struggling, hairless things one by one. Blood dripped from the diving board and spread through the water like smoke. Mist feathered up from the heated pool and the underwater lights reflected in the owl's eyes. Benji went back to bed, pulled the sheets over his face, and cried.

He crammed his wetsuit into a backpack before sunup, grabbed his board, and hitched to Malibu, hopping into a rusty truck bed with some stoic *jornaleros*. They rode in silence with his board across their laps, huddled against the night chill still clinging to Puerco Canyon, and he watched the gunmetal waterline sharpen against the dawn as the pickup shimmied and rattled up PCH.

Benji pounded his fist on the cab and they pulled over to drop him at the Trancas Creek overpass, where LOCALS ONLY had been spray-painted on the cliff face and over the padlocked door of the empty lifeguard tower. He hiked down through the ice plant along the creek as the first sandblasted locals stepped barefoot out of live-in microbuses and old conversion vans guarded by half-wild dogs. They stretched and pissed, a few of them packed bowls and cracked Pabst Blue Ribbons—breakfast of champions.

He paddled out with them, past the breakers, out where the Garibaldi and giant sea bass milled in the swaying kelp, and straddled their boards like a picket of Mongol horsemen. They rode double overheads until noon, Benji playing conservatively until he had some sense of the pecking order, but he caught his share and held his own. When the sets played out around sundown, they built a pallet bonfire and Benji peeled his wetsuit down to his waist to let the flames bake the cold from his ropey muscles until only sea salt remained, like dandruff on his bare shoulders.

Benji lost track of how many nights he spent out there where the continent was sliding into the ocean, each day folding into the next. There were only waves, weed, and the warmth of the bonfire. He wasn't ever going back, doubted if Big Ben was beating the bushes for him anyway.

PRESENT

The living room was ghetto fabulous, choked with pricey crap from places like the Sharper Image, a snooker table, a jukebox, and a stylized litho of Elvis and Marilyn at some diner with a real neon sign. A fence would have kept his wares in a garage or storage unit. Ben figured this guy had just been pathologically acquisitive.

Framed photos hung among the neon beer signs. Ben saw a foggy old snapshot of a young boy receiving his first communion. Next to it was another photo of the same boy in his teens, squatting in front of a tricked-out lowrider with four homies in ironed flannel shirts buttoned up to the throat. They wore matching bandannas and wraparound shades—all five of them throwing up Florencia. Another group of photos depicted the same guy, now in his early forties. Hard time etched deeply into his lean face. Three teardrops tattooed under his left eye. In one photo he was holding a candle, marching alongside Edward James Olmos. In another, a grinning Magic Johnson was handing him a charity check the size of a bus bench.

Grant poked his head into the kitchen and whistled. "Any signs of forced entry?" he asked, pinching his nostrils shut.

"Nope, he either knew them or they bamboozled him somehow." Marquez shook his head. "Must have really hated this motherfucker to do him like this."

Exposed to the outside air, the dead man's bloated belly suddenly popped like a balloon, expelling a cloud of sweetish gas. That did it. Ben lurched across the kitchen, leaned over the sink, and let his lunch fly into the basin.

"I hold these truths to be self-evident," Marquez said, sounding strangely pleased. From the doorway, Grant screwed his face into an uncanny imitation of Marquez's permanent scowl and held his index finger under his nose to simulate a mustache. He mouthed the words as Marquez spoke them, lip-synching a speech he must have known by heart. "It's better to be rich than poor, better to be tall than short, better to have a big dick than a small one, and it is better to be alive than to be dead."

"Yes, sir." Ben coughed, wiping his mouth. Where did he come up with this shit?

"I can't do anything about your money or your prick, Professor," Marquez said. "But if you do what I tell you out here, I promise to keep you alive."

Marquez radioed the RTO to tell them he had the suspect in custody, but he needed additional units to secure a second crime scene. Then he used the house phone to call the station and told the watch commander to get another homicide detective rolling. Vintner sent a middle-aged Asian guy named Chuin. Detective Bae Chuin was five-foot *nada* with a potbelly and bifocals and he combed his black hair across a widening bald spot.

"Miguel, what the fuck?" Chuin uncapped a bottle of Old Spice and dabbed a few drops on to his handkerchief. "Have you seen my desk lately? Neither have I, can't find it under all the crap. This one will make sixteen open cases I'm carrying and I'm starting to forget what my kids look like."

"They're ugly," Marquez said.

"You hearing this barbarian, boy?" Chuin poked Ben in the ribs with a chubby index finger. Still tender from Tony's body shots, Ben grunted involuntarily. "No respect for his elders, I come out of the showers last month and this spick motherfucker wants to rub Buddha's belly for good luck. Ha-ha, big locker-room laugh, but now every superstitious gun-fighter in division has to get some before he leaves the barn. I come home chafed and my old lady thinks I have something on the side, like I have time for pussy. I don't have time to sit on the crapper with a racing form like a civilized man anymore. Get used to long hours, boy. You're partnered up with the original shit magnet." Chuin clamped the damp handkerchief over his mouth and nose as he stepped into the flyblown kitchen. "I'm serious, kid. I mean this man is cursed." He eyed the body, scanned the photos on the wall, cocked an eyebrow, and looked at the body again.

"Hey, I knew this guy," Chuin said through the handkerchief. "Last couple years, he was a bagman for the *Eme,* but he was a hope-to-die shooter back in the day. I'll clear four or five old DRs on this asshole. His MO was to blast witnesses." Chuin made a gun of this thumb and forefin-ger. "Bang! Enough wits come up dead and the survivors suffer acute memory loss. They used to call him Wizard, like in the movie. 'Nobody sees the Wizard. Not nobody. Not no how.'"

"Cute," Marquez said.

"This is the third *Eme* taxman in as many weeks that's gone to the big tortilla factory in the sky," Chuin said, shaking his head. "Coroner's office is starting to look like a tattoo parlor."

"Same MO?" Marquez asked.

"Yep." Chuin nodded. "No forced entry. All the victims—I use the term loosely. I mean, couldn't have happened to a nicer bunch of guys—All tortured to death, like somebody was asking them, '*Dónde está* the fucking dope money, Julio?' Nobody's tried this in years, not since Crazy D popped those wholesalers on the West Side."

"You got any theories, Detective?" Marquez asked.

"One," Chuin said. "But I don't think you're going to like it."

Marquez charged Ben with babysitting the driver of the Bonneville while he and Chuin held the crime scene. Ben walked the guy out front and sat him in the back of the black-and-white. It was slow going. The dude couldn't put any weight on his ankle and he was still doubled over from the beanbags. Ben cranked the air-conditioning and opened the glass partition, so he could talk to the guy from the front seat. "Name?"

"Deandre," he said. "Lamar." Ben watched him through the rearview mirror. He was older than his passenger had been, but not much, nineteen or twenty, tops. A DA might let him plea to aggravated manslaughter. If he survived inside, this kid would be in his mid-thirties by the time they let him see daylight again. "I didn't know about that dude inside the house."

"Nobody said you did," Ben said, and he believed Lamar. If he'd known there was a dead body in the house, Lamar would have hidden somewhere else. "You bang?"

"Boot Hill Mafia," he said, straightening up in his seat.

"What do they call you?"

"Baby Nickel," Lamar said. Ben punched his name and gang moniker into their appropriate fields on the MDT. "Hey, I seen you," Lamar said, his voice climbing. Ben watched through the mirror as Lamar's pain-clouded eyes widened. He leaned forward in his seat. "You that half-a-mouthpiece Jew bitch used to wipe Darius's ass for him."

The air inside the black-and-white felt suddenly close, like the inside of a sub that has gone too deep. The stench from the kitchen had somehow seeped into his wool uniform and his throat tightened, making it hard to breathe. Caught on my first day out, he thought, all of it unraveling just that quickly. "You're mistaken," Ben told him feebly, glancing around at the other cops working the scene. All the windows were rolled up, but he wondered if any of them were standing close enough to hear Lamar.

"Working for the Man now," Lamar said, as though relishing the perversity of it. "Now, that is a fuckin' trip, nigga. Crazy D's had every Crip in Cali gunnin' for your ass and for the kind of ducats he was laying down, niggas were shootin' folks way up in Fresno just because they looked like you. They'd fax him these photos like, 'Yo, D, is this the guy?' And you're right here in his backyard, hiding behind a motherfuckin' badge."

"I don't know what you're talking about," Ben said, wiping the first facets of panic-sweat from his forehead. He swallowed dryly, tasting the bitter residue of his own bile. "My name is Halloran."

"Sure it is." Lamar smiled. "Sure it is."

1985–1995

When Darius was about twelve, he confessed to Jax that he didn't know his own birthday, so they settled on one together. To make it official, Jax gave Darius his very own ventilator, a MAC-10 with an extended magazine and the serial numbers neatly drilled off the receiver. The MAC was a lot of gun for a little boy, but Jax took him out to the desert and taught Darius to hold low with both hands, get his whole body behind the gun and make it sing.

Once Darius had demonstrated his control of the weapon, Jax took him on his first drive-by, rolling up on a Family Blood Shrike party in a stolen Toyota. Jax cut the headlights, watching a couple of Shrikes out on the front porch, two forties of Old E and a blunt between them. "Don't worry about savin' ammo, D," Jax told him, letting the car idle forward along the dark street "We can always get more."

When the car came flush with the house, Darius popped up from the backseat, spraying the MAC-10 out the open window with a sound like coarse fabric tearing. The two Shrikes on the porch lifted right out of their Nikes, knocked back through the picture window behind them. Jax floored it and they were in the wind. In the backseat, Darius stared down at the hot weapon in his hands, watched sensuous curls of smoke rolling out of the barrel, and fell deeply in love.

A year later, Darius stopped his bike right in front of the lead limo of a funeral procession for Tray, a Shrike who'd been gunned down on Cen-

tral a few nights before. The whole procession was forced to a stop, like tanks in Tienanmen Square. When the lead limo flashed its brights and honked at him, Darius pulled his birthday MAC from his waistband and dumped fifty rounds straight into the limo, the bullets unzipping the car's windshield, obliterating the driver and all three passengers, Tray's parents and his thirteen-year-old sister bone-flecked pulp from the shoulders up.

Darius appeared in Juvenile Court, riding a detained petition for murder at the age of thirteen. There was a lot of get-tough-on-crime-in-an-election-year posturing about trying Darius as an adult, but nothing came of it. This kid was the orphan son of a crack whore, unable to read or write. The judge sent Darius to the Summerfield Home for Boys.

Summerfield was a sprawling Spanish rancho in the Mendocino foothills that had been donated to the state, surrounded by razor wire, and converted into a progressive juvenile detention facility. That first night in Summerfield, coyotes cornered a jackrabbit or something out beyond the chain-link perimeter fence. Darius could hear them from his bunk, not the lonely howl he'd expected, but an alien keening, like the laughter of children. Darius folded his pillow over his ears, but he could still hear them, playing with their kill long into the night.

About half the counselors at Summerfield were semireformed homeboys, OGs from all the major hoods, hired on as soon as they finished parole. The idea was to staff Summerfield with counselors who had come up on the same streets as their wards, mentors the kids would identify with and respect, but Summerfield hadn't counted on what the state auditors would later call the Fagin effect; these nominally reformed gangsters cliquing up with the kids, and recruiting shakedown crews from among their wards. First of every month, the new meat paid their canteen money up the chain to a roving shakedown crew, the crew in turn breaking off a hunk for their OG counselor. Before the state trashed the mentor program, the Summerfield Bunkhouses became South Central minus the firepower, the gangsters going all *Lord of the Flies* after lights-out, settling street beefs with their hands and feet and sharpened mop handles.

The other counselors were well-meaning white broads with master's degrees out of places like Smith, the kind of women who kept a lot of cats. Most of them were fucking the older boys, their closed-door tutorials a campwide joke. By sixteen, Darius had grown tall and muscular and he was number one on the Earth Mother Hit Parade, the women stepping over each other to pick some forbidden fruit at the peak of ripeness. Olivia Green, Darius's reading tutor, was a flabby-legged woman who braided her red hair down to her tabular ass, wore Birkenstocks, and kept goddess stickers on the bumper of her car and a dreamcatcher hanging from the rearview. "You're like Brad Pitt made of dark chocolate," Olivia once told him, her shapeless body shining with their commingled sweat. For some reason, that made Darius want to strangle her.

Olivia taught him to read, and after Darius had read everything in the camp library, she sent out for books just to keep him quiet. He read Herodotus, *Plunkitt of Tammany Hall*, *The Prince*, *The Autobiography of Malcolm X, Up from Slavery, Think & Grow Rich*, and everything he could find by Harold Robbins. Books became his drug of choice, his instant transportation, but where crack had eaten his mother right off the bone, books let Darius pack on unseen muscle. While the rest of the boys were still set-trippin', still stabbing and gouging and bludgeoning each other over a few sweat-soggy dollars like they were the last morsels in the belly of a slave ship, Darius saw past the ghetto for the first time in his life. He felt like the first of Moreau's animals to put on a pair of pants while the rest of them were still rutting in the mud.

When he turned eighteen, the judge kicked Darius out of the Summerfield just as he had promised he would. Jax was waiting out front to pick him up in his long-ass Cadillac. By then, Jax had turned forty, no mean feat for a black man in the hood, and a certified miracle for any gangbanger. Jax was still as bad as you want and then some, but he had lost a step or two getting there. Darius, on the other hand, had grown red in tooth and claw.

"My nigga." Jax smiled, hugging him up.

Darius hugged Jax back a little harder than he needed to and whispered into his ear, "I ain't your nigga no more, Jax. You mine."

Jax must have expected this reversal, even welcomed it as part of the natural order. He didn't bat an eye, just went right on hugging. "Your world, D," Jax whispered.

Darius hit the ground gunning. The first item on his agenda: gather a handful of the best shooters he could find. "Mix me a crew," he told Jax as they headed south on the 101. "Smashers only. I don't want no junior jive-ass, stick-up kings tryin' to make their bones out here. I'm talkin' leave-no-witness-above-ground, bloodthirsty Boba Fett niggas. Keep it tight, two, three guys tops, and tell them it's BYOG. I ain't got time for toy shoppin', hear? Want to get this party started, like yesterday."

Jax wasted no time rounding up a war party, recruiting stone killers from as far south as Calexico, where Jax found the legendary Poway Charlie sitting in a night-black *sureño* bar, nursing a bottle of Indio with his back to the wall. Jax had always heard the dude had some kind of Samson thing going with his hair. He wore it long and loose, a cream-rinse cascade framing his heart-shaped face like a black velvet cowl. He had delicate features, full lips. Poway Charlie was bitch-pretty, but damned if that border brother couldn't put a bullet through a flipped peso at thirty paces.

Contestant number two was a one-time Shotgun Crip called Sleepy Loc, so named for the heavy-lidded expression he wore when shit got bloody, like the sound of gunfire soothed him in some way.

Rounding out their triumvirate was Daddy Python, a Boot Hill OG Jax had known since grade school. Daddy Python had had his juvie record sealed and he'd gone to the Gulf with a Marine force recon unit. Now he hired out his gun to the highest bidder.

"The lick's not a bank or an armored car," Darius told his new crew over a plate of wings at an after-hours club on Vermont. "We're hittin' a sling spot, a dope pad."

Daddy Python and Sleepy Loc shook their heads, no fucking way, and even Poway Charlie looked skeptical. That was until they heard the plan.

The next morning, they waited in an idling cargo van at Sixty-third and Brynhurst, in the Rollin' Sixties Hood. The van was stolen and cold-plated out of Riverside County, tailpipe chuffing steam into the predawn stillness. They sat in silence, windows cracked to keep them from fogging up. Then Darius's digital watch alarm chimed straight-up 0400 and they charged the house, five men in black ski masks and surplus-store fatigues, Daddy Python swinging his sledge against the front door hard enough to take it off the hinges, Darius taking the street out of his voice to shout "Police! We have a search warrant!"

The crusty-eyed Sixties inside the pad had been through search warrants before. They knew the drill, hands on their heads, dropping to their knees in the living room while these narco cops rifled through their place, maybe brought a dog in to sniff out their stash. Only the in-house shot-caller, an OG Sixty called Crisis, smelled bullshit in the air, but by then it was too late. Watching these men knife open his couch cushions, hastily stuffing the hidden dope cash not into evidence envelopes, but pillow-cases, Crisis got a bad feeling. Then Crisis caught sight of the Jheri curl spilling from the back of one of the cops' ski masks.

"Hey, Jax," Crisis said, rising from his knees. Poway Charlie fired a three-shot burst from his AR-15, the first round laying open Crisis's throat, the next taking his jaw off at the hinges, the last round blowing most of his thinking cap onto the carpet. Sleepy Loc put the rest of them down, head shots when they would stand still for it. No one even called the cops until the smell got to the neighbors a week later.

Darius funneled his taste of the money into his new venture, Lethal Injection Records, which owed much of its early success to the earning power of its tent-pole act, DJ Post-Mortem and his WAN (Wild Ass Nigga) Posse. DJ Post-Mortem, formerly Duncan James Mortimer, a bona fide South Central homeboy, made the transition from small-time Boot Hill Mafia gangbanger to big-time gangsta rapper with absurd facility. His debut album, *Barbequed Pork,* which featured the hit single "Cops: The Other White Meat," went double platinum. Lethal Injection was suddenly an industry force to be reckoned with. Darius made the cover of *The*

Source, the press calling him a hip-hop Hammurabi and the heir apparent to Suge Knight's dubious legacy.

Then DJ Post-Mortem caught an acute case of the greedies and got himself hooked up with some hotshot entertainment lawyer. Darius received a nastygram from said lawyer stating Post-Mortem's intention to terminate his contract and sign with another label.

That same afternoon, this attorney pulled out of Sports Club L.A. in his little convertible Porsche and there was Jax, reprising his basehead roll on the concrete median at Sepulveda and Santa Monica. When the lawyer's Porsche pulled up next to him, Jax dropped his cardboard WILL WORK FOR FOOD—GOD BLESS sign, vaulted into the passenger seat of the Porsche, and shoved his nine into the guy's face. Staring at the business end of the nine, Mr. Seven Figures pissed all over his custom leather seats.

"Drive," Jax said.

Barbecues and pool parties were common at Darius's stately pleasure dome on Mulholland Drive. DJ Post-Mortem got wind of an old-school barbecue at D's crib and drove over from Studio City with no thought of his impending flight from Lethal Injection. His mouthpiece had said he'd handle that, make it right with Darius. That was what you paid a lawyer for anyway, so you didn't have to trip.

Sure enough, no one was trippin' at the party. Nothing going on but whiskey, weed, women, and some of the sweetest barbecue that Post-Mortem had ever tasted. You didn't need teeth to eat it. You could suck that shit right off the bone like a mutherfuckin' Popsicle. Post-Mortem busted a bib and some Wetnaps, bellying up to the table until all the shirt-tail guests, the models and actresses, had trickled away into the night. Only Darius, Jax, and Darius's hard-core homies, Daddy Python, Sleepy Loc, and Poway Charlie, remained. Post-Mortem was forced to unbutton his pants the way he had at his momma's Thanksgivings back in the day.

"Damn, that's some mad-ass barbecue, D," Post-Mortem groaned. Sopping a bit of juice from his plate with a broken roll, he popped it into his mouth. "Tender as a mutherfucker."

"Jax 'cues a mean swine," Darius agreed. He was seated across the table from Post-Mortem, studying him. "And we been savin' you the choicest cuts, my nigga." Darius motioned for Jax to bring over a covered basket and Jax laid the steaming basket on the table before Post-Mortem. "For the road."

Post-Mortem took a long whiff, smiled, and lifted the lid off the basket. The steam cleared and he saw his attorney's severed head and hands inside. The attorney had a baked apple stuffed into his mouth.

Post-Mortem's face went flat. Darius and Jax grinned at him and he knew, somehow, that they would kill him if he spit up. He swallowed hard, banishing the overwhelming urge to vomit. "On second thought, D," Post-Mortem said carefully. "I think my eyes were bigger than my stomach."

"You're goddamned right they were, nigga." Darius reached into the basket and wrenched the baked apple from the attorney's cracked, shining lips. "But I'll have Jax keep these here in the Sub-Zero in case your eyes get big again." Darius crunched down on the apple and grinned as the juice ran down his chin.

PRESENT

Ben came out of the Starbucks downstairs from his studio on Ocean Avenue with his coffee and newspaper and found Ignacio and Jaime leaning against Carcosa's new black Jaguar like they owned it. With their matching mullets and gold-rimmed shades, they looked like something out of an Andy Sidaris movie—direct to video.

Jaime and Ignacio were fraternal twins born to an ill-starred family of farmers in Sinaloa. In their teens, Jaime and Ignacio had run away to join a Tijuana circus that set up on the weekends in front of the jai alai courts on Avenida Revolución. Throwing knives was their bag. Carcosa caught their act one night and hired the brothers on the spot, told them any *cuchilero* who could handle a blade like that ought to be carving for the cartel.

Ignacio let his thin brown cigarillo fall to the asphalt and crushed it under the heel of a snakeskin boot. "He wants to see you," Ignacio said with no particular menace, just telling Ben the news. Ignacio hooked his thumbs into the matching snakeskin belt around his acid-washed jeans and drummed his fingers against his thighs. The barest grin appeared on his face, deepening the knife scar that ran from the right corner of his mouth to his right ear.

Ben nodded, knowing they had followed him here from his apartment. It shamed him to think he had walked the two blocks to the Starbucks without his Spider Sense tingling because observation was supposed to be a crucial skill in his new line of work.

Ben shrugged and walked toward the Jag, but Jaime stepped in front of him, crossing his tan arms over his chest. The sleeves of Jaime's knit shirt stretched tight over his jailhouse triceps. He wore mirrored sunglasses to cover the little black teardrop tattooed at the corner of his left eye. Jaime held out his callused hand, palm up. "You get it back when we're through," Jaime said, referring to the five-shot .38.

"We both know it doesn't work that way," Ben said.

"Oh, yeah." Jaime smiled. "So how does it work, Officer?"

"I keep the gun," Ben said.

"We could take it from you," Jaime said.

"We'd end up shooting each other in front of all these people," Ben said, glancing around the parking lot. "And the old man wouldn't like that."

"Fine," Jaime snapped. "But you can't bring the coffee."

"I just bought it," Ben said.

"Leather interior," Jaime said.

"It has a lid," Ben said.

"He's not going to spill it," Ignacio said. "*Vámonos.*"

Ben climbed into the backseat, into that sexy new-car smell and sipped his coffee while Ignacio drove them up the 405 to Sepulveda.

"So, what's he like?" Jaime offhandedly tossed out the question, like he didn't care about an answer, not quite pulling it off.

"Marquez?" Ben asked. Jaime nodded solemnly. For years in the pen, Jaime had heard fish stories about Marquez, his cellmates spinning dime-novel bullshit to fill the dead space after lights-out. "He's like . . . you know how in movies the cop jumps on the hood of the bad guys' car?" Ben said. "And the bad guys are all 'The sonofabitch is crazy!' That's Marquez, man."

"For real?" Jaime asked, clearly pleased.

"Swear to God," Ben said. They headed up a series of winding switchbacks through the mountains to Bel Air Crest, passing the palatial homes of pro athletes and producers before stopping at Carcosa's reinforced iron security gate. A tall guard with a Bonelli auto-loading shotgun slung across his chest opened the gate to allow the Jaguar to continue up Carcosa's serpentine driveway.

Carcosa's home was the kind of conceptual abomination found only in southern California and southern Florida, like a Spanish mission and a Venetian palace had collided somewhere in the ether and the wreckage had been collected and rearranged into a postmodern space station roughly the size of Rhode Island. While the house itself was not to Ben's taste, it commanded one of the finest views in Los Angeles County. On a clear day, the Hollywood sign, Century City, Santa Monica, and Catalina were all visible from Carcosa's home. Carcosa had kept peacocks, but the coyotes took them.

Ignacio parked the Jaguar under the marble portico, and they led Ben around the north side of the house, past the tennis courts to the black-bottom swimming pool.

Ben felt someone watching him from the house. He glanced over his shoulder at the balcony overlooking the pool and glimpsed her, phantomlike behind the translucent bedroom curtains. A breeze rippled the curtains and she was gone, but he knew she'd been there by the way Jaime and Ignacio studied the patio. There had always been rumors about Serena and her father.

Jose Carcosa floated dreamily along the surface on one of those ultra-buoyant, thin foam rafts. He wore dark sunglasses and neat black swim trunks. His thick body had a languid aspect of repose, but Ben knew the man wasn't sleeping. A warm Santa Ana smelling of chaparral rippled the still water around him. Eucalyptus leaves floated on the surface.

Ben stood at the edge of the pool. Jaime placed the flat of his palm between Ben's shoulder blades. "In you go, Benji," he whispered. Jaime didn't push, but he didn't let Ben back away from the edge either.

"I didn't bring any trunks," Ben said.

"He wants to talk to you," Jaime said, and slowly extended his arm until Ben was forced to step off the edge onto the first step of the wide stairs into the shallow end. The water wasn't bad, but he was going to have to clean and oil his gun when he got back. He took the rest of the steps, feeling the cool water leaching his jeans until he was standing on the bottom—in up to his navel. Holding his arms out from his sides, Ben slogged awkwardly over to Carcosa. If he had been wearing a wire, the water would have instantly killed the power. Carcosa said police work can get in your blood, like malaria. You may think you have it under control, but it can come back without warning to give you a fever.

"I told them not to touch you," Carcosa said when Ben was standing next to him in the pool. Ben hated not seeing Carcosa's eyes under the sunglasses. Sweat clung to Carcosa's upper lip, the black hair brushed neatly back from his forehead and the curly patch on his chest, which had begun to frost with gray. He wore a Jesús Malverde medal.

"They didn't," Ben said.

"How is the thin blue line?" Carcosa asked casually.

"About what you'd expect," Ben said.

"Darius knows," he said.

"How?" Ben asked.

"Some fucking *mayate* you arrested," Carcosa said.

"Lamar," Ben said.

"That's him," Carcosa said. "He recognized you, called Darius from County, hoping to trade the info for bail."

Ben pictured Darius receiving the collect call from Lamar. He imagined Darius's features ossifying as the muscles in his face tightened around the news. A wolf raises his hackles and a shark lowers his pectoral fins, Ben thought, but with Crazy D, homicidal intent is expressionless.

"Darius wasn't laughing." Carcosa frowned. "But I have him under control. That's not why I brought you up here."

"So why *did* you bring me up here?"

"I ever tell you about the time I walk into this tittie bar in Tijuana?" Carcosa asked him.

"Sounds like the beginning of a joke," Ben said.

"I'm just a *chiclero,* you understand?" Carcosa ignored him. "Pushing my way past the Marines and the whores, and there's Ochoa, lieutenant for the Arellano-Felix cartel, *encargado de la Plaza de Baja.* I tell him I want to take merchandise across. I want to be his mule. I was just a kid, you understand, sixteen. Ochoa laughs and says he doesn't need me. Guy next to him in the booth stands up to throw me out and I open his throat with a straight razor. Guy's wiggling on the floor and making these weird gurgling sounds. I can hear the whores screaming behind me. The Marines run out of the bar and I tell Ochoa, '*Ya me necesitas.* Now you need me.'"

"Some joke," Ben said. He already knew this story by heart, but Carcosa loved to tell it. He had first heard it from his dad and then he had heard it again in the academy, complete with a gory slide show and newspaper clippings copied on to overhead transparencies. Ochoa gave Carcosa the job muling product through a fresh tunnel under the border into El Centro. Once in El Norte, Carcosa worked his way up from mule to enforcer, from enforcer to midlevel dealer and from midlevel dealer to distributor. In 1988, Carcosa made a play for control of the stateside operations of the cartel and all hell broke loose. East L.A. ran red for almost a year, and when the smoke cleared, Joe Carcosa was the last man standing.

By 1992, Carcosa had begun to funnel cash into commercial real estate and development, a chain of 99-cent stores, a security firm, and Lethal Injection Records. Over the next four years, while the DEA fooled around with useless wiretaps and misplaced surveillance, Carcosa went legit (well, almost legit, as good as legit) right under their cornpone noses. That was the official story anyway, but that night in Vegas Carcosa had told him a different version.

The DEA hadn't bungled their investigation, not according to Carcosa. Their bosses had just called them off, allowing Carcosa to establish himself as a semilegitimate American businessman. Of course, Carcosa had a fluid definition of *legitimate,* and over the years Ben's father had been more than happy to help him push that envelope. Big Ben had always admired treachery as a necessary skill applied for material gain and Joe Carcosa was the embodiment of applied treachery. Dad called him the Mexican Machiavelli, Horatio Alger with an Uzi in his briefcase.

"I need your help with something," Carcosa said, his voice suddenly heavy with insinuation, not needing to remind Ben that, push come to shoot, Carcosa was all that stood between Ben and Darius. Finally, we come to it, Ben thought. The reason Carcosa had sent his boys to haul him up here, not to lecture him, or warn him about Darius, but to work some angle—the rest just Carcosa blowing smoke, same as always.

"Someone murdered three of my employees, decent men, honorable. They butchered my men like animals." Carcosa lowered his shades. "They *stole* from me." Ben had almost forgotten how black his eyes were, shark's eyes, same as his daughter's. "What I heard is two *chongos* wearing oval badges, but I don't know. Hear anything more about it, you pick up the phone, *mijo.*"

10

1985

Benji had never understood how in movies guys were always waking up on the beach with no recollection of straggling out of the water, but that's where he'd flopped when Carcosa toed him in the side with his loafer. Benji rolled over and sat up, half his face covered in sand. He squinted. The sun was high and Carcosa's white suit was so radiant that it was hard to look at him. Benji's head throbbed and he shivered in his wetsuit. He didn't bother to ask how Carcosa had found him. Maybe one of the lifeguards had tipped him, or maybe one of the gulls.

The storm had strewn junk over every square foot of breach. Broken glass, pulpy wads of paper, two-liter soda bottles, and hunks of drywall were scattered over the sand.

"*Puedes levantarte?*" Carcosa took Benji's hand and helped him to his feet. Benji wobbled, but didn't fall. He felt stiff and a little hungover, but otherwise okay—except for the weird tickle in his gut. "*Acompáñame.*"

They walked north along the waterline. Jaime and Ignacio stayed behind them at a discreet distance. The tide flowed in, soaking Carcosa's white trousers halfway to the knee. He paused, smiling like a kid, and wiggled his toes inside ruined Gianfranco loafers.

"First time I came to the States," Carcosa said, "I came across the river after a storm like this, almost drown in there, in others people's shit, Benji. Crawled up the bank and the *migra*'s waiting. They put the boots to me and sent me back." Carcosa picked up a flat rock and skipped it into the face of a wave. "I promised myself that I'd never let anyone kick me like that again, like some kid's goddamned dog."

Plovers hurried around a half-buried tricycle with sea grass streaming from the spokes of its front wheel. Sand fleas swarmed and settled as Benji stepped over a tangled patch of kelp.

"Did my father send you?" Benji asked. That tickle in his gut felt more like something chewing its way out.

Carcosa raised his eyebrows and Benji recoiled. Okay, he thought. I guess you don't send El Jefe. El Jefe sends you. The next wave carried in a fiberglass camper shell, upended it, and left it on the shore in front of them. An uprooted eucalyptus wallowed like a mastodon in the surf.

"You don't belong out here, *mijo*," Carcosa said. "You're not one of these burnouts." A sharp breeze carried the faint smell of rot. Benji's insides were on fire. Farther up the beach, bulldozers plowed the garbage into high berms. Gulls circled and their piping cries carried on the wind. The birds crowded around something in the sand. As he walked closer, Benji saw the gulls were picking at a dead bichon, its fur matted and muddy. Benji clutched himself, fell to his knees and vomited. "Easy, *mijo*," Carcosa said. "Let's get you cleaned up." He motioned to Jaime and Ignacio and they carried Benji back to the car.

Benji had picked up some kind of parasite in the water and Carcosa brought a doctor in for him. He spent a month recovering in Carcosa's guesthouse, waking to the cries of the peacocks. The twins seemed to sense Carcosa taking another half-wild orphan under his black wing, just as he'd taken in Jaime and Ignacio years ago, and they took it upon themselves to indoctrinate Benji. When he was on his feet again, Jaime and Ignacio taught him how to throw a knife and after a few days he got good enough to stick the target at twenty feet.

When his strength came back, Benji swam laps in Carcosa's pool. Serena sat on the edge, watching him. She was probably eight or nine, and she looked gangly, almost mannish in her one-piece suit, a Band-Aid on her left knee. "Hey, Serena."

"How long are you staying with us?" She kicked her legs in the water.

"I don't know." Benji folded his arms over the side of the pool and rested his chin on them.

"Where's your dad?"

"Home, I guess."

She nodded. "I don't know how to do a kick turn."

"It's easy," he said. "I'll show you." She came up coughing on the first try, water in her nose, her straight-across bangs plastered to her forehead, and a blotch of snot in her left nostril. But after twenty minutes she had it. "See? Told you it was easy," Benji said. Then he dunked her and let her dunk him.

That afternoon, Benji sparred with Jaime in the outdoor ring behind the guesthouse. Ignacio said Carcosa had once financed a middleweight contender and he'd let the guy train here, delighted in his victories the way the owner of a thoroughbred might, but the young man had thrown a fight to zero out a debt and Carcosa had to put him down. He'd arranged for the fighter to die honorably in the ring, his shattered nasal bones driven into his brain by a Korean who was not Korean but Japanese and was not a boxer but a disciple of a subtler art.

Tall for his age, Benji had reach on Jaime, but that was all he had and Jaime didn't exactly kid-glove him, but he didn't try to take his head off either. Ignacio coached him with the focus mitts, taught him to slip a punch, and even throw a few combinations. Sparring became part of his daily regimen, but Benji had no idea they were preparing him to be sacrificed.

He came out to the ring one afternoon and found Carcosa waiting for him in it. Carcosa had unbuttoned his shirt and hung it over one of the ring posts. He stepped out of his loafers and stood barefoot while Jaime slid the gloves over his hands. "Has he told you about the trophy case?" Carcosa asked as Jaime laced his gloves with ritual care.

"Yes," Benji said. Ignacio held the ropes apart for Benji. Climbing into the ring with Carcosa was like stepping onto an altar. Ignacio laced the gloves over Benji's hands and Benji slapped them together.

Big Ben had actually told Benji about the trophy case four times, once on Carcosa's yacht, once on a flight to Cancun, and twice at the house. It was the story Big Ben told on those rare, introspective drunks of his. He always started it the same way: "I'm going to tell you something, Benji." There'd be tears in his eyes, like it was killing him to reveal this. "Something I've never told anyone before in my life."

All through Scarsdale High, Big Ben said, he'd been ignored by girls and tortured by boys. The ruling WASP lettermen, the strapping sons of the country club set, routinely beat Big Ben for the compound offense of his blubbery waddle, his wit, and his outstanding scholarship—what a colleague and fellow tribesman would later call Big Ben's intransigent Jewishness. One lunch period, some Scarsdale football heroes dragged Big Ben screaming and sobbing into the locker room, stripped him, wrenched his arm behind his back, and forced him to walk naked across the quad. That night, Big Ben said, he broke into the school, shattered the trophy case, and smashed every trophy inside.

Deep in Dewar's, Big Ben offered this story as the justificatory trauma that forever defined the course of his life. It had a beat and you could dance to it. All the broad-shouldered, lantern-jawed cops, those Yankee Doodle Dandies Big Ben had ruined over the years, bore more than a passing resemblance to the bullying shits who'd tortured the fat little Jewboy.

"He is still smashing their goddamned trophy case," Carcosa said. Jaime and Ignacio climbed out of the ring and disappeared around the side of the guesthouse.

"Don't apologize for him," Benji said. When he held up his gloves for Carcosa to touch them, Carcosa threw a vicious left hook that knocked Benji sideways into the ropes. Before Benji could recover, Carcosa hit him with two left jabs and a hard right that put him on the canvas. He was old, Benji thought, but there was a lot of *sicario* still left in Carcosa.

Benji used the rope to pull himself to his knees and tried to shake the pixies out of his eyes. "Why are you doing this?"

"Exercise," Carcosa said, but he wasn't even breathing hard.

"I'm serious." Benji stepped away from the ropes and put his gloves up.

Carcosa circled him. "Maybe I see a little of myself in you," he said, closing in on Benji. "Of course, you're not as handsome as I was, and you're not as tough, but you have *ganas,* and I expect big things from you, Benji."

Carcosa ducked Benji's jabs, slipped his right. When Benji tried an uppercut from the outside, Carcosa came over with a right hook and Benji went down again.

"Your father hates all his mistresses," Carcosa said. "Did you know that? He hates them because those same cruel cunts wanted nothing to do with him in school, wouldn't even deign to drop a pity valentine into the Kleenex box on his desk. Still they would have nothing to do with him when he was managing a fucking Radio Shack in Van Nuys, I can tell you that. And he hated your mother most of all because he'd loved her."

A year into their marriage, Carcosa said, Big Ben had done the unthinkable. He'd shattered the comradely politeness of their model-for-millionaire arrangement when he'd actually fallen in love with her. Not with his typical disdainful flamboyance, but wide-eyed, Icarian, and irreclaimably gone on her, Big Ben had dared to ask his wife to love him back.

"He dared by having a child with her," Carcosa said. "And he sees her every time he looks at you."

"I'm not going back," Benji said. He tucked in his arms and bulled forward, trying to wrap Carcosa up. Carcosa danced away, drove two fast jabs into his forehead and, when his head snapped back, put an uppercut under his chin. Benji fell backward.

"Yes, you are," Carcosa said, stepping on Benji's chest. "You are going home and you are going to law school. You're going to become a DA, maybe a U.S. attorney, and someday you're going to marry my daughter, *mijo.*"

11

PRESENT

Marquez saw the kid popping Advil before roll call. With last night's adrenaline spent, Marquez figured the kid's gut had to be killing him, but the kid hadn't banged in sick and he didn't bitch about it. Maybe he was harder than he looked.

Right out of roll call, they arrested some *borracho* for wife-boxing. His old lady had a fat lip and a cut under her swollen eye that was going to need a needle and thread, but she wailed and pleaded in Spanish, begging them not to take her husband away. The kid handed her all the required bilingual pamphlets on domestic-violence shelters and restraining orders, but she tore the pamphlets to pieces and ground them under her heel.

"No fucking way she'll testify against him," Marquez told the kid after booking her husband. "The DA won't file and those two will be at it again next week. One of these nights, he'll knock her one that she doesn't get up from and the sob sisters will come out of the woodwork to ask why the department didn't do more to protect her." Marquez spat. "Back in the day, we'd take a guy like that out back and tune him up, tell him the next time he touched his old lady, we'd kill him."

"Did that ever work?" the kid asked him.

"You'd be surprised." Marquez smiled.

Then he spotted good old Ronny riding down Sixth Avenue on a wobbly bicycle he'd probably cobbled together from scavenged parts. "Have I taught you how to conduct a proper investigative stop on a narcotics suspect riding a bike?" Marquez asked the kid. He killed the headlights and slowed the car, pulling alongside the pedaling basehead.

"No, sir."

Marquez lifted his baton from his lap and threw it out the open window of the black-and-white. His baton speared the bicycle's front wheel and lodged in the spokes. The entire frame of the bike bucked, lifting the back wheel and pitching Ronny over the handlebars onto the asphalt. He flopped in the street like a stunned fish.

Marquez got out of the car, pulled his baton out of the spokes, and hung it on his belt. Then he hauled Ronny up by his collar and brushed him off. Ronny made extra cash cleaning the stables down on 132nd and Fig and you could always smell horseshit on him. "You okay, Ronny?"

"Marquez?" Ronny grinned, shaking his head. He cackled. "Shit, kill my ass. Shit." Ronny looked like a scarecrow, tattered clothes hanging loosely from his bony frame. His skin was the grayish color of soot and looked so thin as to be membranous, like the wings of a bat were stretched over his skull and bones. Ronny's fingers had been cracked and blackened by years of butane flame. An open seeping blister furrowed the center of his bottom lip where he had placed the hot glass pipe again and again. His front teeth had been devoured by acrid cocaine vapor on its way to his lungs. Haunted eyes stared out of deep sockets in his haggard face.

"Ronny's a goddamned legend in Seventy-seventh," Marquez told the kid. "He's the only asshole to ever pull a piece on Tim Rourke and live to tell it." This was way back when Marquez was a rookie and Ronny was still spry enough to pull armed robberies. Ronny had drawn down on Officer Rourke, but Rourke, a champion shooter, had fired first and sent a .38 slug flying into Ronny's open mouth. Miraculously, the bullet had lodged in Ronny's palate, near the back of his throat and Ronny had survived, but the hole in Ronny's palate never quite healed over and Ronny used the old wound as a cubby to secrete his rock cocaine.

South Central had been full of zombies like Ronny since cocaine base made the scene in the eighties. Cocaine hydrochloride concentrated by heating the drug in a baking-soda solution until the water evaporated. It made a cracking sound as it cooled, hence the name. Crack vaporized at a low temperature, so it could be inhaled through a heated glass pipe to deliver an intensity of pleasure previously unknown to human beings. They tasted some kind of chemical apotheosis and then wandered the streets and alleys like extras from a George Romero movie.

"Where's your pipe, Ronny?" Marquez asked him. Ronny reached into his breast pocket and pulled out a small glass cylinder with some wire mesh jammed in one end. Ronny held the cylinder between his thumb and forefinger. The glass was fogged with the yellow residue. "Get rid of it," Marquez told him.

"Shit." Ronny sighed, shaking his head sadly. He dropped the glass pipe onto the asphalt and crushed it under the heel of his ragged sneaker.

"Rock?" Marquez asked.

Ronny opened his mouth wide, like he was getting a physical, allowing Marquez to shine his flashlight into the bullet hole. "No," Ronny said.

"Cash?"

"Ten bucks," Ronny said, shaking his head at the injustice of it all.

"Where were you going to buy?" Marquez asked him.

"Shit," Ronny said, but his resistence was perfunctory. This whole exchange had the long-worn rhythm of street ritual. Ronny knew he'd give it up, but Marquez let the poor guy keep some of his hood dignity.

"Come on now, Ronny," Marquez said. "I already know you got that paper in the system for possession."

"Pink house on Dauber," Ronny sighed. "Between Fifty-eighth Place and Fifty-ninth on this side. I just knock on the front door."

"South of Fifty-eighth?"

"Yeah, south, shit."

"How many inside?"

"Just one that I seen," Ronny said and winked at Marquez. "Light-skinned dude got PIRU and BLOOD tattooed right here?" Ronny traced his burned fingertips under his eyes. "Sound about right?"

"Little Quiet," Marquez said for the kid's benefit. "He strapped?"

"I expect he is," Ronny said, glancing at Ben. "Shit."

"You're a gentleman and a scholar, Ronny." Marquez palmed a few folded bills and handshake-passed the cash to Ronny the way you'd grease a maître d' for a good table. "Fix your bike." Ronny buttoned the bills into his breast pocket.

"Hey, we had a stinker yesterday over on Five-eight," Marquez said. "Turns out the guy was *Eme*."

"Tax man." Ronny nodded. "I'm already knowin'."

"Got anything?"

"Nothin' solid," Ronny said. "Shit, Marquez. Gimme a minute."

"You can have two," he said. "For old times."

"Ask Little Quiet," Ronny said. "He be on this side, but nigga's foul enough to know somethin', be talkin' to the crows and shit."

"Oh, I'll ask him," Marquez said. "You got my number?"

Ronny rattled off the phone number in a bored singsong. Per department policy, uniformed personnel were strictly forbidden from keeping informants, but everybody had them anyway. You couldn't get any work done out here without a few deep throats in the division. So, like a lot of guys in patrol, Marquez carried his own snitch phone. He dealt with a Lebanese subagent who had a table at the Slauson Swap Meet, paid cash for a piece-of-crap little prepaid cellular, and the dude gave him a decent deal on his minute cards. That way his snitches could hit him up day or night and if IA got wind of it Marquez could always shitcan the phone. It was a trick he'd learned from gangsters trying to stay ahead of wiretaps.

"Call me as soon as you hear something," Marquez said.

"Oh, I'm double-oh-seven on this motherfucker." Ronny touched his finger to his nose and winked, like he was on his way up the chimney.

They left Ronny to tend to his ruined bike and drove to the end of the block to park the black-and-white on Fifty-eighth Place. "We walk from here," Marquez told him. "Turn down your radio."

There were few functioning streetlights in South Central. The bulbs were often shot out and the city did not rush to repair them. On some streets, the resultant darkness was almost liquid in its totality.

They stalked across the front yards on the west side of Dauber. For a big man, Marquez moved almost soundlessly. Ben blundered after him through hedges, over low fences, and around parked cars until they reached the pink house. The roof had buckled in places and the paint on the garage was peeling. A five-foot cinder-block wall surrounded the back-yard. Marquez and Ben squatted behind a brown Eldorado that rested on blocks in the driveway.

"Here's the plan, Professor," Marquez whispered. "You set up in the backyard, get some cover, and wait. I knock on the front door. If this ass-hole runs out the back, just keep him contained, but don't get excited and come charging in the back door because we'll have cross fire. I'll holler if I need you up front, but don't you dare come through the house."

"Yes, sir." Crazy, Ben thought. Even he knew that they needed at least another unit as backup to take down a dealer like this, but Marquez was an old-school copper and probably still believed two guys could handle anything out here.

Ben swung his legs over the cinder-block wall, dropped into the over-grown backyard, and crept slowly along the side of the house through the riot of high crabgrass and chickweed. Quavering blue television light pulsed from the bedroom window, and he dropped to his belly to crawl beneath it. The yard was a decaying reliquary strewn with dented beer cans and malt liquor bottles with their labels faded and peeling. A child's plastic pool leaned warped and cracked against the far wall and a ruinous couch sagged, moldering in the middle of the yard. The couch had sprouted cudweed, and sprits of prickly lettuce pushed up through its ul-cerated cushions.

That couch afforded the only suitable concealment in the yard, so Ben dropped to one knee behind it and waited, watching. He strained to see through the screen door at the back of the house, but he could make out only a rectangle of near-perfect darkness. Something stirred off to his left and Ben angled his Beretta at the sound. An oafish gray possum emerged from behind the plastic pool. It trundled sulkily through the weeds and wiggled under the porch. Ben's constricted breath hit the night air in steamy plumes.

Then he heard the pounding of Marquez's fist on the front door. "Police!" he shouted. "We have a search warrant!" Unbelievable, Ben thought.

The screen door banged wide open. Little Quiet charged down the back steps and would have vaulted the couch on his way to Mexico, but Ben drew down on him and shined his Streamlight in the guy's face. "Show me your hands!" Ben shouted.

Those prison tattoos under his eyes looked inflamed in the bright light. He stood in weeds up to his shins and bared his teeth at Ben, or rather, in Ben's general direction. With that light in his eyes, Ben didn't think Little Quiet could actually see him. Thank God for small favors, he thought.

Little Quiet was gangster chic in a black Nike cap, a red Tommy Hilfiger pullover, and oversized jeans. He had a gold incisor like the one Madonna wore a few years back, but it looked better on him. The screen door had lost a hinge. It hung at a precarious angle and banged against the jamb behind him.

"What's your probable cause, bitch?" Little Quiet grinned and Ben saw his right hand slip around behind him to reach into the rear waistband of his jeans. Here it comes, Ben thought. The adrenaline sang in his ears and the hairs on his forearms prickled.

"Don't!" Ben warned him, touching the trigger. He put the sights of his Beretta aligned squarely between the words TOMMY and HILFIGER on Little Quiet's chest. Ben needed to see both his hands. They'd hammered this into him in the academy. Eyes wouldn't kill you. Mouth wouldn't kill you. But you had to treat hands as independent creatures, both capable of sudden wickedness. He knew all this and he couldn't see that fucking hand.

If that hand came out with a weapon, he knew he'd have less than a second to process the info and press his shot, but it would take longer than that for the electrical impulse to travel from his brain to his trigger finger. And by then it would be too late.

Listen, he thought. Assume your aim is true. It may not be. You may miss him altogether because now you're shaking like a fucking hype with the dries, but just assume your shot finds its mark. You press your trigger and hit this asshole square in the chest with a nine-millimeter hollow-point parabellum round, but it doesn't knock him down. He may be dead on his feet and not know it yet. If he's juiced, he may not even know he's been hit. The bullet will take several seconds to stop his heart, time enough for him to squeeze the trigger on his little friend. At full auto, a MAC-10 or a TEC-9, two perennial South Central favorites, can both fire about three hundred rounds per minute. So, in the few seconds it takes for his heart to stop, Little Quiet empties a heaping helping of his fifty-round magazine into your face and you're fucked.

What if that hand comes out of his waistband with some strange shape in it, Ben thought. Is it a Walkman, a wallet, or something that can kill you? If it's a gun, you're dead. If it's just some harmless object, you could spend the rest of your life in federal prison because once your brain sends that gun message to your trigger finger, there's no calling that bullet back.

Little Quiet's right hand came out from behind his back holding a tricked-out TEC-9 with a threaded barrel shroud and a fifty-round magazine. Ben felt his trousers sucking up into his puckered asshole. "Drop it!" he said, slowly squeezing, not jerking, the trigger. The hammer on his Beretta clicked back and he fought to stay on target with tremors moving through his body.

The guy must have heard the hammer on Ben's Beretta click because Little Quiet dropped the TEC-9 into the weeds in front of him. "Turn around and get your hands on your head," Ben told him. As he turned, Ben lowered his Beretta, eased the hammer back, and blew out a long sigh.

Little Quiet's hands, honed by years of street fights and three-card monte, moved too fast for Ben's eyes to follow. Ben saw Little Quiet's hands go to his head as Ben had instructed him, but he didn't see him lift the Nike cap off his head with his left hand, his right hand taking hold of the compact .30-caliber pistol he had tucked beneath his cap. By the time Ben saw his second gun, Little Quiet was already turning to shoot him with it.

Marquez's thick fingers clamped like bolt cutters around the wrist that held the pistol. He wrenched that wrist at an impossible angle, forcing Little Quiet to bend forward. Then Marquez drove his knee up into Little Quiet's face and burst his nose like a ketchup packet. The .30-caliber fell into the weeds. Marquez kicked his legs out from under him and Little Quiet did a hard face-plant onto the back porch. Marquez stepped between Little Quiet's shoulder blades and put some weight on him, dropped a knee into the small of the gangster's back, cuffed him, and patted him down. He pulled a black plastic film canister out of Little Quiet's back pocket.

"Possession for sales," Marquez said. He shook the canister in Little Quiet's face, the rocks rattling inside. Marquez tossed Ben the canister and Ben popped the gray cap. There were maybe thirty decent rocks in there, about five hundred bucks' worth of cocaine base. He could have stood on any corner in this neighborhood and made his five hundred in about twenty minutes. "Add ADW on a police officer and your parole violation and you should be out by the time we've colonized Mars."

"*Eme* tax man got zapped yesterday." Marquez ground his boot heel into Little Quiet's kidney to let the guy know he wasn't talking to himself.

"What's that got to do with me?" Little Quiet said.

"You might've heard something about it," Marquez said. "Inquiring minds want to know."

"Fuck you."

"Hey now, I'm offering a one-time special here," Marquez said. "You open your hymnal and we'll forget you pulled on dipshit here. You'll just be looking at the violation, Keith."

"I'd be looking at a death sentence," Little Quiet said. "Everything you need's in my other pocket, punk ass, just every mutherfuckin' thang. I want a supervisor out here to take pictures of my face. No, scratch that. I want your fuckin' captain, dog. Race profiling, violatin' my civil rights, excessive force, I just call up my Jewboy and he snatch your tin behind this cowboy shit. I should really thank you for the settlement I'll get on this." Little Quiet laughed. Blood ran down his face and dripped from his chin. "The city's gonna buy this nigga a big house in Baldwin Hills and your skinny white ass be pullin' me my frappacinos down at the mutherfuckin' Starbucks."

Marquez fished around in Little Quiet's other pocket and pulled out a dog-eared business card. Ben couldn't see it from where he was standing, but he didn't have to. He recognized the logo. The card read:

BENJAMIN KAHN
ATTORNEY AT LAW

"No shit," Marquez said in a tone that let the gangster know he was impressed. He took his foot off Little Quiet and moved to stand in front of him. "Big Ben's your lawyer?" Little Quiet nodded with an imperious smile. Marquez raised his eyebrows and frowned, as though chastened by this news. Then he dropped Big Ben's business card on to the porch, unzipped his trousers, and pissed on it. Steam rose from the urine-spattered concrete. "Hey, you want your card back?"

The gangster just stared at Marquez, his jaw clamped shut. He must have recognized Marquez now. This was that cop they all talked about, the *vaquero* who just didn't give a fuck.

Marquez lifted Little Quiet's TEC-9 out of the weeds, stripped the magazine out of the weapon, pulled back the slide, and let the chambered round fall into his open palm. Hollow point. He repeated the process with the .30-caliber, stripping out the mag and then popping the round out of the chamber. They sealed both guns and their ammunition into separate evidence envelopes.

Ben and Marquez hauled Little Quiet to his feet, led him around the front of the house to the car, and put him in the backseat. Then Marquez opened the trunk and they secured the bagged guns, ammo, and film container full of rock cocaine inside.

When he shut the trunk, Marquez turned to Ben. His hand lashed out like a prizefighter's jab and struck Ben's sternum hard enough to knock him off his feet, but he didn't let Ben fall. His hand closed, snatching a bunch of Ben's shirt in his fist, and he yanked Ben close to him, shouting into his face. "You looking to die out here, Professor?" He held Ben close enough to smell the coffee and Red Man on his breath. His face filled Ben's vision. The pores around his wide nostrils looked grainy and puckered.

"You let your fucking guard down because he dropped that nine," he barked. "You've got to be smarter than that if you want to play out here. You carry two guns. I carry two guns. So, where is it written a gangster can only carry one strap at a time? Where?" His spittle flecked Ben's cheeks. "They put guns under hats, in their socks, in the hoods of their sweatshirts, under their balls where they think you won't search. I once booked a guy had a .22 derringer crammed up his ass.

"I'm not looking to write up another dead probationer," Marquez said. "That report takes forever and it's a lot less paperwork for me just to fire your ass. Step on your meat like this again, I'll send you the fuck home." He let go of Ben's shirt and Ben staggered back from him, using the back of his palm to wipe flecks of spittle from his cheek. Ben's face felt hot and his eyes stung with shame.

"Now, about young Mr. Wallace, here's what's going in the arrest report: we were on routine patrol when we saw a male black we recognized as the parolee-at-large known as Little Quiet in front of the pink house on Sixth Avenue." Marquez paused, lightly brushed his mustache with his index and middle fingers, as though considering the plausibility of his narrative. "When we attempted to detain him, he ran from us. We chased him through the house and caught him in the backyard. I tackled him and he busted his nose on the back porch. We recovered the guns and dope from his person *after* we cuffed him."

Ben gaped at him, struggling to take this all in, to get his mind around it. Marquez dug out his pouch, socked a fresh wad of Red Man into his jaw, chewed meditatively and spat. "Quit looking at me like a baby with a load in his diapers," he said. "A plus B equals C. This how it works out here, Professor."

12

1988–1989

After Benji's mother had skipped, a cast of waitresses, models, actresses, weepy drunks, and flight attendants had drifted through their lives like guest stars in a bad sitcom, Big Ben's parade of paramours culminating in Gretchen Maddox. Gretchen clung to the Kahn Empire with greater tenacity than her predecessors. She was a miracle of evolution, a self-contained engine of survival with small, foxlike features and the world-weary insouciance of a gangster's moll. According to Big Ben, she'd been one of those Lone Star urchins who'd worn a burlap sack to school and a childhood of muddy poverty had left her hungry.

Gretchen had grown up in Pecos City, Texas, called herself a double-wide debutante. Her daddy had been killed in a roadhouse outside of town when she was nine. He'd come out of the gents' to find her momma soul-kissing some Mexican, broke them up, and got a boot knife between his ribs for his trouble. Died on the dance floor with the peanut shells, pull tabs, and sawdust.

Gretchen had taken the bus out here from Texas with her high school sweetheart, one of hundreds of kids who step out of the Greyhound station at Hollywood and Vine each year with stars in their eyes and end up as someone's cautionary tale. Her boyfriend's songwriting career took him to the front of the Mann Chinese, where he sat on the sidewalk, picking Joni Mitchell tunes while people dropped spare change into his guitar case. By the end, the guy just slept all day in their roachy extended-stay motel on Cahuenga Boulevard, shooting the money that Gretchen made stripping into his arm. The guy eventually gave up and loaded himself a hot shot.

A creepy albino named Strange used to come sniffing around the club, looking for new porn talent, but Gretchen figured those movies would take her to the same place her boyfriend went and she told Strange thanks but no thanks. She did some softer stuff for late-night cable, hustled to auditions, and landed a part in a Troma picture, another for Sidaris, and, her magnum opus, a speaking part in Roger Corman's *Carnivorous Cave Girls*.

When Big Ben introduced her to Benji for the first time, Benji just stood there gaping until Big Ben drove an elbow into his ribs. He hadn't realized his future stepmother was *that* Gretchen Maddox, the peerless princess of *Cinemax After Dark*. Benji was seventeen. She was twenty-six.

Big Ben said Gretchen's biological clock was at Def Con 2, the woman keen for him to have his vasectomy reversed, but he would never cede that power to her. Their mutual alienation by Big Ben was all Gretchen and Benji had in common at first and they'd had little to say to each other.

Benji was more or less certain she'd eventually rotate out of the house like all the rest. And Gretchen did her best to tiptoe around the sullen teenager with the Kurt Cobain hair, the way you'd ease around a dog you weren't sure about, but she'd blanched the afternoon he'd come home from his first English riding lesson. She'd had no idea Benji was learning to ride because Big Ben didn't consult her about matters concerning the kid. Benji's grades, his friends, his curfew or the lack of it, were off-limits.

But somehow the sight of Benji with his crop and jodhpurs, her instinctive certainty of their wrongness for him, triggered a flare of maternal outrage. "Give me that," she snapped at him, yanking the crop from under Benji's arm. She was trespassing here and they both knew it, making him her stepson once and for all with the protective audacity of her disapproval. She wrinkled her nose, made a show of holding the crop up between their faces like it was some dirty magazine she'd found under his pillow. "Only fags and Kennedys ride English, kid."

She took him riding without consulting Big Ben, a bold stroke. They rented horses at Mandeville Canyon Corral and rode single file up the barranca. Gretchen picked up a trail along the dry creek bed, and the horses wound upward through high mesquite and toyon, brown legs pancaked with sweat and trail dust. Gretchen pointed out coyote scat and cougar sign, deep depressions where pads had pushed into the creek bed. A squadron of white pelicans passed over them without a sound, graceful hunters from a world before the Satwiwa, nothing like the grubby clowns he'd seen begging baitfish at the Santa Monica Pier.

At the ridge they stood in the saddle and shaded their eyes to look out over the Channel Islands. She told him how Mary Pickford and Douglas Fairbanks had bought a narrow tract of land from Pickfair to the ocean just so they could ride up here together.

Benji and Gretchen rode the ridge once a week after that, their conversations at first limited to what they saw on the trail, Gretchen pointing out the Wilson's warbler and horned toad. They talked movies and music—they were both into Pearl Jam. After a few months she was telling Benji things she'd never told anyone, the crucible of sexual abuse that had driven her out of Pecos, her roughneck uncles with their whiskey breath and calloused, scorpion fingers, how it was like she was snakebit after that and some men could smell it on her.

Benji told her how he'd lost his virginity to a girl in the senior class, how he'd lasted about thirty seconds and he thought maybe something was medically wrong with him.

"Pshaw," she said. "You'll get the hang of it. Besides, it's not even about that. It's about, I don't know. The way I see it, men'll act low down, debase themselves in every kinda way, but the dignity of their cock has to be preserved at all costs. Their whole lives are about protecting it and they get all hung up on the female orgasm, but here's the big secret, kiddo." The wind came up, carrying the weird tobacco scent of the kelp beds, and blew her hair across her face. She pushed it away. "You can train any lug to make you come," she said. "That can be taught, but you can't teach them to listen to you. They either know how or they don't. Mostly, they don't."

13

PRESENT

Marquez saw the kid in the locker room before roll call, straddling a splintery bench, polishing his new boots with an old T-shirt. Spit-shined boots were an LAPD tradition, but Marquez himself had never mastered the process and considered it a waste of time. "You polishing those boots with a fucking Hershey bar, Professor?" Marquez snorted, striding past the kid. "Look like a cat shit on them." Then, taking some pity on the kid, Marquez leaned in close to him and whispered. "Oh, for Christ's sake, just pay a cobbler five bucks to shine the goddamned things."

The annual uniform checks had come in and that nibble of city money turned roll call into a fucking hootenanny. Marquez knew for a fact half of these hand-to-mouth dudes were already so deep in debt on their watercraft and aboveground pools that they'd end up retiring straight into security work, forced to spend their last years on earth chasing sullen teenagers away from the Del Amo Mall, but here they were giddy with the prospect of new rims for their truck or maybe a second-hand set of free weights. They were all amped up like a pack of welfare junkies. He'd seen that same dreamy look on a thousand baseheads, swaggering out of Nix Check Cashing on the first of the month, the younger ones always padding their fresh rolls with dollar-sized strips of newspaper. He'd watched that cockiness fade to despair as the last crisp bill was peeled away to reveal the worthless newsprint beneath, Uncle Sam's monthly gift pissed away on pussy and porch booze.

Someone had drawn a huge dripping cock on the dry-erase board and labeled it Chief Burns. Paper airplanes and the gallows jokes were flying. "How do you make a girl cry twice in the same night?" Guerra shouted, dabbing Mother's Mag Polish onto his gleaming badge. "Use her teddy bear to wipe the blood off your dick." Groans and a few chuckles, some female slapped the back of Guerra's head hard enough to make him drop his badge.

"An' how do a ghetto mamma know her daughter on the rag?" Jones asked, screwing up his face to squawk like a basehead. "Her son dick taste funny." That one actually got a few belly laughs. Then Callaso caught two fat roaches and guys were racing them across Vintner's desk, laying a dollar a heat until Vintner showed up, looking serious as a heart attack.

"Roll call," Lieutenant Vintner said. "Everybody shut the fuck up." He donned his reading glasses to read through the rotator: a stolen Sentra was rolling around the division with flames painted on it, should make it easy to spot. The Five-Deuce Hoovers and the Neighborhoods were still feuding to the tune of six dead in two days. The department ombudsman will henceforth be referred to in all official department correspondence as the ombudsperson. "If anyone finds a pair of Oakley blades," he said, "they're Garcia's."

"Have we gone over ambushes yet?" Marquez asked the kid after Vintner dismissed them. He reached into his trusty pouch of Red Man, fished out a hefty load of chaw, and socked it deep into his cheek near the hinge of his jaw. "You wind up in a foot pursuit, you ought to be thinking ambush. Capping a copper wins these assholes a lot of juice on the street, and it makes them fucking royalty in prison. So, when you chase some knucklehead down alleys and over fences, don't assume he's just scrambling to get away because he may be leading you into something nasty.

"Mike Garret, guy I worked with in Southeast, chased this PJ Crip into Imperial Courts one night and got set up," Marquez said. "The fucker had strung razor wire across the breezeway about head high and smeared the wire with black shoe polish so you wouldn't see it in the dark. Garret chased that cocksucker full bore through the breezeway. Wire damn near sliced his head off."

"Jesus," the kid breathed.

"Garret can't really talk anymore," Marquez said. "He has to use this weird little box makes him sound like a fucking robot, but at least he lived. This kid Cardozo wasn't so lucky. Last year, Cardozo chased a Five Deuce Hoover down an alley off Fifty-first Street right here in the Seventy-seventh. The Hoover had a layoff man with a sawed-off twelve-gauge waiting at the other end of the alley. When Cardozo chased the Hoover out the end of the alley, his layoff man gave Cardozo both barrels of bad news right in the face and the double-ought buck split his head open like a fucking cantaloupe. His teeth and skull and shit were all over the alley." Marquez spat tobacco into his styrofoam coffee cup.

Marquez and the kid got stuck on a deuce traffic collision later that night. Señor Borracho stumbled out of Club Tiburon and took his rattling Toyota truck up Florence, punched the red light at Vermont, clipped a Cadillac, and wrapped his Toyota around a light post. The impact launched him out the driver's-side window. He was lying in the street when they rolled up. Marquez figured he'd be DRT, Dead Right There, and they'd at least get some on-call court time out of it, but the guy just had a few bumps and bruises. There was something invulnerable about the boneless way drunks flopped around in a wreck. He'd once seen a deuce kill a family of five and stumble away from the crash with a fat lip.

After they'd booked the drunk, Marquez drove the kid into Eight Tray territory and they jacked some Neighborhood Crip called C-Love, but the little bastard rabbited on him.

Marquez and the kid were right on C-Love's ass when he cut and ran north through a narrow alley, his left arm pumping as he ran. C-Love kept his right hand in the pocket of his jacket and Marquez kept watching for it, expecting that hand to come out with a pistol. The burned-out hulk of a stripped Volkswagen bus blocked the alley and when he couldn't go any farther, C-Love's hand came out of his pocket holding something black and Marquez almost shot him where he stood. Then C-Love turned and chucked the film canister over the wall. The canister must have been packed solid with rock cocaine because it was heavy enough to sail for a half a block. No way to find it.

Marquez grabbed C-Love's shoulders, pulled him down, and brought his knee up into his solar plexus. C-Love dropped, gulping wind. He had to know the rules. You run from the Five-Oh, you're going to get tuned up. Besides, Marquez thought, little puke almost made him swallow his chaw.

But C-Love stayed down too long and seemed to be having a hell of a time catching his breath. He was a lot younger than Marquez remembered, that North Carolina jacket putting phony pounds on his scrawny teenage frame. He might have panicked just at the sight of Marquez, figuring maybe that knee was just the beginning of a serious beat down. Marquez helped him up out of the mud, cuffed him, brushed him off, and told him to take slow, deep breaths. C-Love nodded woozily, eyes bulging at Marquez, but his breath still rattled and he looked unsteady on his feet.

"I don't get it," Marquez said. "I didn't even thump him that hard."

Ben patted a lump in the front of C-Love's North Carolina jacket, reached into his left front pocket, and pulled out a white asthma inhaler. C-Love nodded, eyeing the inhaler pleadingly. Ben jammed the thing into the kid's mouth and squeezed a long blast out of it, watching the C-Love's eyes go half mast with relief as his lungs opened and his breathing slowed.

"Jesus." Marquez flicked C-Love's ear. "Why the fuck didn't you say something?"

"Don't know." C-Love shrugged, staring mope-faced at his new Adidases. "Scared, I guess." He couldn't have been older than seventeen and he was handsome in a winnowy, insubstantial sort of way. There was an almost spectral quality about him. "Ain't like I was out here servin'," C-Love said, his breath still rattling between words. "I mean, earlier yeah, but when you hemmed me up I was on my way to my girl's house, get me a fuck and some Fatburger."

"You're deep in the Eight Trays, here, *mijo*." Marquez spat. Even the hardest of the Neighborhoods wouldn't dare come this far into enemy territory on foot. Marquez glanced at Ben as he uncuffed C-Love, his look saying this poor dumb kid was a fucking ghost.

"I know." C-Love shrugged, his dainty shoulders swimming in the North Carolina jacket. He took another puff from his inhaler and smiled. "But I'm a *lover-lover*. Yey ain't even my thang no more," C-Love said. "But we savin' to move out to Houston. My girl got people out there can hook me up with a job."

"Yeah, okay." Marquez shook his head, absently picking a dead leaf from the shoulder of C-Love's jacket. "But Jesus Christ, kid, keep your head down out here."

"Hey, I be like a ninja, walkin' through walls and shit." C-Love winked at Ben, put his hood up, and struck a karate pose. "In and out before anybody know I been here." Then he turned and melted into the shadows of the alley.

Marquez and Ben cruised through the alleys between Western and Vermont, hoping to flush some quarry worth chasing. Tires splashed darkly through standing water that stank of human waste as the car plowed through fetid hillocks of garbage left in the alley to rot. Graffiti marred both sides of the alley. The jumbled glyphs passed Ben's window like a zoetrope. *Placas,* roll calls, and hit-ups ascribing old vendettas to boys long dead. Black spray paint overwriting red, red crossing out blue, blue crossing out red crossing out blue, red, blue—generations of indecipherable scrawl smearing bruiselike over sagging fences and crumbling walls.

"Dogfight," Marquez said.

A company of shadows gathered in the alley in front of the black-and-white, maybe a dozen of them in a loose circle. They hooted, pumped their fists, and laughed. Crumpled bills and a bottle exchanged hands. Ben only glimpsed the muscular tempest within the circle. For a moment the two dogs locked in combat seemed to be a single creature, a Cerberus these men had somehow conjured from the fabric of the night.

Marquez hit the lights and siren and the men scattered, scrambling over the fences on either side of the alley. The two pit bulls remained, oblivious to all but each other. The oily sheen of blood on their mottled coats made the dogs look eerily reptilian in the headlights.

Marquez and Ben got out and stood over the dogs. One dog held the other's throat clamped in its jaws, splayed its forelegs for leverage, and shook its blunt head from side to side. The other dog looked dead on his feet. Blood matted the fur of its neck and spattered the concrete.

The victorious dog's eyes sickened Ben; no trace of the expected savagery in them. The dog's eyes rolled and searched in the same anxious way a good horse's do, wide open and eager to please.

"Stand back," Marquez said. He drew his .45 and blew a hole through the dog's skull. The dog stood frozen, like a pointer, and collapsed with his jaws still clamped on his opponent's throat. The loser staggered a few steps and sat on its haunches with the dead dog still clinging to his throat. Then the loser began to lap at a wound on its flank.

"He's suffering," Marquez told Ben.

"I—I can't," Ben whispered.

Marquez sighed, stepped to the loser, and shot it through its head. The dog fell sideways and lay still. "They breed them for this," he said. "Train them for it from the time they're puppies. Not their fucking fault."

They heard the staccato roar of an automatic weapon. Ben had practiced enough to recognize the clanky percussion of an AK-47 churning out a hundred rounds per minute. The sound came from behind them, back in Eight Tray Hood. Marquez and Ben ran back to the black-and-white, Marquez broadcasting the shots fired heard in the area to get some units rolling their way.

It had been a drive-by. Witnesses said a male black in a blue baseball cap shouted "Eight Tray," pointed the muzzle of an AK out the passenger window of a blue Olds, and sprayed, leaving two teenagers down in the front yard. C-Love must have been dead before he hit the ground. A 7.62-millimeter ball ammo had chopped through him at 2,350 feet per second, cutting through everything he couldn't do without: liver, lungs, heart, spine. He'd crumpled in the front yard. Bright blood pumped out of the ragged holes in him, seeping into the grass so that the area around his body was already swampy with it. Blood welled up around Ben's boots and they sank into the mud as he stood over the body. Bits of chewed-up Fatburger, blown out through C-Love's back as the rounds tore open his stomach, were scattered over the bloody grass along with the singed stuffing of his North Carolina parka.

The girl didn't look like she was hit as bad as C-Love. She'd taken a single round, maybe a ricochet, just that dime-sized puncture in her side and no exit wound that Ben could see. Her pulse was still strong under his fingers. She was a pretty black girl of about fifteen with baby fat just giving way to a woman's true shape. She had braided hair and the kind of wide mouth that might have risen easily into a smile.

Responding units got the crime scene taped off and held back the crowd so the ambulance could get to them. The paramedics loaded her onto the ambulance, cut off her clothes, and jammed some instrument into her poor sexy mouth that was supposed to get her breathing again. Ben rode in the ambulance with her, standard procedure in case the victim makes any dying declarations about who did it, but she wasn't talking.

The paramedics worked on her all the way to County USC. At the hospital, they cut into her beautiful body and reached inside to massage her heart. Nothing worked. A young doctor in a Hawaiian shirt pronounced her dead, and they all stripped off their bloody gloves and walked away from her. The girl was naked and for the first time Ben noticed her Eight Tray tattoos. Blood soaked the sheet beneath her and the incision they'd cut to reach her heart looked like a gaping red mouth. Her cracked ribs were exposed. "Look what they've done to you," Ben whispered to the dead girl. "What a mess they've made of you."

Ben reached Marquez on the radio and told him the girl was dead. He gave him the name of the doctor who pronounced her and the girl's intake number. They still didn't have her name. Marquez was still back at the scene waiting for Homicide. He told Ben to sit tight and grab a bite to eat. Sure, Ben thought, like some fucking Fatburger. The cafeteria was closed, but Ben bummed a cup of bitter coffee from Hospital Security. The doctor in the Hawaiian shirt found him before he had time to finish it.

"You came in with that GSW, right?" Ben nodded. "Her mother is here," the doctor said. "She described the girl's tattoos precisely." He clapped Ben on the shoulder. "You ready to make the notification?"

"I thought you guys did all that," Ben said. The doctor shook his head.

"I can help you," the doctor said. "But you know more about what happened to her than I do." The doctor took Ben through the emergency room and led him into a small private office where the girl's mother was waiting on a bland couch. She was in her early thirties. She and the dead girl could have been sisters. She must have had her at fifteen or sixteen. They would have been like two children growing up together, trying to figure it out together. The doctor closed the door behind them, and he and Ben sat in the two chairs opposite the couch. The woman's eyes shone with such force and hope that for a moment it was like the dead girl was reaching out from behind her mother's face.

"My name is Officer Halloran." He took a deep breath, conscious of the stale authority in his own voice, just like a real cop. "Earlier this evening, my partner and I responded to the scene of a drive-by shooting. Your daughter had been shot. I rode in the ambulance with her, but . . ." He faltered and the doctor took over for him.

"We continued to work on her after she arrived here, but we couldn't revive her," the doctor said. "The bullet struck her heart and she was killed almost instantly." The doctor paused for a moment. "There wouldn't have been much pain."

The woman brought her fists to her forehead and clenched her jaw. "Goddamn," she hissed. "Goddamn her young wild ass." She looked furious, as if dying had been her daughter's ultimate rebellion, her final revenge. Then the woman moved her hands to cover her mouth and the tears finally came. Her grief materialized like a physical entity, a muscular thing suddenly present in the room with them. Ben watched the creature choke that false anger out of her. "My baby," the woman cried. Ben leaned forward and reached out to rest his hand on her shoulder. As soon as he touched her, she crumpled forward out of her chair, falling against him. She clutched him, face buried in his chest. "Oh Lord, my baby girl." Her racking sobs shook them both. Ben said nothing. He just stroked her hair, distantly aware that he wasn't pretending to be a cop anymore.

An hour later, Marquez picked him up from the hospital. South Bureau Homicide had taken over the crime scene and the investigation. The detectives would need a first responder's statement from him, but Marquez took one look at Ben and told him he could write a statement later if he wanted. "You okay?" Marquez asked him.

"No, sir," Ben said.

Marquez pulled the black-and-white over to the curb and turned to face Ben. "It's not yours," Marquez told him. "And don't even think about picking it up and taking it home with you because none of it belongs to you. It's theirs. Leave it right where you found it, you hear me?"

Marquez bought them a hit-and-run call on St. Andrews, their second traffic of the night, because it was close to the homicide scene and the suspect vehicle was a blue Oldsmobile, same as the one from their 187. Maybe they'd get lucky. The car had run aground in St. Andrews Park, its front end buckled against the jungle gym. Ben keyed on the blue ball cap on the passenger seat. Bright boy, Marquez thought, go to the head of the class.

They picked up the blood trail leading away from the car, the spatter looking motor-oil black on the moonlit asphalt, turning candy red in the beam of his Streamlight as Marquez followed the trail away from the crash, straight across a corner lot and up Eighty-seventh Street. Jesus, whoever he is, he's losing a ton of sauce, Marquez thought. Still, the unwavering trajectory of the trail itself encouraged him. As a rookie, he and Rourke had followed the blood trail of a stabbing victim, and you could tell the guy was dying by the reeling way the trail doubled back on itself, circled itself, the poor fucker moving just to move. He'd finally dragged himself into some oleanders, probably knowing it was over by then, the guy seeking only a private place to die.

But the trail here was different, straight and full of purpose. This victim was moving with a destination in mind, maybe with some hope for survival. Marquez picked up the pace. He and the kid followed the trail to a smallish Spanish bungalow with an immaculate lawn. A semi parked in the gravel drive along the side of the house. The front door was standing open, spilling light out across the lawn.

There were plastic covers on the living-room furniture and plastic runners over the carpet. Leno was interviewing the Spice Girls on the television. A TV tray lay on its side, a potpie facedown on the carpet. The old guy had probably knocked it over jumping out of his La-Z-Boy.

Their victim, male black, twenties, sat on his knees in the center of the room, arms hanging limp so that the backs of his hands rested against the carpet. His father kneeled in front of him, gripping the kid's shoulders the way you would a child who'd just darted out in front of a car. The victim's sleeves bunched under the old man's fingers. Bruises would be coming up under his clothes, but Marquez doubted if this kid felt anything. There was a neat entry wound in the back of the kid's head and no exit. His bowels had already gone.

"Twelve-A-Forty-five," Marquez said into his rover. "Let me have an RA unit for a male black—"

"His name is Ronnell," the guy whispered. "He is my son."

"—conscious and breathing," Marquez continued.

"This is my son."

"—suffering from a gunshot wound to the head."

The kid's head slumped forward and the guy shook him. "Stay with me, Ronnell." He had the kid's head in his hands now, trying to keep him upright. "You hang on now, son." He pressed his forehead against the kid's, using his fingers to force the kid's eyes open. Some pinkish foam bubbling out of his nose and mouth now. The guy used his shirt to wipe it away, but it just kept coming.

The first paramedic through the door took one glance at the kid, popped his gum, and looked inclined to pronounce on the spot. No one tried to separate them.

"Sir," Marquez said softly, "did Ronnell say anything to you when he came in?"

"Sorry," the guy whispered. He was hugging the dead kid now, rocking him gently. "He told me he was sorry."

"Our victim here's an Eight-Tray Gangster," Chuin said. They were standing out on the guy's front porch, watching SID photograph the blood trail. "Probably our shooter from Gramercy. We just pulled an AK out of his trunk. I'll have it drug-fired tomorrow, but a sawbuck says it's the weapon that punched your lovebirds in that drive-by."

"Payback's a bitch." Marquez spat.

"Three clearances," Chuin said. "Easy-peezy. Christ, if we let them alone they take care of the shit themselves."

"You're starting to sound like Keyes," Marquez said.

"What do you hear about that other thing?"

"I've got Ronny looking into it," Marquez said.

"Well, hell," Chuin said, "I may just take my vacation."

14

The first time Big Ben gave his son the Some-Day-All-This-Will-Be-Yours speech, Benji was still a senior at UCLA, clerking for the old man while he studied like a mad monk for the LSAT. "I mean it, Benji," Big Ben told him, absently scratching the salt-and-pepper chest hairs curling out of the open V of his shirt. His eyes looked a little misty, but it was probably the dope. "Everything I've built belongs to you, my man."

By then, Big Ben had had his frizzy hair chemically straightened and slicked back into a gleaming ponytail. He swiveled his high-back leather chair and swept his hand over the Century City skyline, visible from his office window. The remainder of a joint smoldered between Big Ben's thighlike fingers. Big Ben had this deliberate way of talking when he was stoned that made everything he said sound like a slightly ominous joke. "What do you say?" Big Ben asked, passing Benji the joint.

"Thanks," Benji said, just to be saying something. Benji still not sure if his offer was some kind of backhanded curse, but knowing in his bones he would never take over his father's firm. He hadn't been accepted to law school yet, but that wasn't up for discussion. He was going to be a DA. Carcosa had spoken.

"You know, I wasn't much older than you when I hung my shingle out at some shitass little strip mall in North Hollywood," Big Ben said. "Right next to this Hong Kong handjob house that Vice raided like every other day." He told his son how he used to take a thermos of coffee and a police scanner and sit up all night in his crappy little Corolla with the floor so rusted out he could see the highway rushing beneath him, just listening for the L.A. cops to catch drunks barreling down Laurel Canyon on their way back from the discos. This fat little guy waddling into the middle of their traffic stops in his off-the-rack suit and frizzed-out Art Garfunkel do.

"I'd start in on the cop about how the walk-the-line test was *verkocht* because the asphalt was uneven and that big flashlight had disoriented my client," he said. "*My* client, Benji. Never seen the bastard before in my life, but that's how I came at those pigs, what you'd call a presumptive close. And the souse isn't about to argue with me because here I am keeping his ass out of the pokey. I don't remember how many clients I actually got that way, enough to pay my rent and keep me in Top Ramen for a while, but that wasn't the point. Word got around.

"After the cops got wise, it was open season on the fat kike," Big Ben said, an old bitterness coming into his red-tinged eyes. "This was back when Gates was still tall in the saddle and I want to tell you, there wasn't a kid glove on that department. They used to bust out my taillights with their Billy clubs and then cite me for it. One night, a couple of Hoss Cartwrights tossed me in their trunk and drove me up the grapevine, dumped me out around the Tejon Pass. They roughed me up some and I had to hitchhike home in the goddamned snow, but I was back out there the next night like nothing had happened."

After successfully keeping a couple of television actors out of jail on what should have been dead-bang possession beefs, Big Ben's bulldog reputation gained momentum. Soon, every Hollywood producer with a bad boy in his stable was calling Big Ben in the wee hours with a wee problem. *Of course, we all know fifteen can look twenty-five at that time of night . . . No problem, how the hell were you supposed to know it was in there? It's not like you packed your own suitcase . . . So, she drowned. She was a heavy drinker, went for a midnight swim and never came back. Case closed.*

His abilities as a fixer earned Big Ben access to the entertainment industry's innermost circles, but it was working with L.A.'s poor black community where Big Ben struck it rich. "While all the yuppies were out dancing to Lionel Richie, crack turned South Central into Beirut," Big Ben would say. "People were singing 'I'd like to buy the world a coke' and everybody loved that bloated little black kid on *Diff'rent Strokes,* but the moment June Cleaver sees Cool Breeze ditty-bopping down her street with a boom box on his shoulder, she's on the horn screaming rape to the cops."

The remaining descendants of L.A.'s Protestant establishment, the vanilla suburbanites, demanded protection from what they saw as a rising tide of chocolate crime. "And the LAPD protected them, if you'll pardon the pun, in spades," Big Ben told him. "They shot something like eighty people a year, Benji, shot poor Eulia Mae Love eight times because she wouldn't let the meter man shut off her family's power. Hell, the LAPD choked a dozen black guys to death, and Gates said they died because blacks have different arteries than *normal* people. You believe that shit?"

Big Ben was one of the first lawyers to see an untapped gold mine in the city's combustible racial strife. "I'll be the first to admit it, Benji," he said. "*Schvartzes* commit the lion's share of the robberies and murders in this town—black-on-black crime. And if I know it, you can bet your sweet ass every cop on the street knows it. That's why the hotshots are drawn into the ghetto. The young ones are the real money trees, Benji. Yankee Doodle Dandies, looking to make a difference out there or maybe just hooked on the rush, they pile up messy arrests faster than you can say 'punitive damages.'"

Young black men account for over 60 percent of your arrests. You've been targeting black men for your entire career, haven't you, Officer?

Objection! Relevance!

Your Honor, this officer shot and killed a scared young man armed only with a baseball bat. I think the jury has a right to know if this officer has a past history of racism.

Objection!

The scared young man in question had been a Playboy Crip and a three-time loser nicknamed Scatter for his facility with a sawed-off shotgun. Scatter was coked out of his gourd at the time of the shooting, and the baseball bat he wielded was embedded with blood, skull fragments, and patches of human hair, Scatter having just bludgeoned his uncle into the dark land. Scatter's grandmother, now Big Ben's client in a wrongful-death suit, had barricaded herself in her bedroom and called the police, screaming that her grandson had gone crazy and was trying to kill her. When officers arrived, Scatter charged them with the bloody bat and they blew him out of his socks. Big Ben got the grandmother seven hundred grand and put a third in his pocket.

After the Rodney King verdict, Big Ben and his son sat in his office and watched the riots on national television. The rest of the building had been evacuated after they started looting Wilshire Boulevard, but Big Ben insisted Benji stay to celebrate. The local news carried most of it live from their helicopters. Big Ben cut the sound, cranked one of his Grateful Dead bootlegs, and they watched the city burn to "Estimated Prophet." From the office window, Benji could see slanting black mantas of smoke and ash drifting across the 405.

"I'm telling you, kid, accomplishment is bullshit," he said. "Don't ever get sucked in by accomplishment. That's the real opiate of the masses." They hauled Reginald Denny out of his truck and shattered his skull with a hunk of concrete. "See? Boom, that's real power, Benji," Big Ben said. "The power to unmake, the power to tear down. Power to the people, man." He threw up a mocking Black Power salute while Football Williams danced a jig over Denny's body.

Later that night, watching that rippling red curtain on the horizon, the fulgent shimmer of a neighborhood in flames, Big Ben clipped the end off a cigar and lit up. "Manna from heaven, Benji." He smiled and blew smoke rings. "You watch. This thing is going to make us a fortune."

Big Ben did not actually represent Rodney King. If he had, he liked to say Rodney would have walked away with a lot more lettuce than he eventually did. Still, the fallout from Rodney King proved an enormous boon to Big Ben and others. The gates of Rome were at last laid open and the city attorney didn't want Big Ben anywhere near a jury. All Big Ben had to do was pick up the phone and the city attorney would settle out of court for the price of a split-level ranch in Encino. Big Ben had the city attorney on his speed dial. He called it making a withdrawal from the Bank of Los Angeles.

It was during those halcyon days after the riots that Joe Carcosa called Big Ben at home to tell him about Darius. For years, Carcosa had been laundering money through Lethal Injection Records. "This kid's going places and he'll need someone like you when he gets there," Carcosa told Big Ben. "You should sit down with him."

Darius was on time to the minute. He carried a leather-bound copy of *Ivanhoe* in his right hand with a tasseled bookmark about two-thirds into the book. He wore a close-fitting, black vest buttoned over his bare chest and pleated black trousers with a fob pocket. A black silk ribbon attached his antique pocket watch to his belt, and as he stepped into the waiting room, he made a great show of clicking open the gold watch to check the time, then snapping the watch closed and slipping it back into his fob pocket in one practiced motion. Ben thought the Phileas Fogg thing was a little much.

"Mr. Washington, I presume." Ben stood to greet him, extending his hand.

"Please." Darius smiled, transferring *Ivanhoe* into his left hand to free his right. "Call me Darius." Darius was maybe a few years older than Ben, beautiful rather than handsome, with a high, smooth forehead, upturned eyes, faintly Asian cheekbones, and flawless teeth. He resembled an articulated figure carved from solid black marble.

When Olivier played Othello for the Royal Shakespeare Company in greasepaint as dark black as Darius's natural skin, British theater critics called his performance *dangerous*. Later, when Benji was getting to know Darius, Darius got a big kick out of telling him about that production. "Like a lighter shade of Moor might not have smothered Desdemona."

"May I get you something?" Ben said, nodding to the wet bar.

"No, thank you."

"Good book?"

"I prefer *Rob Roy*," Darius said. "Sir Walter Scott was actually a lawyer. He got a cushy legal job that gave him time to write his poetry. Ever read *The Lady of the Lake*?"

"No," Benji said. Darius shrugged.

"Byron sort of edged him out, so Scott turned to the novel."

"Oh," Benji said, wondering if Darius knew how transparent this Alistair Cooke act was. Benji pressed the intercom to tell his father that his appointment was here. "You can go on in." Darius thanked Benji, stepped into his father's office, and closed the door behind him.

Benji lifted an empty Baccarat glass from the wet bar and tiptoed to the office door. He pressed the open end of the glass to the door and put his ear against it, figuring it was after hours. If someone happened to walk into the waiting room, he could just put the glass to his lips, pretend to be draining the last of it—very Encyclopedia Brown. He hadn't done this for years, none of Big Ben's clients were interesting enough to risk it.

"Don't slide that 'fight the power' shit on me," Benji heard Darius tell his father. He sounded like a different man, taking his dialect elevator down to street level for Big Ben. "I wanted Atticus Finch, I'd check him outta the fuckin' library. I know Little Deuce is dirty because that's what I pay him to be, but he's just supposed to run product to my street-level dudes and bring the Benjamins straight back to me. Now I find out that fool's a contract killer in his spare time, puts my operation in jeopardy."

"I believe I can get the evidence against him excluded on the grounds that the police had no right to pull Deuce over in the first place," Big Ben said, his tone placating. "The stop sign the officers claim Deuce ran doesn't even exist. Case dismissed."

"But all that noise about the fruit of the poisonous tree don't mean a thing if I can't retrieve my merchandise." Darius said "merchandise" like they were talking about a kilo of Concord grapes.

"You don't get your dope back," Ben said flatly.

"Then what the hell am I paying you for?" Darius hissed. "That nigga's been a liability from day one and this was his last bad on my dollar. Deuce can press vanity plates up in Corcoran for the rest of his dumb-ass life, but I wash my hands of that nigga right here and now."

"Just hear me out," Big Ben soothed, working another angle, handball again. "We get the evidence excluded. Then we turn around and sue the city for the civil rights violation under color of authority. That's good for three-quarters of a mil."

"Of which you take a third," Darius said quickly.

"That's still five hundred grand in your boy's pocket," Big Ben said, letting his voice get a little playful now. "Of course, you're free to recoup your loss from Deuce any way you guys want to work it out."

Benji heard the delicate sound of ice cubes clinking in the waiting room behind him and whirled to face a lean black man at the wet bar, the glass nearly slipping out of Benji's hands at the sight of him. The guy had just materialized there to fix himself a gin and juice like it was the most natural thing in the world. He wore his hair in a wet, Rick James Jheri-curl do that draped down to his shoulders and left an oily film on his blue Members Only jacket. Black parachute pants tucked into black Reeboks. His eyes were hidden behind dark Ferrari sunglasses. Benji would have put this guy into his forties, but with his gaunt features cloaked by those oily curls and sunglasses it wasn't easy to tell.

The guy held a camera bag on a nylon strap across his chest, but the weight and shape inside the bag were all wrong for any camera on the market. He'd have an Uzi in there, maybe a MAC-10. Benji had met enough of his father's clients to recognize the casual aspect of a practiced killer. The man in the sunglasses smiled, stirring his drink with a yellowish finger.

"Good evening," Benji said, smiling too broadly, the facial equivalent of a frightened dog rolling onto its back to let a stranger scratch its belly. "Do you have an appointment?" Benji stepped warily across the carpet, keeping his eyes on the guy as he moved toward the desk like he was checking the appointment book. The guy didn't answer, just sipped his drink, and stepped back from the bar to face Benji full-on, in the half-mocking manner of a gunslinger in a Hollywood saloon.

"Let's see," Benji said, leaning over the reception desk. He began to leaf through the appointment book with his left hand and palmed the stainless-steel letter opener with his right, the only item in the office that even resembled a weapon.

The man came slowly forward and drained the rest of his drink, sucking an ice cube out of the glass to crunch on it. He set the empty glass between them on the desk. "You gone stick me, bwoy?"

Just then, Darius stepped out of Big Ben's office, closing the door behind him. "I see you've met Jax." Darius grinned. "My road dog."

"This brave's got some medicine in him, D," Jax said, hooking his thumb at Benji. "Thought I was some badman come for Daddy and this white boy was fixin' to stick me."

"God damn." Darius raised his eyebrows at Benji. "I'm beginning to like you already."

PRESENT

The California sun pounded South Central with extreme prejudice. Day Watch had to shoot three mad dogs—ghetto elk—before noon and more prowled the streets, loping miragelike through the rippling heat, foaming and snarling at shadows. "Even gangsters ought to have enough natural sense to stay out of this shit." Marquez squinted at the heat rippling off Normandie Avenue and spat brown juice into his cup. "Makes everybody nuts."

Marquez turned east up Hughes Avenue. "I want to check with some of these dudes from DP," Marquez told Ben. "Shot caller owes me a solid."

The Damu Princes looked somehow quaint in their old-school embroidered varsity jackets, holdovers from the bygone era of the Slausons and the Businessmen, back before crack, before zip guns became AKs.

A dozen DP reputables were throwing bones in a friendly driveway midblock. You could tell the game had been going awhile by the ducats on the deck, some of the players using spare mags as paperweights to hold down their winnings. Typical street craps: the dice were almost secondary, lost in a trading-floor cacophony of hedges and side bets. The money changed hands in a blur, winners holding the bills pimp-style, fanned like peacock feathers in their palms. There were body-checks and a few slap-fights to settle halfhearted claims of cheating. A bottle of Hennessy made its way around the circle.

Two runners broke from the game as soon as Marquez and Ben

stepped out of their black-and-white. Security, Marquez thought. A game like this would need at least two shooters to cover it. The Princes were plenty poisonous, but all that loose cash on the concrete had still been known to tempt takedown crews to try their luck.

Ben reflexively started up the driveway after the two runners. "Leave 'em be," Marquez told him, watching the kids hit the fence like a pommel horse, splitting east and west in the alley. It might have been a flanking move, two dudes looking to hang in the cut and double back on them, but this didn't have that kind of vibe. More than likely they'd just ditch their burners somewhere in the alley and pick them up again after One Time had moved on.

The big baller in this bunch was an OG called Boscoe who didn't miss many meals—three bucks and some silver on the boy. Boscoe was on parole for witness intimidation, just a few weeks shy of discharge, and his hard-earned prison muscle had long since turned to Crisco, but he carried it with class. Boscoe wore his braids in crop-circle patterns, capped with red beads. The guy saw Marquez and Ben coming up the driveway, but made like he was too busy rolling to notice them.

"Boscoe," Marquez said. "A word."

"Word's all I got time for," Boscoe said. High voice for a big guy.

"Two." Marquez smiled. Boscoe sighed theatrically, swept up his winnings like a close-up magician, folded the bills once, and slid them into his pocket. He grabbed the bottle by the neck and walked to face Marquez at the edge of the lawn, well clear of the game.

Last Christmas's plastic figures were still standing on the burned lawn in front of the house, a sun-faded Santa and his reindeer, Mary and Joseph mooning over the Baby Christ—each with a forty-watt bulb up its ass. Boscoe's big pit was chained to a palm in the yard, quietly gnawing the belly out of Frosty the Snowman. Marquez wondered if Frosty was still plugged into an outlet, figuring the mutt would find out soon, begin to dance around.

"How's your grandma?" Marquez asked, calling in his chit.

"Day by day." Boscoe shrugged. "You know, she survivin'." Boscoe downed two fingers of Hennessy and handed the bottle to Marquez. Marquez tilted the bottle to his lips, eyes locked with Boscoe's for three long swallows. Not many Mexicans out here would drink after a *mayate,* Marquez giving the OG his due props.

"Some fools took down a tax man," Marquez said, pressing the bottle back into Boscoe's big palm. "Other side of Slauson. Did him pretty hard."

"Uh-huh." Boscoe nodded. "Did two, three of them is what I heard. They been talkin' 'bout it on the other side." He tilted the bottle toward Normandie, sloshing a little juice into the grass.

Boscoe'd had a Boot Hill celly up in Lancaster, guy named Sleepy Loc, and they still hollered back and forth across Normandie once in a while. *Eses* had outnumbered brothers inside, and the racial imbalance made strange bedfellows on the tier. Boscoe and Sleepy Loc had been caught up in a prison riot and circled the wagons in the rec room, Crips and Bloods slashing side by side, going Thermopylae against a brown tidal wave. They'd both survived, served their bids, and paroled on back to the Balkans, but sworn enemies or not, Boscoe and Sleepy Loc still kept in touch. It was like walking away from a plane crash; come out the other side of the shit and you need an occasional touchback to quiet your mind.

"*Díme,*" Marquez said.

Boscoe shook his head, eyes shut, some pressure there in need of trepanning. "Been hearin' some beepy-ass shit, my nig," he said. "Upside-down-type shit, like after the riots, remember? For a minute, folks swore up and down the Five-Oh was out here pullin' drive-bys." He finished the bottle, tossed it.

"I remember," Marquez said. The pit bit another hunk of white plastic out of Frosty and something about the dog's dumb contentment ruffled Marquez, like cold water through his own plumbing.

"Okay," Boscoe said. "Well, now, my boy from the other side? He sayin' doan open the door for an oval badge, blood. He say just stay bool, keep your nappy head down, and the homies gone inherit the earth." Boscoe smiled uneasily, pushed up his sleeve, and held his arm eye-level between them so Marquez could see the hairs standing at attention. "I'm scared, Marquez," he whispered. "No joke."

"Was that guy bullshit?" Ben asked as they pulled away.

"God, I hope so," Marquez said.

The radio squawked. "Twelve-A-Forty-five, handle the screaming woman at two forty-six East Seventy-sixth Lane in apartment four. Code Two high incident Eleven Thirty-eight."

The apartment building was a squat shoe box of crumbling cinder block partitioned by thin drywall into four sad dwellings. Ben followed Marquez to the fourth apartment. The brass 4 had been pried from the door for the few pennies it would fetch, but the wood behind the missing 4 had not yet faded to match the rest of the door. Marquez and Ben stood on either side of the door and listened. Marquez pounded the door with his fist. "Police," he said. "Open up."

A scream came through the door. Marquez stepped back from the door, as though the sound itself had knocked him backward. He drew his pistol and kicked the door once, twice. The wood pulsed, but would not give. "Both together," he said. "On three." Another scream pitched out of the apartment. Ben stepped next to Marquez and drew his pistol. He counted to three and together they slammed their boots into the door. The jamb split and the door swung open. Marquez and Ben swept into the dim apartment and separated, weapons level.

Ben scanned the single room for threats. Under the sagging, popcorn-plaster ceiling, he saw a hotplate and some papers on a wobbly card table, a moth-eaten couch. A sweaty teenage girl with a swollen belly shrieked in the middle of the floor. She lay spread-eagle with her dingy sundress hiked up over her thighs and bunched in her fists. The floral pattern of her sundress and the dirty carpet around her were soaked with something viscous. She looked at Ben with wide glazed eyes and shrieked again.

"Oh, shit," Ben breathed, and kneeled at her feet. Her coarse black pubic hair was soaked and her vulva was engorged like an eye. Marquez snatched a torn cushion from the couch and kneeled to place it under her head. He keyed his radio. "Twelve-A-Forty-five, we're going to need an RA to our location for a female black, approximately fifteen years of age, conscious and breathing. She's in labor."

"I don't think this kid's going to wait for the ambulance," Ben said. "And I don't know nothin' 'bout birthin' no babies, sir."

Marquez took a handkerchief from his pocket and mopped the sweat from the girl's taut brow. "What's your name, sweetheart?" he said.

"Jackie." The girl gasped and gritted her teeth. Her nostrils flared and she screamed again.

"Ah, I see feet," Ben said, trying to summon everything he had ever heard about breech birth. He knew it was dangerous, but he couldn't remember why. Could the baby suffocate or something?

"Shouldn't you see a head first?" Marquez whispered.

"These are definitely feet, sir," Ben said. Jackie cried out. Her body heaved and bucked. A tiny penis and the gentle curve of a belly followed, trailing a bluish cord. Ben placed his palm under the baby's slick bottom to keep him off the filthy carpet. Jackie panted and groaned. Her body seemed to sag and her head lolled on the cushion. The baby hung there, his progress halted. "Jackie, you have to keep going," Ben said. Her eyes fluttered. "The baby really needs to come out now," Ben said. He reached up to clasp her wrist. "It's very important." She grimaced and arched her back. Her jaw locked and tears streamed along her cheekbones. When the baby's arms came through, Ben saw the way the cord was around him.

The baby popped out bright blue and misshapen. The cord was tight around his neck. Ben worked two fingers under the loop and slipped the cord up over his head. The baby didn't seem to be breathing. Ben lifted him and brushed his little chest with the tips of his fingers.

"Give him here," Marquez said. He gripped the baby's ankles, held him upside down, and slapped him on the behind. The baby squalled, but Marquez did not smile as he handed the wailing baby to Jackie and she cradled him to her breast.

Marquez leaned against the black-and-white with a soggy burrito as big as Ben's forearm, brushed the flies off it, and shoved the business end of it into his mouth. He chomped the burrito as cleanly as Ben's father would have clipped the end off a Cohiba. Ben hadn't opened his own grease-soaked wax-paper package on the hood of the car. He felt sick. "They're fucking out babies every goddamned day down here," Marquez snorted. "Forget it. Not our problem." But Ben could see he was jazzed about the delivery.

The radio crackled: "Twelve Cycle Twenty-two." A bike cop trying to catch his breath. "We need backup at Florence and Western for a male black under the influence of PCP."

Marquez chucked his burrito into the alley. "Get your head in the game," he said as Ben slid into the passenger seat of the black-and-white. "Fighting a shermhead's like fighting the Incredible Hulk with a cattle prod up his ass." He drove like a TV cop, blowing through intersections, jumping the concrete median to slalom through oncoming traffic, and leaning out the open window of the car to bellow at pedestrians while he drove down the sidewalk. Marquez stopped the black-and-white in front of the drive-thru Burger Palace at Florence and Western. "*Dios mio,*" he growled. "Look at this dog-and-pony show."

Seventy or eighty gawkers already clogged the intersection and more were coming. Most of the hood was already out of doors anyway, half crazy from heat and hooch. Street vendors in sweat-stained work shirts and baseball caps gathered with their borrowed shopping carts bearing *elotes,* wilted roses, overripe strawberries, bagged oranges, and peeled mangos on sticks. The usual skeletal baseheads and winos craned their heads next to a surly crew of gangbangers in oversize jerseys and clownishly loose-fitting jeans. Lots of them had video cameras, everything from those bulky, first-generation VHS antiques to the latest digital wonder. The homeboys jostled for position, throwing wild elbows like they were fighting for rebounds on the Venice courts. A few climbed onto the hoods of parked cars for a better view. Spontaneous fights broke out in the crowd. A woman screamed.

"Bad juju," Marquez said, meaning it. A kid not more than twelve jammed a butterfly knife into the front tire of a parked black-and-white. Someone threw a water balloon filled with piss at a motor cop and it exploded against the motor cop's chest, splashing up into his face. The motor cop cursed, trying to blink the sting out of his eyes, arms out from his sides, gaping down at his soaked uniform. The crowd whooped and brayed. They toppled some vendor's pedal cart and foggy chunks of dry ice tumbled onto the hot asphalt with about fifty Popsicles. Kids scrambled into the street. When the vendor tried to stop them, someone broke an empty bottle of Hennessy over his head.

At the sight of Marquez, the crowd came alive in a chorus of pop-eyed whoofing, swaying, and dancing, long arms pushing upward—*raise the roof.* "Officer Marquez in the *hizzee!*" Some gangly kids in the crowd cranked their fists in the air. "Heyyy! Hooaa!" Marquez wading into the clamor with his head bulled forward like a human cowcatcher. The crowd parted instantly for him, scrambling out of his path. The cameras turned to take him in as Marquez strode past them with Ben following squire-like in his wake. When he had pushed through the crowd into the intersection, Marquez spat. "Dupriest Jenkins," he said. "He used to play ball for SC, decent kid, but he and his brother like to smoke sherm and fight cops."

Dupriest Jenkins was what Rourke would have called a grit-eatin' freak. He stood six-seven and weighed at least three hundred. He was naked and his top-heavy muscles shined with sweat. Little commas of coarse dark hair curled out of his heaving chest. Some fat on him, Marquez noted, just enough to make his ham-hock tits shake as he howled and gibbered. Some bike cop snuck up behind him and tried to take out his legs with his asp baton. Dupriest grabbed him by his belt and collar, lifted the flailing cop over his shoulders, and hurled him at a nearby black-and-white. The cop somersaulted and landed hard against the windshield of the car.

The windshield spiderwebbed. Dupriest picked up the cop's mountain bike by the rear wheel and swung the bike like a scythe. The handlebars caught a patrol cop in the shoulder and knocked him over a parked car. The crowd cheered and hooted. Dupriest cast the bike aside and howled.

Sergeant Patty Pendergast, a.k.a. Patty Cream Cheese, was in charge of the scene. "Somebody get a Taser up here!" Patty shouted, already sounding panicky. Ben could hear the rotors of LAPD air units orbiting the scene and news helicopters from three of the local stations hovering in the airspace above them. What happened here was going to make or break Patty's career, and she knew it.

"Sarge, I've dealt with this kid before and that Taser isn't going to work!" Marquez shouted, moving closer to her. Another young probationer rushed up with the Taser and paused, standing between them. "Put that thing away, son," Marquez told him gently. "You're wasting your time."

"*You* shut your goddamned mouth!" Patty shrieked at Marquez. Her eyes were nearly as wild as Dupriest's.

"Slow down," Marquez told her. "I'm on your side."

The young officer looked at Marquez expectantly. Patty stepped in front of Marquez and stood on her toes to get in the young officer's face. "Don't look at him," she screamed, trembling now. "He's not in charge here. I am. Deploy that weapon now."

The kid stepped forward and shot Dupriest in the chest with the Taser. Twin darts sank into his chest, the juice crackled, and Ben glimpsed a thin blue arc sizzling between the wires. Ten thousand watts should have had him dancing, but Dupriest just tore the darts out of his chest, mugging and howling for the crowd. Patty looked on the verge of tears. Her hands were balled into tight little fists at her sides.

Marquez cupped his hands around his mouth and spoke directly into Patty's ear so that she could hear him over the crowd. "Patty, listen to me," Marquez said. "The crowd's riling him up. We need additional units to contain—" She swatted his hands away.

"Beanbag, stand by," Patty shouted. Another young cop waded warily into position with his beanbag shotgun at port arms. At her command, he leveled the weapon and pumped four beanbag rounds into Dupriest, his broad belly rippling like a water bed with each impact. He staggered, but did not fall. Dupriest lunged, snatching the beanbag shotgun out of the cop's hands. He gripped the shotgun by the barrel and swung it like a bat, catching the cop in the face. The crowd roared as the cop dropped to all fours, spitting blood and teeth on the pavement. When his partner bent to help him up, Marquez drew down on Dupriest, but Dupriest cast the shotgun aside, linked his hands, and brought them down like a hammer on the partner officer's back. Both cops lay in a heap at his feet.

Before Marquez could stop her, Patty charged Dupriest with her baton. Marquez and Ben ran after her. Dupriest ducked Patty's swing and wrapped her in a bear hug, lifting her off her feet. Patty struggled with her arms pinned at her sides, legs kicking. Her baton clattered to the pavement. Dupriest turned his head slightly, as if to kiss her. His open mouth covering the right side of her face. Patty let out a sputtering scream as Dupriest bit down and Ben heard the gristly crunch of flesh and muscle tearing away from her skull.

The crowd went suddenly quiet, the only noise coming from this kid, about twelve, perched atop a graffiti-covered mailbox, shouting, "Hoa shit, hoa *shit*!" The kid's delicate hands flew to cover his mouth, as though stifling laughter, his eyes wide in horror and delight.

Ben pounded away at Dupriest's arms with his baton, but he wouldn't turn Patty loose. Blood ran down her face and neck. Marquez swung his baton hard, cracking Dupriest on the back of his head, but Dupriest didn't seem to notice. Patty's screams stretched into a maniacal aria, her mouth pulled into a lopsided diagonal as the left side of her face was torn completely open, everything from her eye to her jawline just gone.

Marquez swung a second time, connecting with Dupriest's skull. Still nothing. Patty's left eye was wide with shock, but her left eyelid, now disconnected and sagging from her facial muscles, looked almost sleepy, hound-doggish. Ben could see the working of her jaw. Her fillings gleamed in the sunlight, her tongue like a sea cucumber probing blindly over exposed bone.

Marquez swung a third and fourth time, splitting Dupriest's skull open in a misty red cloud. Dupriest's eyes rolled back and Patty's torn cheek fell out of his slack mouth like a raw steak. Dupriest toppled forward, his face hitting the pavement. His big legs twitched as his bladder and bowels let go.

16

1995

Cabe Risley worked a black-and-white in Rampart Division with Arlander Carver for ten months before Carver introduced him to Darius. By then, Risley and Carver were already running most of the block action east of Alvarado right out of their black-and-white. The MacArthur Park *negocios* pumped twenty-four/seven and crack was the number-one hit on Casey's Countdown. The *mercados* couldn't keep baking soda on their shelves. Cooking crews, mostly fresh illegals hunkered over hot plates in bodega kitchenettes, couldn't get the shit off their cookie sheets and out on the street fast enough. If crack wasn't your thing, there was Mexican brown, black tar, gack, chronic, whores, bootlegged videos, fireworks, stolen cigarettes, and counterfeit *licencias*. It didn't matter what you were selling, as long as Risley and Carver had their taste. And if any assholes got squirrelly, or refused to break a little something off for the Boyz in Blue, they wound up in prison, deported, or dead.

Like this rustler out from the Texas Syndicate who got too big for his britches: greedy little dude stomped the fuck out of his product and wound up killing a dozen junkies before word got out the shit was poison. Carver and Risley paid the dude a predawn visit just to kind of remind the little shitass that the Five-Oh giveth and the Five-Oh taketh away. Risley tossed him off the freeway overpass at Vermont and he landed in the path of an eighteen-wheeler. By the time CHP got to the scene, mongrel dogs had dragged pieces of the dude into the ice plant on the shoulder of the Hollywood Freeway. "Okay," Carver said. "I think you're ready to meet D."

When Carver swung by Risley's pad in his Benz, base thumping but not bumping because it wasn't going to be that kind of day, Risley had on his freshly pressed purple Canali suit over a black collarless silk shirt and crepe-soled shoes with no socks. "I said dress to impress, nigga." Carver sighed, shaking his head at Risley. "You look like the motherfuckin' Joker." Carver wore a muted Brooks Brothers suit and he looked a little like Sidney Poitier in *Guess Who's Coming to Dinner*, but suit or no suit, Risley figured only a dead white man would ever let Carver near his little girl.

"Just drive," Risley grunted.

A big-ass Boot Hill OG named Daddy Python stopped them at the mansion's front gate. He gripped a clipboard in his meaty hands and had his signature chrome-plated .357 Colt Python jammed into his waistband. "MTV Cribs be shootin' the rumpus room segment today," Daddy Python told them, baring a mouthful of polished gold. "So y'all can hit the service entrance with the rest of the fuckin' house niggers."

Beyond the eucalyptus grove at the east side of the mansion, the service entrance was barred by a sliding chain-link gate topped with razor wire. A red plastic sign on the gate warned of high voltage in five languages. As the Benz drew closer to the gate, Risley saw the web of electrified coils winding through the chain link.

The gate slid open and four Boot Hill Crips dashed across the gravel drive to surround the Benz, AKs angled straight into the car, but *surround* was the wrong word because it implied cross-fire problems. These guys just flowed right into a two-by-two cover formation, creating a field of fire that would chop through the Benz in seconds. Scandalous motherfuckers have been practicing, Risley thought, and he reached for the trapdoor where Carver had a Glock hidden behind the dash, but Carver grabbed his hand. Barely moving his lips, Carver whispered to chill the fuck out.

Two of the BHMCs ordered them out of the Benz, kicked their legs apart, and patted them down hard. Rougher than they needed to be, Risley figured, their filthy dick-skinners all over his Canali because they knew he was Five-Oh. The third guy searched the Benz and checked the car's underside with a convex mirror mounted on castors, but he somehow missed the dash trap. The last guy hung back and held down on them with his AK until the search was done. Then he mumbled something into a walkie-talkie and waved them through the gate on foot.

Carver led Risley past the famous infinity pool where Naomi Campbell and Tyra Banks had once posed with Darius for the cover of *Vibe*. The pool had been drained, and a cleaning crew now stood on the bottom. Men in white coveralls hosed ropey spatters of blood off the sides of the pool and mopped the blood and fur from the colored tiles that formed the Lethal Injection logo. "He drains it for dogfights," Carver told him.

Carver flipped a toggle under a long planter box, trying to act casual, but looking pleased as a pig in warm shit when the hidden elevator doors slid open. Pissing on his territory, Risley thought, Carver wanting to show Risley how close he was to the throne. No one knew how many LAPD coppers moonlighted as "security consultants" for Lethal Injection Records, a dozen that Risley knew about, and locker-room gossip held that twice that number did special favors for Darius—a veiled society of fixers with one foot in a black-and-white and the other on the red carpet. Darius called them his secret police.

"We'll take the back way," Carver said. "Darius keeps his jaguar at the top of the stairs." Risley and Carver stepped into the elevator, Risley doubting the practicality of the thing even as he marveled at the blue damask walls and padded benches. A motor hummed somewhere in the bowels of the mansion. Risley touched the demo CD in his pocket, wondering how he would work his demo into the conversation without sounding desperate. Then the elevator doors hissed open and Risley was suddenly standing in the man's master bedroom. No wait, he thought. Just give me a hot second to pull my shit tight. I'm not ready.

In the years to come, Risley would play this encounter over and over again in his mind, torturing himself, punishing himself with every shameful detail. Risley would say his own lines aloud, sometimes giving himself a faggoty lisp. Later, Risley even tried crafting new lines for himself, imagining different outcomes. But in the end, the thought of what might have been was just another way of punishing himself.

The room smelled like pussy. An empty bottle of Krug upside down in a Tiffany ice bucket. A box of Count Chocula dumped on the floor, brown cereal already ground into the carpet, the count leering madly at the ceiling, like he'd seen a few things.

Jax, Darius's hoary old half-breed bodyguard, stepped in front of Risley, his face all keloid scars and sharp angles. He wore an old-school Adidas tracksuit with Jheri-curl stains at the shoulders and the piped satin sleeves pushed up to the elbows. Jax crossed his arms in front of his chest, going all Sitting Bull on Risley, showing off the Boot Hill tats that covered his oaken forearms. West Side mommas still scared their bad-ass kids with stories about Jax.

Darius James Washington, president and CEO of Lethal Injection Records, Inc., lounged on his unmade California king, watching *Thunder-Cats* on the biggest projection television Risley had ever seen. It was like a movie screen that took up an entire wall of the room. Risley shielded his eyes, blinded by the projector as he crossed the room. Two thousand square feet if it was an inch, wall-to-wall blue shag carpet. Framed posters of *Cotton Comes to Harlem* and *Black Belt Jones*. Platinum records. The far wall adorned with Masai shields, masks, beaded collars, lion-kill spears, and an authentic Simi sword, which Risley instantly coveted as a king's weapon.

Darius was eating Count Chocula from a huge stainless-steel bowl, his eyes flying half-mast with bored satiety. The monogrammed silk bathrobe tied loosely at his narrow waist, open to his navel, and riding up over his dark thighs.

"Arlander here tells me you're down for the cause," Darius said, shoveling in another spoonful of Count Chocula. When he spoke, Jax moved aside, but Darius did not take his eyes from the television. He gripped the spoon in his fist, still eating like a kid.

"Boy's mad-niggerish," Carver assured Darius.

"Shit," Risley said, smiling. "You know I'm hood."

"I heard that." Carver chuckled, playfully punching Risley in the shoulder, something he'd never done before. Carver's gushy tone put Risley off balance—so much fear behind it, Carver's eyes darting from Darius to Jax through all this shuck and jive.

"Ain't nothin' else a nigga can be," Risley said, wincing inwardly at his own false tone. He was trying too hard, coming across like a straight punk.

"Uh-huh." Darius nodded slowly, as though considering the wisdom of this. Darius lifted the bowl to his lips, gulped the chocolate milk, and nested the empty bowl in the rumpled sheets next to him. Eyes still fixed on *ThunderCats,* Darius distractedly dragged the sleeve of his robe across his chin, wiping away the rivulets of brownish milk.

Then Darius turned to Risley, all the foggy, postcoital languor now gone. Risley wondered if he'd maybe said too much, if Darius would smell church on him, marking him as some kind of Oreo wannabe, a college boy who'd learned the word *nigga* from Ice-T. Risley couldn't move, couldn't look away.

Darius held Risley's gaze as he slowly untied the sash of his bathrobe and opened the robe to reveal his half-erect dick. "Think you can get your lips around that?"

"What?" Risley felt his limbs go numb. An odd piece of arcana surfacing in his mind, like a phrase pushing up against the window of the Magic 8-Ball, something he'd once read about the death of Houdini—dude escaped locked safes dumped in the East River, but ended up dying from a sucker punch.

"You so motherfuckin' down? You so motherfuckin' hood?" Darius took his dick in his hand and stroked himself fully hard. "Show me." He wagged it at Risley, taunting him. "Get down here and kiss the ring, nigga."

"What the fuck is this?" Risley heard himself say. The room spun.

"Listen, D," Carver stammered. "This—"

Jax moved behind Carver with the quickness of a big cat, enveloping him. He tilted Carver's chin upward with the broad blade of his buck knife. Carver froze, arms held away from his sides, afraid even to swallow. "You keep your fingers out the Kool-Aid," Jax whispered in Carver's ear, scraping the knife under Carver's chin like a barber, the blade popping beads of blood from Carver's ingrown hairs. "Let your boy here do for hisself."

This was some kind of initiation ritual, Risley thought, but testing what? His commitment? His manhood? For his full-time loyalty, the LAPD offered Risley a modest salary and a walk-on part in a losing battle where everyone who mattered called him a traitor to his race. Darius was offering him money, power, the fragrant proximity of fame, and the taste of bitches he'd only seen in magazines.

Risley turned to Carver. With Jax's knife still pressing his throat, Carver kept his eyes locked on the ceiling. Knife or no knife, Carver had no interest in witnessing this.

"Come on then, nigga," Darius said, swinging his parted legs over the side of the bed so that he faced Risley head-on. "I ain't got all day."

Outside his own body now, Risley saw himself step forward and kneel in front of Darius. Get it over with, he thought distantly, feeling bile rise to the hinges of his jaw. Pretend it's something else. Risley scooted forward on his knees, slowly reached his hands up to place his palms on Darius's thighs.

"Whoa!" Darius sprung off the floor, crab-walking backward across the huge bed, scrambling away from Risley. Darius wrapped the silk robe around himself, suddenly modest. "Goddamn!" Darius's wide eyes searched the room for a witness and found Jax. "Ol' boy was really goin' *do* it. He was like—" Darius pinched his eyes shut, mimicking Risley's openmouthed grimace. "Damn, this motherfucker *dirty.* So dirty he make shit hold its nose." Darius threw his head back and brayed baritone laughter until tears ran down his angular cheeks.

Risley decided then that he had to kill this man.

17

PRESENT

Lieutenant Vintner sat at his desk in the 77th Watch Commander's Office, absently thumbing through last night's Probable Cause Disclosure forms. On the wall above his desk hung an RD map of the division with push-pins marking recent homicides, a brace of LAPD Bench Press Competition awards, and a framed photograph of Ronald Reagan wearing a 77th jacket.

Ben stood at attention in the doorway, clearing his throat.

"Sergeant Portillo from Internal Affairs has some questions for you about yesterday," Vintner told him. "He's waiting for you in the Community Room." Vintner took off his glasses, frowning up at Ben. "Be careful with that one, son."

Ben walked down the corridor, stepped into the Community Room, and took the only available seat, opposite Sergeant Portillo at the long conference table. Portillo: a darkly handsome, compact man with thick brown hair and deep-set brown eyes. He wore a well-cut blue suit and a yellow tie with a chain. He had a black smudge on his forehead, some kind of Catholic thing. Portillo seemed disgusted by these surroundings, a Roman forced out here among the Gauls.

Portillo busied himself queuing up his tape recorder, appearing not to notice Ben as he entered the room. He double-checked the cassette, placed it back in the recorder, flipped his yellow legal pad to the first clean page, and smoothed the sheet with a sweep of his palm. Then, extracting a Cross pen from his breast pocket, Portillo held his pen poised—not quite touching the pad. Only then did Portillo acknowledge Ben's presence in the room. He hit the red button on the recorder.

The white fluorescent lights buzzed over the soft hum of Portillo's tape recorder. Ben's eyes darted to the revolving reels. Catching this, Portillo reached across the table and paused the tape.

"You seem nervous, Officer," Portillo said. He had a thick accent—maybe Cuban. "If you would prefer, I can conduct this interview at a later time." An obvious trap, Ben thought. If your suspect appeared rattled, stewing would only further erode his defenses.

"I'm fine, sir," Ben said. Portillo hit Record again.

"You have the right to remain silent," Portillo began. When he finished the Miranda admonition, Portillo said, "As of this moment, the allegations against you and your partner are insubordination and excessive force. However, by the conclusion of my investigation into this matter, charges may include anything from improper tactics to unbecoming conduct." Translation: your narrow ass is now mine, white boy. And your employment with this department will continue at my whim. "How long have you been assigned to Officer Marquez?"

"I've been with him since the academy," Ben said.

Portillo nodded, jotting something on his legal pad. "During that time, have you heard any sexist remarks from Officer Marquez that would indicate he is less than respectful of female police officers?" Portillo paused, flipping pages to glance at his investigative notes. "Specifically, have you ever heard Officer Marquez refer to Sergeant Pendergast as 'Patty Cream Cheese' or 'Fatty McButterpants'?"

"Never," Ben said, inwardly appalled at his own heedless fealty to Marquez.

"Have you ever observed Officer Marquez commit any misconduct whatsoever?" Portillo asked. Another rookie trap, Ben thought. If he admitted having observed Marquez commit misconduct and hadn't already come forward about it, he was screwed. Failure to report misconduct was itself considered misconduct by the LAPD. On the other hand, if Ben answered no, he risked being caught in a lie.

"No," Ben said flatly. "I have never observed Officer Marquez commit any misconduct."

Portillo reached across the table, and shut off the tape recorder. He dropped his pen on the pad.

"Let me give you a little piece of free advice, Officer Halloran," Portillo said, his Latino accent drying up. "One cop to another, I have no argument with Officer Marquez's results, but his methods are going to land him in federal prison. You know Marquez topped the List of Forty-four, right?"—the Christopher Commission's infamous list of officers who'd received six or more complaints of excessive force. "This is the new LAPD and you don't want to throw your career away protecting a dinosaur like Miguel Marquez."

"Officer Marquez probably saved Sergeant Pendergast's life," Ben said, the heat unbidden in his voice. "I thought guys were supposed to get commendations for that sort of thing."

"You don't get it," Portillo said. "Marquez's fucking career is long over. That goddamned Mexican's just too pigheaded to turn in his badge and go home."

"Then you don't need my help putting a case on him," Ben said. "Do you?" He pushed his chair back and headed for the door.

"What if I told you your black-and-white was wired?"

Ben stopped midstride, hand hovering at the door handle, but didn't turn around. Portillo ejected the interview tape and popped another one into the recorder. *"Hey, I seen you."* It was a high-quality digital transfer, and Ben instantly recognized Lamar's voice on the tape. *"You that half-a-mouthpiece Jew bitch used to wipe Darius's ass for him."*

Ben froze with his face inches from the door like he'd been hit in the neck with a poison dart.

"These old gunfighters are creatures of habit." Portillo sighed smugly.

Ben heard the dry whisper of wool against wool and he knew Portillo was crossing his legs, settling back in his chair with his fingers laced behind his head. "They'll check the same rickety old shop out of the kit room every shift just like clockwork.

"I'm the one who pulls the memory card after end-of-watch, dubs it, logs it," Portillo said. "I'm the one who had to tell SID their recorder fucked up and gave us dead air on your first day out."

Ben swallowed. His throat clicked. "What do you want?"

"We want you to rein him in," Portillo said. "We know you can't control him. Just try to keep Marquez from stepping on his meat long enough for him to flush out the guys who killed Wizard."

"Jesus." Ben closed his eyes and leaned his forehead against the cool door. "You're *Eme*."

"I'm a shadowboxer," Portillo said. "Just like you."

Marquez headed up to the Watch Commander's Office after the kid didn't show for roll call, figuring he'd drive code 3 out to the beach to break the kid's balls if Ben had banged in sick. Then Marquez smelled horseshit in the corridor outside the Watch Commander's Office. He paused and sniffed the air where the waist-high patch of paint had been stripped from the wall, scraped away by a thousand pairs of handcuffs from arrestees leaning against the wall while the watch commander logged them in. Marquez pulled the clipboard off the hook and flipped through the pages. *Chinga.* A couple of P2 dogs working a Z car had popped Ronny for his dope warrant. Marquez knew the guys, both good kids, hard chargers who'd picked up an easy Frank at their end-of-watch looking to pad their recap and maybe milk a little overtime out of the booking process.

"I can't be in here," Ronny told him through the door. He was in the last tank on the right, waiting to be booked. He wore a moth-eaten Navy peacoat and fingerless weight gloves, his nose almost touching the little window, face ashen under the fluorescents. Marquez thought Ronny looked oddly spooked for a guy who'd spent more than half his life in lockup.

"No shit, double-o-seven," Marquez said.

"Naw, I'm serious," Ronny said. "It's not safe in here. Why you gone do a nigga like that, Marquez?"

"Hey, I didn't fucking arrest you," Marquez said. "But you were pushing a cart up Fig at end-of-watch. Jesus, Ronny. What did you think was going to happen? You might as well be wearing a Code Six Charles sign."

"Shit, I ain't talking 'bout no bullshit-ass warrant," Ronny said. "You got me out there on the clock, Hardy-Boyin' this Mexican murder like it's another day at the office. You didn't clue me I was crackin' the Seventh Motherfuckin' Seal. Shit, Serpico, you couldn't warn a nigga?"

"I told you, the dead guy worked at McDonald's," Marquez said.

"Shit, buy my little rock from this G over on Blessed," Ronny said, licking his cracked lips. "Been knowin' this dude since he in diapers so we cool and I just gettin' my gossip on, kinda slidin' the shit into conversation. Motherfucker went boo-boo on me, wavin' his burner like he didn't even know a nigga. Shit. Dude revoked my pass, bounced my old ass off the block."

Ronny beckoned him closer, and Marquez put his ear against the seam of the heavy door. "It was cops killed him," Ronny whispered. "Wasn't it?"

Marquez walked back down the corridor, carried the clipboard into the Watch Commander's Office, and pulled the door shut behind him. "Ronny's in the tank," Marquez told Vintner.

"I know," Vintner said. "He's got a warrant."

"I need to cut him a skid," Marquez said.

"IA's in the station," Vintner said. "Your buddy Portillo's putting the screws to your P1 in the Community Room. It's a bad time to bet, brother. Scared money never wins."

"I'm good for it," Marquez said.

Vintner pulled his glasses off, dropped them on the blotter in front of him, and rubbed his palm over his face. "Hurry the fuck up," he said. Marquez handed him the clipboard. "Kick him to the curb." Vintner brushed Wite-Out over Ronny's name. "Now, before Portillo's done with your partner. Go on, I'll square it with the Z unit."

After his IA interview, Marquez and the kid caught a shots-fired at the liquor store at Seventy-sixth and Main, in the heart of the Swann's Hood. The four assholes who had gathered in front of the place scattered from the black-and-white, sprinting down alleys and over fences, but they'd left their homeboy behind, curled up on the dirty sidewalk in front of the store. The kid was maybe sixteen, rolling around on the concrete with his eyes pinched tight, holding his right foot in both hands. His Nike Air had a bullet hole through the top of it and another jagged hole where the round had punched out through the rubber sole. The kid's foot was leaking all over the sidewalk, his blood shining purplish red under the blue neon LIQUOR sign. "Some crabs crept up, Kitchen, I think, put a cap in me," the kid hissed though gritted teeth, bravely fighting back tears. "Officer, I need a ambulance."

"Know what I think," Marquez said. Squatting over the kid, he reached under the kid's T-shirt to finger the scorched hole in the front of it. "I think you had a strap in your waistband, pulled it out to show your buddies." Marquez nodded up at the liquor store. "Maybe you were getting ready to hit this place, got the gun hung up in your T-shirt, and shot yourself in the foot."

The paramedics laughed and taunted the kid as they loaded him onto the gurney. One of them cut his shoe off and tossed it out onto Main Street. Then they peeled off his blood-soaked sock, chuckling as they bandaged his ruined foot. It had been a large-caliber weapon, .40 or .45, the gangster's foot misshapen by the expanding hollow point. He'd be crippled for the rest of his life, Marquez thought, which wouldn't be long now. Limping around the hood, this dipshit was going to present an irresistible target for any rival set—already dead and he didn't know it.

Marquez could count the gangsters he'd seen go that way, guys who seemed to have lived through a drive-by, and then didn't. Hood pride and infection killed most of them, like that Harvard Park Brim who survived a .30 caliber round in his gut. Too proud to go back to the doctor after they discharged him from Daniel Freeman wearing a colostomy bag, the dumb fuck just let the bag fill up until it poisoned him.

The ambulance eased away from the curb, its sirens perfunctory. Ben and Marquez stood in front of the liquor store, watching them bear the wounded kid to King/Drew in no particular hurry. "Sir, a guy from IAD interviewed me before roll call," Ben said, just blurting out the words in a kind of clumsy confession. "I guess you know that."

"Portillo," Marquez grunted. Ben waited for more, wanting to tell Marquez that he'd toed the line, that he'd been a good partner and kept his mouth shut, but he felt whorish. Silence stretched between them as passing traffic kicked the bloody sneaker husk around Main like roadkill.

"Well," Ben said. "Anyway—"

"She was pregnant." Marquez spat and squinted, his eyes still tracking the bloody sneaker across Main. "She stayed in the car that night because she didn't want anything to happen to the baby."

"Huh?" Ben wrinkled his nose. At first, he didn't know what the hell Marquez was talking about. "I don't—"

"Everybody out here fucks their female probationers, Professor," Marquez said. "I mean *everybody*. You take your Code Seven up at the rock garden, top of the parking structure, the trailers on St. Andrews, whatever. It's kind of an open secret. The brass just looks the other way because they all did it when they worked a black-and-white."

They watched a northbound cargo truck, its side panels covered in a slurry of East Coast Crip graffiti, punt the torn sneaker on to the far curb. A mongrel pit sidled along the sidewalk, pausing to lap the dirt-caked blood from the sneaker's blown sole.

"Patty didn't even tell anybody she was pregnant until after the fight,"

Marquez said. "Vintner could have fired her, could have fired us both, but he had her transferred to West L.A. to protect me."

"So, it was yours?" Ben asked, his head swimming, the words out before he could call them back.

"Mine or Portillo's." Marquez shook his head, spat again. "She got rid of it before we had a chance to find out."

The dog picked up the sneaker, shook it, and carried it up Seventy-sixth Street.

"Our shop's wired," Ben said.

"What?"

"Bugged," Ben said.

"Bullshit," Marquez said.

"Portillo told me," Ben said. "Played me a tape."

"Wait a minute." Marquez turned to face Ben. "I don't get it. Why would he tell you? That doesn't make any sense."

"Sir, I'm—"

"I mean why would Portillo tip his hand now when all he's got on me is guttermouth?" Marquez said. "What aren't you telling me?"

"I'm contaminated, sir," Ben said. "Seriously, I'm . . ." He shook his head. "I'm radioactive. If you want to trade me in for another P1—"

"Yeah, yeah." Marquez spat. "Fuck you, Professor. You're not getting off that easy."

They traded their black-and-white in after they cleared from the liquor store. Then Marquez took him to church for Ash Wednesday at St. Rafael's Parish, just west of Mount Carmel Park. Ben had never been inside a Catholic church. He was expecting something magisterial, but this church was spare and a little grubby. An Irish priest delivered a Spanish Mass. Ben and Marquez sat in the back, by far the tallest people in church. For most of the Mass, kids played peekaboo with Ben from the pews in front of him.

The parishioners filed out of the pews to receive their ashes. Ben and Marquez followed a stoic father pushing his daughter's wheelchair up the aisle. She had an oblong, asymmetrical head, limbs bound to her wheel-chair. Her lips were crusty and never closed. An oxygen tube ported into her throat. In Santa Monica, Ben thought, they'd have seen you on the ul-trasound and you'd be a genteel abortion. He wondered if maybe the girl would have wanted it that way.

Up close the priest looked jowly and forlorn. He said to Ben in En-glish, "Repent and believe in the Gospel." And then he smudged soot over Ben's forehead with his thumb. "Ah, yeah, okay," Ben said, feeling Mar-quez's eyes on him. "Amen." He made a passable sign of the cross, did an about-face. Getting into the black-and-white, Ben checked himself in the sideview mirror. The primitive black X on his forehead looked more pa-gan than Christian. He still preferred the idea of waiting on Mossiach. It must have been troubling for these people to believe He'd already blown through town and left them such a mess.

Marquez and Ben answered a burglar alarm at a nonprofit medical clinic on Fig. Crammed into a narrow storefront between a Spanish video rental place and an Afrocentric nail salon, the clinic had limped along on grants and volunteerism, still the closest thing to first-world health care for a lot of people living south of Jefferson. Most of them, desperately poor or scared of the INS, and they sought healing from neighborhood *curanderas* and bindles of black-market Tijuana antibiotics at the Slauson Swap Meet. "Probably some basehead in there, scrounging for Vicodin," Marquez spat.

The motion detector inside the place had tripped a silent alarm, but the front door was still locked and the windows weren't broken. Ben saw something moving inside, an upright shadow rippling and shifting be-hind the pebbled-glass window. He snapped his fingers at Marquez, pointing at the window. Marquez stepped back, kicked the door, and they swept through the doorway, weapons and flashlights raised.

The waiting area was furnished with mismatched plastic schoolroom chairs. Bilingual warnings about prenatal care, immunization, and dia-betes tacked up over cheap paneling, the stagnant air reeking of ammonia. Ben and Marquez stepped through the shadowy corridor into the pitiful examination room, something like a wartime infirmary. Tattered blue curtains separated the empty cots, the ammonia smell yielding to the stench of sickness. Dim stains shaded the unmade linens.

Ben heard her breathing before he actually saw her. Her slight shape gradually distinguished itself from all those right angles in the darkness. He shined his flashlight on her, but the young woman cowering against the wall at the far end of the examination room was still not immediately familiar. She wore a bloodstained T-shirt and stretch pants. Her hair was matted with blood. "Let me see your hands," Ben told her.

She used the bed to support herself, stood, and staggered along the wall. "Help me," she slurred. Then she gripped a hanging curtain, stumbling forward like a foal, popping the metal rings and pulling the curtain down with her. She collapsed in a heap on the tile floor in front of Marquez.

"Basehead?" Ben asked.

Marquez kneeled over her, brushed her delicate jaw with the tips of his fingers, gently turned her head to the right. Her left eye was swollen almost completely shut. "Yeah, but she's just had the living shit knocked out of her," he said, shining his penlight into her right eye. "Concussion."

"Where's my baby?" The woman panted. Her eyelids fluttered open, and she stared up at them. "Where's Jamaal?"

"Jesus, it's *her*," Ben said. "It's Jackie."

Marquez radioed an ambulance for Jackie and used the clinic's phone to landline Lieutenant Vintner, telling Vintner they had a Critical Missing. "All the units you can spare to start a grid search," Marquez said. "Code Two."

Vintner, in turn, would notify Detective Headquarters Division, get some dicks rolling to the scene. Then he'd called the watch commander at Air Support Division, requesting birds over the area as soon as they could get them up. Within minutes, Vintner would declare a Citywide Tactical Alert, holding over the PM Watch units from Newton, Southeast, and Southwest Divisions for the search.

After he hung up with Vintner, Marquez dug a card out of his breast pocket and called a guy he knew out in Lancaster who kept bloodhounds, but the guy said he was going to be at least an hour getting out to the scene with his blue ticks.

Two uniforms followed the ambulance to County USC to wait with Jackie while she underwent a CAT scan. Detectives were supposedly on their way out to the hospital to interview her, but Marquez didn't know how much information she had to give them. "Doctor called and told me to come in with the baby," she'd told Marquez as the paramedics wheeled her gurney out of the clinic. "Baby was fussy. Maybe colic. It was late, but he said . . ."

"How late?" Marquez asked her, holding her hand in both of his.

"Nine, I think," she said. Her voice sounded dreamy, distant, probably slipping into shock "Like nine. Maybe nine-thirty." It was a quarter after eleven now. "Doctor said he needed to examine Jamaal," she said. The paramedics opened the rear of the ambulance, folded the wheeled legs of the gurney up, and as they slid her gurney into the ambulance, a sudden awareness cut across her shock. Her eyes snapped and she gripped Marquez's hand hard, screaming into his face. "Where's Jamaal?"

Vintner arrived in the South Bureau Response Vehicle, a black-and-white Suburban equipped with multiple phones, fax, televisions, a dry-erase board, flares, cones, crime-scene tape, and cameras. He set up the command post at Florence and Figueroa and had the black-and-whites respond there for assignment. Vintner dispatched units in four-man teams to search the area on foot. "Anything bigger than a breadbox," Vintner said. "No exceptions." Officers moved methodically from house to house, checking occupied homes, unoccupied homes, filthy apartments, dumpsters, garages, toolsheds, and abandoned cars.

Mounted units arrived from Metropolitan Division, pulled their horses out of trailers, and mounted up in pairs to join the search. Air units orbited the area, using their Forward Looking Infra-Red to scan the ground for telltale body heat. News vans from Fox 11, KTLA 5, and Univision pulled up to the command post and a fat sergeant from Media Relations went in front of the cameras to brief them in English and halting Spanish.

Even some Menlos put on their coats and shoes, and came outside to help in the search, hitting up the homies on prepaid phones. Vintner used his block captains from the Neighborhood Watch Program to organize the civilian volunteers into supervised search teams.

When some asshole tried to stop officers from coming inside his house without a search warrant, a female officer named Walsh gently told the guy these were exigent circumstances, kicked his testicles up into his throat, and stepped over him to search his house. She and her team found some phony credit cards and a couple of assault rifles, but no baby.

Vintner told Marquez and Ben to tape off the clinic. As the first responders, their instructions were to wait outside and preserve the crime scene until detectives arrived, but after about five minutes, Marquez got sick of waiting for the dicks. He ducked under the yellow tape and opened the door to the clinic.

"What are you doing?" Ben asked.

"Sir," Marquez said.

"Sir, I thought Lieutenant Vintner said—"

"This is bullshit, a clusterfuck," Marquez said. "I'm not going to stand around here while some detectives pound their puds."

Ben eyed him carefully, Marquez was suddenly transparent to him. This wasn't some impotent dog-and-pony show. They were heavily mobilized here. Half the department was out beating the bushes, but Marquez saw South Central as his private game preserve and what he really wanted was for the rest of the beaters to go home so he could hunt alone.

"Sir—"

"Jackie strike you as the millionaire next door?" Marquez cut him off. "Because unless they plan to ask for a ransom, I don't figure this kid has a whole lot of time." Ben glanced around, ducked under the tape, and followed Marquez back inside the clinic.

"Work the problem, Professor," Marquez said. "Jackie walks into the clinic, suspect brains her, takes the baby, and locks the place up with her inside."

"Maybe he figures she's dead and no one's going to find her until they open the place up tomorrow," Ben said.

Marquez nodded. "Figures by then, he'll be long gone," he said. "But she regains consciousness, starts moving around in there, trips the alarm."

"An employee." Ben snatched the Rolodex off what passed for a reception desk in the waiting area. "Someone with keys and the alarm code." Ben flipped through the Rolodex, found Dr. Susanne Worley's home number. She answered on the third ring.

"Doctor Worley?"

"This is she." Patience and professional clarity. She would have been used to phone calls in the night, panicked voices rousing her to tend their sick and dying.

"This is Officer Halloran of the Los Angeles Police Department," Ben said. "I'm sorry to bother you at home, but there's been a break-in at the clinic. I need some information from you. Do any other doctors work at the clinic, any male doctors?"

"No," she said, not even asking him for ID or a callback, Ben figuring break-ins at the clinic were a common occurrence. "Just Carla, the nurse-practitioner." Worley paused. "Oh, and Aaron, of course, and myself."

"Who's Aaron?" Ben asked.

"Aaron's been helping out part-time around the clinic for a few months, cleaning, maintenance, phones, blood pressure, and temperature," she said.

"What's his last name?"

"Farber," she said, defensiveness sharpening her tone. "Aaron's a family friend. He's been trying to clean up his act and leave that life of negativity behind him." Gangster or addict, Ben thought, it can't be that easy. Ben flipped through the Rolodex to find Farber's address: 1324 West Angel Street—Archangel Crip Territory.

"What time did you close the clinic today, Doctor?"

"I left the clinic around eight," she said.

"But Aaron stayed," Ben said.

"Aaron always stays to clean and lock up, Officer." She sounded terse, not wanting Ben to get the wrong idea about her employee. "Yes, working here is a condition of Aaron's probation, but we've been lucky to have him at the clinic."

Ben hung up, tore Farber's card out of the Rolodex, and handed the card to Marquez. "I know this guy," Marquez said. "He's an Archangel Crip. They call him Wacc. This isn't his style. He's more of an armored-car guy."

"We ought to chat with him, sir." Ben said. "Now would be good."

Marquez hadn't been down Angel Way in months, and he couldn't remember the last time he'd answered a radio call on this block. He hardly recognized it anymore. The homes looked freshly painted, the yards well tended. Newer cars were parked in most of the driveways. Even at night, little brown kids rode their bikes up and down the sidewalks and his border brothers played pickup soccer in the street. Marquez knew he was supposed to be happy about this sort of transformation, but the new-and-improved Angel Way made him nostalgic for the bad old days.

Back in the day, Marquez remembered, the Archangel Crips had been as hard as they come, big ballers and broad-daylight bloodspillers, the kind of game you brought in tied spread-eagle to the hood of your black-and-white with sirens wailing—a Frank Buck parade through the hood on your way back to the station—letting the Waziri know you had their backs. Bwana much warrior, him mighty hunter! Hush, my darling. Don't fear, my darling. The lion sleeps in the county lockup tonight.

Now the Archangel Crips were on South Central's endangered-species list. Median home prices had decimated the gang in a way the cops and the Hoovers never could, pushing them out to Riverside and San Bernardino while these Mexican families moved into their homes. What the hell would he do with himself if all of South Central cleaned up this nicely? A guilty part of him hoped it would never happen in his lifetime. Marquez and his kind would Betamax in a big hurry, tossed in a pile with the rest of the city's outmoded crap.

Marquez parked the black-and-white a few houses down from Wacc's pad, the shingled duplex with a basketball hoop bolted to the garage. A couple of kids were playing an after-dinner game of horse. One of them no-look passed Marquez the ball as he was coming up the driveway and he made an easy layup.

Marquez and Ben paused at Wacc's door, just listening. All they heard was a television tuned to live coverage of the Command Post on Fig—a good sign. Marquez wrapped on the door with his Streamlight, identified himself, and heard Wacc scrambling around in there, another a good sign, but you never knew. After all, the guy was on probation for dope. He could just be stowing his shit. "Open the door, Aaron," Marquez called.

"Marquez," Wacc called back, sounding genuinely pleased. "That you, man?" Marquez backed away from the door and kicked it open. He and Ben swept into the room with their weapons at low-ready. Wacc put his hands up, backed against the far wall of his tiny living room. He looked scared alright, but Marquez figured the guy was entitled. The Popo had just kicked in his door, after all.

"Heya, Aaron," Marquez said. "Long time."

"*Hell,* yeah," Wacc said, turning his back to Marquez, hands laced behind his head, extending the man some professional courtesy. "You never come 'round no more." Wacc was a lot leaner than Marquez remembered him. He hoped this guy hadn't caught the ninja on his last trip through the system. Marquez didn't wish that shit on anyone.

"Nothing happening down here these days," Marquez said, patting him down and cuffing him, not tossing Wacc around too much because the same goes back.

"Shit, I heard that." Wacc sighed as Marquez guided him over to sit on the couch. Marquez ransacked his kitchen, throwing open cabinets and pulling out drawers. There was a box of fish sticks in the freezer and some leftover Chinese and a two-liter bottle of red soda in the fridge. Ben tossed the bedroom, but all he found was dirty laundry, an empty KFC bucket, a dog-eared *Playboy* with Faye Resnick on the cover, and a skull-shaped bong. Ben handed the magazine to Marquez.

"What'd you do with that kid, Aaron?" Marquez leaned against the wall, casually leafing through the magazine, tilting it to let the centerfold fall open. "I'm not fucking around here, man."

Wacc shook his head. "I'm already knowin'," he said defeatedly.

Ben scanned the room, thought he saw something under the couch. It couldn't be what he thought it was. Ben sensed Wacc stiffen as he squatted to pick it up and he felt a surge through his chest the moment he had it in his hand. Ben held the cut hospital bracelet up to Wacc's face, turning it so Wacc could read Jamaal's name, watching those watery eyes widen and then go hard. "You reached for my gun," Ben told him quietly. He drew his Beretta, put the business end between Wacc's eyes. "We struggled for it here in your apartment and I had no choice." He thumbed back the hammer.

"He's down in the crawl space." Wacc sighed, his body sagging with relief. "Off the hall closet, I just put him down there when I heard you outside. I swear I didn't hurt him none."

Ben holstered up and ran down the hall, swept the junk off the floor of the closet, and threw open the square hatch. He almost cried out when he saw the baby motionless in his white plastic bassinet. Ben grabbed the handle and lifted him out of the crawl space. Biting his bottom lip, he supported Jamaal's head, unsnapped his blue jumper, and carefully ran his fingers over Jamaal's puttylike limbs. The baby blinked his eyes and yawned, shaking his little arms in the air. He didn't seem to have a mark on him. Ben put him back in his bassinet and carried him out into the living room. "He looks okay," Ben said.

"I told you I didn't hurt him," Wacc said.

"There could have been rats down there," Ben whispered, gently rocking Jamaal. "I don't understand. What did you want with him anyway?"

"That bitch come into the clinic talkin' 'bout how she need some money," Wacc said. "I told her to get the fuck on. She got the kid there in his little . . ." Wacc nodded to the secondhand bassinet. "I told that bitch she best get off that glass dick. Can't have a baby out on Fig in the middle of the cold-ass night." Wacc shook his head slowly, tight jawed with disgust. "Nappy-ass crackhead bitch tried to sell me her baby, Marquez," Wacc whispered through his teeth. "Tried to sell me her own son. And the baby, he cryin' and shakin' and you see how kinda fucked up he is? And I just got . . ." He swallowed hard. "I don't know. I just went off. Bow! Bow! I hit her, took the kid, and smashed out. That's the truth on Archangel Crip, Marquez. That's on hood, cuz, on everything I love."

"Oh, for Christ's sake." Marquez sighed. The all-around senselessness of Wacc's story rang true. This guy was just another hand-to-mouth hustler, probably thought he'd gotten too goddamned smart for the pen. But seeing that baby tonight, a kid double-fucked at birth with a zombified mom ready to toss him away for a five-dollar rock, Wacc had abandoned his street sense and acted on impulse. The guy thought he'd been doing the right thing, taking Jamaal in like some mongrel pup.

"This wasn't a kidnapping, sir," Ben said.

"It was an adoption," Marquez said. He parted the vertical blinds with two fingers to check the street. "Okay, here's the breaking news, Professor. We're not even here. An unknown female black flagged us down, directing us to a noisy dumpster on . . . *mmm* . . . let's make it over on Vermont. Lo and behold, there's Jamaal in the dumpster, but our citizen's in the wind. Samaritan or *sospechoso*, who gives a fuck? We got the kid, right?"

"A plus B equals C, sir." Ben smiled.

"You cool with us leaving you out of this one, Aaron?"

Aaron nodded. He was crying openly now. "Can I maybe just hold him a minute, right quick before you go?"

After end of watch, Marquez met Chuin at one of his uncle's strip-mall massage parlors on Olympic, well south of the Thirty-eighth Parallel, deep in the neon jungles of Korea Town. Chuin's uncle met Marquez in the lobby. The old guy wore a bullfrog frown and a bristly gray flattop you could have served tea on. He was tight-lipped, even for a Korean. In fact, Marquez couldn't remember ever hearing the guy speak.

Chuin was alone in the steam room, sitting on the green tile bench with a towel around his waist, mist rising from his narrow shoulders. Marquez had seen the tattoo before, but he was always stunned by its intensity, its power. The dragon covered Chuin's entire back, wet scales gleaming, eyes bright red.

Chuin's family was K-Town royalty with heavy connections on both sides of the Pacific. As a kid, Chuin had done some light extortion and lit a few small-scale insurance fires for the Fuk Ching, but he'd fallen in love with a virtuous woman at Cal State Northridge and walked away from the family business after graduation. He was still an honorary member, an old skeleton the department overlooked because Chuin could still float through K-Town like a ghost when he wanted to, and even RHD was deaf and blind anywhere west of Berendo without him. You'd still hear rumors about him once in a while, but Marquez knew better. The man bled LAPD blue and still sang his wife to sleep at night.

"Ronny says it was cops," Marquez said.

Chuin bowed his head in defeat or deep thought. The long black hairs of his neat comb-over tumbled off his head and hung from his temple, making him look strangely monkish.

"How do you want to play this?" Marquez asked.

"I want to blow the dirty *shib seki* out of his socks." Chuin ladled water over the rocks, and a fresh cloud of steam mushroomed to the ceiling. "But hey, man, that's just me."

"Be nice to know how far up it goes before we move," Marquez said.

"Be nice," Chuin said. "Can you trust this kid?"

"He feels solid," Marquez said.

"I'll ask around," Chuin said. "No offense, but you've been wrong before, man."

18

1995

Gretchen played old Hank Williams tunes in the kitchen while she fixed Benji a late breakfast—their Sunday thing, a column of ash sagging from her Carlton 100 as she slid the spatula under another leaden flapjack. She always fried them in bacon grease in her great-grandmother's seasoned cast-iron skillet. The skillet, she'd told him, was one of the few possessions she'd brought with her on the Greyhound from Pecos to Hollywood and she'd used it to conk a masher in Barstow.

Gretchen was up for the part of Phyllis Dietrichson in an R-rated, straight-to-video remake of *Double Indemnity*. Her agent said the director was a huge Roger Corman fan, loved Gretchen in *Cave Girls*. Since her primary contribution to *Cave Girls* had been to jiggle in a rawhide bikini, Benji figured this was the director's way of saying he wanted to sleep with her, but he didn't share this opinion with Gretchen. She was supposed to read with Eric Roberts the next day, and she had Benji running lines with her for most of the morning. Gretchen could hardly contain herself. She had very pale skin and when she was excited, her neck flushed pink.

"Don't let's start losing our heads, that's all," Benji told her, around a mouthful of flapjack.

"It's not our heads," she said, plopping another one on to his plate. "It's our nerve we're losing."

"We're gonna do it right." Benji smiled. "That's all I said."

"It's the waiting that's getting me," she said, letting her body come toward Benji a little, making it look as though some irresistible force was pulling her.

"It's getting me just as bad, baby," Benji said, pouring the syrup. "We've got to wait."

"Maybe we have, Walter." She put the skillet in the sink and ran the faucet. "Only it's so tough without you. It's like a wall between us."

"Let it go, baby," Benji said. "I'm thinkin' of you every minute." They both started giggling, and the phone rang. She picked it up, probably hoping it was her agent, told the caller to hang on, and then handed the phone to Benji.

"Ben, it's Darius."

"Oh, you're looking for my dad," Benji said. "He's—"

"I'm having some folks over this afternoon," Darius said. "Wondered if you might like to join us."

"Me?"

"I'm sending a car over," Darius said and hung up.

Darius sent over a blue Rolls-Royce Corniche driven by a former middle linebacker for the Los Angeles Raiders. Twice on the way over, Benji thought about jumping out of the car at a red light, but that seemed childish.

Darius lived in a 7,000-square-foot mansion overlooking the Franklin Canyon Reservoir. His front gates bore the Lethal Injection Logo. Security cameras, pivoting on tiny servos, followed the Rolls up the winding brick driveway. Woofers pounded the walls of the canyon with a tectonic bass line. The car stopped under a wide portico supported by Greek columns, which Darius had painted Crip blue. Benji followed the driver up the wide front steps. "Are you carrying any weapons?"

"God, no," Benji said.

"Hand me your glasses, watch, keys, and belt," the driver said. Benji did as he was told and walked through a metal detector into the great room, the driver handing the items back to him without a word. Benji followed him into the dining room. He knew Darius had paid cash for this place, but he couldn't shake the impression of a barbarian horde settling into a castle after driving out its inhabitants.

Automatic pistols and revolvers rested on nearly every flat surface in the house. Five AK-47 Kalashnikovs, two of them disassembled, arrayed on the glass banquet table. A SPAS-12 automatic shotgun leaned in one corner of the dining room, and a Browning sniper's rifle with an exquisite scope and bipod stood on a windowsill. Benji counted four Uzis, three MAC-10s, three TEC-9s, and a Steyr AUG nestled among the overstuffed cushions of a blue leather couch.

The house was full of Lethal Injection talent and hangers-on. Former football players, promontory men thickening to bovine proportions, drank with Crips sheathed in crude tattoos and penitentiary muscle. Benji was invisible to these men, as inconsequential as the regimental beastie. But scattered among them, he saw another group of rawboned, strutting poseurs who seemed agitated by his presence, cagily stalking the periphery of the party like coyotes prowling just outside the spill of headlights. He'd seen their watchful arrogance before in court while clerking for his dad. They might as well have been in uniform.

Beyond the dining room, the house opened into a high, latticed atrium. Gauzy tapestries draped from crossbeams down to the sunken floor. Veil-like partitions rippled and swayed in the canyon breeze. Embers of patchouli and sage smoldered in wide, iron braziers on low tripods. Through the rising smoke and gossamer-thin tapestries, Benji took in the tangle of bodies among the heaped cushions.

He saw dead-eyed white and Asian women in heavy makeup and permanent eyeliner, writhing expertly, their skin strained around immense breast implants. Yesterday's porn stars, Benji thought, rented from Strange. Watching them, Benji remembered what Gretchen had told him about Strange, how he recruited them as young as eighteen for girl-on-girl movies, just a lark to get ahead on rent. Then he'd ease them into straight porn, a chance to put some real money away. The next movie would have to be anal. Of course, Strange provided them with pharmacological remedies for their shame, their salaries diminishing as their beauty faded until one morning they'd wake up, twenty-five going on forty. Then Strange would put them out to pasture, turning them out for gangster parties and Christ knew what else.

"There's an anthropologist from UCLA in there someplace, says she's writing a book on gang culture." The driver chuckled. "She has a big ass." Benji didn't see the anthropologist, but he saw several black girls barely old enough to drive. Groupies, the driver called them ghetto bitches, ditching school to come here. A girl who looked like she belonged in a plaid uniform performed oral sex on a man with BLOOD KILLER tattooed on his chest while another man penetrated her from behind. The two men high-fived each other. As a teenager, Benji had imagined orgies were about the shared exuberance of fucking, the illicit fun of strange flesh, but this was closer to rape—a transgressive ritual of subjugation, some kind of pagan affirmation of brotherhood. Homeboys over bitches. Pimps up, ho's down.

"Welcome to hell." Darius appeared next to him, tying the sash around his blue silk robe, acting the ghetto Caligula, but Benji thought it was just that. Acting. Benji thought Darius actually looked embarrassed. "Want to take a dip?" Darius nodded to the scrum. "Good for what ails."

Benji hesitated, revulsion winning out over lust. "I don't think so."

"Suit yourself." Darius shrugged, leading Benji out past his infinity pool with the Lethal Injection logo on the bottom. Darius stepped cautiously around the water because, as he would later confess to Benji, he had never learned to swim.

Beyond the pool, Jax leaned against the trunk of a banyan tree, dragging his bone-handled Bowie knife across a whetting stone. He did not look up as they passed. At the edge of the garden stood a rabbit hutch stuffed so full of jostling bunnies that their fur pressed against the chicken wire. Darius unlatched the door and selected a lop-eared white rabbit with pink eyes. He gripped it like a kitten, by the extra skin behind its neck, to carry it into the house. Benji followed him up the curving marble staircase to the second floor. The rabbit bounced along agreeably, clown feet pedaling empty air.

Benji froze on the landing at the top of the stairs. A jaguar lounged on an ottoman, leashed to a D-ring in the marble floor by a liberal length of heavy-gauge chain. The jaguar regarded Benji with imperious contempt, as if it was worship the big cat demanded instead of food. Benji watched the languorous rise and fall of the jaguar's breathing and the tail snaking slowly through the air. One foreleg dangled from the ottoman and claws leisurely scraped the floor.

Darius held the rabbit behind his back, but the cat must have scented it, because its face wrinkled back over curved teeth and its whiskers fanned upward like the tail of a peacock. Darius beckoned Benji around the edge of the landing, tiptoeing past a cross of blue duct tape on the floor. Benji assumed that X marked the limit of the Jaguar's chain. The marble around the tape was stained and spattered. Benji pressed his back against the wall. "Don't move," Darius whispered, placing the rabbit down on the X. "Watch this."

The jaguar's yellow eyes fixed on the rabbit, all the lassitude coalescing into a deadly assemblage of muscle. The rabbit looked too scared to run, its heart beating through its fur. "Ulaga," Darius said.

The cat moved too swiftly for Benji's eyes to track, but he was conscious of the rabbit enveloped as if by dense smoke. Then the cat was back on the ottoman, licking the back of its splayed paw. A few tufts of white fur and surprisingly little blood remained. "*Ulaga* means 'kill' in Swahili." Darius smiled, leading Benji into his master bedroom.

"You have to bring him a bunny every time you come upstairs?" Benji asked.

"I don't *have* to," Darius said, sounding a little defensive. "I can go up the back way if I want." Darius had purchased the jaguar to be his ultimate sentry, but like a powerful djinn, something in the cat had defied ownership. Engorged on blood, the creature had grown haughty and insistent, even lordly. Now the jaguar exacted these tributes from Darius as a kind of toll, and Darius entered his own bedroom only at the creature's pleasure. Still, Darius wouldn't get rid of the thing because to do so would mean admitting the jaguar was beyond his control.

Darius had a king-sized water bed with an African-print comforter, a big-screen projection television, a collection of antique Masai weapons, and the kind of sound system the army uses to shake dictators out of their homes. Inside his walk-in closet, Darius slid some of his clothes aside to reveal a four-by-four safe with a cooler resting on top of it. Darius opened the cooler and plucked out a raw Ball Park frank, jammed the hot dog in his mouth like a cigar, and squatted to work the combination. Benji averted his eyes until he heard the heavy door. A strange, loamy odor escaped the safe.

"Jesus," Benji breathed, taking in the bearer bonds, bundled cash, record contracts, and tightly sealed bags of what he assumed was coke, but what shocked him was the dinosaur in the safe, sitting in a shallow pan of water.

"Picked him up in New Orleans a few years back," Darius said. The creature inside craned its coarse neck, lifting a pointed snout to open its huge mouth. It had a ridged carapace about two feet long, the curved beak of a triceratops. "Alligator snapping turtle, goes about two hundred pounds, take your hand off neat as you please." Darius carefully dropped the hot dog into the creature's yawning black mouth. "I know what you're thinking, overkill, right? But Ben, too many niggas down there want what I got." Darius waved his hand toward the landing, Benji not sure if the vague gesture was meant to include his own houseguests. "A lot of home-invasion crews cut the power to a house when they hit, but these here, Ben? These protect me with or without electricity."

While the turtle stretched its neck to swallow the hot dog, Darius reached over its head and lifted a small package of folded butcher paper from a shelf in the back of the safe. He unwrapped the butcher paper, then a layer of bubble wrap, and gingerly handed Benji the clear plastic case. It was Boba Fett, the Kenner Star Wars figure. Benji remembered saving five proofs of purchase to send away for him, playing with Boba Fett for years until his paint wore away, but there was something different about this one. He was raw, alive somehow.

"You're holding the only known kit-bashed Boba Fett," Darius said with undisguised reverence. "In 1979, Lucas told Kenner about this kick-ass character he was putting in *Empire,* so Kenner rushed to make the figure. This was their first prototype. See how they cobbled him together? Stormtrooper's arms. C-3PO's chest. This bad boy didn't come off an assembly line. Sculptors actually put this one together by *hand.*"

"Beautiful," Benji said.

Darius beamed. "I didn't get a chance to play Star Wars too much as a kid," Darius said. "Had a lot of other things on my plate, you know, but I always dug Boba Fett." *A lot of other things on my plate*—Benji knew he was played here, Darius pouring salt on his tail, but he sensed something else too. The criminal had fashioned a snare of his own lost childhood, but the lost boy only conned Benji because he needed a secret sharer. Darius was both, and to Benji, that would always be his genius. He could make you fear him and want to protect him at the same time.

PRESENT

Marquez wouldn't have been surprised if the Short Stop just dried up in a few years, its hard-core regulars whittled by heart and liver disease, and all the new guys too shit scared of the career-killing debauchery that went on here to even come near the place. The fucking and fighting, guys stumbling out onto Sunset, cranking rounds into the night sky, like they were trying to shoot the ass off Jesus Christ. Rumor had it, those faggot-ass scandal chasers from the Justice Department had enough wire running through the bar to stretch to Catalina and back. And who the hell wants to swap war stories with some fed's mike up his ass?

For now, Payday Wednesday was still a Holy Day of Obligation for any copper with some time on the job and a story to tell. Five years was the minimum for admission. Try strolling in here with less than a nickel on the job and a couple of silverbacks from Metro would toss you out on your candy ass. And if you're CHP, don't even think about coming in here. Ponch himself couldn't duck into the Short Stop to use the head. They'd put the boots to him. It was that kind of place.

Marquez took a chance walking the kid into the Short Stop that night, figuring he had enough juice to put the kid on waivers for tonight. Grim, defeated faces took in the kid's vestigial buzz cut the moment they crossed the threshold, smelling rookie a mile off. Glassy eyes narrowed. Mouths curled, grumbling curses.

The pope here was a red-faced robbery detective named Karris. Karris was deep in his sixties, the ruddy bloom on his nose like a death clock. The sleeves of his shirt cuffed to the elbows and his tie jammed into his back pocket. Blotchy forearms rested on the bar, corralling his drink. The bar stool beneath him looked like part of his body, and they'd probably bronze it when the guy died. Karris peered at the kid through watery eyes. "You're in the wrong place, son," Karris said, drawing the words out to make sure the kid got the message, probably figuring this rookie deserved fair warning that he was about to lose some teeth. The barmaid gently touched Karris's arm, but he shrugged her off and nodded toward the juke.

Michaels, the big black motor cop pretending to scroll through selections on the juke, looked up, and ambled over to the kid. Marquez remembered Michaels as a scrapper from his days playing for the Centurions. Michaels still had triceps the size of Nerf footballs and his old 77th T-shirt fit him like a second skin. Stretched over his chest, the printing on the T-shirt read: VIOLENT MEN FOR A VIOLENT SOCIETY. "You heard the man," Michaels said, coming straight at the kid. "No rookies."

Marquez stepped between them, nose to nose with Michaels, and heard the sound of a dozen chairs scraping against the scuffed floor as guys all over the bar slid back from their tables and stood. If the regulars smelled fear now, he and the kid were going to end up punching their way out of there. "He's all right." Marquez spoke almost softly, but it was like those old E. F. Hutton commercials and they fucking well heard him. "One of us." Michaels's face softened almost imperceptibly and he turned back to the juke. One by one, the men who had stood sat back down. Marquez sighed, elbowing the kid. "Let me buy you a drink."

An old bullet hole pocked the front door. Out-of-season Christmas lights rimmed the ceiling. Glass cases along the walls displayed badges, shoulder patches, and police caps from all over the world, framed pictures of retired LAPD officers, small shrines to officers killed in the line. The walls plastered with peeling bumper stickers: DIAL 911—MAKE A COP COME and

WE SUPPORT CHIEF GATES. The dartboard had an aerated picture of Chief Burns with black-marker fangs taped over the bull's-eye.

Ben and Marquez stowed their off-duty pieces in one of the gun lockers below a stained-glass sign. Marquez twisted the lock, pocketed the numbered key, and led Ben to an empty slot at the bar.

The barmaid was in her fifties and had probably been a crumbling beauty at seventeen. Sun-brittle hair and Naugahyde skin. A tight Dodgers jersey over ponderous breasts, calling each man by his first name. "Viva Villa," Marquez told her, holding up two fingers. She raised her penciled eyebrows, shook her head, pulling a plain bottle from the bottom shelf. The bottle was three-quarters full of colorless liquid, a brown and curling piece of masking tape for a label. VIVA VILLA printed on the tape in wide black marker. She set up two shots and the stuff fumed like nail-polish remover. "Bathtub tequila," Marquez said.

"Any risk of blindness?" Ben asked.

"I take full responsibility," Marquez said, sliding a glass to Ben. "*Salud.*" They tossed them back in unison. Ben grimaced. His eyes watered. Tequila scorched its way down and picked a fight with his lunch. Ben gripped the edge of the bar. *I will not vomit in front of these men. I will not vomit.* Marquez closed his eyes for a second, grinned, and slammed his shot glass back on the bar. Ben set his glass down next to Marquez's, and it wobbled on the bar like a top. "*Otra vez,*" Marquez said, motioning to both glasses.

"You sure, Miguel?" the barmaid asked. "Boy Wonder here looks a little green around the gills."

"He's just thirsty is all," Marquez said, clapping Ben on the back. Ben coughed. The barmaid eyed him sadly, shrugged, and set them up again. This one went down a little easier.

Around eleven, the women streamed in like someone had blown a factory whistle. Big-haired badge fuckers and cop groupies hoping to get handcuffed tonight, a pack of hungry-eyed East Los Latinas in small black skirts searching for a pension-and-benefits man to knock them up, and an anxious clutch of USC girls dressed to the nines and looking like they might bolt for the door at any minute. "Look at 'em." Marquez leaned into Ben. "Like a bunch of rubes just walked into a cathouse for the first time."

Ben watched her, apart from the pack with back to the bar, hands jammed in her back pockets, shifting her weight from one hip to the other in time to Warren Zevon's "Indifference of Heaven." She looked small, almost childishly so, blond hair dyed blue at the ends like a gas flame. She shot him wide-set, sleepy blue eyes, mouth impertinent, ready to pop her gum in his face. Freckles smattered like nutmeg over a tiny upturned nose. Marilyn Monroe meets Peppermint Patty in a tight camouflage T-shirt and black leather pants with cigarette burns on them. "You don't look like a cop," she told him, lifting her White Russian to full lips, Ben going weak-kneed at her milk mustache. The listless display of colored lights in the juke flashed from orange to red.

"Haven't been one very long," Ben said. Was he slurring? They talked about the things you talk about in a bar while the Short Stop unraveled around them, the party gaining a kind of centripetal force. The juke played Hank Williams's "I'll Never Get out of This World Alive," and he thought of those Sunday mornings with Gretchen.

Grant, the K-9 officer from Ben's first day out, had challenged one of the SWAT guys to a game of Edward Whiskey Hands—which contestants played with a bottle of Bushmills duct taped into both fists. One rule: Nobody moves until the bottles are empty. The loser: whoever pukes or passes out first. The SWAT cop had already pissed himself, but he hung in longer than Grant, who lurched away from the table to pitch his lunch into the corner.

"Want to get some air?" She was quick, impact preceding the sound of a gunshot, gripping Ben's bicep for emphasis, brushing her hip against his fly. She'd chewed her shiny little cocktail straw down to a twisted nub.

He watched some guys from Metro tackle Grant. They stripped him naked and handcuffed Grant to the light pole in front of the bar. He was still out there, laughing his ass off, when she led Ben out to the parking lot.

"Miguel." Someone shouted to Marquez through cupped hands. He rotated on his stool, nine to three, slow to get a fix on the voice through the smoky clamor. Michaels pumped out twenty strict push-ups with one of the USC girls straddling his back. Some guys from Major Crimes pitched craps against a wall in the poolroom, kneeling around the game like hunters before a small fire.

"Miguel." Another cup-handed shout zeroed him in. I'm just like Jim Bridger, he thought, squinting happily across the bar, shoot twice and I'll find you. The barmaid was waving an old rotary phone over her head, cord draped over her shoulders, black handset dangling between her breasts. "Phone call, honey."

Marquez, warm and walleyed with a gut full of tequila, reached for the handset half expecting to hear his wife on the line, the clenched fist of a woman balling his ass out in rapid-fire Spanish. But the fugue was over before it started, reality jabbing through the booze. Carmelita had left him years ago. Tired of his drinking, tired of his anger, tired of wondering if they'd lose their house to the suit, she'd lit out for Phoenix, never touched back with so much as a postcard. Remembering her brown shoulders, the cinnamon taste of her, Marquez had a moment of boozy grief that lodged in his throat and made his eyes water. He swallowed, jammed the receiver against his left ear with his palm flat against his right, ignoring the barmaid as she twisted and dipped out of the tangled cord. "Yeah?"

"How long you been at the pisswater, Miguel?" He knew the voice, but couldn't summon the face, just needed a few more notes to name that tune.

"The fuck is this?"

"Who do you think, wetback?"

"Chuin," Marquez said, smiling. Behind him, a few guys broke away from the crap game to bet on an arm-wrestling match. "Get your coolie ass down here and let your old dad buy you a *bebida*."

Somebody's .45 went off in the men's john, the report sharp even in the din. "The hell was that?" Chuin's voice crackled. He was on his cell, probably skirting a dead spot somewhere. Two drunks stumbled out of the john in a cloud of cordite smoke, making like they hadn't heard a god-damned thing.

"Nothing," Marquez said. The shot had sobered him a little, blowing some of the dust off his shelf. "You get with Situation Mike, man?"

"That's why I'm calling," Chuin said. "Mike said he didn't know shit about our dead tax collectors."

"That's why you're calling?"

"No, listen," Chuin said. "Mike told me he knew your boot, and I did some checking. That kid isn't who he says he is, man."

"Yeah, but who is?"

"Oh, boy." Chuin sighed. "You *are* fucked-up. Pinch yourself or something, okay?"

"Okay," Marquez said. "I'm pinching."

"Your boot's real name isn't Halloran," Chuin said. "It's Kahn, as in Benjamin Kahn. You're rolling with Big Ben's son. He's in deep with the guys at Lethal Injection. He's tight with Crazy D. People think he was that third guy in the car at the Wiltern, but nobody's been able prove it."

Marquez closed his eyes. His legs turned liquid, and he locked his knees to keep from going over. He breathed through his nose, waiting for his guts to arrange themselves around it. When he opened his eyes again, his vision was clear.

"You still with me, brother?"

"I don't care," Marquez said without a trace of slur.

"What do you mean, you don't care?" Chun shouted. "Are you fucking reading me here? This is Risley all over again."

20

1996

Chuin had pleaded with Marquez, tried to bribe him with everything but his daughter's virtue, but Marquez was dead set on this loan to Rampart Narcotics. Everyone in town knew Rampart Division was bad juju, Chuin said, off the edge of the map. Here there be dragons, my main man. Street dealers were dropping out here like sorority girls in a slasher movie. Last week, another *marielito* gak dealer had bobbed up on the shimmering surface of the lake, his body blue and bloated, gold teeth gleaming where the crawfish had eaten away the guy's lips. Now even the independents, the broken-down OGs shilling bindles of stomped-on kid's stuff to finance their own habits, were scared to work their regular corners. Rumor had it there was a bona fide boogieman out there, a *cucuy* systematically wiping out his competition, and anybody moving any weight through MacArthur Park was paying obeisance the new landlord.

Of course, it didn't help matters that enough blow to put Don Henley into orbit had walked out of the Rampart narcotics locker in the last year—not a single theft, which might have been written off as an aberration or mistake, but a steady trickle of coke that had fled the property room like sand from an hourglass.

"My conclusion," Chuin said, "is that this boogieman wears an oval badge. But even if it is him, you don't want to get involved in that kind of hoodoo shit, man. You want to do dumb things? Okay, fine. Stay in Seventy-seventh and do dumb things."

When he couldn't talk Marquez out of the loan, Chuin put in his own 1.40, following Marquez to Rampart to work the buy team alongside him.

"What makes you think I need a babysitter?" Marquez asked.

"Because you are a dumb Mexican, ill suited to cloak-and-dagger stuff," Chuin said haughtily, taping the harness mike to Marquez's bare chest. "As a wily Korean, however, I was born to it. Now, hold still. Christ, you smell like pickled Pancho Villa. You been giving yourself tequila enemas or what?"

"Trying to blend." Marquez belched, buttoning his grimy work shirt over the wire. Then he slipped on his poncho. Last month, he'd come home to an empty house, the place stripped bare, and a short note on the fridge. Since then, he'd been sleeping alone in his stucco bungalow on West Edgeware Road. Nothing left in the house but an old air mattress and that creepy picture of Christ, holding out his crowned heart, with eyes that followed you wherever you walked in the room. Last night, blind drunk and bawling, he'd shot a hole straight through the Savior's crowned *corazón*.

Marquez headed through MacArthur Park, staggering along the matted grass bank of the lake, doing the *borracho* shuffle not so much because they might be watching him as to get into character. He slipped on some goose crap, falling hard into the moist grass. Ducks on the bank, sleeping with their heads tucked under greasy wings, shook themselves awake and stepped unhurriedly into the water. Marquez watched them sail across the still surface past the guano-covered paddleboats.

He made his way up Alvarado. The street vendors were just setting up, rolling out their blankets. Mestizo women arranged bootlegged videos and *norteño* CDs over dingy blankets they'd spread out on the sidewalk. Marquez passed a couple of guys unloading painted ceramic statuettes of monkeys on surfboards and clumsy renderings of the Blessed Virgin. The truth behind these crude statuettes, Marquez knew, was that they had once been a smuggling gimmick. The Arellano-Felix cartel had pressed refined coca into these molds, sending them north by the thousands. After the DEA caught on and the smugglers ditched the molds, poor migrants still filled them with cheap plaster and sold the statuettes as tourist trinkets.

Marquez slumped against the cinder-block *pupusería* at the mouth of the alley, just south of Temple Street. He sipped coffee from a styrofoam Winchell's cup, looking like another blue-collar border brother waiting to catch the bus uptown.

After a few minutes, his mark, a walk-alone 24/7 street pinto called Tanque, stepped out of the alley, sniffing the air like a feral cat. Tanque had this straight-backed Frankenstein strut because he carried a sawed-off gauge slung barrel-down along his spine. He'd sliced open the back of his shirt, then resewn it, so the shirt would tear in half Hulk Hogan–style if he needed to reach the shotgun in a hurry.

"*Que onda, huey?*" Tanque smiled jaggedly, missing a couple of big ones right up front. Tanque's remaining choppers were nearly black, corpse-gray gums puffed with infection. Goddamn, Marquez thought, this *ruco* clears five hundred a day, easy. You'd think he could find his way to a cash-and-carry *dentista* once in a while.

"*Compa'.*" Marquez nodded to Tanque, nursing his Winchell's *wariche* like he had more important things than five ounces of hubba on his mind. The chase cars would be in place by now, covering the four winds with a two-block cushion. Marquez made his play.

"I need five, *carnal*," Marquez said. "Today, *ahorita*."

Undercover Narcotics 101: make a few token buys from a street daddy to gain his trust, then ask for more volume than the guy can deliver. If he trusts you, you work your way up the totem pole, from dealer to whole-saler, from wholesaler to trafficker. If he doesn't trust you, if he smells *chota*, it's a short trip. The last plainclothes guy to work MacArthur Park wound up with his tongue pulled out through an ear-to-ear arroyo in his throat.

"*Estás seguro?*" Tanque said, scoping Marquez as though seeing him for the first time, a nice long mud check to see if Marquez flinched. Marquez waited, half expecting a *cabeza* full of double-ought buck, not sure how he felt about it.

"Firme," Marquez said, sipping his coffee.

"Get your ass to the Pioneer Chicken on Alvarado," Tanque said. "Ten minutes."

Marquez made his way up Alvarado to the Pioneer Chicken, taking his time getting there, not wanting to appear too eager. He stood in the parking lot, watching the drive-thru line of stuttering pickups packed with *jornaleros,* working men who had no truck with corner cons, their sun-blunted faces sizing Marquez up and dismissing him as a piece of Mara saddle trash. This was going nowhere. Marquez was about to call it when he heard the bumping stereo that made his hackles stand to.

A gold Benz with tinted windows and spinning rims lurched across the parking lot and stopped in front of him. Marquez couldn't make out the driver through the midnight tint and part of him wanted to bolt for some cover, but he stood his ground as the electric window came down.

The driver: male black in his late twenties, wearing a blue felt cowboy hat, blue silk shirt buttoned all the way up with a bolo tie. The guy had on mirrored shades with gold chips imbedded in the frames. Boot Hill Mafia Crip, Marquez thought. This is my guy, the wholesaler, the boogieman.

"Don't get greedy, dog," the driver said. He smiled wolfishly at Marquez and pointed a Ruger nine-millimeter out the open window. Marquez stood alone in the parking lot, a million miles from any cover.

He flipped the poncho back over his shoulder and reached for the Beretta Cougar he kept in his front pocket, but he drew too late, hesitating, like part of him wasn't sure how he wanted this to come out. He felt the bullet tear through his neck as he drew the Cougar, bringing the gun up on target as he was going down. He managed to squeeze one off before he hit the pavement. The left lens of the driver's mirrored shades exploded, blood and pinkish matter running down the side of his face. He slumped over the wheel and the Benz smashed into the drive-thru menu.

Marquez felt the blood pumping warm and soundless from his open throat. His head lolled and he saw the sluicing red flow pick up a cigarette butt and carry it away. A woman screamed. The chase cars swooped and he heard them shouting for the crowd to stand the fuck back. Now Chuin was over him, his big round face blocking the sun, both hands jamming his poncho over the spurting wound. "Aw, man, you pissed yourself," Chuin told him, his voice husky with effort. "You really want to die with a lapful of piss?"

Risley badged his way past the two Metro guys posted outside the Recovery Room in the Trauma Center at County USC. He hated hospitals, the sourness that got into your lungs, every breath metallic. Risley ducked behind the vinyl curtain. Marquez was still under anesthesia. A monitor attached to stickers on his chest. IV. Endotracheal tube. Velcro restraints bound Marquez's wrists and ankles to the bed rails to keep him from unconsciously pulling out the tube.

Risley smiled, leaning over the bed, Dracula to Mina. "*Someone left the cake out in the rain,*" he crooned softly, lips close to Marquez's ear. As he sang, Risley traced his fingers along the accordion oxygen hose—too thick to just kink. He could have unplugged the monitors, dis-attached the hose from the endotracheal tube, and simply held his hand over the opening to block the airflow—easy-peezy. But Risley figured Marquez deserved better than a straw death. Humming, Risley carefully brushed the blood-crusted hair from Marquez's face. "*And I'll never have that recipe again.*"

"Radio check." Risley put his hand in Marquez's. "You readin' me?"

A fluttery squeeze.

"Roger that." Risley pulled a chair over next to the bed, swung it around to straddle it backward, and crossed his arms on the chair back. "Now, riddle me this, Batman," he said. "How come you get to toss Constitution every shift? Fourth Amendment, what's that? *Hey, we doan need no stinkin' Miranda.* How come that's all just goddamned cricket? How come that's getting it done out here. But I take it to another level and you come at me like I'm Pol Fucking Pot."

Risley took a deep breath. He'd come dangerously close to shouting, resentment spilling out of him in a pantomime of bug-eyed neck-popping.

"Who made you Pope of the Popo, huh?" He lowered his voice to a bedroom whisper. "Just who the fuck are you to tell me where the line is?"

Another squeeze, this one firm. Heart rate climbing on the monitor.

"You know as well as I do somebody was going to have to put that produce on the street, Miguelito," Risley said. "And I worked Narcotics long enough to know what the fuck I'm talking about. Didn't matter what we did. Wiretaps. Informants. Task forces with a new badass acronym every other week. Didn't make a damn bit of difference. Somebody's always going to supply that demand.

"So I'm asking you, serious now," Risley said, "Would you rather have Eighteenth Street runnin' Rampart? MS? 'Cause I'm here to tell you those are some murderous motherfuckers, partner.

"See, with me in charge out here the goddamned trains ran on time," he said. "I kept the peace, made sure the shit wasn't poison. Sure, I had to put a few of 'em down, but these were stone assholes to a man, and I'll be damned if I'll apologize to you for doing what I had to do out here. Can't make an omelet without blah blah blah, brother. I thought you of all people would understand that."

The monitor beeped. Marquez suddenly squeezed his hand hard, grinding his knuckles together. Risley was trying to pry it loose when the respiratory therapist came in to check the ventilator settings and Risley pretended to hold Marquez's hand in both of his. "You're going to be okay, partner," he stage-whispered, not having to fake the tears because his hand was killing him now. "You hear me? You're going to make it."

The respiratory therapist split and Risley twisted his hand free. He stood up, shaking it out. "You know homicides were actually down on my watch," he said, pacing around the bed. "Way down. How many dudes on the job can straight-face claim they've impacted crime, actually saved lives? How many? Can you? I'm a better cop than you were on your best day. I brought order out of chaos. Brought Jesus to these motherfucking Indians and you're all up in my shit for it.

"Because of you there's going to be blood in the street again. I'm stepping down, lying low for a while. And you know *los lobos* gone be tearing each other to pieces over the mesa I built. Drive-bys. Dead kids. Poison dope. Savages, just the way I found 'em.

"Now, I want you to think about that in here," he said. "All that innocent blood spilt over your wounded pride. All that mess and you haven't even stopped me. Didn't even come close. All you did was inconvenience me, Miguel. And that is just sad, man."

21

PRESENT

Through an Israeli night scope, Risley watched the kid stumble out of the Short Stop with some skanky-looking bitch on his arm. Risley fooled with the dials as they climbed into the Jetta, switching the image from standard night vision to infrared. Their combined body heat made the rocking car look like a Jap lantern, glowing yellow-white as they found their rhythm, fading to orange when they'd finished. Cool effect, Risley thought, glad he'd liberated the scope from that Armenian capper out in Vegas who had no more use for it or anything else.

She and Ben climbed into the back of her Jetta, wrestled, groped, and kissed hard. She left her shirt on, but pulled her leather pants down to her shins. Ben reached between her legs and felt the silver stud through her clitoral hood. "Does it hurt?"

"You tell me," she said, moving into his lap. She gripped the backs of her thighs, pulling her knees up against her shoulders. The soles of her sneakers rubbed against Ben's ears. They sandwich-fucked until she cried out, biting the heel of his hand. Ben caught his breath, climbed out of the car, staggering to the wall for a piss. She got out, sat on the hood of the car, and lit a smoke.

———

"I'll be goddamned," Risley said, watching the kid climb out of the Jetta to piss against the building, his stream like lava flow on the infrared. "Mike was right." Risley's guts began a slow, Möbius churn. "It's him."

Risley had just assumed the kid would be dead by now—law of averages—but this wasn't like seeing a ghost. He'd always hated those Bizarro comic books featuring parallel-universe stories, the ones where Batman robs banks and the Joker fights crime. The stories offended his sense of order, made his goddamned head hurt. Seeing the kid here unsettled him in that same looking-glass way. Big Ben's boy wasn't supposed to be out here. He was supposed to be hiding out in the Yukon, on a kibbutz, at the bottom of a fucking lake. So what the hell was he doing here in the belly of the beast?

"No fucking shit," Mapes grunted sullenly, only half in the game. "Ain't that what I said?" He shoved the dripping remains of his Fatburger into his mouth, and followed it up with a long pull on his strawberry shake.

"What did you say?" Risley hissed, snapping his head from the scope's padded eyepiece to glare across the front seat at Mapes.

"Jesus, Cabe," Mapes stammered, hunching his massive shoulders against an expected blow. "Okay? Goddamn, I didn't mean—" He coughed, bits of burger tumbling out of his mouth.

"You got too many teeth in that head, nigga, that it?" Risley let his fist hover, sword of Damocles, ready to pound some act-right into this feeble-minded motherfucker. "Yeah, you gone think clearer with some of those big ones in your lap." Risley lowered his fist and raised it again just to see the big man flinch.

This was Carver's fault, Risley thought, shaking his head in disgust. Risley wouldn't have been saddled with this talking tub of hog fat if Carver hadn't gone off the reservation. They'd had a good thing going with Lethal Injection, lying low and playing the angles, waiting for their shot at Darius. But Carver had been too goddamned greedy to give up his own dime-store dope dealing, and he'd gotten himself capped by that crazy Mexican down at the Pioneer Chicken. After that, Risley had thrown a yoke over Mapes, figuring he still needed a blocker if he was going to carry this ball into the end zone. Mapes had seemed a logical choice, ox-strong and twice as dumb, but even a pack animal will cop attitude if you slack his reins. Spare the rod.

Risley had always told himself he was just biding his time working for Darius, plotting his ultimate revenge, but he was digging the whole scene too—digging the premieres, pool parties, and chartered jets to Vegas. Darius, whose unpredictable fits of ghetto largesse were almost as legendary as his homicidal tantrums, had even given Risley the keys to his seventy-five-foot sportfisher out of Long Beach. "Fuck do I care." Darius had laughed. "I got other tub toys, my nigga." Fronting him, but Risley knew Darius wouldn't go near the boat because that ghetto-ass nigga couldn't swim.

As assistant head of Lethal Injection Security, Risley had done mostly old-fashioned pipe-hittin', the kind of smashmouth ghetto work Darius would have preferred to do himself, but rarely had time for now that he was an entertainment mogul. It had been easy money, hardly work at all—like the time Risley and Carver shook down a wayward promoter, tearing the silver stud out of the guy's nose and making the guy swallow it along with a bloody piece of his own nostril. Or the time those dagos at Columbia had buddy-fucked Darius, secretly courting one of Lethal Injection's performers, and Darius had ordered Risley and Carver to break into Tommy Mottola's office suite and shit on his desk blotter. Or that time the *Enquirer* had threatened to run photos of DJ Post-Mortem and his latest thirteen-year-old paramour, Risley had hauled the photographer out of bed, breaking both his legs with a fireplace poker—compound fractures that had left the splintered bones poking through the guy's pajamas like bloody fangs.

Carver had never once mentioned the incident in Darius's bedroom, but it had been there between them whenever their conversation lagged and part of Risley hadn't been a bit sorry when Marquez shot Carver dead at the Pioneer Chicken.

The disgrace of that first meeting with Darius still hung over Risley like an old debt, binding him to Darius, his bane and benefactor, the man Risley hated and loved beyond all reason, Risley's idol and the punk motherfucker who'd punked him like a bitch. But it hadn't been shame that kept Risley answering D's pages, or fear, or even the money. The truth of it was part of him wanted to impress Darius as much as he needed to kill him. Part of him had been secretly pleased when Darius survived the Wiltern because Risley wanted to be face-to-face when Darius's clock stopped.

Even now, close as he was to making his move, it wasn't the heavy ordinance but the daring scale of Risley's plan that excited him. Risley pictured Darius kneeling bloody and broken in the blasted rubble of his mansion, smiling up at Risley, one warrior king abdicating to another, Darius finally knowing how badly he'd underestimated him.

"What do you think he's doing here?" Mapes murmured, nodding across Sunset. The big man couldn't hang with long silences.

"Let's go ask him," Risley said.

"Want my number?" She leaned her head back to blow smoke into the damp night air, like she didn't care one way or the other, just being polite. Ben scribbled his number on a gas receipt from her glove compartment. They kissed again and she bit his earlobe before she drove away.

He lingered in the parking lot, taking in the night sky, the shouts and laughter inside, the occasional rush of traffic on Sunset Boulevard. He wondered where Gretchen had wound up, if she'd found someone.

He was heading back into the bar when a white Lincoln Navigator that looked bigger than his apartment jumped the curb in front of him. A decorative black light pooled on the asphalt under the vehicle and DJ Post-Mortem pounded from the speakers, the bass shaking Ben's sternum. The Navigator's vanity plate read EETMEIA. Holy shit, Ben thought, I'm out here alone. He tried to dodge around the back of the Navigator, but they were too quick for him, slipping jackal-like from the open doors. Risley cut a dashing figure in his fedora, double-breasted lightweight Prada suit, and Bruno Magli shoes, all white to match the Navigator. No shirt under the white jacket, displaying a chest and abs that belonged on a Calvin Klein billboard over Times Square. Mapes: physically larger, yet somehow less substantial than his partner. He was clean shaven and wearing a bright blue Armani suit with a black T-shirt. Small blue-tinted, octagonal glasses low on his broad nose.

"You a long way from Santa Monica, mayonnaise," Risley said, stepping in to block Ben's path. He slid his arms akimbo, spreading his suit jacket open. Ben saw the chrome .45 jammed down the front of his pants. *Shit. Shit. Shit.* His off-duty piece was still stashed in the locker inside.

"What do you want?" Ben staggered back. Mapes circled around behind him.

"That's my line," Risley said. Broken blood vessels around his eyes like a Thomas Guide. He'd gone a few nights without sleep. Mapes giggled.

"This supposed to be funny," Risley said. "Is that it?" Mapes pinned Ben's arms behind his back. Risley slapped Ben in the face three times fast, forehand, backhand, forehand, hard enough to bloody his nose.

"Hey, get the fuck out here," Grant called into the bar. Ben had forgotten about him handcuffed to the pole out front and he didn't think that Risley had even noticed him there until Grant shouted, "Officer needs help!"

Marquez and Michaels were the first ones out the door, a dozen more charging out after them. Mapes released Ben's arms and Risley spun to face Marquez. "Gun!" Ben shouted, but Risley already had his chrome polished LAPD badge out, hanging from a gold chain around his neck.

"Code Four, Code Four," Risley said. "Everything's cool."

"The hell it is," Marquez said, stepping in front of him.

"Just having some fun with your new boot, Miguel." Risley spread his arms and smiled. "Just like old times, brother." Ben finally got his personalized license plate. EETMEIA. Eat me, IA, an open taunt directed at Internal Affairs Division.

Marquez stepped forward and fired both his palms into Risley's bare chest. Risley's head snapped and the fedora fell into the street as he stumbled back against the Navigator. Something with teeth flashed across Risley's eyes and for a moment Ben thought Risley would go for his .45, but he only smoothed his jacket. "Step off." Risley bared his even teeth at Marquez. "I'm wearing your pension, motherfucker."

Mapes moved to flank Marquez, but Michaels intercepted him, squaring off with the big man. Mapes turned to Risley, his eyes asking how Risley was going to play this.

"You're both going to be wearing your teeth in a minute," Marquez said. Most of the bar had emptied into the street now, cops fanning out around the Navigator like a herd boxing out predators. "Don't let me catch you fucking around in Seventy-seventh either," Marquez said. "Everything south of Vernon is my property, and it's still legal for me to hunt my own land."

Risley glanced around at the crowd, sighed, picked up his fedora, and made a show of brushing the grit from it. He nodded to Mapes, and the two men slid back into the Navigator. "See you around, Miguel," Risley said just loud enough for Marquez to hear. He shot Ben with his finger and thumb. The Navigator lurched over the curb, roaring down Sunset Boulevard toward Rampart. Ben could hear DJ Post-Mortem thumping for blocks.

Marquez and Ben left the Short Stop and wandered up Sunset to Stadium Way past the old academy, Marquez leading him up a narrow dirt track to a small mesa overlooking Dodger Stadium and the downtown skyline. The timber remnants of the old academy confidence course stood on the mesa like dinosaur bones silhouetted against the night sky. Beyond them, Ben could see the planes backed up from LAX to Barstow like distant planets shifting into tacit alignment.

They climbed part of the confidence course and sat on a gallows-like platform. Marquez reached for his bag of Red Man, hooked out a wad with his index finger, and socked it into the left side of his mouth. He offered Ben the bag. Ben pinched out a tiny, flaking wad of tobacco, placing it between his cheek and gum as he had watched Marquez do about a thousand times. Then Ben leaned over the side of the platform and vomited into the dirt.

Marquez looked like this was more or less what he had expected. He spat a measured squirt of tobacco juice into the weeds and gazed out over Dodger Stadium, lit up like an empty space station. "This used to be my folks' barrio," he said. "When my dad was a kid, the LAPD came into Chavez Ravine one morning to *relocate* his family so the O'Malleys could build their stadium. He ended up in a shanty at the river for a year.

"When I told the old man I was coming on with the department, he about shit," Marquez said. "Cursed me and spat on my shoes."

"He ever come around?"

"Nope." Marquez shook his head, shrugged, and spat.

"It was a different department when I came on," Marquez said. "This used to be a good job, a man's job, until it all went to hell and the city started handing out these fucking settlements like government cheese. Free money, come and get it. All the city attorney had to hear was 'LAPD' and that was good for at least a hundred grand."

Only a hundred grand, Ben thought. Those Kmart settlements weren't his dad's clients. Big Ben didn't even come to the table for under a quarter of a million.

"One night, my partner and I got in this vehicle pursuit," Marquez said. "Two P-stones, both one-eight-seven suspects, in a stolen CRX. One of these assholes, Coke Dog? He hangs out the sunroof of the CRX and starts capping rounds at us with a MAC-10. My partner took one in the vest and our windshield shattered, but I could still see well enough to drive. CRX cut left and Coke Dog couldn't hang on. He fell out of the sunroof. Now, we were right behind the CRX, I mean *right* behind it, making about seventy when Coke Dog flopped on to Fig and I wasn't about to swerve into a light pole to keep from hitting this piece of shit. So, I ran his ass over, made Coke Dog a paraplegic.

"Another unit caught the CRX," Marquez said. "Everyone knew Coke Dog and his buddy were good for the homicide, but Coke Dog had dropped his MAC-10 somewhere on Fig when he fell out of the car and we never recovered the gun."

Ben was silent. He remembered the suit from his days clerking for his father. The suit named Marquez, Risley, and the much-maligned Los Angeles Police Department, Big Ben ranking it among his well-tended money trees. *This one's a payer, Benji, a fuckin' money tree. All it needs is a little water. They don't have a gun and we've got a crippled* schvartze *who won't look half bad in front of a jury if I can get him to take the cornrows out of his hair and go easy on the fuck words.*

And Ben remembered Coke Dog trying to look tough in his sideways cap and bloodred jersey while his play-cousin wheeled him into Big Ben's office, but whatever kind of hard-core street-terror Coke Dog had been before his injury, it was impossible to look tough with his piss draining into a bag on his leg. The unsettling way Coke Dog slumped in his wheelchair calling to mind a bear freshly caught in the jaws of a trap. The chair had him from the waist down, but Coke Dog hadn't yet learned not to struggle against it. Ben remembered Coke Dog's sullen acceptance of Big Ben's pitch, the childish way he held the Mont Blanc when he signed the retainer agreement after pretending to read it.

"It was a deadly-force situation and the department found my actions justified, but Coke Dog sued the city and Big Ben made him a fucking millionaire," Marquez said. "Now Coke Dog owns that Jolly Burger on Inglewood and the P-Stones run dope out of it all day long.

"I'm here to tell you I was plenty pissed, but Risley . . ." Marquez shook his head sadly. "Risley went bonkers. Guy'd played by the rules his whole life and he couldn't afford a decent house in Boyle Heights, but now that shitass son of a bitch who'd shot him had a mansion in West Hills and the pinko congresswoman from his district called it a civil rights victory for African-Americans everywhere.

"Risley'd come up west of Crenshaw. Good family. They went to church with the chief and I guess somehow managed to steer clear of the worst of the gang shit. He knew all those guys, yeah, but Risley? He's basically a middle-class kid and I don't think they ever accepted him. He ran track at USC. I think he tried acting for a while, wanted to be a rap star. I guess the chief helped Risley get on the job after some other things broke bad for him.

"He was the best I ever trained," Marquez said. "Cunning, Jesus. If he couldn't come at them straight on he'd flank them, tunnel in under them. The guy was unstoppable and he had charisma to burn, which doesn't hurt you in court.

"He got pretty hung up on all those hip-hop assholes and it worried me some." Marquez halfheartedly hammered his fist down on the platform. The planks groaned beneath them. "When Risley hit the street in Seventy-seventh, the folks down there, people he'd grown up with, called him Uncle Tom, slave, house nigger. It got to him after a while," he said. "Well, that and Big Ben's suit, like I said."

Ben leaned over the platform and vomited again. A deep understanding had thickened the air between them, like infidelity known but not yet named. Now it came to Ben where he'd seen Marquez before that first day in 77th. He'd served Marquez with a subpoena for the suit. He'd actually gone to his home before sunrise and slapped the subpoena into his thick palm when Marquez had opened his front door.

Ben wiped his sleeve across his mouth. "How long have you known?"

"Since that first week," Marquez said. "At least part of me did. I knew I'd seen you somewhere before, but I couldn't remember where or when. Chuin just called me tonight. I guess he talked to this hype snitch hangs out at Ventura and Lankershim—"

"Situation Mike." Ben sighed.

"Yeah, said he'd heard Big Ben's boy had changed his name and put on a badge, hiding in plain sight," Marquez said.

"It's all true," Ben said.

Marquez was quiet for a moment.

"When I was a rookie, I had this hard-ass TO, Rourke?" Marquez said. "He brought me up here after I'd shot some blanks at this gangster, scared the little asshole into shitting his pants," Marquez said. "What Rourke told me, what he said was you can wear a badge for thirty years, but you're not really a cop until you break the law.

"See, the right thing isn't always the pretty thing or even the legal thing. I've seen you out there, man, and I don't care who or what you were before. You're a cop now, Ben, whether you like it or not. And I think maybe that's a little like being a Catholic, you can't ever get shorn of it."

"Rourke sounds all right," Ben said.

"He was a piece of shit." Marquez spat. "Half in the wrapper most nights. We got in a pursuit one night and that son of a bitch was driving blind drunk. I thought he was going to kill us. I mean, this guy used to slap a double rubber on his prick and fuck every strawberry on Fig. On duty, I shit you not. Vice just looked the other way because he was this big department legend. They finally pensioned him off and he choked on his own puke at his retirement party, right down there in the rock garden." Marquez spat. "Couldn't have happened to a nicer guy."

They were quiet for a time. Marquez brushed his fingers over the scar under his jaw. "So, anyway, about a year after Risley transferred to Rampart, I started hearing these rumors," Marquez said. "About a *cucuy* running loose out there, a boogieman."

A ragged coyote padded out of the wild oleanders and stood with its feet splayed in the dirt track. Blood painted its slender muzzle and its eyes glowed yellow, catching the distant lights of the city. Blood dripped from the coyote's fangs, spattering the dirt like an auger foreboding. Tufts of steam puffed from its nose. The coyote sniffed the air and moved on.

"You're bleeding again," Marquez said. Ben touched his nose and his fingers came away red. He pinched his nostrils shut and leaned his head back, watching the stars swerve overhead, while Marquez told him about the Carver shooting at the Pioneer Chicken in Rampart.

"When I came out of anesthesia, Chuin told me I'd just killed an off-duty Los Angeles police officer," Marquez said. "This guy Arlander Carver. I told Chuin he was full of shit, couldn't be." Marquez hesitated, running his fingers over the scar on his neck. He'd already done so much talking, but the kid was drawing it all out of him somehow, the way a poultice draws puss from a wound.

"Goddamned shame," Marquez said solemnly. "Chuin showed me this picture in an old issue of *Vibe*, taken backstage at a DJ Post-Mortem show in Atlanta. You can see Risley, Carver, and Mapes kickin' it backstage with Post-Mortem's crew. They're all pimped out in Crip blue, you'd never in a million years know these guys were cops. Risley's throwing up Boot Hill Mafia in the photo like it's the thing to do.

"So, after my shooting, Chuin went to the sixth floor with all this stuff he'd dug up, took it all right to the chief," Marquez said. "Burns told him to leave it alone. It's above your pay grade, Detective. He had Chuin transferred off the case, bounced out of RHD. Chief insisted Carver get a department funeral with full honors. Then he had the department pay off Carver's family—seven hundred and fifty grand. Man, Chuin was so burned up about it he even went to those fags at the *Times*. The *Times* people told him they had it covered, thanks but no thanks, Detective, but be sure to call us the next time your officers beat on somebody."

"Chief had me on the desk pending my Shooting Board," Marquez said. "After the first board cleared me, he tossed the ruling, handpicked a second board of all black officers, but they cleared me too. He let me back on the street after that, but Portillo's been a wart on my ass ever since."

"Portillo's dirty," Ben said. "Tied in with the *Eme* somehow."

"Figures." Marquez laughed bitterly.

"Why would the chief cover for Risley?"

"Hell," Marquez said, "I thought you might know."

Ben shook his head.

"The chief's son got popped in Vegas," Marquez said. "This was right before I went to Rampart. Feds got him for trafficking. Kid had a trunkful of evidence coke."

"Out of Rampart?"

"I don't know," Marquez said. "Feds were supposedly working out some kind of deal when the kid got killed in a walkup. Two rounds amidships, one in the *cabeza*. LAPD failure drill, what we used to call the Mozambique."

"Risley?"

Marquez shrugged. The planes had all landed, the eastern sky fading like a bruise. The birds had started up and now they could hear early-morning traffic on the Pasadena Freeway.

"I think this is going to get worse before it gets better," Ben said.

"Always does," Marquez said.

22

1996

Tyice Craig, the bellicose gangster rapper known to fans everywhere as Certain Death, was a Blood gangster out of New Orleans whose album *Bomb-Ass Gangsta* lost out to DJ Post-Mortem's *Barbequed Pork* for Hip-Hop Album of the Year. "I don't even trip," Certain Death assured his fans. "But losing to bitch-ass crabs be worse than getting my shit pushed in."

The East Coast–West Coast feud cleaved the rap world into warring factions, and Certain Death regarded DJ Post-Mortem and Lethal Injection Records as his mortal enemies. He came at them in magazines like *The Source* and *Vibe*. A Blood from down south, Certain Death professed hatred for all West-Side Crips and he derided Lethal Injection Records as a "weak-ass label" that produced only "pussy-ass commercial rap." Finally, in his single "Flatbackin'," he called Darius's mother a "straight rock ho" and dismissed DJ Post-Mortem as a "cum-drunk faggot."

DJ Post-Mortem took up Certain Death's gauntlet during an interview with Kurt Loder on MTV. "We representin' the West Side," Post-Mortem said, throwing Boot Hill Mafia Crip signs into the camera. "We walk the walk out here, bwoy, and you better bow down or we'll bury you." When Loder casually remarked that Post-Mortem sounded like Nikita Khrushchev, Post-Mortem, who thought he was being compared to "that bony-ass swimsuit modelin' bitch," threatened to slap the taste out of Loder's mouth.

Gretchen said she worried Benji was getting in over his head with Darius and his friendship with Darius would exact a price, one he wasn't prepared to pay. By then, Benji had half convinced himself the whole East Coast versus West Coast rivalry was just playacting to sell albums. "It's just like professional wrestling," Benji said.

"The hell it is," she said. "When I was still stripping, I watched two Bloods stomp a guy to death because he tossed some hundred-dollar bills on their table. It was a gesture of disrespect and they killed him for it, right there in the Tropicana."

"I don't think you should hang out with Darius so much," she said, drifting dangerously into parental waters. "He's not a nice guy."

"Neither is my dad," Benji said.

"How true." She sighed, frowning elaborately. They had an unspoken agreement not to talk about Big Ben, and Benji could see he'd upset her by mentioning him now. "But your father never killed anyone, kid."

Benji thought about the cop, the defendant in one of Big Ben's latest lawsuits, who'd just blown a hole up through his soft palate into his brain. Big Ben had just laughed the dead man off. Benji was going to say something to Gretchen about it, but what would be the point? He knew he would just upset her. Gretchen seemed increasingly fragile these days. She'd been twenty-seven for three years now and Big Ben hadn't budged on the baby issue.

"I just don't want anything to happen to you," she said, taking Benji's hand in both of hers.

"I'll be fine," Benji told her.

Perhaps the greatest pleasure of Benji's friendship with Darius was Big Ben's staunch disapproval of it. His father rarely took the time to object to anything he did, let alone attempt to censure it, but he grumbled for hours on end that he didn't want Benji fraternizing with his clients. "I don't like mixing my peas and carrots," Big Ben said. "Besides, it's dangerous, Benji. You're like that bird that stands in the crocodile's mouth and picks shit out of his teeth. What are you going to do when he gets tired of holding it open for you?"

Even Carcosa failed to mollify him. Carcosa looked at Benji's friendship with Darius as a cultural-exchange program. Darius offered a kind of portal through which Benji glimpsed another world, and Benji was content to be swept along, carried into the stream of another life with no sense of where it might lead.

Every Tuesday, he and Darius played chess in Darius's game room. Darius had had a set custom-made for him. The pawns were haggard little baseheads. The rooks were gangsters and the bishops were pimped-out street dealers. Darius had made the knights cops because they can jump you no matter who you are. The queen had been stylized to resemble his own sainted mother and the king was, of course, Darius himself.

DJ Post-Mortem slumped on the couch, slurping strawberry soda, and watching *Beavis and Butt-head* on Darius's big-screen television. After *Beavis and Butt-head*, MTV aired the world premiere video for "150 Percent Authentic," the new single from the white rap sensation, Sarsaparilla Whiskey. He was a square-jawed former underwear model in big sunglasses and a glittery, Buster Crabbe jumpsuit. His shock of blond hair was gelled straight up so that his head looked like a Monument Valley mesa.

"Ridiculous," Darius snorted.

As DJ Post-Mortem heard the first bars of "150 Percent Authentic," he spat and coughed until strawberry soda came out of his nose. Then he jumped up off the couch like something had bitten him. "Thieving-ass cracker!" he shouted, hurling the bottle at the television. The bottle shattered against the screen and red soda ran down Sarsaparilla's face.

"The clicker is right in front of you," Darius said calmly.

"Those are my songs, D," Post-Mortem wailed, pointing furiously at the screen. He stamped his foot, on the verge of tears. "Back when I didn't have two dimes to make me a nickel sandwich I sold my best tunes to that Nazi motherfucker. Now look at him."

At Darius's request, Big Ben sat down with Sarsaparilla's attorney the following week to explore the issue of Post-Mortem's songs. When they were done exploring, Big Ben called Darius to tell him Lethal Injection was shit out of luck. Post-Mortem should never have sold his songs to

Sarsaparilla, but in doing so, he'd relinquished any claim to them. They were Sarsaparilla's songs now.

Carcosa's unorthodox solution was to book Sarsaparilla Whiskey to play a set at his daughter's *quinceañera*. Sarsaparilla didn't play private parties as a rule, but Carcosa said the guy's agent, Patrick Cordova, owed Carcosa a favor from the days when Patrick was still Paco. Paco said okay, but it would be a short set and Carcosa would have to provide security. Carcosa told Paco security was never a problem.

"You know Carcosa's daughter?" Darius asked Benji on their way to the party.

"Serena and I kind of grew up together," Benji said. He didn't mention Carcosa's creepy scheme for their arranged marriage. It would have sounded ridiculous. "She's been in a Catholic boarding school up in Ventura for the last couple years."

"What's she like?"

"Spoiled brat," Benji said. "Has Carcosa wrapped around her finger."

Carcosa had paid a service to decorate the outside of his house with thousands of star-white Christmas lights that you could have seen from space. Lights looped through the bars of the front gate and salted the gardenia hedges along the driveway. Tiny lights were fastened to big sycamore trees by wire ties so that the lights traced the fractured path of each limb. More lights lined the many eaves and windows of the main house.

Under the portico at the top of the driveway, one of the red-vested valets offered to park Darius's Suburban, but Jax wouldn't hand over the car to anyone without a fight, so he waited in the car while Darius and Benji went inside, signed the guest book, and let someone take their coats and gifts.

Still more tiny lights wrapped the silk plants in Carcosa's massive living room. White crepe paper and decorative piñatas hung from the high ship with Darius as a cultural-exchange program. Darius offered a kind of portal through which Benji glimpsed another world, and Benji was content to be swept along, carried into the stream of another life with no sense of where it might lead.

Every Tuesday, he and Darius played chess in Darius's game room. Darius had had a set custom-made for him. The pawns were haggard little baseheads. The rooks were gangsters and the bishops were pimped-out street dealers. Darius had made the knights cops because they can jump you no matter who you are. The queen had been stylized to resemble his own sainted mother and the king was, of course, Darius himself.

DJ Post-Mortem slumped on the couch, slurping strawberry soda, and watching *Beavis and Butt-head* on Darius's big-screen television. After *Beavis and Butt-head*, MTV aired the world premiere video for "150 Percent Authentic," the new single from the white rap sensation, Sarsaparilla Whiskey. He was a square-jawed former underwear model in big sunglasses and a glittery, Buster Crabbe jumpsuit. His shock of blond hair was gelled straight up so that his head looked like a Monument Valley mesa.

"Ridiculous," Darius snorted.

As DJ Post-Mortem heard the first bars of "150 Percent Authentic," he spat and coughed until strawberry soda came out of his nose. Then he jumped up off the couch like something had bitten him. "Thieving-ass cracker!" he shouted, hurling the bottle at the television. The bottle shattered against the screen and red soda ran down Sarsaparilla's face.

"The clicker is right in front of you," Darius said calmly.

"Those are my songs, D," Post-Mortem wailed, pointing furiously at the screen. He stamped his foot, on the verge of tears. "Back when I didn't have two dimes to make me a nickel sandwich I sold my best tunes to that Nazi motherfucker. Now look at him."

At Darius's request, Big Ben sat down with Sarsaparilla's attorney the following week to explore the issue of Post-Mortem's songs. When they were done exploring, Big Ben called Darius to tell him Lethal Injection was shit out of luck. Post-Mortem should never have sold his songs to

Sarsaparilla, but in doing so, he'd relinquished any claim to them. They were Sarsaparilla's songs now.

Carcosa's unorthodox solution was to book Sarsaparilla Whiskey to play a set at his daughter's *quinceañera*. Sarsaparilla didn't play private parties as a rule, but Carcosa said the guy's agent, Patrick Cordova, owed Carcosa a favor from the days when Patrick was still Paco. Paco said okay, but it would be a short set and Carcosa would have to provide security. Carcosa told Paco security was never a problem.

"You know Carcosa's daughter?" Darius asked Benji on their way to the party.

"Serena and I kind of grew up together," Benji said. He didn't mention Carcosa's creepy scheme for their arranged marriage. It would have sounded ridiculous. "She's been in a Catholic boarding school up in Ventura for the last couple years."

"What's she like?"

"Spoiled brat," Benji said. "Has Carcosa wrapped around her finger."

Carcosa had paid a service to decorate the outside of his house with thousands of star-white Christmas lights that you could have seen from space. Lights looped through the bars of the front gate and salted the gardenia hedges along the driveway. Tiny lights were fastened to big sycamore trees by wire ties so that the lights traced the fractured path of each limb. More lights lined the many eaves and windows of the main house.

Under the portico at the top of the driveway, one of the red-vested valets offered to park Darius's Suburban, but Jax wouldn't hand over the car to anyone without a fight, so he waited in the car while Darius and Benji went inside, signed the guest book, and let someone take their coats and gifts.

Still more tiny lights wrapped the silk plants in Carcosa's massive living room. White crepe paper and decorative piñatas hung from the high ceiling. Soft white doves cooed in a dozen white wicker cages placed around the room. Waiters moved among the guests with trays of shrimp cocktail and champagne.

If Darius's life was a conscious refutation of White America's notion of success, then Carcosa's life was an imitative celebration of it. Carcosa saw himself as another Joe Kennedy, a privateer patriarch, who had planned to someday sire a legitimate American dynasty, but Serena was his only issue. This party was Carcosa's schizophrenic attempt to reconcile his criminal origins with the propriety of a Mexican tradition. Benji knew he'd never be able to pull it off, but you had to admire the man's determination to bluff it out.

"This looks really uncomfortable," Benji said, seeing that the party had already hemorrhaged into two groups. The other parents from Serena's school were upstanding citizens: doctors, architects, financiers, an ACLU lawyer, and even a local congressman. The hoods looked even stiffer than the straights. Carcosa's underworld colleagues knew how much this party meant to him, and nobody wanted to be the *cabrón* who accidentally said "Fuck" and made some dowager gasp. Carcosa flitting from group to group, making introductions and reviving dead conversations. Benji watched Carcosa turning oil and water into wine. Carcosa wore his ill-gotten wealth and status with an air of laconic bemusement and, like Cary Grant, Carcosa made it all look easy.

Darius and Benji walked straight for the buffet where tamales were stacked in chafing dishes around a glistening ice sculpture of the Blessed Virgin. Light refracting through the ice gave the sculpture a spectral glow. "Check her out," Darius said. Upon closer inspection, Benji found the ice sculpture was not a rendering of the mother of Christ, but an uncannily accurate image of Carcosa's own wife, who had died giving birth to Serena. The melting droplets gave the illusion of tears. "He's got her stuck over here babysitting the fucking tamales," Darius said. "I'd be sad too."

"I'm not hungry anymore," Benji said.

Jaime and Ignacio sidled up to them at the buffet. The two most formidable leg-breakers in Carcosa's employ looked positively stricken. They loitered shoulder to shoulder and seemed to be scanning the room for a place to hide. "We're thinking about tunneling out," Ignacio whispered.

"Take us with you or we'll blow the whistle," Benji said. Jaime plucked a brown cigarillo out of his silver case. Before he could light it, Carcosa appeared out of nowhere and snatched the cigarillo out of Jaime's mouth. Carcosa stood nose to nose with Jaime, bared his teeth at him, and hissed something in Spanish that Benji couldn't make out. When Ignacio tried to calm him, Carcosa backhanded Ignacio in the face. His hand was fer-de-lance quick, and Benji didn't know how many people saw it. He looked away while Jaime and Ignacio slouched out of the room.

Carcosa turned, seeming to notice Benji and Darius for the first time. *"Ah, mis hijos."* Carcosa smiled and lunged awkwardly, hooking Benji with his right arm and Darius with his left, to wrap them both in a rib-cracking hug. Darius tensed and then seemed to go with it. Benji could hear the air rushing out of him. Carcosa's cologne made Benji's eyes water. *"Mis únicos hijos." My only sons.*

Big Ben arrived then with Gretchen on his arm in one of her deadliest Diors. He had four of his private investigators in tow. "What the hell did he bring *them* for?" Benji asked, but Carcosa had already moved to greet him. If you harbored any romantic illusions about private investigators, Benji thought, the PIs working for Big Ben would shatter them for you. Not a fedora among them, Big Ben's errant knights just a bunch of pasty, paranoid chain-smokers who resembled nothing so much as sickly teamsters. They were mostly thugs who'd been kicked off different municipal police forces for being sadists, drunks, wife-beaters, or compulsive gamblers. Though officially employed to gather intelligence, these guys earned their pay illegally tapping phones, spooking witnesses, spreading disinformation, and destroying evidence for Big Ben's clients. He only brought them along when he was expecting trouble.

The other girls from Serena's class filled out their gowns in ways that made Benji feel a little guilty for even looking. Even without the heels, most of the girls would have been taller than the boys in attendance. They wore their curls piled on their heads and more makeup than their parents would have allowed for any other occasion. Benji guessed most of these girls had had their hair and faces professionally done for this party, the makeup applied with more subtlety than most teenagers can manage.

The boys gathered in a tight circle. They looked like a herd of pimply antelope huddling close to each other for protection. Some of them were still a year or two away from the full brunt of puberty, and they seemed caught between worlds. They fretted stiffly with their church suits, palsied by discomfort and embarrassment.

The DJ stood on his little stage, tapped his microphone, and called for attention. "Ladies and gentlemen," he said in English and then Spanish, "allow me to present Señorita Serena Magdalena Carcosa."

Serena appeared beside her father under an arbor of white balloons, and the room erupted in applause. She had one hand on her father's arm. In the other, she held a delicate fan, which she used to cover her flawless smile. Then Carcosa moved aside and allowed his daughter to step forward into the center of the room. Every eye in the place was on her, but anyone could see she was used to the attention, even demanded it.

The last time Benji had seen her, she'd been a kid, what? Twelve? Three years had sculpted that awkward brat into the kind of young woman that vaqueros used to kill each other over.

They sang "Happy Birthday" and "Feliz Cumpleaños" while Serena pirouetted slowly and Benji caught himself searching her white gown for hints of the girl he'd known, but there was no trace of child left in her. When they had finished singing, Serena held the hem of her gown and curtseyed, bowing deeper than was necessary, Benji willing his own eyes away from her décolletage. Serena smiled, eyes shark black behind her coquettish veil.

Furniture was cleared from the living room for dancing, and the DJ kicked off with some disco. The girls giggled, twirled, and imitated John

Travolta. The boys kept their backs to the wall as though expecting an attack. None of them budged until, one by one, their mothers menaced them away from the wall and the boys stepped onto the dance floor the way you'd cross a patch of thin ice.

Darius couldn't take his eyes off Serena and she knew it. She danced with three or four boys, but seemed to be performing just for Darius, angling her body to afford him the best vantage, Benji wondering where she'd learned to move like that.

"She's fifteen years old," Benji reminded him.

"There's grass on the field," Darius said, watching her dance.

"Jesus," Benji said. "You can take the boy out of the ghetto . . ."

"Look at her," Darius said. "And you tell me what's wrong with it."

"Carcosa will have the *Eme* put a green light on you before you get to second base," Benji said. "That's what's wrong with it."

"Who's gonna tell him?"

"Just don't involve me," Benji said. "Not as a beard, not as an alibi, I don't want to know anything about this."

Sarsaparilla Whiskey was an hour and a half late for his set. When he arrived in his glittery costume, complete with shoulder pads and oversized sunglasses, the girls screamed and mobbed him. It wasn't easy to tell with his sunglasses, but he seemed to be searching the middle distance for something, probably a mirror. Nobody was going to confuse this guy with a Rhodes scholar. He couldn't have been much over six feet, but with his blond hair gelled straight up, he looked taller. He pursed his lips and sucked in his cheeks. Someone had probably told him that expression made him look dangerous and sexy, but Benji just thought he looked like an old woman trying on a hat.

Sarsaparilla required no sound check. He took the stage and lip-synched his entire set right off his own album, but none of the kids seemed to mind. Here was Sarsaparilla Whiskey in the flesh, giving them a private concert. For his final number, he took Serena's hand and brought her up on stage to dance with him to "150 Percent Authentic."

During the song, Benji noticed his father's burly private investigators moving through the crowd to position themselves around the stage, Benji expecting them to turn away from the stage to keep all the kids from smothering Sarsaparilla after his set, but they all faced the stage, focusing their attention on Sarsaparilla. Benji asked Darius what was going on.

"Just be cool," Darius told him.

Sarsaparilla took a bow and kissed Serena on the cheek. He stepped jauntily off the stage, four PIs surrounding him like Secret Service Agents. If he was aware that he was being corralled, Sarsaparilla didn't seem alarmed by it. He just waved to the cheering kids and let Big Ben's men steer him out of the living room, like a man being carried out to sea by a riptide. "Ladies and gentlemen," the DJ said, "Sarsaparilla Whiskey has left the building." Then the DJ cranked up Sir Mix-A-Lot's "Baby Got Back" and the kids went on dancing.

Nobody seemed to notice that Sarsaparilla hadn't actually left the building. Instead of leading him out the front door, Big Ben's men had forced Sarsaparilla into a side door that led to Carcosa's motor court. One of the PIs stayed behind, a former sheriff's deputy pensioned off on some kind of weight-lifting injury. The guy folded his arms with finality, blocking the doorway with his thick body. But after a few minutes, the man nodded to Carcosa and moved aside, allowing Carcosa to step through the same door. As he disappeared through the doorway, Carcosa turned and nodded to Darius. "That's our cue," Darius said to Benji, draining the rest of his champagne.

"What cue?" he asked, but Darius was already snaking through the crowd, making his way to the door. Benji hurried after him. Whatever was happening, it was happening fast. He should have suspected they'd have something prearranged like this, but why hadn't they shared their plans with him? Maybe his father hadn't trusted him. Maybe Carcosa had wanted to shield him from whatever was going to happen. Maybe the fewer people who knew the better. Maybe Darius figured when it actually went down he'd still be able to count on Benji's suicidal curiosity to pull him into it.

The big PI blocking the door stepped aside to let Darius pass, but Benji hesitated at the threshold. He saw Gretchen watching him from the bar. She was standing next to Big Ben, one hand resting lightly on his shoulder, her Oscar turn as the attentive wife while Big Ben traded business cards with one of the other guests. She pretended to sip her drink, and shook her head at Benji, mouthing the word "Don't."

"Come on, then, nigga." Darius beckoned him from the darkened corridor beyond the door. The PI held the door open for him. He looked back at Gretchen. Her eyes glistened. *Please. Don't.*

"In or out," Darius said.

Benji mouthed "Sorry." Gretchen turned away from him, and he followed Darius down the rabbit hole. He heard the door lock behind him.

Carcosa's Wal-Mart-sized motor court had been built to house his ever-expanding collection of rare and classic cars. It featured a walk-down pit and a cherry picker. Reading from left to right, he'd collected a 1949 Jaguar XK-120 Roadster with an alloy body, a 1970 Oldsmobile 442 Coupe, a 1995 Porsche 911 six-speed Carrera, a 1963 Maserati 3500 GTE Sebring, a 1956 Austin Healey 100-M Le Mans, a 1962 Ferrari 250 GTE, a 1958 V8 Thunderbird Coupe, a 1965 convertible Mustang, a 1975 V8 Grand Torino, a 1962 Mercedes 190SL Roadster, a 1960 four-speed MGA Coupe, a 1958 BMW Isetta, a 1967 Triumph TR4, a 1973 Twin-Cam Lotus Europa, and a 1984 Ferrari 308 GTS, just like the one Magnum used to drive. Carcosa employed a full-time mechanic and a detailer to keep his babies washed and waxed.

Benji saw Sarsaparilla as soon as Darius and Benji entered the motor court. Benji stopped in midstride, choking back an ill-conceived warning or a call for help. Darius seized Benji's triceps and forced him to keep walking.

"I said be cool," Darius whispered to him. "This is just business."

Between the third and fourth rows of Carcosa's gleaming cars, Sarsaparilla Whiskey hung upside down from an engine hoist, twisting like a game fish. His hands and feet were bound and someone had stuffed an oily rag into his mouth. Jaime and Ignacio were carefully wrapping Sarsaparilla in crepe paper. Sarsaparilla was all bug-eyed piss-panic, and probably too dumb to get the joke anyway, but Jaime and Ignacio were making him into a human piñata.

"Ninety minutes late," Carcosa said. He had taken off his jacket and rolled up his sleeves, holding an aluminum baseball bat between his legs while he tied a blue bandanna over his own eyes. "And you lip-synch your shit like this is some high school talent show." Sarsaparilla made desperate, beseeching noises, but Carcosa just shook his head almost sadly. "Very disrespectful," he said, picking up the bat.

Jaime and Ignacio spun Carcosa around three times to disorient him and one of the PIs pushed Sarsaparilla so that he swung like a pendulum. Sarsaparilla fell silent as Carcosa stepped blindly forward and cocked the bat. He swung, missing Sarsaparilla by inches, but the bat put a huge dent in the door of his 1995 Porsche 911. Carcosa reoriented himself, swung and missed again, this time shattering the windshield of his 1970 Oldsmobile 442 Coupe. *Mierda.* He hissed and set up for another swing.

"Choke up on it," Ignacio offered.

Sarsaparilla pushed with his tongue and spat the rag out. "Fuck!" he sobbed. "Please stop! Jesus, I didn't mean to disrespect you." Sarsaparilla wept, his tears running up his forehead into his crispy hair. "I'll make it right."

Carcosa untied his blindfold and cast it aside. He winced when he saw the cars. "Little late for that," he said, leaning on the bat, Benji praying this had all been a bluff to scare Sarsaparilla and Carcosa had missed intentionally, but who the hell would trash his own cars like that?

"I'll do another concert," Sarsaparilla pleaded. "Anytime you want."

"I don't think so," Carcosa said. "But I'll tell you what would make me happy: if you returned those songs you stole from DJ Post-Mortem."

Sarsaparilla hadn't stolen those songs. He'd lawfully purchased them, but he didn't argue the point, maybe not as dumb as Benji thought. "Sure," he said quickly. "I mean, they're *his*, right?"

"*Claro que sí.*" Carcosa winked at Darius. "I'll have them cut you down and you can sign the papers before you leave."

PRESENT

TJ finger-spun his binoculars until the jungle cat in the Dodgers hat was sharply in focus. Dude was on foot, just ambling up Blessed Way like it was Main Street, USA. He looked familiar, but the bill of his cap shaded everything north of the fifty and all TJ could make out for sure was a Lando mustache and a strong chin, so he could have been anybody. The walking woodpile with him looked like one of those chain-saw sculptures of Bigfoot.

"Call it in," TJ said, cool as a cola Slurpee. Bodhi Bomb hit Send on the preprogrammed number and handed over his cell. "Coming up the block," TJ said into the phone, calling the play for Mushmouth and Tech-Nick, Get Some's curbside sentries.

"Rollin'?" Mushmouth asked.

"Strollin'," he said.

"Singleton?"

"Deuce," he said. "Flaco and Gordo."

"Anyone we know?"

"These niggas ain't in my Rolodex, cuz."

Risley made the two toucans perched midblock. They were both proned roach-tight to the flat gravel roof of those two-story Tiki apartments next to Get Some's pad. In their slate gray hooded parkas, these dudes would have been nearly invisible to a passing ghetto bird. Risley knew they already had him, but he didn't trip. These two were only spotters—Get Some's Apache early-warning system—Bodhi Bomb and Tehachapi Jack, who everyone just called TJ. Between the two of them they'd have the block covered from Budlong to Normandie.

Risley and Mapes were technically on duty today and it delighted Risley that the city was paying him for this outing. They still worked a SPU unit in Rampart. It was a uniform gig, but their sergeant let them roll in plainclothes if they gave him half a reason. For that matter, the old guy pretty much let them make their own hours, disinclined to fuck with them because they still brought in the numbers.

"Get Some's gettin' jumpy in his old age," Risley said under his breath. Get Some had installed a new Bedlam fence, one of those iron arrowhead numbers. A clean Escalade truck was parked in front the fence, two wheels up on the sidewalk and two in the street. Eight grand easy for the after-market rims, another five sunk into the sound system pumping out DJ Post-Mortem's postmortem hit "Lobo," a gangsta-rap tirade that improbably sampled snatches from the theme to *Sheriff Lobo*.

A Boot Hill Mafia Crip called Mushmouth sat on the Escalade's open tailgate with a Bonelli Black Eagle shotgun resting across his thighs, sucking a blunt and bobbing his head to Post-Mortem's bass line. The guy wore a ski mask pulled down to his nose, leaving his mouth exposed. They called him Mushmouth after the Fat Albert character, but Risley knew he wore the ski mask because his momma, three sleepless nights into a freebase marathon, had burned his face with a hot iron when he was a baby and his grafts never quite cut it.

Mushmouth's road dog, the one they called Tech-Nick because of his gadget fetish, stalked back and forth in front of the truck, pausing now and then to strike movie-poster poses with his Bushmaster Bullpup. Wrong roscoe for the job, Risley thought, the weapon probably chosen for its wicked looks alone. Tech-Nick had a pair of surplus Russian night-vision goggles pushed back on his forehead, the cumbersome goggles there for show because it was fucking four in the afternoon.

These weren't your usual dipshit dope lookouts, not the kill-crazy cannon fodder you let get chewed up in bullshit block-to-block feuds.

PRESENT

TJ finger-spun his binoculars until the jungle cat in the Dodgers hat was sharply in focus. Dude was on foot, just ambling up Blessed Way like it was Main Street, USA. He looked familiar, but the bill of his cap shaded everything north of the fifty and all TJ could make out for sure was a Lando mustache and a strong chin, so he could have been anybody. The walking woodpile with him looked like one of those chain-saw sculptures of Bigfoot.

"Call it in," TJ said, cool as a cola Slurpee. Bodhi Bomb hit Send on the preprogrammed number and handed over his cell. "Coming up the block," TJ said into the phone, calling the play for Mushmouth and Tech-Nick, Get Some's curbside sentries.

"Rollin'?" Mushmouth asked.

"Strollin'," he said.

"Singleton?"

"Deuce," he said. "Flaco and Gordo."

"Anyone we know?"

"These niggas ain't in my Rolodex, cuz."

Risley made the two toucans perched midblock. They were both proned roach-tight to the flat gravel roof of those two-story Tiki apartments next to Get Some's pad. In their slate gray hooded parkas, these dudes would have been nearly invisible to a passing ghetto bird. Risley knew they already had him, but he didn't trip. These two were only spotters—Get Some's Apache early-warning system—Bodhi Bomb and Tehachapi Jack, who everyone just called TJ. Between the two of them they'd have the block covered from Budlong to Normandie.

Risley and Mapes were technically on duty today and it delighted Risley that the city was paying him for this outing. They still worked a SPU unit in Rampart. It was a uniform gig, but their sergeant let them roll in plainclothes if they gave him half a reason. For that matter, the old guy pretty much let them make their own hours, disinclined to fuck with them because they still brought in the numbers.

"Get Some's gettin' jumpy in his old age," Risley said under his breath. Get Some had installed a new Bedlam fence, one of those iron arrowhead numbers. A clean Escalade truck was parked in front the fence, two wheels up on the sidewalk and two in the street. Eight grand easy for the after-market rims, another five sunk into the sound system pumping out DJ Post-Mortem's postmortem hit "Lobo," a gangsta-rap tirade that improbably sampled snatches from the theme to *Sheriff Lobo*.

A Boot Hill Mafia Crip called Mushmouth sat on the Escalade's open tailgate with a Bonelli Black Eagle shotgun resting across his thighs, sucking a blunt and bobbing his head to Post-Mortem's bass line. The guy wore a ski mask pulled down to his nose, leaving his mouth exposed. They called him Mushmouth after the Fat Albert character, but Risley knew he wore the ski mask because his momma, three sleepless nights into a freebase marathon, had burned his face with a hot iron when he was a baby and his grafts never quite cut it.

Mushmouth's road dog, the one they called Tech-Nick because of his gadget fetish, stalked back and forth in front of the truck, pausing now and then to strike movie-poster poses with his Bushmaster Bullpup. Wrong roscoe for the job, Risley thought, the weapon probably chosen for its wicked looks alone. Tech-Nick had a pair of surplus Russian night-vision goggles pushed back on his forehead, the cumbersome goggles there for show because it was fucking four in the afternoon.

These weren't your usual dipshit dope lookouts, not the kill-crazy cannon fodder you let get chewed up in bullshit block-to-block feuds.

Mushmouth and Tech-Nick were supposed to be the kind of hard-core heat you hired when the shit-to-fan ratio was high. Get Some was probably afraid the *Eme* was going to get hep to Risley's little tax rebate, but homeboy was just wasting disk space on worry because Risley had it all under control.

Mushmouth and Tech-Nick brought their guns up to track Risley's approach, letting the slack off their triggers when they saw it was him. They lowered their weapons, mortified. Goddamn right, Risley thought. He'd come unannounced and in civvies, but these busters still should have known better.

DJ Post-Mortem bellowed from the speakers: *Pigs profilin' my homeboys while their cocaine infects us. Slam your head on the hood 'cause they still disrespect us.*

With a single, fluid uppercut, Risley brought the flat of his palm up under the loading port of the Bonelli. Closing his fingers around the entire receiver, Risley yanked the weapon out of Mushmouth's hands.

Beat your punk ass for kicks—say they gotta correct us.
Least the Crips and the Bloods don't pretend to protect us.
Now, don't run tell your broker, cuz, this ain't no prospectus.

Risley flipped the Bonelli, caught it in midair, and drove the stock into Mushmouth's face—like a shovel breaking hard-packed earth. Mushmouth fell backward into the truck bed, blood welling under his ski mask. Tech-Nick tried to back away with his Bushmaster held at port-arms.

Doctor Martin had a dream that was dead on arrival.
Poor brothers live a nightmare, killed by the Five-Oh.

Risley tossed the Bonelli to Mapes. Mapes caught the shotgun by the barrel and swung it like a bat, catching Tech-Nick full in the face. The blow lifted Tech-Nick off his Filas. His Bushmaster clattered on the street and his night-vision goggles skittered across the pavement.

This crunk-ass nigga's just been kickin' it old school.
But Wolf's hour's comin' and I'm a wolf in the fold, fool.

Tech-Nick reacted quickly, rolling and scrambling toward the Bush-master. Mapes kicked the weapon under the car and stomped down on Tech-Nick's scrabbling hand hard enough to split the skin. Tech-Nick yowled, clutching his bleeding hand.

Lobo, cuz. Lobo Enscondito.
Superfly-ass bandito.
Muy discreet-o and fleet of feet-o.

Mapes changed his grip on the Bonelli, pressing the muzzle into Tech-Nick's cheek, and Risley dropped his knee between Tech-Nick's shoulder blades.

"Pull on me again and you'll wake up in the Spook House," Risley whispered to him. "With them dogs chewin' your black ass. And you *know* that's real."

"Won't happen again, sir," Tech-Nick stammered.

"I know," Risley said and let the kid up. Risley stepped through the gate, calling out at the house. "Yo, Get Some, Avon callin', cuz."

The front door opened not a foot before a pit bull charged out of the blackness, a muscular hobgoblin trained not to bark a warning. The creature sprang, launching itself into Risley's chest, and nearly knocked Risley into the iron fence. The dog licked Risley's face, wagging its nub tail. He'd given Chronic to Get Some when he was still a pup, the pick of the litter, and the dog still remembered Risley.

Gethsemane Guyton, a.k.a. Get Some, stood on the porch in his boxers and an open robe, shaking his head at his fallen soldiers. He was about Risley's height, not a lot of meat on him. Get Some had been slinging since the late Cretaceous, ought to have squirreled some Scrooge McDucats by now, but he was still hood-posted on Blessed Way, still doing his grocery shopping at Tam's Burger, still having his momma cut his hair, still two steps away from prison and one from the coroner. Tote that barge, Risley thought. Lift that bail.

Financial planning to a lot of these motherfuckers meant jacking a Jack in the Box when the drawer was fat before shift change, but in fairness, lack of foresight wasn't the source of all Get Some's money woes. Get Some also had a protein problem. Poor guy shot photon torpedos and he'd sired seventeen—count 'em—seventeen kids from nine different baby mamas. Even Costco wasn't giving away Huggies these days, and this motherfucker was always strapped for cash. Most of his women got along with each other, but a few were like those tropical fish you couldn't keep in the same tank. Baby Mama 7 didn't dig Baby Mama 4. Baby Mama 2 was Baby Mama 4's sister, so she didn't get along with Baby Mama 7. Baby Mama 9 and Baby Mama 7 where both Belizean so 9 had 7's back. Get Some's life played like one of those logic games you find on standardized tests. And he got high a lot which only made it worse because he sometimes got the women mixed up, forgot which kids went with which. His women were always beating his ass behind the shit. Baby Mama 4 once clouted him with a baseball bat after he mistook her for Baby Mama 3. Last year, 7 and 4 got into it after 4 braided the hair of one of 7's kids. All their scratching, kicking, and extension pulling was scaring the kids, but when Get Some tried to break them up, Baby Mama 9 (at least he thought it was 9) shot him in the leg.

"What's crackin, cuz?" Risley smiled.

"Why you gotta squeeze a nigga's mutherfuckin Charmin, cuz?" Get Some said, hands jammed in the pockets of his robe. "Those ain't lapdogs, homie. Shit, cuz, I train 'em to bite."

"Then train 'em right," Risley said, heading up the front walk with Chronic happily sniffing his shoes. "They both old enough to know better."

They hugged on the porch and Risley followed Get Some back into the house. Mapes posted out front. Other than the elaborate hydroponics, the pad was typical late-century ghetto: discount Prince Living Room Set, ostrich plumes jammed into faux African pottery, dining room as dirty clothes hamper. Get Some was on the dark side of thirty, but his tastes had frozen around fourteen. His walls were decorated with posters of DJ Post-Mortem, Pacino in *Scarface,* and a Budweiser Kings of Africa bar mirror. An old episode of *Cops* was running mute on Get Some's bloated, rent-to-own big-screen TV. Get Some had his Egyptian hookah and pile of moist doujah set out on a swap-meet coffee table.

Risley cleared away the Tam's wrappers and sat on the edge of the couch. Get Some flopped in the love seat opposite, packed the clay bowl of the hookah, and flicked an engraved Boot Hill Zippo. Get Some hit the cobra once before offering Risley the hose. Risley shook his head, eyeing the crossbows placed around the room. "Make a nigga paranoid," he said.

"On hood, cuz," Get Some said, hitting the cobra again.

"I keep hopin' the shit'll lower my motherfuckin' sperm count." Risley chuckled.

"You get right with the albino?" Get Some asked.

"It's set up for next week," Risley said. "In the river."

"Then why we jawin' now?"

"Got me a Curious George," Risley said, tilting his chin out toward the street. "I need your dogs to bite him for me."

"Another badge?"

"Uh-huh," Risley said.

"Who?"

"The *vaquero,*" Risley said. "Don't care how you get it done, but get it done *mañana.* He ought to leave out of roll call around three."

Risley had been ninja-fucking one of the 77th records clerks for the better part of a year, a fat woman who smelled like bubble bath, but worth the sweat because Petunia Pig faxed him copies of all the schedules at the start of each deployment period. So Risley knew when the hard cases would be out hunting and when the B-team benchwarmers and station queens would be manning the tiller. He planned all his south-end excursions accordingly. More important, he knew having those schedules would come in handy if he ever had to zap a cop.

"Marquez?" Get Some coughed a cloud of smoke. "Aw, *hell* no."

"What the fuck did you say?" Risley whispered, leaning forward.

"Naw, cuz," Get Some said. "Fuck that."

Risley drew the blue-steel SIG P226 from his waistband, a single-use piece he'd snatched out of Property for this trip, something he could blast and dump in the river.

"I misheard you is what just happened," Risley said. "'Cause otherwise, cuz, you're just about two cunt hairs shy a Crip heaven." He thumbed back the hammer and leveled the SIG at Get Some's chest.

"Damn, cuz," Get Some said softly. "You got me twisted, homie. I don't—I can't be in this predicament, cuz. No way."

"And, ooh, motherfucker you just lost one," Risley said, caressing the trigger. "Calm down, baby. Think about your answer now, cuz."

"This whole Darius lick is whack, cuz." Get Some raised the hookah's hose in a plea for sanity. "You can't just cut a nigga open and climb into his skin. That ain't the business."

"Oldest business there is, cuz," Risley said. "That's like the *original* business. If you can kill a man and get away with it, you get to keep his shit. Whole country was founded on that." Risley eased the hammer back and placed the SIG on the coffee table between them. He snapped his fingers. Get Some handed the hose to him.

"Let me ask you something. How many homies you know been killed out here?" Risley said. "Know personally, I mean. Ballpark the shit for me. Thirty? Fifty?" Risley put the hose to his lips, took the smoke deep into his lungs, pushed his shoulders back, and held it.

"Thirty-six," Get Some said solemnly.

Risley exhaled, a conjurer's storm pouring out of his nostrils.

"And how many they solve?" he asked. "I mean, anybody actually go to prison behind the shit? You got niggas in prison on chickenshit robberies, dope, but how many homies you know ever went up on a murder?"

"Tiny Buck," Get Some said.

"Naw, man." Risley waved hanging smoke away from his face. "That hapless nigga fucked around and shot a little kid. Tiny Buck went to prison for poor marksmanship, so that one don't even count."

"Serious now, my nigga." Risley handed the hose back to Get Some. "You can count on one hand anyone you know ever went to prison for killin' another nigga."

Get Some blinked, taking this in. Risley felt sorry for him.

"Spent your whole life caged up here in motherfucking Kandor," Risley said. "Born on this street and you'll die here. You're enclosure's what, twenty blocks square? Just big enough to forget you're livin' in a damn bottle. You lack proper perspective, my brotha, but I'm out there in the Fortress of Solitude. So I'm in a position to know.

"It's still legal to kill a black man in this country," Risley said. "Darius may be a Grammy presenter, maybe one of *People*'s best-dressed, but when he comes up dead nobody gone trip. You watch. LAPD just gone toss him on a pile of a hundred and ninety-two other dead niggers and get the fuck on."

Risley stood, tucking the Sig back into this waistband. Get Some followed him out as far as the porch. Risley stepped down to the lawn and squatted to scratch behind Chronic's clipped ears, letting the dog slop him a good-bye smooch.

"So what happens if a nigga can't handle the shit tomorrow?" Get Some asked, trace amounts of petulance detectable in his voice now, the guy looking to save face in front of his foot soldiers. "You gone arrest me, cop?"

Risley kissed the dog, making like he hadn't heard the question. Then he nodded to Mapes.

Mapes grabbed the dog's hind legs, yanking the dog up like a wheelbarrow. The dog's front legs scrabbled, claws plowing dusty furrows in the packed dirt. Then Mapes arched his back, spinning like a hammer thrower and heaved the thrashing creature up over his head, flinging the dog down over the top of the arrowhead fence. Iron spikes burst upward through the dog's body. Air bubbled from six bloody punctures, steam rising from the wounds.

"See now, I loved that pup," Risley said sadly. Upside down, the dog's limbs paddled the air in a kind of slow-motion swim, its tongue lolling like a wet sock. "And nigga, I don't even like you."

24

1997

Darius fumbled and groped and kissed Serena clumsily, his teeth clicking against hers while he struggled to find their seal. His fingers brushed her insolent nipples, and traced her belly to the black hairs curling over the top of her panties. He begged her to let him touch it, trembling just to see it. Darius was only dimly suspicious of the deft way she spat into her hand before wrapping her fingers tightly around him. He'd expected some precocity from Serena (she was Carcosa's daughter, after all), but he hadn't seen this coming; this almost clinical composure, her sexual poise, the delicate industry of her little fist sliding up and down, consuming him again and again until he bit his lip and came. He lay limp-muscled, panting on his side as though awaiting punishment, dimly embarrassed by his own body pooled like oil across the white bedspread. "You're almost twice as big as me," Serena told him, her black eyes surveying the wreckage of him with equal parts fascination and contempt. "And look what I just did to you, with only my hand."

She dug a clove cigarette out of her Hello Kitty purse. There was stillness in her even now, those shark eyes always verging on boredom, like she was daring him to show her something.

He could have had any woman he wanted any way he wanted, but he needed her and he contrived these furtive assignations to neck with her like the teenager he'd never been. Benji had told him he suspected that was some of Serena's appeal, an opportunity for Darius to steal back the gulag years he'd lost to the California Youth Authority, a chance to stow away aboard the final leg of Serena's childhood. Maybe at the beginning he'd wanted a piece of her youth, but this had all gotten away from him in a hurry, like that skyscraper beanstalk that punches up through Jack's house overnight. Darius wondered if it was like this for DJ Post-Mortem, if this was why his homeboy—livin' the life of motherfucking Riley— fell off the wagon again and again, right into the arms of another nappy nymphet.

From the beginning of their affair, if you could call it that, Darius had found himself desperate to impress Serena. He bought her jewelry, sent her rambling letters. He'd even dressed down *double-gangsta* for this little rendezvous, wanting to thrill her as the deadly outlaw.

One of her schoolmate's parents, a real estate developer and his third wife, were out of town for the week and Serena had somehow gotten her hands on the key to their empty house. So they'd made plans to meet up here in Thousand Oaks some time during the week. Serena hadn't been sure when she'd be able to slip away from the Dominican Sisters who walked the tier and he'd been checking his cell every few minutes to make sure it was working. Jax, seeing how far gone he was, knowing he was walking in front of a firing squad, had refused to participate in any way. "You like a samurai shovin' a sword in your gut," Jax had told him. "And I ain't about to cut your head off for you."

Benji too had sworn he wouldn't get involved, wouldn't enable his addiction to her, but unlike the oak-hard Jax, Benji could be manipulated. And against his better judgment, Benji had driven him up the Ventura Highway, swearing up and down it would be the last time. He'd climbed into the trunk of Benji's Audi to get past the guard at the gated entrance to this neighborhood—another indignity willingly suffered for her.

Now Darius lay on his side, afraid to look at her, lost in the LeRoy Neiman painting hanging next to the bed, some dude at the top of his backswing. "My father wants me to marry Benji," she said, lighting her smoke. She shook out the match. His muscles, still limp, coiled in a convulsion of homicidal jealousy. He sat up in bed. He saw himself putting his thumbs into Benji's eyes, pushing them right through into his brain.

"But I want to marry you." The words tumbled out of him. It was like getting sick all over yourself.

"Jesus." She traced the Boot Hill tattoos on his chest. "Grow up."

She told him she had to get back before bed check and he called her a cab, kissed her good-bye, wondering as the cab pulled away if she would even miss him. Now he was alone in some stranger's house and it scared him. He gently tapped the keys on their grand piano, recently tuned. He wandered the halls, inspected their family photos, lay in the kids' beds, and stared up at the white ceiling. He stayed away from the windows, wouldn't do for the neighbors to see a black man skulking around in here. Good way to get his ass shot. It was getting dark and part of him wanted to burn the whole place down, but he pulled his shit together and called Benji.

"Went to see the new James Bond at that mall down the street," Benji said, after he'd slipped into the passenger seat next to him. Darius hunched low in the seat, cap pulled down. The neighborhood rolling past his window: Greenbelt. Bike paths. Lighted fountains. Koi. Pond turtles. And everywhere he turned, those hideous bronze De L'Esprie sculptures, fiendish children grinning at him from people's front lawns.

"And?"

"It was kinda like sex with an ex," Benji said, clearly pleased with the analogy, probably been working on it awhile.

"What the fuck is that supposed to mean?" Darius saw street lamps, real street lamps, not those piss-yellow low-sodium substitutes, but honest-to-God fluorescents lighting the road like a runway. A man could take a midnight stroll in a neighborhood like this, a man could walk his dog, take his ease here in the dark. A woman could jog out here long after sundown.

"I mean the landscape was more or less what I'd remembered," Benji said. "But five minutes into it I knew it was a bad idea."

"That bad," Darius said.

"Parts were okay, I guess," Benji said. "Michelle Yeoh."

"Have I ever told you about the Spook House?" Darius asked him as they wound their way down out of the foothills.

"No," Benji said.

"Some of these motherfuckers think it's just Loch Ness Monster jailhouse bullshit," Darius said. "Shit, some of 'em prayin' that's all it is, but it's real. Only a handful of homies even know where it is."

"What is it?"

"Fear," Darius said. "Any buster can bust caps, pitch some hot lead through a nigga. GSW, shit, that's an honorable way to go out, but you *disappear* a motherfucker, dump homeboy's headless body on mamma's front lawn with the business end of a road flare shoved up his ass?" Darius smiled, seeing Benji recoil. "See, straight gangbangin' is too *pedestrian* to put the fear in folks anymore. You want 'em to shit they-selves, you got to become a *flesh-eater,* Wild Man of Borneo, a real bone-through-the-nose unga-bunga."

Benji stopped for the light at the intersection of Westlake and Thousand Oaks. "Why are you telling me this?"

Darius was silent, seething. When he finally spoke, he measured each word with a quartermaster's exactitude. "Because if you ever touch Serena," he said, "I'm going to give you the Grand Tour."

Benji looked at him. "Where the fuck is this coming from?"

"Why didn't you tell me Carcosa wanted you to marry his daughter?"

"What?" Benji sighed. "Oh, Jesus. You scared me for a second. He's been saying that since we were kids. Look, I didn't mention it because it doesn't mean shit. It's just noise, man."

"Don't condescend a nigga that way," Darius said. "Don't even think about it."

"I don't even know her," Benji said. "Besides, I have someone."

"Who?"

"Never mind."

"I've done that fuckin' Mexican's dirty laundry for years." Darius punched the dash. "*Years.* Anything he needed done. Didn't matter how gory. And where the fuck were you, my nigga? In school? Naw, man, fuck that. *Fuck* that." Darius threw open his door and started stepping. He left Benji at the light, heard Benji calling after him, but he didn't stop.

Darius walked through the huge parking lot into the new Westlake Promenade, one of those upscale Mediterranean-style outdoor shopping centers with red tile roofs, cupolas, a Toyland clock tower, bougainvillea dripping from decorative balconies. Sur La Table, Bristol Farms, Academy Optical, Bombay, Bed Bath & Beyond. A Cigar Wagon with a green canvas awning and old-fashioned wheels planted on the sidewalk.

Right away he had the prickling sensation of being watched, of being noticed, but not for his celebrity. What had he been thinking jumping out of the car like that? Darius was easily one of the most successful figures in the music industry, topping anyone's list of who's who in hip-hop, but he rarely left the house without a full entourage and he almost never ventured beyond the fence without Jax. There was relative safety in the company of his crew, but it wasn't the fear of attack that kept him indoors without them. Darius could still pitch speed dice or hot lead on any block from Croesus to Crenshaw, drop thousands on Krug for everyone at an after-hours club. What scared Darius, what really put him on check, was white people. And now he was alone and on foot in another country.

Another De L'Esprie sculpture formed the mall's fountain centerpiece. The plaque on the edge of the fountain had a Christian fish symbol and the title "Joy to Life." The statue was of a woman with flowing hair, flowing gown, and a Lon Chaney grin, holding her baby while she flew a kite. The kite was pulling her, the baby, two other kids, and a Coppertone dog right off their feet. Pulled aloft, he supposed, by the transcendent ecstacy of being rich and white. Darius thought these figures looked maniacal, rabid, hungry. A bronze Jack Kennedy–looking statue Darius figured was supposed to be the dad leered at his family from an iron bench.

In a thousand years archaeologists would dig this place up and think it had been a temple where children had been worshipped, Darius thought, and they wouldn't be far off. He saw toddlers in Gap sweaters and Timberland boots. Their parents loaded them into Mercedes SUVs and minivans. They brought their kids shopping with them, took them into nice restaurants where the waiters handed them paper menus and crayons. Nobody whupped their kids in public. He'd never seen anything like it. These folks didn't even seem to curse their kids, didn't yank them around by the arm, didn't shake the shit out of them for squirming or touching something.

He stopped in front of an indoor playground where kids ran a padded obstacle course. Darius stood outside the window, watching employees in khaki shorts and yellow T-shirts spotting for the kids on a zip line. The spotters had a new day-camp affirmation, some encouraging phrase, for each kid. He marveled at the training—the money—that must have gone into this. Darius took one of the glossy brochures from a slot in the door. Christ, he thought. Nothing but Laura Ingalls foothills as far as the eye can see out here and these folks still fork over two hundred a month for their kids to play inside fucking McDonaldland. Probably worried about UV or some shit.

Everyone here was Stepford white, unless you counted Service Mexicans, unobtrusively brown and nearly mute, bagging groceries, parking cars, and bussing tables with the practiced invisibility of English butlers—men who erased themselves for less than minimum wage.

These white men all looked the same. They all seemed to have the same Peter Jennings haircut, the same doughy face, and the prosperously thickening gut of a jock gone to seed. They wore dry-cleaned golf shirts, pressed jeans, caps with tasteful logos on them—Ralph Lauren, J. Crew.

The women all carried expensive purses, matching barettes, watches, belts. Rhinestones on crisp denim jackets, manicured toes poking out of pricey black mules. They wore fashionable haircuts, the dye jobs more elaborate on some of the older models, gray becoming blond. Some of their faces looked surgically taut, a few with the sheen of a recent chemical peel.

There was none of the jittery flailing and woofing you saw in the hood, niggas cutting wild-ass capers just to burn off their constant fear. In South Central, people moved with purpose, stepped with a feral alertness, stayed on top of their shit all the time because daydreaming would kill you out there. But these folks looked carelessly confident, calm, almost drowsy with the anesthetic comfort of their utter safety. And that safety seemed to make them easygoing, munificent. People here smiled and stepped aside for strangers without any life-threatening loss of face. There was none of that postprison bristle you saw in the hood, the Gs puffing up like polecats, taking up more space than they needed because everyone they encountered was a potential enemy. Folks here actually pivoted to let others pass. And when their bodies brushed against each other, the kind of inadvertent physical contact that could and often did result in death in South Central, these people just smiled, said excuse me, and moved on.

That was until they saw Darius, gaped at him like Donald Sutherland at the end of *Invasion of the Body Snatchers,* and he remembered where he was. What he was. Their stares rendered him at once faceless and conspicuous, reminding him this was the deep suburbs, boy, the white world of Applebee's and Little League and crossing to the other side of the street and clutching your purse and finding another ATM. Clerks who asked may I help you with solicitous suspicion. Wary smiles following him like searchlights. Double takes. Folks wondering where he belonged, who he belonged to, how long he planned to stay, how many more like him might be coming here. Of course, they didn't all stare. Some of them didn't look at all, and that was worse, the trouble they went through to avoid his eyes.

He wanted to smash a store window. He wanted to get in their fat faces, wanted to holler, *What the fuck are you afraid of me for? You're the motherfucking Morlocks!* He tried to meet their eyes for a while, match them glare for stare, but he couldn't do it. He walked with his head down, looking for somewhere to hide.

As often happened when he was under extreme stress, Darius was suddenly seized with a bibliophilic Jones, needing to climb inside Conrad or Melville at this moment as bad as his mother had ever needed to hit a pipe. He headed for the bookstore. He'd find a good book, a book to comfort him, a book to sustain him.

He saw a white teenager gone hip-hop near the entrance to the store. As a rule, Darius couldn't stand poseurs, but when he saw the kid was wearing a sideways Lethal Injection ball cap, DJ Post-Mortem T-shirt, and oversized jeans—playing player with a cell to his ear in front of the Barnes & Noble—Darius caught himself hoping he'd be recognized. He would have been happy to sign an autograph right now—just for the human contact. The kid looked up and his eyes widened, but not with recognition. He looked scared.

Darius moved past the kid into the store, a deep breath to take in that familiar smell, the smell of order, of civilization. In the hood, only winos slept in public, but he saw people had nodded off right here in the bookstore, slumped in comfy chairs with magazines open in their laps just as they would at home. A clerk was coming at him now, a college-age girl with a nose ring, going out of her way to make him feel welcome. Darius cut away from her, fearing the kid would try to steer him into African-American Interest, not sure what he'd do to her when she did. He was having a hard time catching his breath. His chest hurt.

He bolted for the Starbucks inside the store, nearly stumbled on the steps to the raised dais, and got into line. He was sweating. He could see his face reflected in the pastry case. He was roughly the hew of the espresso brownies. Sheryl Crow piped out of a speaker in the ceiling.

He ordered a venti drip, fumbled for his wallet. His hands were shaking and he slopped some of his coffee onto the counter. The baristas pretended not to notice, probably figured he was gearing up to rob them. He turned away from the counter, headed for the bar. There were about twenty tables but every one was taken and no way was he going to take the empty chair next to the guy with a laptop or the new mom feeding a yogurt parfait to her baby.

He didn't realize he'd left his wallet on the counter until a little girl, maybe seven, tugged on the seam of his jeans. "You forgot this," she said, holding up his wallet. Darius squatted so that he was eye level with the girl. She had a soapy, sour-cream-and-geranium smell.

Darius opened his wallet, peeled off a C-note, something nice for the kid, let her bring home the Barbie Dream House courtesy of Crazy-D. The girl hesitated, her hand drawing back from the hundred, remembering she shouldn't be accepting anything from a stranger, and he felt ashamed. He knew it had been a ghetto move, but he wasn't playing pimp here. There was just no way to explain to this kid what her simple kindness (barely that, more like simple *politeness,* fucking grade-school good citizenship) had meant to him. Just enough humanity to prove to him he wasn't invisible, and he wanted a gesture of grandiosity equal to his rush of gratitude.

He was squatting there, holding the money out to the kid, when the girl's mother turned from the steel counter, expecting her daughter to be right beside her, scanning the restaurant in that instant way mothers do. Darius caught sight of the kid's mother in his peripheral vision, her face aimed like a gun at his head. "Stop," she shouted. "Don't touch her." And he felt a spasm of humiliation that nearly stopped his heart.

"Hey, good evening, ma'am," he soothed as the woman charged him, letting her do her lioness thing, figuring he could still calm her down, make her understand. "I was just, look . . ." He stood up, backing away as the woman yanked her child away from him. The kid looked scared now. "Listen," he stammered. "Please, just . . . listen." The woman spun away, putting her body between him and the girl—like he'd been trying to hurt the kid or something—and he snapped. "Bitch," he growled. "Don't you turn your back on me when I'm fuckin' talkin' to you!"

He could tell by the way they came through the doors that someone had hit the silent robbery alarm. Ventura County Sheriff's Deputies hot-footing it through New Fiction with shotguns angled at the floor—ready to bring their muzzles up on target, punch a softball-sized hole in him, and send him flying into the pastry case.

"On the floor," the point man barking at him. He was a black guy, gym rat, probably played some ball back when. "On the fucking floor now!"

The tile floor was clean and cool against his face. It had been years since he'd proned himself out for the Five-Oh—asphalt angels, they used to call it—but it was like riding a bike. Didn't matter how much time had passed since your last pop, you never forgot how to prostrate.

Darius sat handcuffed on the hard plastic seat in the back of the sheriff's cruiser. The helicopter was overhead. One of the movies had let out, and the crowd on the sidewalk was filing in. Some of them pointed, like he was a captured animal. The black deputy, whose nameplate said HAWKINS, asked him his name. When Darius told him, the guy laughed, said he was bullshitting. Darius said the guy was free to check his ID. The guy asked him if he was under the influence. Darius shook his head.

A sergeant showed up in a black-and-white SUV, a gray-haired guy with the bearing of a former Marine. And Darius saw Benji break out of the crowd to intercept the guy. Benji introduced himself, handed the guy a business card. The sergeant squinted at the card, looked Benji over. Then Darius saw him talking to the girl and her mother. The sergeant squatted down to talk to the girl, placed his hand on her shoulder to ask her something important. The girl shook her head emphatically. The sergeant conferred with Benji, the two of them walked over to Darius, and the sergeant opened his door.

"Appears we had a misunderstanding," the sergeant said, helping Darius out of the car. He told Darius to place his hands on the back of his head as he removed the handcuffs. Once the cuffs were off, the guy took two steps back from Darius before telling him he could put his arms down.

"I told him I was your attorney," Benji whispered.

"Get me home," Darius said. He felt woozy, feverish, as Benji led him to the car. Benji drove them out of the parking lot and headed for the Ventura Freeway. Twice on the ride home, Darius made Benji pull over so he could throw up.

PRESENT

Sundown. Yellowed palms clacked dryly over MacArthur Park. A holdout *helado* vendor pushed a dry-ice cart up the sidewalk, thumbing a tinny bicycle bell. The Mara kids dangled their bare legs from enameled fire escapes above Alvarado, watching brown bats hunt mosquitos over the lake.

Slammed DeVilles and El Caminos on rims were slotted down the slope from Park Boulevard. Chrome and candy apple covered every patch of city grass west of the lake. Doors blazoned with airbrushed Aztec warriors poised over prostrate sacrificial virgins. You could have walked across those hand-waxed hoods without touching the ground, but then some *vato* would probably kill you for defiling his ride.

Ben drove west on Wilshire, cut down Park View Boulevard, and ran straight into a pair of motor cops out of Central Traffic, figured they'd come to impound forty or fifty illegally parked lowriders—a recap to end all recaps. Then one of the motors popped the stand of his Harley and came around Ben's side of the car, cranking his hand for Ben to drop the window. The guy cocked his hip and leaned down to rest both hands on Ben's door, a big tactical no-no. He was an older cat with a bristly mustache, some booze coming up under his skin.

"Help you?" Soft eyes dropping to size Ben up, dismissing him for a wayward *turista*. Shit, this dude had probably been writing movers before Ben was born, his street sniff long gone. Guys sell their kids for a motor spot, the take-home ride, and tit jobs working security for location shoots, easy money.

"I'm here for the . . ." Ben nodded toward the MacArthur Palms Hotel.

The motor cop looked him over again, wrinkled his nose. "That's not a nightclub, son," he said.

"I know," Ben said.

"I mean, that's a seriously private party," the cop said.

"I know," Ben said.

"Well"—the cop lifted his hands from Ben's door and shrugged—"anyway, it's twenty bucks to park." He dug into the pocket of his uniform leather, pulled out a fat roll of bills wrapped in a rubber band. Ben stared at him.

"You lookin' at something there, friend?" The cop flashing his teeth, eyes poison.

"No, sir," Ben said, shifting in his seat to dig a twenty from his wallet.

"Thank you." The guy slipped off the rubber band, folded Ben's twenty over the top, snapped the rubber band back over the roll, and socked it into his jacket. "Drive safely in the City of Los Angeles."

Ben steered over the curb and parked along the sidewalk. He pulled his Beretta from under his seat, performed a low-light chamber check with the weapon down between his knees, and slid the Beretta into his waistband at the small of his back. He jogged across Park View Boulevard toward the hotel's Palladian glass doors. The MacArthur Palms had been built sometime in the twenties, gone to shit, been restored and registered as a historic landmark. The place now hosted weddings, Oscar parties, and L.A.'s underground cockfighting championship.

The shouldering smells of sweat, *carnitas,* and chronic hit Ben as he crossed the transom into the main lobby. The place was packed. Big ballers and shot-callers here representing every brown barrio south of the Kern River, shaved heads gleaming. Collared shirts with just the top buttons buttoned, hanging open over bone-white cotton wife-beaters, creased three-quarter Dickies shorts, knee-high white socks, and Bruce Lee creepers. From the visible ink on their arms and faces, Ben could see sworn enemies standing shoulder to shoulder, rival gleekas tossing their hood beefs for the evening to honor the Man on the Mesa. A gamecock had slipped its pen and wandered underfoot in the lobby, looking like another dazed party guest.

Las Víboras del Norte, a local *norteño* group, performed in the grand ballroom. Wearing their signature snakeskin suits, with matching snakeskin hatbands, belts, and boots, Las Víboras belted out a home-grown *corrido* of Carcosa's early years as a cartel *sicario*—hard-core lyrics about bloody shootouts with the DEA socked into a simple accordion polka. Ben thought he might have heard this one, but it was hard to tell. Young Carcosa, the two-gun barrio Robin Hood, blazed through a dozen L.A. *narcorridos*.

A pair of Tijuana *payasos* juggled torches in the Bronze Room, passing the torches behind their backs and between their legs to pitch them back and forth over the crowd with increasing speed. The flames snapped, gasped, and burbled, the torches spinning end over end. As he moved closer, Ben saw the jugglers' clown makeup—whorish ear-to-ear grins and vertical diamond eyelets—was actually tattooed on their grim faces. He'd heard of that happening to gypsies locked up in Matamoros Prison, some kind of scarlet letter.

Ben made a posse of shitfaced Sinaloan cowboys in their big white Stetsons and Resistols, wearing bolo ties over patterned cowboy shirts, tight Wranglers tucked into hand-tooled boots. They carried nickel-plated hand cannons in shoulder holsters or jammed into their waistbands behind ornate silver belt buckles. One of them must have gotten the idea he could shoot a torch in midair. Guy cranked off four booming rounds with his .50 Cal Desert Eagle, punching quarter-sized holes in the beamed ceiling, before his saddle pards wrestled the gun away from him.

Jacked on mescal and primos, the badass *matanza* monks from Mara Salvatrucha gathered in the corner of the Gold Room like a troop of sullen grizzlies, scratching MS 13 *placas* into the dark wainscoting with their *puñales*—ritual Nahua daggers with the sarcophagi of Catholic saints carved into the wooden handles. A *veterano* called Kreeper sliced a bloody MS into the meaty shoulder of his *carnalito,* who went by the name of Snare. Snare hissed through his teeth and pulled hard on a bottle of cloudy mescal, blood sheeting down his arm into a wide, wooden bowl. Ben watched Kreeper bring the bowl to his lips, tilting it until the bowl obscured his face, the blood sluicing down his chin, soaking his shirt. Kreeper gargled and spat—Gene Simmons style—and the bowl passed among the MS crew until everyone drank.

They'd jackhammered the tiles out of the courtyard to expose the bare earth they needed for the cockpit, the dirt neatly raked and chalked in the old way. It was a standing-room rogue's gallery on the bleachers.

Carcosa and his cortege sat on a railed dais draped with crepe-paper bunting of red, white, and green. At first, Ben thought Serena was sitting with him, but as he got closer Ben noted with some relief that the dusky damsel next to Carcosa wasn't his daughter, just his date for the evening. Ben didn't recognize the other men seated on the dais with Carcosa, but figured they'd come from the Mexican consulate across the street.

Four bodyguards stood at the corners of the platform, facing out toward the crowd. The guards wore tactical body armor and held F88 Austeyr rifles at port arms. Ben figured them for off-duty Mexican Federal Judicial Police moonlighting in *el norte.* He knew Carcosa used PJF tac squads as bodyguards when he traveled (and enlisted them for other chores Ben preferred not to think about).

Ben snaked through the crowd, making his way to the dais, careful to keep his hands in view. He must have crossed some invisible threshold because two of the bodyguards drew beads on him, fingers light on their triggers, exerting just enough pressure to activate their laser sights. Red dots danced on Ben's chest and he froze midstride. Another half-pound of pressure, he thought, and I'm *carnitas* from the waist up.

The crowd, fixed on the pit action, didn't appear to notice anything.

One of the bodyguards leaned over, lightly touched Carcosa's shoulder, and cupped his hand to Carcosa's ear. Carcosa nodded, glanced back over his shoulder. Their eyes met and Benji shrugged. Carcosa smiled, a wolfish smile that did not reach his glittering black eyes. He turned and spoke to the men seated around him. They stood without a word and stepped down from the dais through a hinged section of railing.

The bodyguards lowered their weapons and waved Ben on to the dais.

Ben sat next to Carcosa, but he kept his eyes forward.

"Gameness, Benji," Carcosa said. "See, the cock doesn't fight over a hen, doesn't fight over territory. He fights because it's in him to fight, because fuck you I don't like your fucking face is why."

"My dad calls it chutzpah," Ben said.

The ref was all business, unmoved by all the rabid shouting and waving as he stepped out into the pit in his crisp guayabera, black chinos, white socks, and black dress shoes polished to a high gloss. He stood in the center of the pit and beckoned the cockers for the next bout.

"*Claro.*" Carcosa nodded. "Your father is game, Benji. Doesn't fight for money or pussy, doesn't fight for headlines. He fights because he has *fuck you* in his soul. Gameness. The man couldn't stop if his life depended on it."

The cockers came from opposite sides of the pit, cradling their birds, whispering to them and brooding over them as the birds jerked their heads and muttered calliope curses. The birds had long, thick legs and a distinct, clawlike curve to their beaks. Rust-colored feathers trimmed tight against their tapered bodies, fed on cracked corn and alfalfa pellets soaked in chicken blood. Their combs and wattles had been neatly dubbed.

Carcosa sighed, uncapped the bottle of Patron, filled two glasses, lifted one, and nodded to Ben. Ben picked up his glass. "*Salud,*" Carcosa said.

"*L'chaim,*" Ben said.

The cockers faced in the center of the pit to bill their birds, each man holding his fighter with both hands. The men lunged at each other in a kind of halting dance, swinging their birds forward, then back. The birds stretched their necks, straining forward as if to kiss until their bills clicked together.

"What's on your mind, Benji?"

"I came to tell you I'm through," Ben said. "I'm not working for you anymore."

Gamblers shouted across the bleachers, waving fisted bills, fingers signing odds in a wagering pantomime unknown to Ben. At the far end of the pit, odds men scratched the house figures onto an antique chalkboard.

"Because?" Carcosa waited.

"Because I'm a cop," Ben said.

"I see." Carcosa smiled indulgently. "Knocked from our horse on the road to Damascus, were we?"

"Something like that," Ben said tightly, chafing a little in spite of himself.

The cockers opened the cigar boxes where they kept their gaffs, .223 cartridges pounded flat, sharpened for hours against an electric whetting stone. The cockers drew their gaffs and lashed them to the birds' legs with leather thongs.

"Listen to me, *joven*," Carcosa said, his hand resting heavily on Ben's knee. "When they put you in a car with this man Marquez, I'll admit I was concerned for you. He has big Mexican balls, this *charro*. But when this pairing was brought to my attention, I chose not to interfere. Leave him be, I said. My Benji is too smart to fall in love."

Brought to your attention, Ben thought, by Portillo, or somebody else?

"Was I wrong?" Carcosa frowned. "Have you fallen in love, Benji?"

The ref nodded to each cocker in turn, then gave the signal to pit the birds. The birds clashed, slashed, pecked, smashed breast against breast with a leathery thud.

"I found something I might be good at," Ben said. "Something that matters."

"Then I'm very concerned for you, Benji." Carcosa shook his head slowly.

The cockers swept up their birds. Ben watched one of the cockers lick the blood from his bird's eyes, the bird's head pecked down to the skull in patches. The man blew up the bird's neck, rippling its blood-glossed feathers, then worked his thumb into the bird's beak and blew down into the bird's open mouth. The cocker put the bird's entire head inside his mouth, puffing out his cheeks to force air into the bird. With each breath, the bird's body swelled like a bellows. Finally, the cocker turned his back to Carcosa and discretely twisted the bird's head off.

The ref squatted to pass his kerchief over his black shoes, wiping away dust and blood.

"You see this lovely girl beside me?" Carcosa said, letting Ben lean forward to surreptitiously take in the girl. "It's all right, she is *muy paisa,* this girl. Speaks no English, not a word. Her husband is a good man, a hard worker, washes dishes at the Jonathan Club. He loves his wife beyond reason, Benji, and yet here she sits." Carcosa rested a proprietary hand on the girl's tan thigh. "Because no one has told him the secret I am telling you now."

The next bout began, another pair of birds leaping, slashing, pecking each other to death—the wounded combatants Jackson Pollocking the dirt pit. "Benji, love is just the lie we tell our children because fucking is ugly. The cunt that opens for you will open wider for another." Carcosa caressed the girl's cheek with the back of his hand. The girl smiled, lowered her eyes coquettishly. "If she moans for you then she will moan still louder for another," he said. "Scream for him as you have never heard her scream."

"So please don't fall in love, *mijo,*" Carcosa said. "The world is older, uglier than you suppose. There are no countries, just as there are no marriages. The United States, the war on drugs, the LAPD, they're just the lies we tell to spare ourselves the ugliness of fucking."

"I didn't come here to be lectured," Ben said. "I just came to give you fair warning. I figured I owed you that much."

The cockers gathered up their birds, holding them close.

"He came to give me fair warning," Carcosa said, and he seemed to be addressing the crowd, seeking a witness to Ben's absurdity.

The ref suddenly snatched one of cockers by his wrist. The man yanked his wrist away, bit his fingernail off and swallowed it, but the damage was done. They'd all seen it. The cocker had grown out the fingernail on the little finger of his left hand. Cradling the bird, the man had slipped his fingernail into the bird's rectum to angry up the bird for the next round. The crowd turned ugly. They booed and shouted, giving the disgraced cocker the thumbs-down.

"Now, you see," Carcosa said. "This is very unfortunate. This fucks up a perfectly nice evening. This is cheating." The ref looked to Carcosa. Carcosa nodded grimly. Two of his PJF men vaulted the dais and charged the pit to grab the cocker. The ref fetched a pair of wooden slats from the edge of the pit. Ben saw three semicircles jigsawed into both slats.

The ref fitted the first slat into a pair of true-sunk slotted posts at the far end of the cockpit—Ben hadn't noticed the posts before. Jesus, they were putting this guy in stocks. The cocker cursed and fought. The PJF slammed his hands and head through the jigsawed spaces, then slid the top slat down and locked it into place.

The ref snatched a fresh bird from its pen, gaffed its legs, whispering to the bird as he carried it across the pen to the stocks. The ref placed the bird on the ground directly in front of the cocker's face. Seeing an eye-level enemy, the bird attacked. The man screamed, twisted and flopped, kicking divots into the dirt, but his head and hands were held fast. The crowd whooped and howled as the bird slashed the cocker's face until one of his gaffs hung up in the man's cheek. Caught off balance, the bird flapped and pecked in a mad panic. The ref grabbed the bird and pulled him off the man's face.

"This is his first offense," Carcosa said. "He keeps his eyes."

"Very civilized," Ben said. He stood, lifting the railing. "Tell me something. How many people do you have inside the department?"

"More than enough." Carcosa kept his eyes on the pit. I never laid a glove on the old man, Ben thought. I've never really even been in the same ring with him.

"Then why?" Ben asked. "Why me?"

"Your father had something I didn't, *mijo*." Carcosa shrugged. "I saw a chance to take it from him."

26

1997

Darius invited Benji to the gala launch party of his new gangsta-rap magazine, *Thug*. He booked the Wiltern Theater on Wilshire Boulevard, had it redecorated in Crip blue for the occasion, and packed the venue with enough beautiful bodies to put the fire inspector into cardiac arrest. Revelers freaked and grinded all night while Lethal Injection staples like DJ Post-Mortem, Erika Badon't, and Stash Capone belted out their earsplitting hits, their collective body heat and the pungent haze of marijuana turning the theater into a sweat lodge.

Darius, Jax, and Benji sat in a corner booth. An unending stream of people approached Darius with accolades and entreaties, seeking an extension on some loan, a record deal, or maybe a cocaine franchise. Darius had come to suspect the feds and other enemies were watching him, so parties like this became his boardroom. He hid in the open, conducting his business transactions in the clamorous privacy of a crowd because all the noise would render useless any hidden recorder.

Around midnight, Darius signaled to Jax that he no longer wished to be disturbed, Jax sliding out of his seat to stand in front of the booth. One look at Jax blocking their way to the booth, and people decided their business with Darius could wait. Jax looked like a malevolent cigar-store Indian in an El Debarge wig.

Darius dug another Adderall out of the pill bottle in his jacket pocket. Amphetamines, Benji thought. Some Beverly Hills shrink was making a fortune on Darius. The guy had him on speed, sleeping pills, anti-depressants, anti-anxiety pills. Jax didn't approve of his Elvis num-nums either, but Darius refused to listen to either of them. He seemed to be losing a lot of weight. "Keep this on the down low," Darius said, dry-swallowing another pill. "We're getting married after she graduates."

Benji turned to Jax, like what the fuck is he talking about? But Jax refused to look at him. "What about Carcosa?" Benji asked, swirling his ice cubes with a blue plastic Lethal Injection stirrer.

"I'm going to ask for his blessing," Darius said. "I'm playing this one straight. I haven't even touched her, Benji. Not once. At first, I thought she might have a Jody on the side, but she's just *muy católica.* You know, 'below the chin, it's a sin.' "

"You're fucking with me," Benji said, wondering if he and Jax could place Darius somewhere for observation. His delusions were going to get them all killed.

"I'm serious as a drive-by," Darius said. "I'm going to get baptized. I know that sounds whack, but if I don't, she says I wind up in limbo with the bad guys from *Superman II.*" Benji was pretty sure the Catholic repository for whoremongers and idolaters was a few tiers south of limbo, but he didn't want to spoil the mood here.

"I want you to be my best man, dog." Darius smiled, drumming his fingers on the leather-bound copy of *Ivanhoe* in his lap.

Benji felt like Darius had sucker-punched him, but asking Benji to be his best man was only Darius's left-handed jab, his power punch yet to come. Benji's glass jaw was still unprotected, a perfect target for Darius's shattering right cross.

"What about Jax?" Benji asked him.

"Already ran it by him," Darius said. "He doesn't trip on that shit."

Of course not, Benji thought, because it's never going to happen. "I'd be honored, Darius," he said, hoping Darius didn't feel patronized by his pasted smile. "But what in the name of God will I do for your bachelor party?"

"Look, there's somethin' else I have to ask you," Darius said. "You've got another year of law school, and after you take the bar, I want you to be my Robert Duvall." Darius knew the word as well as Benji did, but he was playing the earthy homeboy for this pitch and he must have figured "consigliere" would sound out of character. "You and Jax are the only solid I got, and Jax isn't going to last forever."

"Isn't there anybody else?"

"You mean anybody black," he said. "Nobody I trust."

"I've always suspected you were a closet racist," Benji said.

"I'm a realist," Darius said. "I know every nigga claimin' he's down with me is just waitin' for his chance to take what I got. Like pit bulls, everybody waggin' their tail when I come around, but if I ever slip and fall, they'll be climbin' over each other to tear me apart. Today's supplicant is tomorrow's usurper. It's like the man says, even a dog can shake hands."

"You already have an attorney," Benji said. "A good one."

"Word," Darius conceded. "Your daddy's all that, but he's always scopin' for himself and I need a cut man to stay in my corner for all twelve rounds. You had my back out there in Klan country, and I haven't forgotten how you stuck by a nigga out there. I'm never gone forget that.

"See, Benji, I'm into this publishin' shit now," Darius said, popping another pill that Benji didn't recognize. "By the time you're out of school, I'll be slidin' into cable programmin', clothin', fragrances, video games, maybe producin' my own movies. Last week, I went to the Ivy with a couple of Saudis who might want to bankroll a hip-hop theme park."

"By the time I get out of school," Benji said, "you'll be growing out your toenails and saving your urine in jars."

"What I need is a partner to watch my back twenty-four/seven," Darius said.

"You already have Jax," Benji said.

"I need you, Benji."

Here at last was Darius's power punch, his John Wayne haymaker. Benji rocked back on his heels, trying to roll with it, but it was no damn good. It wasn't like he couldn't feel himself being manipulated. Darius wasn't a sneaky puncher and their friendship was no mere contrivance; Darius's plan required the bond only a real friendship would forge.

Benji had always had the nagging sense that he was being groomed for something. Darius wanted someone almost as smart as Big Ben, but not too smart, because he needed someone he would be able to control. And the genius of it was Benji didn't care. He was still touched by Darius's trust, somehow honored that Darius had finally found a use for him.

"I'll think about it," Benji told him and that seemed to satisfy Darius for the moment.

DJ Post-Mortem reeled out of the crowd and stumbled against their table, knocking glasses over. Dried vomit covered his chin. "D, this lime's out of juice," he slurred morosely. "Played the fuck out."

Jax grabbed a fistful of Post-Mortem's collar to keep him from going over again. "Boy's crunker than shit," Jax said.

"Let me tell y'all about *this* depraved motherfucker," Darius said, talking about Post-Mortem like he wasn't even there with them, which in a sense the guy wasn't. "Boy got more goddamned pussy than any natural man got a right to, fine pussy, fat pussy, freaky pussy, rainy-day pussy, model pussy, actress pussy, Madonna pussy. Motherfucker needs to store his unused pussy off-site, feel me? But he don't care, not this'ere. See, what this boy needs, the really-real medicine this sick-ass chester *got* to have, is *teenage* pussy."

Darius shook his head, tracing lines in the tablecloth with his manicured fingernail, like Post-Mortem was a complex equation. "And homie?" He sighed. "I have *admonished* this prodigal nigga about his ham-slidin' issues, in one ear and out the other. Nigga films himself stuntin' thirteen-, fourteen-year-old girls, shit winds up on the Internet, and who you think pays out those hush-ducats?"

"Idi Amin," Benji said.

"His latest performance," Darius said, good and hot about this now.

"He goin' for the motherfuckin' Oscar, pokes this poor girl down her mudhole, just as filthy as you please. Then he *pisses* all over her. They fixin' to take back his Image award and I'm about done cuttin' quiet-checks to cover all this Humbert Humbert shit."

"Come on, let's get his narrow ass home." Jax led Post-Mortem by the collar, and the four of them snaked through the crowd to the exit. Jax had left Darius's black Suburban parked in front of the Wiltern marquee in the passenger-loading zone with the keys in the ignition. No question that the Suburban would be waiting when they were ready to leave. Nobody fucked with Darius's ride.

They stepped out of the theater and into the cool night air, blue carpet covering the wide sidewalk from the main entrance to the street. A human wall in tight black SECURITY T-shirts stood with their massive arms akimbo behind blue velvet ropes on either side of the carpet. Beyond the barriers, hard-core fans jostled each other for a glimpse at DJ Post-Mortem. Upstarts thrust their demo CDs at him through the ropes and slim young women in stylish cocktail dresses begged to be let into the party.

Then a hand grenade rolled under the ropes and everything slowed way down. The crowd seemed to take in a single gasp, as though bracing for the explosion, but the grenade hissed, leaking dark red smoke. Another grenade sailed over their heads and landed on the carpet in front of Benji. It was followed by another, and another. The air blushed with rolling red smoke.

"Get to the car," Darius said. He opened *Ivanhoe* and palmed his Walther PPK from the hollowed-out pages. Jax let go of Post-Mortem and stepped in front of him. He crossed his arms to reach for the twin shoulder holsters under his coat, and his hands came out with matching pistols. Someone screamed. The crowd surged and broke through the velvet ropes. Two security guards were knocked off their feet and trampled. The stampede swallowed the other guards like a wave, and Benji lost track of Darius. Then Benji heard the fire alarm clanging inside the theater, and guests poured out of the exits in a bustling panic. People ran in all directions, smashed into each other, scrambling over the fallen. Benji couldn't make out the Suburban through the smoke. Had he just lost his bearings or had Darius and Jax already left him?

Gunfire erupted to his left, and Benji dropped into a crouch just as razor-thin trails sliced through the particulate smoke above him. He couldn't actually see the bullets flying, but their vaporous trajectories momentarily etched in the heavy smoke, like torpedoes cutting through deep water.

Post-Mortem collapsed on the carpet in front of him, and Benji crawled to him. He'd been shot twice in the upper chest. Benji held his shoulders while violent spasms racked his body. Post-Mortem might have been trying to talk, but all that came out of his mouth was blood. Darius crouched beside Benji, gripping his arm. "He's through," Darius said. "Leave him be."

Beyond the carpet, figures seemed to coagulate in the swirling smoke, and then vaporize again. Benji counted at least four armed men lurking in the murky red fumes. Three of them wore surplus-store gas masks and red baseball caps. One wore swim goggles and a red bandanna over his mouth and nose. The shooters came through the smoke, trying to flank them.

"Go for the car," Jax said. He stepped over Post-Mortem's body and stood in front of them with his guns at his sides, the pose some matter of pride with him. Jax cowered from no man and if a bullet found him, it would find him standing. "Now," Jax said, firing into the smoke. He planted his feet and pivoted his torso like a turret. Then he jerked to one side like something powerful had tugged his arm, and the gun fell from his left hand.

Benji dashed for the car, opened the Suburban, crawled across the console, and started the engine. He threw it in reverse, wheels jumping the curb, and angled the car between Darius and the stalkers. Glowing bullets struck the Suburban, tracers or some kind of weird incendiery round. Ben could smell the phosphorous. Benji threw it in Park, got out of the car, and grabbed Jax by his collar, tracers plowing the air around him. Darius fired his Walther over Jax's shoulder as Benji fumbled the rear door open. Darius shoved Jax into the backseat and lay on top of him. "Drive," he shouted. "Go! Go!"

Benji hit the gas, cranking the wheel. Rounds pummeled the armored panels in the doors and slammed against the bullet-resistant acrylic windows, but not even the burning stuff got through. Benji felt the left rear tire go soft, but Darius had filled all four of them with foam and the tire held. He drove the Suburban over the concrete median, crushing a sapling, and headed west on Wilshire Boulevard.

Jax sat up. He gripped his left bicep and blood welled between his fingers. Benji heard sirens approaching. "Get off the main drag," Jax said.

"I'll take you to a hospital," Benji told him.

"No," Jax said. "Take me back to the crib."

"Doctors have to call Five-Oh on every hit who walks into the ER," Darius said. "Just take us home. We can take care of this."

They brought Jax into Darius's house and sat him at the kitchen table. Darius pulled a big stainless-steel salad bowl out of the cabinet and slid the bowl under Jax's arm to catch some of the blood. Then Darius uncapped a full bottle of Tanqueray gin and handed the bottle to him. Jax put the bottle to his lips and took a long pull. He paused to breathe and took another swig. When he'd finished half the bottle, he slid it across the table to Benji. Benji tilted back the bottle, swallowing as much as he could handle, then swallowing some more. Jax smiled.

Darius went into the pantry and came out with his toolbox and a case of Winchester .45-caliber target rounds. He took a pair of pliers out of the toolbox and used them to pull one of the bullets out of its brass casing. Then he turned the shell casing over and used his index finger to tap the gunpowder out onto a sheet of newsprint. He repeated the process again and again, dumping the powder in a growing pile. "Family remedy," Jax said, and took another long swallow of gin.

Darius used one of Big Ben's business cards to rake the gunpowder, consolidating the pile. "Jax's great-great-grandmomma was a Mescalero Apache," he said.

"My great-great-grandmother was a Warsaw washwoman," Benji said. "I think she would want us to call an ambulance."

Darius handed Benji a pair of blue-handled scissors. "If you want to help, cut him out of that shirt," Darius said. "It's ruined anyway."

Benji stood behind Jax, slipped one blade of the scissors under his collar, and cut down through the shirt until he reached the tail. Once he had the shirt in two pieces, Benji carefully peeled the blood-soaked garment away from his body. He'd never seen anything like Jax's skin, his torso an ugly carapace of mottled keloid scar tissue.

In prisons all over the state, enemies had stuck Jax with any kind of cell-made shank they could devise. Spoons fashioned into crude stabbing weapons. License plates sharpened into slashing tools and always dipped in shit to guarantee infection. They had a saying inside: fistfights are for free men. Up in Pelican Bay, the white screws in SHU had even pitted him against big oaks from the Aryan Brotherhood, betting on their fights like they were gladiators. Over the years, Jax's stubborn skin had knitted unevenly over countless brutal wounds that should have killed him.

Jax placed a black and mild cigarillo between his lips, and Darius lit it for him. Jax drew deeply on it and blew the smoke out his wide nostrils. "Hurry the fuck up," Jax said.

Darius carefully tore the newspaper around his pile and folded the gunpowder into a small cylindrical parcel that resembled a miniature crepe. Jax took his hand away from his bicep and his blood poured cleanly out of both ends of the wound—entry and exit. Darius grimaced and jammed the parcel into the entry wound, twisting and pushing it. "Don't tear it," Jax said. When Darius had pushed all the way through and both ends of the parcel were poking out of Jax's arm, Jax drew on his cigarillo and held it between his thumb and forefinger. Then Darius put a whole bullet into Jax's mouth and he worked it around like a lozenge until he had it between his back teeth. Jax touched the glowing end of the cigarillo to the parcel. Yellow sparks sprayed out both ends of the wound. Jax grimaced and bit down on the bullet. The kitchen filled with the smell of cordite and burning flesh. Benji heard the jaguar yowling upstairs and figured the cat must have scented all the blood. When the wound had been cauterized, Jax spat the bullet out onto the bloody table. Then his head lolled against his chest and he passed out.

Darius carried the salad bowl upstairs to let the Jaguar lap the blood. Then he called the cell phone of a Rampart cop he knew working morning watch and told the cop to get his black ass over the Cahuenga Pass and round up Situation Mike. The cop and his partner located Mike wandering Ventura Boulevard. They cuffed him, threw him in their black-and-white, and brought him to Darius inside of an hour.

The nameplates on the two cops' uniforms read RISLEY and MAPES. On the street they were known as Batman and Robin for their stealth, inseparability, and their uncanny ability to be at the right place at the right time. As they stepped into the living room, Risley's eyes passed over Benji without lingering. His business was with Darius, and he seemed to dismiss Benji as a mildly distasteful addition to the décor. If Benji had encountered him under other circumstances, Risley would have impressed him as a model officer. His uniform appearance was impeccable and he cut a dashing figure, projecting both sophistication and street cunning. He would have been movie-star handsome in his Billy Dee Williams mustache, but his prominent eyebrows, which threatened to meet in the center, made him look somehow predatory.

Risley's partner didn't seem to notice Benji at all. Mapes lumbered into the room with a troll-like slouch. He was stout, with no appreciable neck, and sloping shoulders. His uniform fit him poorly and his boots were not shined. Mapes was a mouth breather, and his dull eyes held the simple brutality of a sadistic child's. He nakedly worshipped his partner, and Risley seemed to have him on some kind of psychic choke chain. He was sure Mapes took no action without first receiving specific instructions from Risley. Benji filed this info away the way you'd palm somebody's flatware.

Once they removed Mike's cuffs, Darius handed Risley and Mapes five hundred each. The moment Darius turned his back on him, Risley transformed. It was instantaneous, almost lycanthropic, terrifying to behold. It wasn't just the way Risley's eyes fixed on the base of Darius's skull, reacquiring their target. It was in the set of his jaw, seeping out of the pores around his nose, every muscle marinating in murder. Benji recalled what Darius had told him about pit bulls ready to set upon him at the first sign of weakness. *You were there at the Wiltern.* A raw, tight knowing that Benji felt way back in his tonsils—wolf knowledge, Gretchen called it. *Maybe not one of the actual shooters, but you damn well had something to do with it.*

Risley caught Benji staring at him. He cocked his head, eyebrows raised, jailhouse daring Benji to open his fucking mouth. Benji dropped his eyes and Risley punked him with a long, low chuckle. Risley did a slow, runway-model turn, an exhibition of his sleeve-bursting arms, and stalked out the door with Mapes. Benji sighed, relieved to see the cops gone.

As soon as they left, Situation Mike plopped on the overstuffed couch like a bored kid. He wore a torn Harley-Davidson T-shirt, faded jeans, and motorcycle boots. His hollow cheeks and the yellowish tint of his eyes made Benji wonder if the man had some deadly strain of hepatitis. He made Keith Richards look like Eva Marie Saint.

Darius received the bulk of his basin intelligence from Situation Mike. It was Carcosa who had first told him Mike heard things, all kinds of things, and he'd tattle to anyone with the cash to refill a needle. Mike was an equal-opportunity snitch. He'd even talk to cops, if it came to that. They always knew where to find him.

Situation Mike used to ride with the Nazi Saddle Tramps back when the outlaw bikers controlled all the guns and speed that came through the San Fernando Valley—before the feds had pushed them out into the badlands. Back then, when Mike was still young and beautiful, he'd scream up and down the 405 astride a custom bike of his own design. He would run down to San Diego with his saddlebags full of cash and make it back home with the dope in time to catch the sunset from his redwood hot tub. With his bike, his dope, his money, his smile, and thick blond hair spilling over his tan shoulders, Mike had every bored housewife and her teenage daughter in the valley lining up to suck his dick. He had it all. Then Mike tasted heroin and it all went away.

By the time Carcosa introduced him to Darius, Situation Mike was just another hype, pulling small-time burglaries and occasionally forging checks to fix. Mike would meet his man early, usually somewhere on Ventura Boulevard and fix first thing in the morning. That left him the rest of the day to hustle what he could in order to pay for tomorrow's medicine. He had stopped getting high from heroin years ago. Now Mike fixed only to stave off the agony of withdrawal. He would rather die than go through that shit again. It wasn't like he didn't get high on other stuff. If Mike had an especially profitable day, he might treat himself to some crystal meth, but that was dessert. Heroin was his nourishment.

Darius took a baggie of Mexican Brown out of his pocket and weighed it in his palm. Mike licked his lips. Darius had once told Benji that Mike needed his smack the same way Michael Jackson needs Boy Scouts.

"They're a merc outfit," Mike said. He grabbed a handful of blue M&M's from the candy dish on the coffee table in front of him. "Bounty hunters out of the projects, a few ex-cops."

"Who hired them?" Darius frowned.

"Certain Death," Mike said, popping the candies into his mouth. "He's been setting it up for a while, ever since your boy punked him on MTV." If he had known all this, Benji thought, why in the hell hadn't he warned Darius about it in advance. Benji thought Mike was lying through his yellow teeth, just regurgitating some prerecorded bullshit Risley had fed him in the car on the way here, but Darius seemed to buy it retail.

"Where is he now?"

"He's in Vegas, staying in a suite at the Hard Rock," Mike said. "He's hired away six of Farrakhan's security people to guard him day and night."

Darius nodded thoughtfully. He tossed Mike the baggie of heroin and told him to find his own way out. "This East Coast–West Coast shit is getting out of hand," Darius told Benji. "When Jax comes around, he and I'll go to Vegas to negotiate with Certain Death."

PRESENT

To commemorate his twentieth year on the job, everyone in 77th Detectives Bureau went in on a cake and cuff links for Detective Big Mitch Keyes. They made a sign for him: CONGRATULATIONS, DETECTIVE KEYES! TWENTY YEARS AND COUNTING! It was a nominal surprise. Chuin took Keyes out to serve some of his wits with subpoenas and brought Keyes back at the appointed time. Marquez took the kid up to Detectives after their roll call for a quick piece of cake.

Someone had tracked down a photo of Keyes from his academy days. In the photo, he looked lean, handsome, a dashing figure in his new uniform. Nobody'd meant to sucker punch him here. It was the kind of thing where you couldn't have known just how bad it would be—how assaultive—until you saw the three-hundred-fifty-pound Keyes staring at his former self while the whole bureau sang "For He's a Jolly Good Fellow."

The guy had been handsome once. Now he was so abominably obese he had to completely take off his pants to shit, just couldn't get situated on the can any other way. You could duck into the second-floor Christian Science Reading Room any given morning and see Keyes's Big & Tall slacks draped over the stall like vaudevillian bloomers.

My brother, Marquez thought, I'm not far behind you—both of us bound for one of those stucco shoe boxes out in Fontana or maybe Ontario, with bars on the windows and white rocks for a lawn. Hook up with some broad who collects Hummel figurines and take a cruise to Ensenada once a year. Tell the same war stories over and over. Grill some Costco chicken on the patio, listen to AM radio, and bitch about the world going down the toilet. Your whole career reduced to one of those while-you-wait bobble-head cartoons they put on your retirement flier. And your buddies drop in to drop twenty a plate for an open bar at the Rock Garden, get bombed on nostalgia and domestic beer. Then somebody drives you home, and come Monday they're back at work and you're taking trips to the hardware store just to keep busy. There but for the grace . . .

"You okay?" Marquez tried to keep his voice light, clapping Keyes on the shoulder.

"No," Keyes whispered. "Not for a long time."

Marquez had gotten behind on the kid's performance evaluations so he got Ben's P1 Book out of the cabinet, opened the binder in front of the kid, and told him to type up a month's worth of his own ratings. "Don't make yourself look like Jack Lord," Marquez said. "But don't make yourself look like Barney Fife either. And go easy on the three-dollar words. I got a rep to protect here." When the kid was done, he handed over his entries to Marquez. Marquez signed them one after the other, dropped them into Vintner's box, and he and Ben headed out.

Off to the east, you could see purple storm clouds boiling up over the San Gabriels, but the hood sky was brilliant blue, brushed clean by a warm offshore breeze—not the sawtoothed Santa Anas that turned eyeballs to iodine and left every lip cracked and bleeding. This was more like a sigh, South Central relaxing its shoulders. Even the radio was quiet. Fractal dandelions drifted across Slauson Avenue, and for a second you could almost forget where you were.

They answered a few radio calls, a 415 group—baseheads at the Arco station on Fifty-fourth and Normandie, pissing on the pumps in some kind of protest. They handled a Domestic over on the East Side and a 211 on Crenshaw that turned out to be two drunks fighting over a half-eaten burger. Marquez had the guys shake and then bought them each a fresh one.

It was after sundown and Ben said he could use a little nosh himself, so they held on to the call, bought *huarache* and chitlins at Family Soul Mex on Fig, and took the chow with them to watch the Lucha Libre at the old brick firehouse on Florence. The match was packed, Mexican families filing in from as far away as Maywood, but the doorman recognized Marquez and carried some chairs right up front for them. Marquez bet Ben twenty bucks his Graffiti Kid would put Mysterio on his hairy ass. Then, the moment his back was turned, Mysterio hit the Graffiti Kid with a folding chair. Boos and hisses as the Kid rolled out of the ring and landed at their feet. Ben laughed so hard some of his *horchata* came out his nose. "*Híjole,* come on, Jesus!" Marquez stood and shouted. "*Ándale,* you bum!" Mysterio was taunting the crowd and all seemed lost, but the Kid stirred, regained his feet, and charged back into the ring. He took Mysterio down with a spinning forearm shiver, and cheers and applause shook the station.

They were heading back up Florence when Marquez's snitch phone chirped. "*Díme,*" he said.

"Got somethin' for you," Ronny said.

"Yeah?"

"Found this duffel bag in a dumpster behind the wash house on Normandie," Ronny said. "Says 'Calle Respeto' on the side. Some stains on it might be blood."

"Tell me you left it where you found it," Marquez said.

"Naw, man," Ronny said. "I got it with me here at the stables."

"Don't move," Marquez told him. "I'll be there in five."

Marquez took them west on Fig, crossing under the Century Freeway into the County. Ramshackle apartment buildings and seedy motels gave way to industrial structures. Featureless behemoths of brick and cement crowded the long blocks. It was a lot darker here.

"There are stables out here?" Ben asked.

Marquez nodded. "Stables were here first," he said. "I used to ride here when I was a kid. They say Bill Pickett used to keep horses here."

"Who's Bill Pickett?"

"Jesus Fucking Christ," Marquez grumbled.

Marquez killed the lights and parked the black-and-white at 132nd, pulling over next to the train tracks. Sun-warped particleboard and assorted construction castoffs formed a sagging jigsaw fence along 132nd. Even taggers had found it an unworthy canvas.

He reached across the console to key the Convertacom. "Twelve-A-Forty-five we're Code Six at 132nd and Athens in the County," he said. Ben tensed. Marquez usually waited until the last minute to put them Code Six anywhere, let alone clue the RTO in to the fact that they were out here poaching in the sheriff's territory.

"Pop the tube," Marquez told him quietly. "This smells like shit all of a sudden." Ben pulled the Remington 870 from the rack and jacked a round into the chamber. He followed Marquez up a short trail that led from the tracks into the corral. They stepped around bald tires, box springs, and an old stove. Mud sucked at their boots. They passed a rusted Corvette chassis and someone's fishing boat on a trailer. An old Lufkin oil pump seesawed behind a stand of bearded palms. Over the tops of the stables, Ben could see searchlights from the strip club down on Figueroa.

"Ronny?" Marquez called, and a few Tennessee walkers poked their heads out over their low stable doors. Marquez patted them as he passed. The last door on the left hung open.

Ben held on the open door with the shotgun, stepping slowly through the mud. Something dashed out of the dark and Ben almost shot a goat, its frog eyes glowing green in the beam of the flashlight mounted under his shotgun. He angled the shotgun, illuminating the inside of the stable, and saw a pair of sneakers three feet off the ground.

"Marquez," Ben whispered, but Marquez was already pushing past him into the stable, instinctively wrapping his arms around Ronny's legs to take his weight from the beam.

"You're all right, Ronny," Marquez huffed. "I gotcha, buddy."

"Miguel," Ben said.

"Fuck!" Marquez let his arms fall away and the body swung. They'd garroted Ronny with bailing wire and hung him from one of the crossbeams inside the stable, his tongue swollen and purple. He hadn't been dead long. One of Marquez's business cards was safety-pinned to Ronny's shirt.

The boards over them groaned and fine dust trickled down between the slats, someone walking on the roof. Ben shoved Marquez as the rounds bored down at them through the roof, moonlight slotting in through a full-auto honeycomb. Ronny's body jerked as bullets struck it and some of the hay caught fire. Ben and Marquez shooting up through a storm of splinters. Flames climbed the walls. Ben heard running footsteps, a grunt of effort as the shooter launched off the roof into the alley. He ran from the stable, sprinting for the alley. Marquez was behind him, barking out a help call as he ran. Horses were kicking the flimsy walls out of their enclosures, running in every direction.

Ben angled the shotgun at the gate, blasted the lock, and kicked it open. He charged into the alley and headlights filled his vision, an Escalade roaring at him. A guy in a ski mask hung out the passenger window with a MAC-11. The MAC's muzzle flickered—.380s buzzing out at sixteen hundred per minute—wasted because the guy mashed as the Escalade rolled over a pothole. He let his muzzle drop and clots of mud lifted from the ground in front of Ben.

Panicked, Ben short-stroked his Remington. The firing pin dinged an empty chamber, and he dropped the shotgun in the mud, went for his Beretta and fired. Rounds whanged the hood, pocked the windshield. He dove and rolled as the Escalade blasted past him out on to 132nd.

Ben was up and running out of the alley. He hadn't even gotten a plate. Marquez pulled the black-and-white in front of him, slowed but didn't stop as Ben swung open the passenger door. Lights and sirens. They chased the

Escalade north up the train tracks, Marquez broadcasting their location as he drove across 124th, 120th. Cars locked their brakes, tires squealing, as the black-and-white leaped the curb across El Segundo. The passenger fired out the back of the Escalade and rounds skipped off the deck, tumbling up into the Crown Vic's grille. Steam hissed from the radiator.

Then Ben saw the Night Sun wash over the Escalade. The air unit was overhead now, broadcasting their location to responding units. The track split at 117th Street. The Escalade cut west and Marquez followed them across a narrow steel trellis that spanned the Harbor Freeway and dumped them out onto Broadway. The Escalade continued west along the tracks.

"Air 10 to black-and-white on the train tracks," the TFO said. *"Check your six guys. There's a Suburban coming up behind you! Behind you!"*

A guy leaned out the passenger window of the Suburban, firing a TEC-9. Rounds sawed through the Crown Vic's rear window. Glass peppered the passenger compartment and Ben spun around to kneel backward in his seat, palmed the nine into his left hand and fired back out the window, using the post as a barricade. The Suburban swerved, kicking up gravel, but kept after them. Ben went to slide-lock, dropped his mag, and pulled a fresh one from the pouch on his Sam Browne.

Another burst from the guy in the Escalade stitched deep commas across the hood of the black-and-white, punching through the windshield. Ben and Marquez hunched low in their seats, cauliflower florets bursting from their foam headrests as the .380 rounds passed through them.

"Fuck this." Marquez dropped it into neutral, into a squealing bootlegger's turn, left the tracks, and smashed through a chain-link fence, down the ice-plant embankment on to the 105 Freeway. Panic horns and the crunch of at least two collisions as the black-and-white skidded into a four-wheel drift across eastbound lanes. The Escalade and the Suburban pursued them onto the freeway. News helicopters were over the chase now, big carrion birds broadcasting live.

Marquez took them north at the 110 interchange on the elevated four-lane viaduct. The Crown Vic chuffed and shuddered, the radiator belching tufts of steam. Marquez hit the brakes and cranked the wheel. The black-and-white swung laterally and stopped, blocking northbound lanes.

"What're you doing?"

"This'll do," Marquez said calmly. He hit the dash button to pop the trunk, opened his door, and stepped unhurriedly around the back of the car to pull his Urban Police Rifle from its case. Ben took a kneeling position next to him behind the black-and-white. The Escalade and the Suburban were coming side by side up the narrow viaduct now, slowing to a crawl because they saw the black-and-white had stopped. Air 10's Night Sun followed their tentative progress. Even without using the optics, Marquez could see them clearly now. There were two in each ride, all of them dressed down for the mission. They wore North Carolina ball caps and blue bandannas over their faces, except the passenger in the Escalade, who had on a blue ski mask.

"*Twelve-A-Forty-five is Code Robert on the Century Interchange.*" The TFO must have seen the play now. "*Air Ten to all responding units: stay off the viaduct or we'll have cross fire.*"

Marquez seated the mag and pulled back the bolt on the UPR, braced the stock against his hip while he pinched some Red Man out of his pouch. He put the stock to his shoulder, rested his elbow on the hood, and peered through the ACOG sight.

"Can you hit them from here?"

Marquez spat. "Watch."

He emptied his twenty-round magazine in less than ten seconds, sweeping the barrel right to left. The SUV's windshield turned to crushed ice and the gangsters jerked, shuddered, and slumped in their seats. Atomized blood misted the passenger compartment and both cars idled forward, rudderless. The Suburban hit the concrete retaining wall and stopped. The Escalade continued a few more feet. Then the passenger door of the Escalade swung open, and the guy in the ski mask rolled out. He'd been hit in the upper arm, but nowhere else that Marquez could see.

He stared at Marquez, eyes showing white inside the mask. Then he ran across the lanes and leaped off the viaduct into space. They had to be at least eighty feet up.

Marquez and Ben rushed to the edge, Marquez thinking maybe this dude had opted out of life in prison with a swan onto Broadway, but the guy had known exactly what he was doing when he jumped. He'd landed on the sloped roof of the shelter over the elevated Green Line station. Marquez watched the guy slide down the roof and drop onto the platform. Too many people there to risk a shot, and the guy was taking the stairs down to Broadway. They were going to lose sight of him.

Ben braced his boot on the concrete wall, about to jump when Marquez grabbed his collar. "Absolutely not," he said.

Air Ten was on him. Marquez heard the TFO guiding units onto Broadway and he saw a black-and-white streaking up Broadway under the overpass, heard its tires bark. He heard the officers giving the suspect commands, proning him out in the street.

"They got him," Marquez said.

Marquez and Ben did their separate walk-throughs for RHD, the District Attorney's Rollout Team, the city attorney, and the feds, which took them hours because the scene stretched over miles back into the county.

There was considerable debate among the department's LERI quislings whether or not to even treat the chase as a vehicle pursuit for reporting purposes. After all, LAPD officers had been the quarry, a wrinkle that delighted local broadcasters, who ran helicopter footage of the chase long into the night.

Three of the suspects were dead. A fourth was in custody, but there was some confusion about which unit had actually arrested the guy and where they'd transported him. He wasn't logged in at 77th, wasn't in any of the downstairs holding tanks or the detective interview rooms. He wasn't at Southwest or Southeast. For a while they were saying somebody had taken him to Parker Center for RHD.

Marquez and Ben were interviewed separately about the incident in the presence of their league attorney. The department had a policy against shooting at or from moving vehicles, a policy these two officers would seem to have spectacularly violated, firing fore and aft from their black-and-white during the chase. But the league attorney didn't seem too concerned. He figured they had all been IDOL shots, fired in Immediate Defense of Life, so they would probably be found In Policy. Marquez's deployment of the UPR was another question, but the league mouthpiece pointed out they'd been facing superior numbers and firepower.

It was after midnight when the suits finally turned them loose and Vintner told them to go home and get some sleep. They were still down in the locker room when Chuin called on the inside line to tell him he'd finally located the fourth suspect, said he needed Marquez for identification.

Since they'd already changed over into their civvies, Vintner let them borrow a plain car to take out to the scene.

They'd found him inside the tunnel walkway that ran under the Harbor Freeway at Sixty-ninth, between Flower and Grand. Yellow tape stretched across the mouth of the tunnel, the scene's inner perimeter. The outer perimeter was wider, uniforms keeping the media and lookie-loos a block away.

"What'd you bring him for?" Chuin cocked his head at Ben as they approached the tape.

"I can wait in the car," Ben said.

"He's okay," Marquez said.

"He's a fucking changeling, man." Chuin sneered at Ben. "I can see the zipper."

"He's my partner," Marquez said.

"Okay." Chuin puffed his cheeks and blew them out. "Your funeral."

Marquez could see where he'd winged the guy, taken some flesh off his upper arm, but the guy had picked up a few more holes since then. Two rounds placed in his ten-ring and one through his grape—LAPD's Mozambique. The blood pooled around his head was still bright and marbled with yellowish fluid.

"Standard failure drill," Chuin said. "He might as well have signed it for us." Marquez absently touched his scar.

The impact had blown the guy's ski mask off. That or Risley had removed it as a final insult before the coup de grâce. The mask lay next to the body, soaked in his blood.

"You know this kid?" Chuin asked.

Marquez nodded. "Curtis Allen," he said. "Mushmouth."

He had these patchy grafts on his face from being badly burned as a child and he'd worn ski masks a lot, folding his insecurity into a hardass street persona—the way all of them did. Marquez had known this kid for fifteen years. He and Rourke had been the first ones into the apartment the night his mom had burned him with an iron. Marquez had visited Curtis in the hospital, tried to keep in touch with him for a while, but he'd let it get away from him. It was like he just blinked and the kid was a pissed-off teenager claiming Boot Hill Mafia Crips. He'd arrested Curtis half a dozen times over the years, some of it serious. The kid always pretended not to remember him.

"So where's IAD?" Marquez asked Chuin. "Where's Special Operations Section? Who's on this?"

"Fucking Committee to Reelect the President," Chuin said, nodding to the RHD huddle at the crime scene. There were some feds prowling around the tape. They looked younger, softer, and they wore better suits than the detectives. "Their official position is the guy wasn't ever picked up. Our dicks don't like it, but that's the word from Mount Sinai. They're saying the suspect slipped away in the confusion and—"

"What?" Ben said. "Killed himself?"

"Don't give them any ideas," Chuin said. "No, party line is he succumbed to his wounds."

"Yeah, right," Marquez said. "Ran thirty blocks with a big hole through his head."

"I don't understand," Ben said. "There were choppers, cameras. The whole world saw this guy being taken into custody."

"It happened under the overpass," Chuin said. "So the choppers missed the actual arrest, but you can see the shop right on the guy's ass when he runs under there."

"And?"

"And it's a Rampart shop," Chuin said.

"Son of a goddamned bitch," Marquez said.

"I tried to warn them, did I not?" Chuin said. "A year ago. No, shit it's been over a year now. 'Mildly interesting, Chicken Little, we'll look into it.' Now the sky is falling and the department's only interested in damage control. People are getting eaten out here, man, and these creeps still won't close the beaches."

"What if I could catch you a songbird?" Marquez asked, some gears catching behind his eyes. "A music box tied up in ribbon, delivered right to your doorstep?"

"Have to do it on the down low," Chuin said, glancing over his shoulder at the RHD detectives.

"Just between friends," Marquez said.

He and Ben ducked under the tape and walked out into the street in front of a bandit cab. When the driver slammed on his brakes, Marquez threw open the right rear door and slid into the backseat. Ben jumped in after him. "We're commandeering this cab," Marquez told the driver, socking a fresh pinch of chaw into his cheek.

"We are?" Ben asked. The interior of the bandit cab stank of patchouli, doujah, and sweat. Wooden beads dangled from the rearview mirror, incense burned in an ashtray on the dashboard. The driver looked pretty FOB, maybe West African, sweating through a loose, patterned tunic. Marquez nodded and told the driver, "Take Fifty-fourth down to Budlong and head south to Blessed Way."

"No trouble," the driver said, meaning either it will be no trouble or I want no trouble.

"We're going to drop in on Gethsemane Guyton," Marquez said, smiling tightly. "Get Some from Boot Hill Mafia. Dope, guns. Shady little son of a bitch couldn't keep his nose clean if you dunked his head in a bucket of bleach. He's been slinging out of that pad for years, but nobody's ever put a solid sales case on him," Marquez said. "Narcotics had an informant dumb enough to wire up on him once, and he did a county lick for possession, but I think their informant turned up gutted in a dumpster on the East Side somewhere." Marquez shrugged. "Jury hung on the sales case."

"Great," Ben said.

"Get Some's not a shooter, he's a planner," Marquez said. "Well, tell you the truth he's not even much of a planner, but he's always kept these go-to guys around to do his dirty. Mushmouth was part of Get Some's crew."

The cab headed west on Fifty-fourth Street and south on Budlong Avenue. Baseheads huddled on the corner of Budlong and Fifty-fifth Street, warming themselves around a shopping cart full of burning garbage. One of them held a glass pipe to his lips.

"Hang a right and take it slow," Marquez told the driver. "But, you know, not *too* slow." Then he popped the cover off the dome light and unscrewed the bulb.

Blessed Way was a graveyard for stolen rides; half the cars on the darkened street had been stripped to their frames. The burned hulk of an old ice-cream truck rested on its side in front of a boarded-up apartment building, bamboo sprouting through its busted windshield. The cab slalomed through oily shadows, easing between the rusted cars balanced on cinder blocks. "Shall I extinguish the headlights?" the driver asked. He hunched behind the wheel, eyes darting.

"You cut the lights and they'll think this is a drive-by."

The cab drifted past abandoned houses, onetime gangster crash pads, covered with Boot Hill Mafia Crip graffiti. The city had put up a wooden sign condemning one of the abandoned houses, but someone spray-painted FUCK SLOBS over it. Through broken windows, Marquez saw the jack-o'-lantern flicker of pitiful campfires burning inside the rotted houses. He could just make out the baseheads and piss-bums squatting at the flames—haunted faces bathed in burbling orange light.

"That's the house up on the left," Marquez said. Get Some's pad was a lopsided, gravel-roofed modular with peeling green paint, a showplace compared to the rest of the block. The spiked iron fence looked brand-new. Mangled British Knights and Chuck Taylors hung like bats from telephone wires over the house.

Ben and Marquez crouched down in the backseat of the cab. "Let it idle forward, but don't stop," Marquez whispered to the driver. "If they see brake lights, we're fucked." He pulled his door handle and elbowed Ben. "You ready, Professor?" Ben nodded.

Marquez let the cab drift past the house. Then he kicked open his door and rolled out of the cab onto the street. Ben followed him out, tearing both knees out of his pants when he hit the asphalt. The cab kept going. Marquez and Ben lay prone in the middle of the darkened street, maybe twenty feet away from the fence. Marquez pushed up on all fours and spider-crept toward the house, moving like a Comanche scout.

There was something caked on the arrowhead spikes of the fence that might have been blood. The gate was not locked. Marquez slowly pushed it open and they crept inside, heading for the house, the yard mostly bare earth strewn with liquor bottles and patches of dry crabgrass. Ben heard the overlapping murmur of televisions from inside the house.

Ben caught movement behind the blinds. He and Marquez darted quietly to the porch, taking up shooting positions on either side of the front door. The door cracked, spilling a thin track of blue-tinged light across the yard. Marquez slammed his shoulder into the door, forcing it wide open and knocking Get Some back into the living room. Ben criss-crossed in behind Marquez, scanning the living room for other suspects. Get Some scrambled to his feet. Marquez took aim at Get Some's chest and ordered him to lace his fingers behind his head.

"You got a warrant, cocksucker?" Get Some smirked. Marquez adjusted his aim, pointing his .45 between Get Some's eyes.

"Sure," Marquez said. "Now turn around."

Ben moved in to handcuff Get Some, patting him down, nothing on him but a cellular phone. Marquez slid a rickety wooden chair out from under the kitchen table and shoved the chair against the backs of Get Some's legs, forcing him to sit. Then Marquez pushed the chair, with Get Some in it, against the wall.

Ben smelled fear-sweat and the musky aroma of home-grown cannabis. Heavy plastic sheets, pocked with condensation, lined the walls. A lattice of PVC tubing suspended from the ceiling—a drip system feeding Get Some's crop of money trees.

"Give a man some weed and he'll smoke for a day," Marquez said. "But teach a man to grow weed and he'll smoke *every* day."

"Exactomundo, motherfucker," Get Some said. "This shit is for my personal, feel me? On account of my glaucoma and shit."

"You know I'm not here for oregano, asshole," Marquez said. Get Some turned away, watching his three televisions arranged on the living-room floor, each broadcasting coverage of the chase.

"I figure Risley would have had to come to you." Marquez opened the fridge, grabbed a can of Budweiser, and popped the tab, slurping the foam off the top of the can as he tilted it to his lips. "Mushmouth, the other busters? They don't change their chonies without your say-so." Marquez sucked the whole can down and crushed it in his hand. "You killed Ronny." He tossed the can on the floor and began cracking his knuckles. "Didn't you?"

Get Some just stared.

"Check the house," Marquez ordered, and belched, too far off the edge of the map now to think about how they'd explain a firefight if Ben found other homies crouching somewhere in the back. Moving slowly from room to room, Ben cleared the place. Marquez was already working Get Some over in the living room. Ben heard him huffing with effort, the blunt thud of his meaty fists striking Get Some's shoulders, arms, and legs. He was avoiding his face, at least for now.

"Man alive, that's thirsty work." Marquez sighed, cracking another Bud. "Let me level with you, Gethsemane. I'm a little out of shape here and I was kind of hoping you'd just come clean here. Clear your conscience."

"Fuck you, motherfucker."

"Suit yourself."

Searching the house, Ben figured this fool either suffered from crippling paranoia or unquenchable bloodlust. He seemed to be expecting some kind of last stand and he'd rigged the place to repel an attack from any room, heaping mattresses, sandbags, and upended furniture under each window to form desperate shooter's nests—like that farmhouse in *Night of the Living Dead*. Behind every door in the house, Get Some had duct-taped an automatic pistol right to the wall. Even more disturbing, the guy had placed a crossbow under each window, but there was nothing romantic in his choice of weapons. These were the kind of high-tech aluminum crossbows favored by deer hunters, 175-pound draws, capable of launching an arrow at 305 feet per second—nearly as fast as a bullet at short range.

Crossbows were silent, but they held another important advantage over firearms. These weapons fired carbon arrows with stainless-steel broadheads designed to penetrate a ten-point buck's tough hide. Unlike a bullet, which expands and distorts on impact, these arrows would pierce Kevlar body armor. These babies were cop killers.

Ben tossed the bedrooms, not sure what he was supposed to find. The guy was a dope dealer. He had dope shit, scales, cellophane, one of those heat sealers. He also had the largest stockpile of diapers Ben had ever seen.

Marquez paused for another breather, and Ben heard Get Some's throaty laughter from the living room. The guy must have been tougher than he looked. "Mex," Get Some said. "I was playing good cop, bad cop back when Michael Jackson was still black. I *know* you the big bad motherfucker. In a minute, Poindexter be back in here to tell me he can't control your buck-wild ass so why don't I just do like you say."

Then Ben saw one of his father's business cards on the bureau, and something inside him slipped its leash. He walked back into the living room, holding the Barnett Quad-300 crossbow. Marquez whistled lowly.

"You've got it ass backwards, Gethsemane," Ben said. "*He's* the good cop." Ben dug a twenty-dollar bill out of his breast pocket and nodded to

Marquez. "Twenty bucks says I shoot a can off homeboy's grape in three tries."

Marquez smiled, dug a twenty out of his own pocket, and placed it on the kitchen counter next to Ben's. Then he took a fresh can of beer out of the fridge. Get Some pitched his head like a horse dodging a bridle. Marquez clamped his hand around his throat and slammed his head back against the wall hard enough to crack the plaster. He balanced the can carefully on his head and stepped away. All trace of human expression disappeared, leaving only the obdurate prison-yard mask through which he stared back at Ben. His nostrils flared and his Adam's apple jerked like a yo-yo. The beads of sweat popping on his forehead matched the condensation on the cold can. "I want to see my lawyer," he said quietly.

"Wrong. Fucking. Answer." Ben sighted down the barrel of the crossbow and deliberately threw the first shot wide. *Thwack!* The arrow sizzled through the air and thunked into the wall, vibrating like a tuning fork next to Get Some's left ear. His whole body jerked and the can tipped over. Marquez called a time-out and replaced the can.

Ben took off his glasses, exhaled on them, and then used his sleeve to wipe the fog off the lenses. Bracing the crossbow on the floor to draw it, Ben pulled another arrow from the quiver and fitted the bolt into the slotted barrel. Ben sighted down again and pulled the trigger. *Thwack!* The can ruptured, jagged lobes of aluminum peeling back like flower petals as the arrow embedded to its fletching. Hissing white foam cascaded down over Get Some's face.

Marquez placed another twenty on the counter. "Double or nothing you can't put another one in that can," he said. "Get Some, you want a piece of this, man?"

"Fuck you!" Gethsemane spat, coughing foam.

Ben drew the crossbow again, and loaded another arrow, but as he was bringing the stock up to his shoulder, his finger accidentally brushed the weapon's delicate trigger. *Thwack!* The arrow flew low. Ben shut his eyes for a long second, not daring to look. He was sure he'd killed him, severing their only lead. He opened one eye. The arrow had struck the wooden seat of Gethsemane's chair, the broadhead splitting the wood right up to his crotch. A sour bloom of urine spread across the front of his trousers.

"Okay," he said. "I give."

"Thank God," Marquez said. "The suspense was killing me."

"Your boy hit some *eses* a while back," Get Some said. "Tax collectors. Did it in uniform. Just knocked on the front door and *blap*. He been throwin' that money around the hood like he a big pimp. Hearts and Minds, homie." Get Some shook his head wearily. "This shit is deep, dog."

"How deep?" Marquez asked quietly.

"Down there where the motherfuckin' fish glow in the dark," he whispered. "Some Boot Hill niggas had a secret sit and they broke it all down, like whoop-de-woo-woo, shit ain't what shit outta be. I mean, here *we* are on the block, been keepin' it hood all these years. Gettin' killed up over table scraps. Now, where the fuck *he* at?"

"They're going after Darius," Ben said.

Get Some nodded. "Crazy D's hope-to-die road dogs fixin' to bite the shit outta the hand that feeds 'em," he said.

"Who?" Marquez asked.

"Your old partner," Get Some spat. "A few other wicked-ass niggas. Daddy Python, Poway Charlie, Sleepy Loc, a gang of 'em. Met in the Spook House, layin' out when they gone do it. How they gone do it. These niggas bringin' some artillery into the hood, talkin' *regime change,* cuz. No joke."

"How do you know about all this?"

"Marquez, I was right there in the Spook House, drinkin' out that skull with all the rest of them thirsty-ass niggas, what the fuck else I gone to do? They all passin' it around the circle, like where you at, cuz. You know the business, now is the time for all good men to come to the aid of their party. I mean, he who is not with me is 'bout to get his motherfuckin' cap peeled. An' pardon me for livin', motherfucker, but I chose the former. Nobody gets to ride the pine in this game. One way or another, we all gettin' bloody as hell."

A dog barked somewhere down the block. Marquez crossed the room, peering out through a space in the curtains. "Where's Risley getting the artillery?"

"Nazi Saddle Tramps," Get Some said. "The albino set it up."

"Strange," Ben said.

"That's the dude." Get Some nodded.

Then Marquez heard a car pulling up out front and Get Some freaked, bug-eyed at the sound of the big engine of a Crown Victoria. He wriggled in his chair, straining against the cuffs. "It's *him*," Get Some gasped.

Marquez dashed around the house, shutting off all the lights and televisions, plunging the room into darkness. Ben and Marquez squatted by the front window and peered out through the translucent cotton sheet. A black-and-white LAPD patrol car, driving with its headlights off, pulled up to the curb and stopped in front of the house.

"Markings," Marquez whispered. "Look at the markings." A white 02 stenciled on the vehicle's black trunk, the department designation for Rampart Division.

"Don't let them in, Marquez," Gethsemane pleaded. "Man, don't let them get me."

"Shut up," Marquez hissed.

Two dark figures eased out of the patrol car, one lean and one stout. They wore black balaclavas and black coats over their uniforms, scanning the street with the sly caution of nocturnal predators. The lean one squatted on his haunches, the ghetto deerslayer, surveying the dark house. Marquez recognized Cabe Risley even in the mask. He couldn't have seen into the darkened house, but he seemed to be staring right at Marquez. The eyeholes in his mask looked like sockets in a skull. The guy pulled a Scorpion machine pistol out of his coat and screwed a sound suppressor onto the barrel—definitely not department issue.

Marquez slid his .45 out of its holster. Get Some's eyes bulged. Ben drew his Beretta and crawled across the living room on his belly. He positioned himself next to Marquez at the windowsill.

Risley stood very still. Ben could almost see his mind gnawing on the darkened house, tasting something here he didn't care for. He turned and signaled to his partner. The two of them backed out of the gate and returned to their black-and-white. The car did not speed away from the curb, but accelerated slowly, like a big croc sliding off a muddy bank.

1997

Benji made a pot of strong coffee. He and Darius took their mugs outside and sat in the iron bistro chairs under the pergola to watch the sun come up over the Santa Monicas. The light poured into Franklin Canyon like warm broth. Hermit thrushes came to drink from the stone birdbath in the center of the garden. A pair of big scrub jays swooped down into the bath and scared the thrushes off. The jays doused themselves and complained bitterly to each other, but Benji thought their irascibility didn't take away from their beauty, maybe even enhanced it.

"You trust that guy?"

"Risley?" Darius sipped, shook his head. "Hell, no."

"Mike?"

"Mike's a necessary evil," Darius said. "Risley's just plain evil, but they both got their addictions and you can control an addict. Mike's just a hype. Risley? Shit, that nigga's addicted to me." Darius swept his hand over the grounds, the shimmering pool. "He's addicted to this."

The morning news led with the story of the bloody shooting at the Wiltern Theater. A sexed-up Asian reporter in a tight-fitting pantsuit delivered a live report from the scene of last night's carnage. "Los Angeles police say they still don't know what prompted last night's shooting in front of the star-studded launch party for the new hip-hop magazine *Thug*," the reporter said, standing in front of the yellow crime-scene tape strung across Wilshire Boulevard. Behind her, SID photographers shot the blood spatters from different angles and pokey detectives in shirt-sleeves and latex gloves collected shell casings from the sidewalk. "But to-day, the music world is already mourning the tragic loss of one of its brightest stars. Duncan James Mortimer, known to hip-hop fans as DJ Post-Mortem, was wounded by gunfire and pronounced dead at the scene." The producer cut to a few memorable seconds of Post-Mortem's MTV interview with Kurt Loder before running some tasteful footage of coroners zipping Post-Mortem into a body bag and loading him onto a gurney. Darius switched off the television.

Big Ben drove his Mercedes up Darius's long brick driveway around seven. "Your daddy looks hungover," Darius said.

"I don't think so," Benji whispered, watching his father struggle up the wide front steps. *But something's definitely wrong with him.* His father's stride resembled a stroke victim's halting shuffle. Gone was the belliger-ent, saucy waddle that had become his courtroom trademark. His big cheeks, normally flushed russet at the first sign of a challenge, looked drawn and pale. His eyes were the color of iodine, like he hadn't slept in a few days, and he was unshaven. That was what scared him the most: his father, who had shaved every morning of his adult life with a safety ra-zor and horsehair brush, now sported a two-day growth of coarse black stubble.

That's because he knows.

Impossible, Benji reasoned. Big Ben just knew his only son could be riding in that meat wagon next to Post-Mortem. He knew how close he had come to losing his son last night. Any father would be shaken by a close call like that.

He's not any father. Look at his face. He fucking knows.

But as he stepped through the threshold, Big Ben seemed to recover at least a fair approximation of his jocular self. Benji allowed himself an in-ward sigh of relief. Then Big Ben hugged him, kissing him on the cheek. Big Ben normally hugged Benji only when he was showing off for new clients, and Darius had no illusions about their relationship, but Big Ben had never kissed Benji, not once. The strange precision of that kiss made it feel like a blow. The shock must have registered on Benji's face, because Big Ben pinched his cheek gently and said, "Just glad you're still in one piece, kiddo."

Big Ben shook Darius's hand. "I'm sorry for your loss," he said solemnly. "Post-Mortem was a great talent." Darius shrugged. "How's Jax?"

"Popped a couple of Percosets," Darius said. "What do the cops have?"

"Right, right, show must go on," Big Ben said, rubbing his palms together. "Most of their witnesses didn't see anything but red smoke. There are casings everywhere and some blood spatter to indicate you and Jax tagged a couple of them, but they carried away their wounded so right now Post-Mortem's the only victim."

Big Ben said Robbery Homicide Division wasn't going to squander any midnight oil on a glorified gangbanger like Post-Mortem. The guy had sold a zillion albums boasting about what a stone killer he was. "Like the song goes," Big Ben said. "'If you can't bite, don't growl.'"

Darius chuckled in spite of himself. DJ Post-Mortem's most famous contribution to society had been the hit song "Cops: The Other White Meat," a modest proposal to kill the police and feed their fatty flesh to the oppressed poor. No detective was going to put in any overtime beating the bushes for Post-Mortem's killers.

"They're still going to want to interview you," Big Ben told Darius. "They know you were there. If they have to, they'll issue a grand jury subpoena." Darius had enough juice with a select group within the LAPD to delay a warrant for a few days, but not to forestall one completely. "It's better if you appear to cooperate with their investigation."

"Give me twenty-four hours," Darius said. "Then I'll sit down with them."

Big Ben nodded. "We need to discuss something else," he said, sounding oddly formal. His eyes darted to Benji. "And we should speak in private."

Darius raised his eyebrows. Then he led Big Ben into the library. Big Ben sidled after him, as though covering their escape, and pulled the double doors closed. Benji's mind sifted through possible explanations for his exclusion. Maybe, whatever they had to discuss was so highly illegal that his father wanted to protect him from any direct knowledge of it, but he rejected this theory out of hand because his father had never protected him in the past. Perhaps, he was just scolding Darius for putting his son in harm's way last night, but Benji couldn't imagine anyone, except maybe Jax, *scolding* Darius for anything. No, the only likely scenario was that Big Ben had somehow gotten wind of Darius's plan to make Benji his consigliere. Big Ben was probably in there trying to talk Darius out of betting the ranch on his son.

This shouldn't have angered Benji, but it did. Their muffled conversation floated out through the double doors. He heard his father's low voice and Darius's raised in alarm, but he couldn't make anything out. Benji brooded on the couch, flicking blue M&M's off the glass coffee table to watch them skitter across the marble floor. He fully intended to tell them both to fuck off, but when they finally came back out of the library, the look on Darius's face shut him up.

What in God's name has he told him?

Whatever it was, Darius had taken the news like a bullet in the gut, body curling around it, and his hand over the wound. Darius's eyes, normally heavy lidded and expressionless, looked feverish as he staggered out of the library. Big Ben slunk out behind him, wearing an almost comic expression of grief.

Darius refused to look Benji in the eye, not a good sign. "I want you to come to Vegas with me," Darius told Benji blankly. He sounded like Laurence Harvey in *The Manchurian Candidate.* "I need your help with this negotiation."

Tell him no, Benji thought. Nothing good would happen in Vegas. This was why they called him Crazy D, catatonia just a prelude to homicidal rage and Benji didn't want to be anywhere near him when he blew.

Benji could have told him he had to study, didn't have a change of clothes, needed sleep, anything to get out of that trip. All his survival instincts said run while you can, but he couldn't do it. Darius looked so lost, like nothing was familiar to him anymore, and Benji couldn't just abandon him like that. It was a four-hour drive to Vegas. Maybe that was enough time to work some of the poison out of him, enough time to save the guy from himself. Whatever Big Ben had told him, however he'd infected his mind, Darius was still Benji's friend.

Jax drove east on Interstate 15 in a black 1982 Cadillac Eldorado with the moldy air-conditioning cranked. The car was registered to a woman named Esther Cole, who had been dead for six years, but she still paid her DMV fees and her insurance premiums in a timely manner. No one would be able to trace the Eldorado to Darius, a fact not lost on Benji when Darius selected this car for their little trip to the desert.

Jax kept to the speed limit and all three of them wore their seat belts. Darius sat in the front passenger seat and Benji stretched out in the back, watching the ravaged sameness of the Mojave unfurl like a dusty Indian blanket. Ragged creosote, yucca, and gnarled mesquite plants peppered the desert. The baked husks of flying insects stuck to the windshield. No one spoke as they blew through the sandblasted camp towns of Barstow, Calico, Yermo, and Toomey. The same stunted burger joints and unkempt gas stations, flying tattered all-weather pendants, huddled close to the interstate at every exit.

Darius stared straight ahead as the long black hood gobbled the highway. Benji could see the hinge of his jaw pulsing at his temples and he wasn't sure, but he thought Darius might have been grinding his teeth. "What did my father tell you back at the house?" Benji asked him finally. "Darius?"

"Not a goddamned thing," Darius said, barely opening his mouth.

"Well, I'm here if you want to talk," Benji said lamely.

His eyes narrowed in the rearview mirror. "Maybe later," Darius said.

They stopped for gas in a town called Baker, which boasted the world's tallest thermometer and a cinder-block restaurant called the Mad Greek. Benji stepped out of the car, the asphalt sticky under his feet. Rippling waves of heat convection rose from the Eldorado's hood. The digital numbers on the thermometer said it was one hundred eight degrees Fahrenheit. While Jax wiped the dead bugs off the windshield, Benji used the gas station's pay phone to place a collect call to the house. Maybe Gretchen would know what was going on. The line at home was busy. Benji asked the operator to try again, got another busy signal. Then Jax leaned on the horn, calling him back to the car.

They reached the vulgar neon minarets of Las Vegas just after sunset, crossed the strip on Paradise Road, pulling into the parking lot of the Hard Rock Hotel and Casino. The Hard Rock is actually a small hotel by Vegas standards, only six hundred seventy rooms, with five restaurants, including a Mexican double entendre called the Pink Taco, a nightclub, a health spa, and an oasis pool. Benji followed Darius and Jax under the giant neon guitar and into the casino. Once inside, Darius purchased fifteen hundred dollars' worth of chips from the cashier. He handed five hundred to Benji and five hundred to Jax. "Spread out," Darius said. "I'll let you know when we're ready."

The Hard Rock was identical to any other casino, but for the meager collection of music memorabilia, signed guitars, and platinum records arranged along the walls. Benji sat down at one of the blackjack tables with a twenty-dollar limit. The dealer slid him the ace of spades and the eight of hearts. He swallowed dryly. A button-nosed cocktail waitress with an East Texas accent eyed his pile of chips and asked him what he was drinking. "Pepto-Bismol," Benji told her.

"I know they have some in the general store," she said, pointing across the casino. Benji thanked her, placed a chip on her tray, and headed in that direction. On the way to the general store, he cashed in a chip for twenty dollars' worth of quarters and stopped at a bank of pay phones to try Gretchen again. She picked up on the first ring.

"Where've you been?" she asked. "I've been trying your cell." Tremors fragmented her voice, the aftershocks of some seismic upheaval. Benji just assumed she was freaked-out about the Wiltern shooting.

"I don't have my phone with me, but I'm okay," he reassured her. "I mean, we're all still in shock about Post-Mortem, but—"

"What the hell are you talking about?" She sounded irritated, confused, Benji thinking: Hadn't she heard about the shooting?

"Well, what are you talking about?" Benji asked her.

"He *knows*," she said.

Benji clutched the receiver. The cacophonous din of the casino, the clanging and tinkling of the slots, the raucous crap games, the music, and the drunken laughter became suddenly distant. The riot of flashing lights dimmed. This is what happens when you drown, he thought. Thin ice breaks under your weight and you just disappear. The dark water steals your breath and you're pounding your fists against the frozen ceiling, only to find the fissure you fell through has already resealed.

"How did he find out?" Benji asked, but the question sounded ridiculous because part of him already knew the answer. Over time, they would have left a kind of psychic imprint. Big Ben must have come home from work one night and just sensed something he couldn't ignore.

It had started two years ago, the day Gretchen's agent told her she'd landed the role opposite Eric Roberts in the new *Double Indemnity*. As soon as she'd heard, she'd driven straight to Big Ben's office to give her husband the big news. Big Ben was in the middle of a billable phone call when she charged into his office to tell him. "Congrats." Big Ben sneered, mashing his palm over the receiver. "I'm sure that fourteen-year-old boys everywhere will be masturbating like chimps. Now, if you'll excuse me." Watching her ear-to-ear grin melt away, Big Ben waved her out of his office.

She could have gone anywhere to get her leg over, free to eat of any tree in the garden, but Gretchen chose to visit Benji that afternoon, sprawled among law books scattered on his unmade bed, pouring over *Hamer v. Sidway* as the last of rays of sunlight slanted through his bedroom window.

"The flesh loses some elasticity over time, did I ever tell you that?" Her eyes looked puffy, like she'd been crying. "Soil's just not as rich as it was that first time, and you don't get the same friction as you used to."

"Hey, knock it off," he said. He'd always loved her flinty candor, but this was something else, bile bitten in every word.

"That first time, that's as much as you ever have to give somebody and you'll never have that much to give again." She came forward unsteadily, speaking with the halting, deliberate speech of a drunk, but he didn't think she'd been drinking. This wasn't that kind of stupor. "You start to fade a little and there's just less of you to go around each time."

"Stop it," Benji said. He wanted to run from her, wanted to slap her. In the movies, you could slap a hysterical woman, snap her right out of it.

"You tell yourself the others meant nothing to you," she said. "They were all just practice rounds, right?" She laughed bitterly, like a dry sob. "But I swear to God it gets harder to say you've never felt this way before and keep a straight face. You tell yourself you're trading up, not down, but you round that corner into your dirty thirties, kiddo, and you find yourself chasing after these assholes you wouldn't have given the time of day."

"Please stop," he said, and put his mouth over hers. Gretchen peeled her sweater up over her head, tossing it in a corner, and he had the dim recollection of that deft move with the sweater from one of her Troma pictures. "Stop." Benji pushed away. She was naked to the waist now, her eyes holding both a frank challenge and a desperate plea.

"Make me," she whispered.

Just that one time, they said, to get it out of their systems. Then they were promising themselves never again in the house. Like embezzlers, skimming those first dollars out of desperation, with every intention of putting it all back, but it only got easier once that line had been crossed. Finally, he was asking himself how long they could expect to keep this up before they got caught.

"This isn't normal," Benji whispered to her, resting his head on Gretchen's chest. He could hear her heartbeat. His fingers traced her freckled collarbone—freckles that matched the reddish flecks in her eyes. He'd been clinging to his guilt, the final vestige of civilization, but even guilt had slipped away from him. He'd lost everything in her, every command of his domestication, and he was marooned in tangled bedclothes.

"Fuck normal," she said. "A normal life's a waste of oxygen. We're normalized in death. Normalized, emulsified, composted. We'll all be normal then, kid. Trust me."

"I came home yesterday and he had packed up all my things," Gretchen said. "He put a tape in the VCR." She was crying hard now, long racking sobs. "That goddamned synthesizer music and even a cheap title." Benji could hear the self-loathing begin to constrict her voice. Big Ben's squadron of private investigators must have set up round-the-clock surveillance on his own home. Infidelity was their bag and Benji was sure they'd spared no hidden camera. "He must have had them watching us for months. Then he had Strange cut the footage together into *The Wicked Stepmother*." She sniffled bitterly. "I guess I ended up doing porn for that bastard, after all."

"Aw, Gretch, I'm sorry," Benji said. "I'm so sorry."

"I'm going back to Texas," she said.

"I'll come with you," he said. "We can start over somewhere."

"No." Her voice sounded diminished, distant.

"Did he hurt you?"

"Oh my God, you don't understand." She hissed. "I've been trying to warn you for two days."

Darius reached over Benji's shoulder and depressed the metal tab on the pay phone's cradle, breaking the connection. Benji jumped. Then he heard the coins falling inside the phone and knew he'd lost her, his hand slick with sweat as he slowly replaced the handset. *But of the fruit of the tree in the midst of the garden, God hath said, ye shall not eat of it, nor shall ye touch it, lest ye die.*

"It's time," Darius said. "He's on the eleventh floor." Benji turned away from the bank of phones and followed Darius and Jax into the elevator. The doors slid closed and they watched the numbers climb. "How'd you do?" Darius asked him. He sounded almost playful, but he wasn't smiling.

"I lost," Benji said.

It wasn't hard to tell which room Certain Death occupied; a cohort of sinewy black men was standing guard in front of his door. Their rigid bearing and severe expressions reminded Benji of those Buckingham

Palace guards, but their stance was slightly wider, to afford them a martial artist's center of gravity. They wore uniforms, of a kind: bloodred bow ties and dark suits tailored to conceal the presence of weapons.

The Fruit of Islam: Nation of Islam's elite paramilitary corps, formed by Malcolm X during the Black Power movement, recruited in prisons all over the U.S. through the Nation's "counseling programs" for addicts, dealers, and hard-core gangbangers. The Nation takes some of this country's toughest cons, gets them to swear off drugs, pork, and white women, and trains them in the deadly arts. Even Jax didn't fuck with these guys.

The Fruit guard Minister Farrakhan's mansion and act as bodyguards at his public appearances. Farrakhan and his lieutenants also farm their bow-tied soldiers out to half a dozen security firms, separately incorporated but all controlled by the Nation, to patrol housing projects in Baltimore, Buffalo, Chicago, Dallas, Dayton, Philadelphia, Pittsburgh, New York City, Washington, and Los Angeles. If you're black, you can hire out a basket of Fruit for personal protection, but they don't come cheap.

When they saw them approaching, the Fruit calmly unbuttoned their suit jackets and shifted positions, forming a parade-ground phalanx to block the hallway. "Shouldn't we wave a white flag or something?" Benji whispered to Jax.

Darius stepped toward them, reaching into his coat. Upon seeing this, all four men slid their right hands under their jackets, but their expressions did not change until Darius's hand came out of his coat with the money. He handed each man ten thousand dollars. "Take a break," Darius said.

The man standing center right, the one Benji assumed was the leader, held the neatly bound packet up to his own ear and ran his thumb over the money. The crisp bills sounded like shuffling cards, and he nodded to himself. Then the leader slipped the money into his pocket and walked to the elevator. His garrison followed him without a word, but some of that military air was gone now and as the elevator doors closed, Benji heard two of them giggling.

Jax pulled his bone-handled Bowie knife out of the sheath under his coat and stabbed the eight-inch blade into the doorjamb. "Whoa," Benji said, backing away as he leaned on the handle. The door splintered, and Jax rushed into the suite. Darius snatched Benji by the arm and pulled him into the room with him.

Certain Death, wearing only red silk boxers, knelt on the floor and snorted a neat rail of cocaine from a glass coffee table while a tall black call girl with false eyelashes kneaded his thick shoulders. Benji had been hanging around with Darius long enough that he found the idea of just one prostitute kind of quaint, but Certain Death probably didn't want to share his coke with a whole troupe. The girl saw them before Certain Death did. She took her hands from his shoulders and backed away from him, but the long line of cocaine demanded his all concentration, like he was going for a personal best. The girl did not scream. She had survived in this town long enough to know better. She quickly gathered her clothes from the bureau. Darius nodded to her and she slipped out the front door.

They watched him finish. Certain Death came up for air, pushed his dreadlocks out of his dilated eyes, and saw Darius standing over him. "What up." Certain Death sniffled and reached behind him for something under the bed. Darius kicked him in the face. Blood rooster-tailed out of his mouth as his head snapped back and two big teeth clattered on the table. Certain Death slumped to the floor and lay on his side, coughing wetly.

"My momma was a straight-rock ho." Darius picked up one of Certain Death's bloody teeth from the coffee table, examined it in the light, and slipped it into his pocket. "See, I can say that, but you can't."

"I thought we were going to negotiate," Benji said.

"This is how the Israelis do it," Darius said. "I thought you'd appreciate that."

Jax vaulted the bed and cut the nylon cord from the blinds, letting them fall to cover the window. He held the knife between his teeth and straddled Certain Death on the floor, wrapping the cord around the man's hands and feet with the ease of a champion calf roper. When Certain Death moaned, Jax found a dirty sock on the floor and stuffed it into the man's bloody mouth.

"Stop," Benji said.

Darius turned to face him. "*What* did you say?"

"You can't do this," Benji said, taking a step toward him. "I won't let you."

Darius dipped his shoulder, and caught Benji with an uppercut that lifted him off his feet. Darius's fist slammed into Benji's chin. His teeth clicked together, and again Benji felt the sting of that strange kiss from his father. *You don't understand,* Gretchen had said. *I've been trying to warn you for two days.* Benji fell backward, crashing through the glass coffee table like thin ice. The world swam out of focus as he hit the floor next to the bed. Shattered glass crunched on the carpet beneath him. A few shards cut into his back and the pain must have kept him from going out completely. His jaw throbbed and bright colors pulsed behind his eyes. The phone, Benji thought. Get to the phone, but he couldn't make his limbs work. He'd never been hit that hard, and it took all his concentration just to remain conscious. He couldn't even lift his head.

He saw Jax grab a handful of Certain Death's dreadlocks. Jax slid his knife under the flesh behind the man's ear and brought the knife slicing up across his forehead in a single motion. Blood leaked into Certain Death's wide eyes and he whimpered through the sock. Jax lifted the scalp from the skull as his blade glided along under the hairline until he circumnavigated to his first cut and it peeled away in a single piece. Jax held the scalp in front of Certain Death's face. Once the actuality of the dripping mess had registered in his eyes, Jax placed the blade under Certain's Death's jaw and opened his throat. He squirmed and gurgled. Blood soaked through the sock until it looked like he had a rose stuffed in his mouth. He lay still and his redness spread across the carpet like a lengthening shadow. Jax stood and wiped his blood-slaked knife on the bedspread.

Darius stood over Benji, bent at his knees and gripped the coffee table's broken frame. He grunted, lifted the frame off Benji, and tossed it roughly aside. He squatted on his haunches and gently ran his fingers through Benji's hair, combing the glass out. Benji may have been hurt worse than he thought because Darius's hand came away bloody and he wiped his palm on the carpet. Then Darius pulled some wadded-up fabric out of his jacket pocket. Benji thought it was a handkerchief, some kind of makeshift bandage, but when he shook it out Benji saw Darius was holding a lacey pair of women's panties. He dangled those panties over Benji's face like he expected Benji to recognize them.

"What's all this, D?" Jax asked him, nodding to Certain Death's body. "Blood's soaking through the carpet and if somebody's in the room below us . . . Darius?"

"Ocular proof, motherfucker." Darius whispered to Benji through his teeth. He stared at Benji, canting his head sideways in a guileless expression of hurt and confusion. Darius looked like a child who has been given a tetanus shot without fair warning. Tears stood in his eyes. "How could you do me that way, brother?"

You had to admire my old man, Benji thought. The guy had style. Gretchen had told him *he must have had them watching us for months,* but he hadn't really heard her. Had he actually expected his father to spend those months just sulking over his cuckoldry? That wasn't him and Benji knew it. Big Ben Kahn didn't brood; he plotted.

Big Ben had insisted he and Darius speak in private. Then he'd killed his own son right there in the library, just like Colonel Fucking Mustard. "Serena left these in my son's room." Big Ben plays dumb, just tossing out the line while he twirls Gretchen's panties on his index finger. His father had just done what his clients had been paying him to do for years, made one small alteration to an existing pattern of facts, bending reality to his will. Maybe Big Ben seasons the story with some spicy detail. "They've been at it for months. You can practically smell it in the house. Darius, you need to talk to him, for his own good." Big Ben swings the panties in front of Darius like a hypnotist's pocket watch. "Carcosa's deadly serious about that girl's virtue. If he finds out my son's busted her cherry, there's no telling—" Darius snatches the panties away from Big Ben, growling his promise to talk to Benji about it.

"Darius," Benji said weakly. "Listen—"

"No!" Darius shook his head furiously. He squeezed his eyes shut, pushing out the first tears. "He said you'd try to jaw your way out of this." Of course he did, Benji thought. *Don't shit where you eat, kid.*

"D, hold up," Jax said. "We're on short time."

"I slept with Gretchen," Benji said, his head beginning to clear. "Gretchen! He flipped out and this is his payback. Have you even talked to Serena, for Christ's sake?"

"Don't say her name!" Darius roared. "Get her name outta your mouth." He kneeled on Benji's chest, wrapping the panties around Benji's neck. Darius was weeping openly as he took the ends in his fists and pulled. The fabric tightened around Benji's throat, cutting off his air. Benji tried to reason with him, but all that came out was a hoarse rattle. He clawed weakly at Darius's arms, tiny fragments of glass falling away from his shaking hand.

Jax struck Darius in the back of his head with the blunt handle of his Bowie knife. It was a glancing blow, but it had the intended effect. Darius's eyes rolled, his head sagging to his chest. Jax caught him before he fell. Darius's hands let go and the fabric around Benji's neck slackened. He gasped, coughed, and gasped again. Struggling to his feet, he steadied himself against the bureau.

Jax used his thumb to open Darius's left eye. "Help me get him walking," he said. They each hooked one of Darius's limp arms over their shoulders and heaved him upright. Darius reeled drunkenly, but managed to keep on his feet. Together, the three of them staggered out of the room and careened toward the elevators. Benji propped Darius up in a corner of the elevator while Jax hit the button for the lobby. Darius's head lolled and he mumbled something with fuck in it.

"When the doors open, we'll head for the first exit we see," Jax said.

"You're a little bloody, but we can still pass for three drunks if you stay cool."

The doors hissed open and they lurched into the bustling casino lobby, steering Darius straight for the exit. "I told you Patrón the mutherfuckin' Cadillac of tequilas," Jax slurred, and Benji laughed loudly, but the casino was full of drunks and no one seemed to notice the performance. Two frowning security guards in black sport coats politely held the exit doors open for them while they stumbled out into the parking lot.

Jax opened the passenger door of the Eldorado and they stuffed Darius inside. Benji started to get into the backseat, but Jax grabbed his arm. "What the fuck you think you're doing?"

"How am I supposed to get home?"

"You don't want to be anywhere near home when D comes around." Jax shoved Benji away from the car. "Stay out of L.A., get someplace no one can find you because we're damn sure going to be hunting. I've seen the way that girl moves and if she's still cherry, I'm a mutherfuckin' Chinaman."

"Jax, I swear I never touched her," Benji pleaded.

"You think I give a fuck about that," Jax said. "You think I give a fuck about you. I'm with this boy till the wheels fall off, but you bitched up yellow on him in the middle of a war party. I'd a killed you upstairs, but all that blood had already soaked down through the carpet and there wasn't time. If I'd known you were going to be on the menu, I'd a brought up a tarp." Jax slid into the driver's seat, backed out of the space. Benji watched the Eldorado head out of town.

PRESENT

Ben had his post-incident evaluation from Behavioral Science Services in Chinatown. A young psychologist asked him a series of rote questions, seemed to find him relatively free of post-traumatic stress disorder, and sent him on his way with a Return to Duty. When the session was over, Ben drove to Marquez's tiny bungalow on Edgeware Road. Marquez pulled a couple of Tecates out of his fridge and they stood on his back porch under the aluminum awning.

"She ask if you're eating properly?"

"No," Ben said.

"Mine always asks me that," Marquez said and they touched cans. "Here's to PTSD."

They heard a car out front. Chuin came through Marquez's front door without knocking, calling out for Marquez. "I'm out back," Marquez said.

Chuin charged out through the screen door. When he saw Ben, his eyes blazed. He knocked the beer out of Ben's hand and shoved him.

"Hey, hey," Marquez said, stepping between them.

"You dropped a fucking dime," Chuin shouted, firing his finger at Ben. "Ran back and told Daddy, didn't you?"

"I don't know what you're talking about," Ben said. "I haven't spoken to him in over a year."

"You're a lying sack of shit," Chuin said. "Who'd you call? Darius?"

"I didn't call anyone," Ben said.

"What's going on?" Marquez asked.

"Your songbird shit the bed," Chuin said. "He lawyered up, wouldn't talk to me. I told him, 'Play nice, asshole, you're looking at Buck Rogers time here,' but he wouldn't budge."

"So a guy pissed backwards," Marquez said. "It happens, fuck."

"Yeah, but dig this." Chuin glared at Ben. "Get Some was one of his daddy's clients. Apparently, Big Ben called in a big favor and the slippery son of a bitch made bail. Get Some took a cab from County straight to the Sultan Motel on Ventura. You know it?"

"Not exactly Gethsemane's hood," Marquez said.

"He walks into a room cash-rented by two male blacks," Chuin said. "Skinny and fat, no further description. The Sultan's under vice abatement so they've got fixed cameras in the courtyard, but you can't make these dudes on the tape. They keep turning their heads away like they know about the cameras.

"Sometime between nine hundred and nine-thirty there's a struggle. Whore's got one of her commute regulars in the adjacent room and she hears it through the wall, but figures it's just rough trade. Few hours later, the manager's sweeping the courtyard and catches a whiff of something. He keys into the room, takes a look in the bathtub, and loses his Egg McMuffins.

"These fuckers filled the tub with carbolic acid and forced Get Some under with a broken towel rack," Chuin said. "Actually, technically, the guy probably drowned, went out aspirating that crap. But you know, eventually, the acid ate the meat right off his bones. Guy was gazpacho by the time I got there." He turned to Ben. "Am I going too fast for you, rookie?"

"No prints, no nothing," Chuin told Marquez. "These guys wore masks and surgical gloves, dumped them right into the soup, and split. So would you say we've suffered a setback here, Sancho?"

"Shit," Marquez said.

"It's over," Chuin said. "We lost."

Ben turned to Marquez, but Marquez wouldn't look at him. Ben opened his mouth, closed it again, and walked back inside. Then Marquez heard Ben's car peeling away out front.

"What the hell made you think he was ever on the side of the angels, man?" Chuin demanded. "God, you are so fucking arrogant."

"You don't know what you're talking about," Marquez said.

"I know you blame yourself for Risley," Chuin said.

"Get off my ass," Marquez said.

"Admit it," Chuin said. "You turned Frankenstein loose on the city, and you thought this kid was going to make it right for you somehow."

Strange's old wig shop on Hollywood Boulevard was now an adult bookstore and he no longer leased. Strange owned the entire crumbling building outright and, last Ben had heard, the guy was seriously lobbying for its designation as a historical landmark. Farther down the block, the City of Los Angeles, the Kodak corporation, and the Walt Disney Company had spent millions in an attempt to transform the seedy Walk of Fame into the kind of place midwestern folks could bring their families without some transvestite hooker lifting his miniskirt to take a leak in front of the kids while a pickpocket lifts Dad's wallet. Despite this attempt at gentrification and to the enduring chagrin of Hollywood's neopuritan visionaries, Strange's bookstore wasn't just holding on, but thriving. Its trademark vulva, rendered in sizzling pink neon, blinked in the bookstore's window 24/7, a beacon of abiding hope to prurient souls everywhere.

One of those guys that act like hip-hop robots for spare change was doing his thing on top of a plastic milk crate in front of Strange's place, covered from his bowler to his sneakers in silver glitter and sequins. His face was slathered in silver makeup that must have been murder in this heat, and his eyes were hidden behind a pair of those old-school *Risky Business* Ray-Bans. The guy smoothly pivoted his whole torso with his elbows locked at ninety-degree angles. Then he froze, like C-3PO, as though waiting for someone to notice him. No one did. The Walk of Fame was crowded, but the tourists were too busy standing on Patrick Swayze's star to notice the robot and the pickpockets were too busy preying on the tourists to notice anything but cops.

An electric eye chimed as Ben stepped through the open entrance to the bookshop, strolling past the rows of videos, DVDs, CD-ROMs, magazines, and elaborate toys. A husky guy with a goatee on a face like a honey-baked ham stood behind the counter with his thick arms crossed over a bouncer's chest. He wore a tight black T-shirt with the store's vulva logo on it. Ben asked Hamface where he might find Strange.

"Never heard of him," Hamface said.

"He's expecting me." Ben flashed his badge, hoping to lubricate their dialogue, as it were, but Hamface was unimpressed.

"Doesn't mean shit to me," he said.

Ben nodded, turned away from the counter, grabbed the closest browser, and slammed him against the DVD rack. "LAPD," he said. The electric eye chimed like a rapid-fire laser gun as the patrons shuffle-sprinted out the door. He turned the guy loose, and the place was empty in about twenty seconds.

"Listen, asshole," Hamface growled, coming around the counter.

"That's quite all right, Gus." Strange's velvet voice oozed out of a ceiling speaker. The guy made even the name Gus sound salacious. "You may send the young man down. He's a family friend."

Gus pulled the EMPLOYEES ONLY chain aside and led Ben behind the counter to a plain steel door. An eye slit opened in the door, like the ones at the entrance to speakeasies in old gangster movies, and Ben saw a pair of dark eyes behind it flick to Gus. "The fuck is he?"

Gus shrugged. "Strange said send him on down."

Ben heard latches and heavy bolts being thrown. The steel door swung open and filled with another roided-up reject from the WWF, wearing a ponytail and those garish elastic muscle-pants. Ben followed Ponytail down a narrow flight of stairs, breathing the still dungeon musk of mold and perspiration. Ponytail led Ben into a subterranean room, a kind of telemarketing sweatshop with moth-eaten army cots where the girls slept in shifts. Fetid gray water leaked from cracks in the low cement ceiling and dripped into catch basins, buckets, and coffee cans on the uneven, dirt floor. A Yuban can overflowed to form a cloudy puddle in the corner.

Twenty women wearing hands-free telephone headsets sat in front of a low-tech switchboard and read from a series of by-the-numbers phone-sex scripts to lonely callers racking up $3.99 per minute on their major credit cards. A few of the girls appeared to have already memorized to-day's script, leafing listlessly through dog-eared *Marie Claire* magazines while talking their callers to orgasm or credit limit, whichever came first. A brown-haired woman in her midforties barked, "Oh, yeah, honey, fuck my ass!" while popping her gum and carefully painting her fingernails.

A girl at the far table with a gauze bandage wrapped around her head moaned distractedly into her headset while a newborn suckled her heavy breast. She smiled down at her baby as though her unconvincing climax were a private joke between them.

Ben followed Ponytail into a second, larger room, set up like a cheap soundstage. Three pert young women: a peroxide blonde, a brunette, and a redhead, writhed in a choreographed dog pile on a big four-poster bed with black rubber sheets. They wore a ton of makeup and the remnants of some cheap lingerie. The blonde and the redhead wielded imposing dildos.

A single digital-video camera rested on a tripod in front of the bed. Off camera, bored geeks wearing Social Distortion and REM T-shirts sat hunched over computer terminals with nimble fingers flying over the keys. Their computer screens held the image of the action on the bed. "Prague wants Karla and Mandy with the pink dildo," one geek called without looking up. The two women crawled to the front of the bed to perform. "And Cincinnati would like Cindy to eat Karla's pussy," another geek said tiredly, and the redhead rolled over, positioning herself to oblige.

"We take credit card orders from over thirty countries twenty-four hours a day," whispered a saccharine voice behind Ben. "They pay a premium for our live content, all one hundred percent interactive."

Strange had no lips. That was the first thing Ben noticed. He was over six feet tall and ascetically gaunt. Ben had heard Strange was a vegan and a world-class yogi, which may have accounted for the mantid refinement of his limbs. His delicate skin appeared almost translucent and wisps of white hair hung from his scalp like cobwebs. He had a long straight neck and the most prominent Adam's apple that Ben had ever seen. It bobbed when he spoke like a tiny skull. Everything about Strange, from his luminous pallor to his skeletal physique, called to mind the grave. Save for his eyes, which were the deep pink of vascular blood.

The Russian Mob had tried to muscle Strange a few years back. They'd sent former-Spetnaz commandos prowling out of Glendale on turbocharged Ducatis. Strange's argument was that there were enough lonely, horny folks out there for a rich mosaic of cut-rate fuck flicks, but the Russians evidently did not agree. And the story goes: they'd bound Strange in heavy chains, bagged him, shot him, and threw him Rasputin-style into the Los Angeles River. But after he'd resurfaced a few months later looking none the worse for wear, the Russians had left him the fuck alone. They still forked their fingers to ward off the Evil Eye at the mention of his name.

"Benjamin Kahn," Strange said, extending his hand. His manner was effete, almost feminine, but there was venom in his smile. "Amateur star of *The Wicked Stepmother*." Ben took his hand, the palm like parchment. "Shall we talk in my office, where there are fewer distractions?"

The soundproof office was furnished entirely in black leather. Strange sat in a high-backed swivel chair behind his big desk and Ben plopped into an overstuffed couch. A bank of six video monitors behind Strange displayed a multiangled view from his bookshop's security cameras, the sweaty scrum on the four-poster outside, *Bloomberg Financial News,* and a rerun of *Hogan's Heroes.*

"They look a little old for you," Ben said, pointing to the flickering image of the women on the bed outside.

"Ancient history." Strange frowned a Pagliaccio's grotesque pantomime of regret. "The kid stuff has never been more than a cottage industry anyway." The word "cottage" brought to mind the life-sized gingerbread house where the witch lures Hansel and Gretel to be fattened and eaten. Strange had a silver tray of raw oysters on his desk, probably had them delivered from Musso & Frank up the street. He tilted a mottled gray shell and slurped the lifeless flesh from it in one practiced motion. Then he held the tray out to Ben.

"I'm allergic to shellfish," Ben lied.

"Some Absinthe?" Strange pulled the stopper from a rococo bottle and poured himself one.

"Nothing, thank you."

"To business then." He raised his glass, his Adam's apple shifting like a parasitic creature. "What brings you to the second circle?"

"Cabe Risley," Ben said, lifting his shirt to show Strange the Beretta Nine tucked into his jeans.

Strange looked him over for a moment, his crimson eyes glowing. Then he broke into a witch's tubercular cackle, an attenuated finger dabbing a nonexistent tear from the corner of his eye. "I'm sorry. It's just that in some ways you're so like your father. Certainly have his audacity, his . . ." Strange rolled his eyes, pretending to search for the word. ". . . chutzpah."

The phone on Strange's desk chirped and Ben reflexively touched his Beretta. "Put it on speaker," he said.

Strange hit the button. "Yes?"

"Texas wants the big finish for twenty thousand," the voice on the speaker said, one of the computer geeks from outside.

"Method of payment?" Strange asked.

"AmEx gold," the geek said.

"Tell them to sit tight for a moment." Strange released the button. He leaned back in his chair, crossed his legs, and steepled his fingers.

"Cabe is a very ambitious young man," Strange sighed. "He tried to cross the Alps last year."

"At the Wiltern," Ben said.

"And failed to reach the summit." Strange nodded. "Well, who am I to stand between Hannibal and his elephants?"

"You set the deal up?"

"Oh my, no." Strange smiled demurely. "I'm but a poor player. I merely hold the funds in escrow until the transaction is concluded."

"For a percentage," Ben said.

"For a percentage." Strange extended his long arms across the desk, holding his wrists out to Ben. "So, am I under arrest, Officer Halloran? It is Halloran, is it not?"

"Where?"

Strange closed his eyes, tapped his papery index finger to his nonexistent lips. "No," he said. "I don't think so."

Ben drew his Beretta.

"That's been done," Strange said. "And it's beneath you."

"Believe me when I tell you," Ben said, pointing the Beretta at Strange. He thumbed the hammer. "That nothing is beneath me anymore."

"Liberating, isn't it?" Strange smiled. "May I screen something for you, a short subject before we conclude our business?"

"Tell me where it's happening," Ben said.

"I'll tell you whatever you want to know." Strange dimmed the office lights and hit a remote. "After the feature. Now hush." Facetious credits floated over black screens on all six monitors.

CUCKHOLD VIDEO PRESENTS:

BENJI KAHN

GRETCHEN KAHN

IN A SURREPTITIOUS PRODUCTION

The music came up, a techno backbeat, accompanied by a bawdy, synthesized horn section, the score yielding to Gretchen's whimpers.

The opening scene: Benji and Gretchen in the master shower, their bodies slick with soap. Gretchen takes Benji in her hand, turns her back to him, bends at the waist, and deftly eases him into her. Cut to: a shot of Gretchen astride him on the kitchen floor, head thrown back, robe hiked over her thighs. Cut to: Ben's head between her legs, Gretchen's fingers digging in his thick hair. Cut to: Gretchen kneeling in the living room, taking Ben in her mouth. Cut. Cut. Cut. Over and over, bodies churning like a single engine until the languid pace became frenetic. Gretchen's hairstyle marked the passage of months, going from pageboy to pixie, from red to blond to brunette.

On the screen, Gretchen looked desperate and pained. She'd needed him to be different than his father. And he had been. When all was said and done, he'd been worse. Ben had a wild impulse to put the gun in his mouth, put the muzzle up into his soft palate, and pull the trigger. Strange was watching him intently, his breath quickening. Misery was his fetish, Ben realized, the only thing that got Strange off.

"He's meeting them at the river tonight at ten," Strange said. He handed Ben a box of tissue. "Under the Olympic Boulevard Bridge. It's a new moon."

Hamface and Ponytail stood outside the office, both dressed as medieval executioners in black leather S&M masks with zippered slits for eyelets. "You're just in time for the big finish," Strange said and nodded to the players. The two men charged the four-poster. Hamface grabbed the redhead by the hair, sweeping a knife across her throat. She screamed, stage blood pouring from a tube hidden under the knife, covering her breasts as she slumped. Ponytail choked the blonde with huge black-gloved hands. She struggled, shuddered, and went limp. Hamface buried his knife into the brunette's abdomen, the spring-loaded blade retracting back into the handle, creating the illusion that the knife had penetrated her flesh. The brunette bit down on a blood caplet and red fizz burbled from her lips.

"And . . . we're off-line," the geek said. Ponytail and Hamface peeled off their masks. The brunette sat up and wiped the stage blood from her chin. The redhead laughed. Her eyes were hollow and dead. It was Gretchen. Then Ben blinked and it wasn't. His eyes stung.

"Anything the traffic will allow," Strange said, clapping softly. The air down there had grown thick enough to gag on. Ben bolted up the stairs. The guard at the top of the stairs threw back the bolts in the door and held it open for him.

Ben rushed out through the bookstore onto the crowded sidewalk, squinting his eyes against the slanting afternoon light. He didn't pay any real attention to the silver robot until the guy stepped off his milk crate with a target pistol clenched in one silver glove.

Now, he'd heard that with all the adrenaline in a gunfight, a guy could take a bullet and not even know it until the fight was over, the smoke clears, and some paramedic points to the leaking hole in him and says, sir, you might want to let me take a look at that, but he didn't see how anyone could fail to notice a pocket supernova exploding in his side.

There was no sound, just this puff of smoke from the muzzle and the instant knowledge that he was hurt. Somehow, he managed to draw the Beretta and stagger over Charlie Chaplin's and Julia Roberts's stars with his gun leveled in front of him. But the guy was already flickering, juking through the crowd, putting all that soft civilian flesh between Ben and his target. A glimpse of glitter paint, like a steelhead moving upstream. Gone.

Someone turned the sound back on and Ben heard the screams of the tourists scrambling for cover around him. Most just hit the deck. Some of them snatched up kids and tried to shield them with their bodies. A few older Japanese guys in Nike exercise suits just put their backs to the wall and went right on filming with digital cameras.

He looked down, expecting to find blood sluicing from his ribs, but there was only a smoking hole in his shirt. He probed the hole and felt the round, flattened against his Kevlar vest like a flanged coin.

Most of the witnesses were still cowering on the sidewalk and crouched in doorways. No one looked up. He tucked the gun back into his jeans, crossed the boulevard at Highland, and took the escalator down into the red-line station. He heard sirens topside as the train arrived. He stepped through the doors and slumped into the first seat he found.

An hour later, Ben was pounding on Marquez's front door. "What do you want?"

"The deal's going down tonight at ten," Ben said, leaning against the door frame, still short of breath. "Under the Olympic Bridge."

30

1997

Benji needed to ditch the Hard Rock in a bad way. His jaw had swollen badly and blood from his head dripped under his collar, staining his shirt. He tried to hail a few passing taxis, but Vegas cabbies can smell a loser from a block away and they wanted no part of him, so he wandered up Paradise Road with no idea of where he was going.

The neighborhood soured within a few blocks of the hotel, bright neon storefronts giving way to bombed-out semi-industrial buildings with boarded windows and incomprehensible graffiti. Carefully sculpted corporate landscaping yielded to bare earth, cracked and ulcerated, like the skin of a sun-dried corpse. Entropy unrelenting, the way erosion claws away a sea cliff.

A gibbering zombie in a stained army jacket pushed a shopping cart full of crushed cans and other filthy treasures. Passing headlights washed over him and Benji saw his face, covered in sores. Wasted whores strutted past him in wobbly heels, and a furtive dealer ducked out of the shadows to jiggle vials of crank in Benji's face.

A large shadow broke away from the wall and fell in step with him, stalking a few paces behind Benji, just outside his field of vision. Benji sensed some size on him, but the guy's footsteps were light as he closed in. He braced himself for an attack, but the guy must have decided he wasn't worth his effort and melted back into the shadows. Benji figured the only thing that saved him from a mugging was that he looked like a hapless drunk who'd already been rolled.

Benji heard sirens and ducked inside a cavelike bar with a lighted marquee that advertised a hot dog and a beer for $1.50. Damned souls hunkered under milky clouds of cigarette smoke, scowling over flat beers. No one looked up. Some smart-ass had tuned the snowy television mounted over the bar to an old rerun of *Cheers,* the blue light flickering in dead eyes.

This bartender would have no need of a bouncer, three hundred pounds of seedy gristle and meat, shaved bald with a coarse ZZ Top beard covering the lower half of his face. He wore a gray T-shirt, jeans, and suspenders with one of those lumbar support belts. The bartender microwaved a flaccid gray hot dog, socked it into a stale bun, and handed the dog to Benji along with a dusty bottle of Pabst Blue Ribbon. Benji carried his beer and hot dog over to a tabletop Ms. Pac-Man that had probably been out of order since the mideighties.

A vulpine man in a black leather jacket moved cautiously along the wall and bellied up to the Ms. Pac-Man like he and Benji were old buddies. The guy had the glittering eyes of a nocturnal rodent, greasy black hair slicked back from a sharp widow's peak, an obscene smile curling his cracked lips upward to bare tiny teeth.

"You need a woman," he whispered. "I can get you one."

"No, thank you," Benji said.

"How about a man?"

"Leave me alone," Benji said, his blood coming up.

"I can get you a kid if—"

Benji gripped the neck of his beer and broke the bottle across the man's face, flaying open his cheek. No righteousness behind the blow, just an uncontrollable spasm of loathing. The other patrons barely stirred as Benji knocked the guy out of his chair. The guy rolled on the floor, reaching for something in his jacket. Benji kicked him in the gut before he could get to whatever it was. The guy pinched his eyes shut and curled his body into a tight ball on the floor; the instinctive reaction of a cur that'd been kicked its whole life. Benji felt sick.

He heard a sharp rap on the bar, the bartender brandishing a sawed-off Louisville slugger. "Hey, Travis Bickle!" the bartender shouted, gesturing to the door with his bat. "Take your crazy-ass shit outside or I'm calling the fucking cops."

Benji dropped the broken bottle and bolted, bumping a table and knocking over some poor guy's beer on the way out the door, running for blocks, until his chest burned and his legs shook. His temples throbbed. He beat his fists against his eyes, found a battered pay phone outside a liquor store, and dialed the only number he could think of. Carcosa picked up his private line on the first ring.

"Joe, it's Benji," he panted, desperately grateful just to hear the man's voice on the line.

"*Jesucristo,* Benji," Carcosa said. "I've got Jaime and Ignacio looking all over town for you. Your father had a heart attack this afternoon."

Benji gripped the receiver, knuckles pulsing white. His head swam, vision blurred until he remembered to breathe. "How bad?"

"'Mild,' whatever the fuck that means," Carcosa said. "He's at Cedars and he's probably going to be okay, but Darius has people watching the hospital for you. Jaime told me the street price is one hundred and fifty large for your head."

"Didn't waste any time putting the word out." Benji sighed. They would have been heading west on Interstate 15, on their way back to L.A. in Esther Cole's Eldorado, Jax keeping to the speed limit. Darius chirping every Crip from San Diego to Seattle, offering one hundred and fifty thousand—*Bring Me the Head of Benjamin Kahn, Jr.*

"What the hell did you do to him?" Carcosa asked. "Forget it, I don't want to know, but you can't come back to L.A. now, *mijo*. No way."

"I can't stay here," Benji said. "Darius knows I'm here. He has people in Vegas."

"Darius has people everywhere," Carcosa corrected gently.

"And I'm an accessory to—" His eyes stung and he couldn't swallow.

"*Ya te dijo que no quiero enterarme,*" Carcosa said. "*No me importa.* Whatever you've done is in the past, no? Deep, slow breaths, Benji. I can help you, but you have to move fast, okay? Get yourself to the south service entrance of the Thebes. One of my people there will set you up with a room and even Darius won't touch you inside the hotel. One of my special friends will call on you. A friend from the old days, *tu entiendes?*"

"*Claro,*" Benji said, his voice cracking. Drops fell onto the receiver and slipped into the perforations on the plastic mouthpiece with an audible sizzle.

"Then go now," Carcosa said. "There isn't much time. *Vete.*"

Twenty minutes later, the southern loading bay of the Thebes Resort and Casino slid open and a striking, black-haired woman in a dark Chanel suit beckoned him inside. The woman had a Spartan air about her that did not invite conversation, a full head taller than Benji. Her Amazonian body, only hinted at under the suit, was of the caliber you'd find on a swimsuit model or an Olympic sprinter. Clear blue eyes, high cheekbones, full lips, and a deep knife scar that ran across her left eye. Her glass eye slightly out of alignment, but otherwise identical to her remaining one.

She pulled a silk handkerchief from her breast pocket, placed it over her mouth and nose while she led Benji through the hotel's laundry facility. He followed her through roiling gray clouds of acrid steam. Hispanic and Asian women, wearing surgical masks and sodden clothing, hauled the hotel's linens out of industrial washer-dryers. Brown, swollen fingers, bleached raw at the tips, pulled twisted, heavy sheets from the machines for ceaseless sorting and folding. Dirty linens belched endlessly from widemouthed laundry chutes overhead. It was like walking through the belly of a slave ship.

They rode the service elevator to the twenty-second floor, and Benji followed her down a long hallway. The penal sameness of luxury hotels was supposed to be a comfort to weary travelers, but it made Benji feel like a rat in a maze.

At the end of the hall, the woman carded into a suite the Thebes must have kept for Carcosa for when he was in town. Opening the door, she stepped aside, politely inviting him to enter first. Benji had a vision of walking into the suite to find a plastic tarp covering the floor, a dozen Crips laying for him with machetes, but he was too tired to run and if Carcosa had betrayed him, he had no hope of survival anyway. He stepped into the suite, but nobody pounced from the shadows to lop off his head.

"Stand right there," the woman said once they were inside. She pulled a compact digital camera from her pocket and photographed him against the white wall of the suite's foyer. "Take off your clothes. There's a robe in the bathroom. Hand them out to me."

Benji handed her his torn and bloody clothes through the half-open door. "Try to get some sleep and don't open the door for any reason. I will key into your room sometime before dawn with a fresh set of clothes. When you awaken, wait for instructions."

After the Amazon left with his bloody clothes, Benji caught his own reflection in the bathroom mirror, eyes receding into reddish pouches. His jaw looked slightly misshapen, lip split like the skin of a plum. Benji showered, rinsing away the caked blood and picking tiny bits of glass out of his skin. Then he filled the sunken Jacuzzi tub and soaked. He shrugged into the hotel robe and flopped facedown on to the bed. Fresh clothes were waiting when he woke up.

There was a knock at the door. Benji checked the peephole and saw Jaime and Ignacio standing in the hall. He opened the door. Both men hugged him roughly and he wanted to cry. The three of them took an elevator down to the lobby. They walked single file, keeping Benji between them as they made their way through the crowded casino. Jaime bought them each a ticket to the Cannibal Cove aquarium, the casino's newest attraction, boasting the "world's largest collection of seagoing predators." They carried their audio tour wands through the turnstiles and down the escalator. None of them spoke.

The place was lit with those phony Pirates of the Caribbean torches. The walls and ceiling were done in textured concrete, sculpted to look like the bowels of an Aztec temple, jaguars and feathered serpents carved in composite relief and plastic tropical plants like you'd find in a dentist's office. The place felt like a movie set, the kind of lost city Johnny Weiss-muller used to liberate on Saturday afternoons. Jaime led them past crocs lounging under misters, a tank of piggish moray eels, a jellyfish habitat, and the piranha exhibit, the fish eerily still in a tank of knee-deep water behind thick glass. A cheesy sign with a bite out of it dangled from the ceiling of the corridor. The sign promised SHARKS DEAD AHEAD!

Jaime cut left and keyed into a steel door marked EMPLOYEES ONLY—NO ADMITTANCE. Benji and Ignacio followed him into a drab cement hallway that took them past the backs of the exhibits. Benji felt claustro-phobic. The air in here was cool and muggy and reeked of fish. They climbed two flights of steel stairs to a railed catwalk that spanned the shark tank. The tank was huge, a million gallons or more. Their footsteps rattled on the grated steel and the water agitated below them. Dark shapes darted and circled under the catwalk, their boomerang tails whipping the water. Benji figured they used this structure to feed them.

Across the catwalk, Jaime punched four numbers into a keypad and pushed open another door, Benji beginning to wonder how much of this was a bullshit snipe hunt—more of Carcosa's flair for the dramatic.

He followed Jaime down another set of stairs into a huge, climate-controlled office: dark wood wainscoting and Diogenes Club wallpaper, brass desk lamps with green shades, first-edition Ian Flemings on ma-hogany bookcases. An antique globe by the bar, a brown leather couch and club chairs around a mahogany desk.

Carcosa stood silhouetted against the clear acrylic panel that com-prised one entire wall of the office. Sharks soared through the water be-hind him, their bodies latticed with green and violet light, long shadows passing over the office. Twisting greenish patterns wove across the ceiling, shimmering light from the surface of the tank. Carcosa stepped across the big Persian carpet and embraced him. Benji had never been so happy to smell that awful cologne. Ignacio sliced some limes and filled four shot glasses with Patrón. They drank to Big Ben's speedy recovery. Benji felt a stab of guilt and nearly coughed up his shot.

"What is this place?" Benji asked, taking in the framed black-and-white photos of some kind of Special Forces unit, hard men in camouflage paint and tiger-striped jungle fatigues posing around a tattered Nicaraguan flag. Combat medals and a folded American flag behind a glass case. A SOG knife rested on the desk blotter, serving as paperweight and letter opener.

"This office belongs to Mr. Faraday," Carcosa said. "He was gracious enough to allow us to use it while he is away." *Mister* Faraday. Benji had never heard that kind of deferential tone from Carcosa. It made him nervous.

"Who's Mr. Faraday?"

"When Nicaragua fell, and the Soviets were sending their Marxist guerillas up into Mexico to stir up the *campesinos,* who do you think the CIA came to for help?" he asked Benji. "Not the shit-ass *presidente.* He wouldn't go to the toilet without our permission, *mijo.* No, the agency came straight to the cartel. We all broke bread together and drank single-malt scotch and said please and thank you. Then we hunted down every *comunista en el campo.* On May Day, we skinned the guerrillas and let the dogs drag their bodies around the plaza. We stuck their heads on pikes by the roads so *los obreros* would be sure to see them on their way to market.

"And when those *putas* in congress lost their nerve, passed the Boland Amendment, and cut their budget, the CIA came crying back to their old amigos in the cartel," he said. "We hated the communists just as much as they did. So, we cut the agency in. We let them fly it out of Ilopango on their big government planes and they used the profits to finance their black ops and to line their own pockets. These men, if I told you their names, you would know them. You see them on CNN." He laughed. "They all tell you NAFTA is about manufacturing."

Brilliant, Benji thought, I'm drinking tequila in some spook's office next to a giant fucking shark tank. *Normal life, Gretch? Not much danger of that, is there?*

Carcosa lifted a plain manila from the desk blotter, used the SOG knife to slice it open, and dumped the contents on the blotter. A California driver's license with Benji's picture on it, his bruises digitally removed, Social Security card, birth certificate, and credit cards, all in the name of Ben Halloran. "The driver's license and Social Security card are genuine," Carcosa said. "They belonged to a Peace Corps volunteer by the name of Ben Halloran. Mr. Faraday says the poor kid lost an argument with a salt-water croc. There are modest limits on all the credit cards. We're going to need to build your credit history, Benji. That's important."

Benji stared at the cards on the desk, watching the shadows glide over them, but he didn't pick them up off the blotter.

"What's wrong, Benji?"

"It's not that I don't appreciate it," Benji said. "No disrespect or anything, but . . ." Benji glanced at Jaime and Ignacio. They were both avoiding his eyes, studying their shoes. ". . . Okay, what's the catch?"

"Sit down, Benji," Carcosa said. Benji sat. Jaime poured them each another shot, but no one drank yet. A sand tiger slid slowly past, looking like a Cessna with teeth. "You trust me, don't you, *mijo*?"

You're kidding, right? Benji thought, but he nodded solemnly.

"If you're working for me, I can protect you," Carcosa said. "Otherwise . . ." He shrugged his shoulders. "These documents are nothing. You can go to fucking Mars, but Darius would find you.

"This whole business." Carcosa sighed. "This unfortunate business with Darius has presented us with an opportunity."

Us, Benji thought, or you?

"Tomorrow, I'm taking you back to Los Angeles," Carcosa said. "And Saturday morning Ben Halloran will go down to Parker Center to take the LAPD written exam."

"You're joking, right?" Benji said.

Carcosa shook his head. "I wanted you to be my DA, but we'll have to table that for now. I could use a pair of eyes inside the department, Benji," he said. "And you're the only one I trust, *mijo*."

Benji slammed his tequila.

PRESENT

It was almost nine when Chuin picked them up from Marquez's house in his uncle's Cadillac. Marquez placed his elk rifle in the trunk—a Winchester .300 Magnum he'd fitted with an old Starlight scope. He slid into the passenger seat next to Chuin, and Ben climbed in the back. Chuin wore a Dodgers cap and an old army jacket to cover his shoulder holster. Marquez wore his stained poncho, a souvenir from Rampart Narcotics.

Marquez opened the paper bag on the seat between them. "I thought I saw a puddy tat," he said.

"Hands off," Chuin said. "My old lady packed that."

"I did see a puddy tat."

"Eat shit, wetback," Chuin said as he pulled away from the house.

Chuin found Ben's eyes in his rearview mirror. "Miguel's a trusting soul," Chuin said. "I still think you're bullshit."

Ben didn't look away. "You're entitled to your opinion," he said.

"We're off the books tonight," Chuin said. "Nobody knows we're out here. That means open season and the shooting policy's out the fucking window. So if you're setting us up, I won't hesitate. Not for a second."

"Relax," Marquez said.

They took the Harbor Freeway to Olympic and headed east through downtown past Santee Alley toward Boyle Heights. Chuin drove them across the old Beaux Arts bridge that spanned the Los Angeles River at

Olympic, passing ornate lampposts at intervals along the cement railing. Marquez hadn't been back here since the night with Rourke.

Factories disgorged weird milky smoke into the night sky. Water trickled down from the bridge, and the low-sodium lamps cast a bouillon shimmer across the filthy water. The river looked low for this time of year, probably less than a foot.

Chuin pulled into the shadowed alley behind the Kenpo Jeans warehouse and handed Marquez a rover. "We'll be working off Clemars."

"Roger that," Marquez said, adjusting the radio. Clemars was an old LAPD emergency frequency that was usually deserted.

"I'll be scanning Hollenbeck and Central freqs." Chuin tapped his earpiece. "But I don't think we'll have any company. They get the odd Four-Fifty-nine, sometimes a floater in the river, but nothing much happens down here."

Marquez pulled his rifle out of the trunk and headed into the alley, moving low and quick. Ben jogged after him. Marquez handed Ben the rifle while he scaled a cyclone fence. From the top of the fence, he climbed onto the roof of the warehouse. Ben tossed the rifle up to him and followed Marquez onto the roof.

They gila-crawled over the warehouse and flattened against a cement shelf overlooking the river. Marquez rolled his good-luck poncho, placed it over a seam in the cement, and nested the rifle there. Propped on his elbows, Ben spotted for him with a pair of night-vision binoculars. Marquez sighted through the Starlight scope, the optics pulling a greenish image from the ambient light.

Chuin took his position across the river, parked in front of the city asphalt plant. *Radio check.* Chuin's voice on the frequency.

"Loud and clear," Marquez said.

They waited. To the north, traffic shushed along the 10 Freeway. Marquez heard crickets on the riverbank and the diesel engines of big semis lumbering out of the loading docks of Dependable Highway Express. The downtown skyline looked far away

"Here he comes," Ben said. "See him?"

Risley's truck was running without headlights up the center of the L.A. River, tires kicking up rooster tails of yellow foam. Marquez made four riders and two heavily laden pack mules closing on the truck from the north, an eerie procession along the river.

"*I can't believe I'm seeing this shit.*" Chuin said.

Claustrophobia set in as Risley drove under the bridge. Ambush alley, Risley thought, and was glad he'd escrowed his money with the albino. He heard the splash of hooves clopping along the riverbed, and a horse nickering. This last sound chilled him for reasons Risley could not explain. He saw the dark silhouettes of four on horseback, motionless but for the steam coming from their horses' nostrils. They must have come down the Rio Hondo out of the San Gabriel Mountains, picked up the Los Angeles, and ridden the cement river right through the middle of downtown.

"I hear they skin brothers," Mapes said. "Quarter 'em on car bumpers and all kind of creepy-ass shit."

"That's all bullshit," Risley said, but looking out at those four still shadows, he wasn't at all sure.

The Nazi Saddle Tramps were the last surviving members of an über-outlaw biker gang that had once ruled the San Fernando Valley until a massive ATF investigation drove them out into the badlands. Licking their wounds in a cinder-block billiard parlor outside Lancaster, the hectored Nazi Saddle Tramps had done what all desert wanderers do sooner or later, they'd found themselves a messiah.

Swede Hargrove was a Pelican Bay graduate with ties to the Aryan Brotherhood, Brazilian jiujitsu enthusiast, and steroid gourmand who fancied himself a Norse chieftain. He preached a mixture of Fourth Reich mumbo jumbo and pagan mysticism with just a touch of John Ford, and he'd reinvented the Nazi Saddle Tramps as an Aryan horse clan, a transformation that might have been ridiculous if it hadn't been so successful. The Nazi Saddle Tramps slept rough, stayed off paved roads and out of all but the seediest saloons, crossing the San Jacinto on horseback with their saddlebags full of cash or crystal meth.

The Swede still had burnout bikers cooking crank in double-wides and old mining camps all over the desert, from Ocotillo Wells to Boron, gack being one of the only illicit substances not regulated by foreign cartels. No sir, like the Ford and the slinky, their crank was handmade with pride right here in the U.S. of A. And some of Swede's best customers were the brave men and women of our armed forces, because nothing sped up an overseas deployment like, well, speed.

The Swede had contacts in Twenty-nine Palms and at Pendleton who were willing to trade overstocked ordnance for crystal meth. While big Hercules transport planes carried NST-brand crank to troops in the Gulf, Germany, and Korea, the Nazi Saddle Tramps sold government-issue iron from Chula Vista to Crescent City. The Swede sold weapons to gang-bangers, militiamen, and Christian end-times cultists. From time to time, he even sold to those one-time flipouts who'd had enough of their bosses and coworkers.

Of course, Risley wouldn't have dealt with these nuts for guns alone. He could have gone anywhere for burners, could have plucked them out of Central Property on their way to the big smelter and fudged the release forms. Hell, he could have pulled Chink AKs out of a container on the Pedro docks. He knew longshoremen with triad connections, but he needed more bang than his usual sources could provide.

"*Do you have a shot?*" Chuin said.

"Stand by one," Marquez whispered.

The Nazi Saddle Tramps had backshot a sheriff's deputy outside Lancaster last year and left him for the coyotes and Marquez had a good mind to dump these assholes on GP, but he knew better. He could work the bolt fast, but not Oswald fast. Besides, the way he had this figured he'd only have to fire once. Drop one of the riders and the rest would take care of itself. Marquez put his crosshairs on the Conan-looking motherfucker on the paint. He'd put a tunnel through his ten ring, knock him off his horse. The others would see Conan drop into the river and think Risley had double-crossed them. Then their first order of business would be to turn Risley's truck into a colander.

"So we're just going to kill him?" Ben asked. "In cold blood."

"Two very dirty cops and sundry other assholes flatline at an elicit arms deal that went sideways," Marquez said. "End of story."

Marquez let up on the trigger, took his eye from the padded eyepiece, rubbed the bridge of his nose. He passed his hand over his stubble, told himself he just was waiting for his shot. What the fuck was his problem? He'd dropped the hammer seven times, well, eight if you counted . . . He shifted around, hard to get comfortable all of a sudden.

"Anytime now, Miguelito," Chuin said.

Marquez reset, curling his finger around the trigger. Fuck it, these curs needed killing as bad as any he'd known. He'd be doing the world a good turn, right?

Now they came forward into the spill of the headlights and Risley saw the swastikas, thunderbolts, and weird runic symbols painted on their horses. Painted in blood, Risley observed, or some substance meant to look like blood.

The big one on the pinto had to be the Swede. Gray-streaked hair swept back into a loose ponytail and a Fu Manchu stash with the ends woven into proboscis braids that drooped below his chin. He wore twin .45 revolvers on an old-fashioned leather gunbelt and he rested a Norse battle-axe on his shoulder, like the guy was posing for Frazetta's *Death Dealer.*

Swede's number two wore twelve-gauge bandoleers and held a drum-fed shotgun across his pommel. He spurred his mount to swing in along the driver's side of the truck. The third and fourth riders carried AKs straight up, with the stocks resting on their thighs, ursine men on ambivalent mounts.

The Swede tossed his reins to number two, swung his leg over the saddle, and slid off his pinto into the foot-high water. He moved easily for a guy packing so much meat, and he carried his battle-axe the way a lawyer might carry a briefcase. He had Shutzstaffel lightning bolts tattooed on the right side of his neck—though neck was probably the wrong word for the pyramidal junction of tendon and muscle that attached the Swede's prognathus head to his massive body. His trapezium arched like the hood of a cobra, and the guy looked to Risley like he might prowl on all fours when it suited him.

Risley could hear Mapes breathing hard in the seat next to him, the big boy apt to lose his shit right here and jerk the trigger. Not hood, Risley thought. Not hood at all. "Easy, Boo," Risley whispered.

"Evening, gentlemen." Convict culture in that voice, a guy who'd taken some time to read between his prison workouts. The Swede's eyes took in the P90 on Mapes's lap and he smiled, big Texas teeth, the better to eat you with. "Nice night for it."

"He was my boot," Marquez said. "My responsibility. I trained him and he went bad on me."

Ben knew how badly Marquez needed to sever himself from Risley. They'd been partners, joined by acts of vengeance and mercy that had taken them outside the law, and Ben felt a weird flash of jealousy for this other apprentice who'd once stood within Marquez's circle of trust.

"So what, now he's Old Yeller?"

An air horn sounded in the distance. A freight train was coming north along the river, carrying cargo inland from the Pedro docks.

"You got a problem with this, partner?" Marquez hissed, winking his left eye to peer through the scope with his right. "Close your eyes."

And now Ben understood that Marquez hadn't dragged him up here to spot for him. He hadn't brought him here to bear witness for him, or to absolve him. Ben had a sudden image of Certain Death, the way he'd struggled on the hotel carpet with a dirty sock in his mouth while Jax opened his throat. *He wants to be talked out of this.*

"Miguel," Ben said. "Man, this is just what he'd do."

Ben would have been talking about Risley, but Marquez saw the face of his old training officer, the legendary Tim Rourke. Six official shootings, Marquez thought. Plus the one they still didn't know about. It had started with a late-night pursuit of two serial rapists. Their last victim had been fourteen, and they'd taken one of her ears as a trophy. No way Rourke wasn't going to catch them, but Marquez was about pissing himself in the passenger seat because Rourke was driving shitfaced, tilting his flask of Bushmills with one hand and steering the black-and-white with the other. Rourke ended up ramming the guys, forcing their big Chevy van off this same bridge. Marquez remembered watching the van roll end over end, leaving pieces of itself along the cement slope. The van landed upside down in the river, the driver killed in the crash. The passenger wiggled out of the broken windshield. Marquez ran down to the river's edge and held his gun on the guy as the guy slogged through the waist-high water with his hands up.

"Plug that son of a bitch," Rourke shouted from up the slope. "That's an order, Mex. Don't you let that fucker reach the bank, hear me? Shoot him. Shoot!"

The gun boomed in Marquez's hands, the guy splashing backward into the river. Marquez watched the body drift, floating faceup with the rest of the garbage, carried by the dark, muscular water until Marquez lost sight of it where the river curved past the rail yard.

After end of watch that night, Rourke had thrown a kill party for him. Way down among the crumbling warehouses at 135th and Estrella, those hulking wartime ruins of cement slab, brick, and corrugated steel, too remote even for the slouching derelicts and shivering junkies. Once in a while, someone would dump a stiff there to be fed upon by rats for days until someone called it in. It was their secret place, a postindustrial arroyo where they gathered at a garbage fire, passed around bottles, cursed and laughed, and cranked rounds into the air like a band of holdout Comanche come to celebrate another Pyrrhic victory. He'd called in sick for four days after that, puking his guts out, but not from the booze. He'd wanted to quit, wanted to kill himself.

Then Rourke had come out to his house, looked at his wife like she was filet mignon when she answered the front door. And Marquez would remember how ordinary, how mediocre the guy looked standing on his front porch out of uniform with a six-pack of Olympia under his arm. On the job, Rourke was a legend. Out in the world, he was just another dirty old coot with an expiration date on his liver. Marquez hadn't seen daylight in nearly a week, but he'd squinted his eyes against the sun and come outside to meet Rourke, not wanting this man inside his home.

They sat together on the uneven cement of his listing porch and watched neighborhood kids playing soccer in the street. Marquez nursed his beer, pausing to hold the cool can against his thudding temple. His vision shimmered and he knew he was crying but there was nothing for it.

"I'll allow that was a hard one, lad," Rourke told him. "But you did what needed doing and that's what matters. That's all that matters." He rested a papery hand on Marquez's shoulder. "That's the job, son. We face the ugly things, do the ugly things, so the rest of 'em don't have to."

Marquez had reached up to grip Rourke's hand the way a shipwrecked man clings to a broken beam, held on because he'd had nothing else.

"You're not like him," Ben said.

"Come on, plug the son of a bitch and let's go home," Chuin said.

"Jesus," Marquez groaned. He rolled over, away from the rifle, and lay next to Ben with his forearm draped over his eyes. "Oh my sweet Jesus."

Chachunka-chank. The Union Pacific rumbled up the riverbank past the front of the Kenpo warehouse. *Chachunka-chank.* Double-stacked cargo containers rolled by them, almost level with the roof. *Chachunka-chank.*

"You know," the Swede said, playfully eyeing the P90 in Mapes's lap, "I don't usually truck with shit skins, but you fellows come highly recommended."

Mapes shifted in his seat. Risley set his jaw, silently willing Mapes not to take the bait, to hold his fudge and not fuck this up for him. God, he wished Carver were here.

"Well." Risley smiled. "We sure do appreciate you making an exception for us." Of course, he knew Swede's bang customers came in all colors, a business practice he justified because it supposedly hastened the Coming Race War, but Risley just figured the cracker son of a bitch was greedy and possibly not as dumb as he looked.

Two more riders dismounted, removed one of the crates lashed to the mule. They slogged through the water and set the crate down in the bed of Risley's truck. Risley popped the lid. The green tubes were packed in Styrofoam, appealing in their nondescript simplicity.

Chachunka-chank. Chachunka-chank.
   "Disregard," Chuin said. *"Don't shoot. Abort. Abort."*
Chachunka-chank. Chachunka-chank.
   "Miguel, you copy?"
Chachunka-chank. Chachunka-chank.
   "We can't see anything," Marquez said. "The train's blocking us."
Chachunka-chank. Chachunka-chank.
   "I'm calling for backup," Chuin said. *"They got RPGs, man."*

"The deal was for stingers," Risley said. "These things are fucking antiques."

"Inventory problems," Swede said. "Seller reserves the right to substitute with items of equal value."

They pulled the other crates off the mules one at a time and stacked them neatly in Risley's ride. Mapes threw a tarp over them and tied them down with bungee cords. When they were done, Swede dialed Strange on his cell. "Thane of Glamis," Swede said. He handed the phone to Risley.

"Thane of Cawdor," Risley said.

"King hereafter," Strange said, his voice like acid on the line.

Then Swede pressed the blade of his axe to Risley's throat. Risley didn't move. He felt, rather than saw Mapes splashing around the truck with his P90 and held up his hand. "No, hold up," Risley said. "Hold up, Boo."

"One last thing," Swede said. "Tell me about the Chinaman watching us from the asphalt plant."

"He ain't mine," Risley said.

"How about the spic with the long rifle and the white boy watching us from the Kenpo warehouse?"

"Not a clue," Risley said, fighting back a smile. *Marquez.*

The Swede lowered the axe. "Good to know." Swede hit the speed dial on his phone. "Green light," he said.

Ben glimpsed them stalking wraithlike atop the Sears Building, momentarily silhouetted against the green neon sign, surefooted men with heavy assault rifles loping along the roof. Ten stories up, they had firepower and high ground. "Move!" Ben shouted. Tar and insulation spurted up from the roof all around them. Upright explosions of fine gray dust, Ben blinking the stuff out of his eyes even as he gripped Marquez's shirt. They were both sprinting now, geysers of grit chasing them right off the ledge. They leaped from the warehouse to the train.

More rounds sparked the steel as Ben landed on the cargo container. Bullets buzzed past his ear and tugged at his shirt. He dropped onto his belly atop the container, pulled the Beretta from his pancake holster, and tried to get his bearings. He didn't see Marquez. The train carried him under the bridge, out of their line of fire.

Chachunka-chank. Chachunka-chank.

Marquez leaped out into the dark, arms and legs flailing, and landed hard on the train, rolled across the top of the container, his momentum taking him right over. He fell between the cars and lost the rifle. Fuck. Fuck. Fuck. He crashed against the coupling and slid backward, shirt riding up his belly, scrabbling for purchase. His legs dangled over the track. He grabbed hold of some kind of hose and swung himself clear of the train.

He heard more firing and looked across the river. Plumes of asphalt spurted all around Chuin's Cadillac. The car spasmed and bucked. The hood seemed to ripple, blistering under heavy fire. Glimmering clouds of safety blew weightlessly outward. The Caddy's horn blared, wavering.

"No," Marquez said. He ran, lost his footing, and rolled down the concrete slope into the gray water. He drew his Smith, running out into the river and saw Risley's truck heading south. He fired to slide-lock as he ran, wild Hail Mary shots, hoping to detonate one of the crates, but the truck was already out of pistol range. No. Marquez watched it disappear past the rail yard. No. He heard horses splashing north up the river, the sound already growing faint. They were gone.

Please. Please. Marquez scrambled up the far bank, running toward the asphalt plant. Chuin must have ducked behind the engine block. He was wily, right? He'd probably gotten clear of the car. Safety glass crunched under Marquez's feet as he approached the car and yanked the driver's-side door open. The engine was on fire now and in the quavering yellow light he saw everything, even the paper bag in Chuin's lap.

PRESENT

Flashbangs. LAPD SWAT served a search-and-arrest warrant at the Redondo Beach residence of Officer Cabe Risley after sundown. Risley was gone. Detectives from the department's Special Operations Section found little of evidentiary value at the location, apart from Risley's extravagant wardrobe, collection of self-help books, and his album of clippings about Darius Washington. A second team simultaneously struck at the Mapes home in Northridge, finding only Mapes's mother, bedridden with type 2 diabetes. Both Risley and Mapes had lately disappeared from Rampart along with a marked police vehicle, two Urban Police Rifles, several department radios, and the shoulder-fired antitank weapons.

The department quickly fired off a bulletin to be read at roll calls about the appearance and effective range and capability of the M-72 Light Antitank Weapon. Lieutenant Vintner shook his head as he read through the bulletin at p.m. roll call and then announced that he would grant T/O (time off) to any officer under his command, no questions asked. "Anyone who wants to sit this out," Vintner said, looking straight at Marquez. "Anyone."

No one took him up on it.

Diagonals of warm, sooty rain fell across Western Avenue, the storm having sucked up cinders from the Calabasas wildfires as it worked its way south. "He hasn't left town," Marquez said.

"How do you know?"

"Everything he wants is here," Marquez said.

"ADW Domestic Violence at 7660 South Sycorax," the radio squawked. "Suspect is a male black. No further. Assaulting a female black in front of apartment six. No weapons seen. Screaming heard in the background. Code Two High Incident 1138. Unit to handle, identify."

Recognizing the address, Marquez sighed, keyed the mike. "Twelve-A-Forty-five, show us handling." Marquez knew all about the apartment complex. Baseheads squatted in about half the units, Boot Hill cooking crews in the rest. Over the years, he'd answered about a million radio calls there, most of them narco-related bloodletting, everything from addict-on-addict stabbings to multiple-homicide dope ripoffs. He'd even testified at the city abatement hearings a few years back, but wasn't surprised that nothing had changed since then. Crumbling stucco still patched with grayish curds of acrylic, bars over every window giving the whole place a penitentiary look. Nothing short of napalm was ever going to sanitize that shithole.

The complex had been passed around by so many dump-and-run slumlords over the years that Marquez had no idea who actually held title anymore, but the name on the deed didn't mean shit anyway. BHMC graffiti all over the building proclaimed these apartments the property of the Boot Hill Mafia Crips.

Marquez blacked out the car, pulled to the curb at Seventy-sixth and Sycorax, and cut the engine. He and the kid heard her jagged screams as soon as they stepped out into the rain. They tramped across the soupy lawn in front of the apartment complex, Marquez throwing a look back over his shoulder, sniffing for an ambush. Nothing behind him but rain.

When viewed from a helicopter, Marquez remembered, the two-story complex formed a squared-off U, all the units facing a courtyard of cracked, uneven pavement and a dead swimming pool—the last pool in the hood as far as he knew. The other ghetto pools had been paved over years ago by landlords fearing liability, but this one remained. Residents here used the pool as their personal landfill, blindly tossing everything from dirty diapers to dead possums out of first- and second-story windows. The pool stayed bone-dry through the summer and filled with two or three feet of stagnant rainwater every spring, breeding mosquito larvae and Christ knew what else.

A two-story cage and heavy steel security gate blocked the entrance to the complex like a portcullis. In the breezeway on the other side of the gate, Clarence Malone (a.k.a. Nine-Nine) was pounding his old lady into ground round. Fresh blood speckled her T-shirt and Daisy Dukes.

They called him Nine-Nine because he'd started carrying twin stainless nine-millimeters after watching John Woo's *The Killer* on cable; never mind the foolishness of the two-piece spray-and-pray approach to an actual gunfight. Nine-Nine sported his traditional blue bandanna, no shirt, size-fifty Levi's over his thirty-inch waist. He was about the kid's height, but much broader through the chest and shoulders. Fresh out of a stint in Soledad, Nine-Nine had spent the last thirty-three months converting starchy prison chow into churned muscle that gleamed in the rain. Marquez didn't see those signature nines anywhere on him, but he couldn't be sure.

When he saw them stuck on the other side of the gate, Nine-Nine smiled, like an audience was just what he needed to do this bitch right. He gripped the woman's hair, the way a bareback rider gathers the horse's mane in his fist, yanking her head back to show them her face. Her bottom lip had been split open, blood leaking from her mouth and nose. Her right eye was swollen shut, left staring, already resigned to all of it.

Marquez didn't know the woman, except he did, because it was always the same goddamned woman out here. Cause of death: blunt trauma, brain swelling, massive internal bleeding, organ failure, and rotten taste in dudes.

"See the way I do this nappy-ass bitch?" He hooked his other fist around and drove it into her face. Her head snapped back and her knees buckled, but he held her upright by her hair. "See?" Again, his fist connected. More blood spattered the concrete. "All you can do is watch."

Nine-Nine grabbed her throat, slammed her against the dented mailboxes in the breezeway, and drove his fist into her rounded belly. Marquez twisted the doorknob, but the security gate was dead bolted. He kicked it twice, cursing. The bars only rattled. No way were they getting past the gate, not without a key or some heavy pry tools.

The woman was pregnant. Ben saw the fullness of her belly and felt his own guts rime over, like he'd just swallowed a quart of liquid nitrogen. "Stop!" Ben shouted lamely, gripping the bars. "Jesus, just stop!"

"Stop what, motherfucker? Stop this?" Nine-Nine threw another fist into her belly, doubling her over. She groaned.

"Twelve-A-Forty-five I need a unit with the hook and ram to my location," Marquez spoke into his radio. "I need that unit Code Three."

"Twelve-A-Forty-five has a five-minute ETA."

"She won't last that long," Ben said, eyeing the front of the building. The bars on the windows might work as handholds, if they would hold his weight. He could make it to the roof, drop into the courtyard behind them, and take Nine-Nine by surprise. "I'm going over," he said.

"Don't be an idiot," Marquez said, only halfheartedly trashing the idea, part of him ready go with it because it was all they had.

Ben gripped a set of security bars on the window and pulled himself up, bracing the tips of his boots on the narrow sill. He pressed his body flat against the wet stucco, stretching up to the second-floor window. Dirty rainwater ran down the face of the building, greasing his hands, soaking through his wool uniform. His wet Kevlar vest felt like it weighed about fifty pounds. He stood on tiptoes to curl his fingers around the next set of rusty bars, did a half-assed pull-up, and got his right foot up on the ledge of the second-floor window. His arms shook.

A bedsheet had been tacked up over the window. Television light pulsed behind the sheet, and Ben could make out the shape of a kid sitting on the floor with his face about ten inches from the screen. The kid glanced up at him, eyes blunted and bored, like he wasn't at all surprised to see a cop clinging to the bars outside his window. Then he turned back to the tube.

Dark water sheeted down over the eaves. It was like crouching behind a waterfall. Ben stretched again, but couldn't reach the roof, his fingers still a foot short of the eaves. He launched himself from the sill, gripped the lip of the roof, and dangled there. Gritty water poured over his face. He sputtered and coughed, but managed to swing his leg over the lip and roll onto the roof.

The roof was littered with about a hundred broken forty-ouncers, a rusted revolver, and an old Cabbage Patch Kid. Ben looked down into the courtyard and saw the pool's green water moiling in the rain. No sign of Nine-Nine or the woman. He figured they were still in the breezeway. He hung from the roof, dropping into a crouch on the second-floor landing. Ben took the stairs three at a time and came around the corner into the breezeway.

But Nine-Nine was waiting for him.

Marquez's shout of warning reached Ben a millisecond before Nine-Nine's loaded right hook. Ben went down, kicked out at his legs, and saw Nine-Nine fall beside him. It was on: the two men scrambling and rolling and scratching and gouging on the blood-spattered concrete. Nine-Nine drove his knee up at Ben's groin. Ben pivoted, catching it with his hip. Nine-Nine trapped his right hand somehow and Ben whaled on his ribs with his left. Nine-Nine grunted with each punch, chuckling in the intervals between.

"Your gun!" Marquez's voice echoed in the breezeway. Nine-Nine had somehow plucked Ben's gun from its holster, bringing the Beretta up between them with the muzzle angled at Ben's face. Ben clamped the wrist that held the gun and shoved. He felt, rather than heard, the shot, the muzzle flash scorching his face. He saw bright spots, but didn't think he was hit. Ben gripped Nine-Nine's wrist hard enough to feel skin sloughing under his fingernails. He heard sirens, but they still sounded far away. Nine-Nine was pushing the gun toward his head again. Ben struggled against him, but Nine-Nine was much stronger than he was. Nine-Nine's wrist, slick with blood and sweat, twisted out of his grip. Ben pulled the ballpoint pen out of his breast pocket and stabbed the pen through Nine-Nine's forearm. Nine-Nine yowled and Ben saw the gun clatter onto the concrete. Nine-Nine released his hold on Ben's right arm to reach for the gun, which was exactly the break he'd been hoping for.

Ben snaked his right arm around Nine-Nine's neck, locked it in place with his left, and squeezed. Nine-Nine bucked and twisted, clawing frantically at Ben's forearm. Ben choked him with everything he had left, feeling Nine-Nine's Adam's apple jerk in the crook of his elbow. Nine-Nine shuddered, his head slumped sideways, and his arms fell limply into his lap, but Ben knew better than to release his hold. The guy might be playing possum.

Then Ben saw the woman moving across the breezeway, crawling blearily forward. She lifted Ben's gun with both hands. For a moment, he thought she actually meant to hand it back to him. She sat back on her knees and leveled the Beretta at Ben, her arms shaking with the weight of it. "Let him go." The words bubbled softly from her bleeding lips, her left eye dull with shock. "Let him go now or I'll kill you."

"Please don't," Ben breathed.

Two hard swings of the ram popped the warped the safety door from its frame. Marquez was the first one through the doorway. He charged into the breezeway with his big .45 up on target. "Drop it!" he shouted and the thunderclap of the .45 reverberated in the breezeway. The hollow-point round punched between her tan shoulder blades and exploded from her chest, her hot blood spraying Ben's face as she pitched forward. Ben heard his gun skittering along the wet concrete, but he didn't see where it went.

Marquez holstered his weapon, squatted next to him, and placed his hand on Ben's bloody forearm. "It's okay, Ben," Marquez whispered. "You can let go now." Ben's hands fell away. Two burly P2s forced Nine-Nine to the ground and cuffed him. Nine-Nine made sudden, chuffing sounds while the two cops kicked his ribs into splinters.

Ben watched as they lifted her limp arms and roughly handcuffed her.

To handcuff this woman's dead body seemed profane, but the handcuffs were department procedure, straight from the manual.

Marquez helped Ben to his feet. He swayed and Marquez hooked an arm around his waist to keep him from falling, Ben was transfixed by the sight of her bright blood as it rolled over the entryway like candle wax. Her blood, her baby's blood, filled the seams and fissures in the uneven concrete, formed narrow tributaries and flowed into the open courtyard to be obliterated by the pounding rain.

The district attorney's rollout team was the last unit to arrive at the scene. The rain had let up by the time they showed in their new Crown Vics and the DA investigators milled around with their arms akimbo, looking for something to do. The young, redheaded DAI approached the markers, hiked up his trousers, and squatted on his haunches, pretending to inspect the shooting scene the way they do on TV. He rested his forearms on his thighs, let his hands dangle, trying to look pensive. One of the RHD detectives let the guy know he was standing in the victim's blood and told him to quit contaminating the fucking crime scene.

Sergeant Portillo drove under the yellow tape in his hybrid car. He was wearing a charcoal suit and tie, and Ben wondered if IAD had called him at home for this one. Portillo wasn't dumb enough to smile with all these people around, but he couldn't conceal his contentment. He headed straight for Marquez, an unmistakable eagerness in his stride. He'd been waiting a long time for this.

"I already gave my Public Safety Statement to the dicks," Marquez said, without looking at him. "I'm waiting for the league attorney."

"Take all the time you want to get your story straight." Portillo flashed his even teeth. "I'm still going to punch holes in it."

"I do not have to take this fucking shit from you, not for a second," Marquez rumbled. His blood was up, thickening his features. "I was on this job when you were still fucking your socks." He bunched his fists and consumed the distance to Portillo in two long strides, but Portillo had no stomach for a stand-up fight. Ben watched Portillo dwindle to insubstantiality as Marquez closed on him. It looked as though Marquez would swallow Portillo entire, just devour the man by osmotic action.

Two uniforms intercepted Marquez and held him back. They tied up his arms and leaned into him. "He's not worth it," one of the uniforms said, but Marquez bulled them both forward, forcing the uniforms to step backward or be bowled over. He freed his right arm and reached between them to swipe at Portillo. When Portillo shrank back from Marquez's open hand, Ben heard one of the detectives chuckle. Another uniform pitched in and the three of them managed to get Marquez under control.

"Take that badge off, Portillo," Marquez said. "You're not a cop, you're not even a man. You're just a bootlicking cunt."

"I want that man placed under arrest," Portillo shouted. "Assaulting an officer."

"You're the one got him riled." Vintner sighed. "Now, stay the fuck away from him until the man's had some time with his lawyer."

Ben didn't step in, didn't move to help. Vintner had ordered them separated after the shooting. He just sat on the curb, watching in a numb stupor, barely even aware of the young paramedic removing the blood-pressure cuff from his arm. "Hey, keep your chin up, Officer," the paramedic said. The he returned the cuff to his tackle box and walked back to the ambulance.

Beyond the yellow tape, the crowd of onlookers and media parted for a black stretch-Hummer with the Lethal Injection Records logo, a phallic syringe in front of a grinning skull and crossbones emblazoned on the door. Jesus, Ben thought. Not here. Not now. He watched Jax slip out of the driver's seat and walk around to open the back door for him. When Darius stepped out of the Hummer, an awed silence fell over the neighborhood crowd. They stepped aside for him and some of them even clapped.

Darius wore a black leather fez on his shaved head, black turtleneck, and a long black leather coat that billowed behind him like the wings of some flying reptile. He was not a tall man, but he had a straight-backed, regal bearing that made him appear so. Darius ambled with the stately self-satisfaction of a River House gent strolling Trafalgar Square. He walked with a cane, though he had no real need of one. The cane tapped the wet asphalt to precisely coincide with his every fourth step. Then, as he approached Ben, Darius tapped his cane a final time, just hard enough to bounce the cane and snatch it by the neck in midair, like a drum major. He held his black cane like a scepter and Ben noticed it was topped by a leering gold, Lethal Injection skull with ivory teeth and ten-carat diamond eyes that matched Darius's earrings.

Ben stood, straightened his ruined uniform, and walked to meet Darius at the tape. Most of the other cops' attention was still diverted by Marquez and Portillo.

"Rough night, Officer." Darius glanced at Ben's nameplate with evident amusement. "Halloran?" He chuckled silkily. He'd lost a lot more weight, and his eyes seemed to have sunken farther into his head.

"A heeb by any other name." Ben shrugged. "Nice car."

"You know what they say." Darius smiled. "You can take the boy out the ghetto . . ."

"Jax," Ben said, Jax handing him a cordial little nod. Never a slave to fashion, Jax sported his old-school Jheri-curl do down to his shoulders, gold chains, and a blue satin Adidas warm-up suit. It wasn't a nostalgia trip for him. He'd just been in and out of the pen so many times that he gave up trying to keep his threads current. And Jax honestly figured Kool and the Gang was as cool as it was ever going to get and it might never get that cool again, so why fix what ain't broke?

"Just happened to be in the neighborhood," Ben said.

"Something like that," Darius said.

"Come out to gloat?" Ben asked. "Or kill me, what?"

"Naw, man," Darius said. "Carcosa said you got the Stockholm syndrome. He said you still Patty Hearst, but you put that costume on and now your head all fucked up. You *think* you Tanya, and you out here robbin' banks and shit."

"Yeah, I guess I've chosen to stay and fight," Ben said.

"Hell, I ain't mad atcha," Darius said. "Shit, my nigga, I'm glad you found a home." He smiled sadly. "Maybe I'll apply. We could be partners."

Ben laughed a little, but he wanted to cry. He'd deluded himself into believing that he and Darius were somehow on equal footing, Ben marooned by his privilege as surely as Darius had been orphaned by his poverty.

"You know about Risley?"

"I mighta heard somethin' about it," Darius said.

"It's no joke," Ben said. "I mean, I saw the rockets myself."

"Good lookin' out." Darius nodded.

"Darius, you know I didn't—" Ben started, but Darius held his *stop* palm up between them.

"Let me tell you a story, my nigga," Darius said. "Your daddy come out to my place in the middle of the goddamned night, leaned on the buzzer a good while. Crazy motherfucker even tried to climb the gate. I figured he was drunk, sent Jax out there to run his fat ass home, but he wasn't havin' any. *Had* to talk to me. Couldn't wait for a civilized motherfuckin' hour. I'm out there on the flagstones in my robe and I'm here to tell you a nigga was *cold*. I'm like, 'What the fuck you got for me can't wait till morning, fat man?' Your daddy hits his knees, talkin' bout how he used me, turned me loose on his own blood, cryin' like a motherfucker. Offered me his life in exchange for yours." Darius smiled. "You believe that shit?"

"Doesn't sound like him," Ben said.

"That's what I thought," Darius said. He looked straight at Ben, slowly reaching across the tape to clasp Ben's shoulder. "I called them off, Ben." He sighed. "I grant you clemency." Darius hung his head, and let his hand fall away from Ben's shoulder. "You're free."

"What does that mean for you?"

"Means Jax and I goin' walkabout." Darius smiled. "Maybe France, I don't know. I'm tired of L.A., my nigga. I'm like homegirl in *Grand Hotel*. I want to be let alone a minute."

"You're serious?"

"Few days for me to get packed." Darius shrugged. "Jax? He travel pretty light. Anyway, in case I don't see you . . ." Darius pressed something into Ben's palm. "Keep your head down out here, homie." Darius smiled, turned, and followed Jax back to the car. "It's crazy out on these streets."

Ben opened the parcel. It was Darius's Boba Fett figure.

PRESENT

Under Special Order 23, all officers involved in a shooting or categorical use of force shall be referred to Behavioral Science Services, located on the third floor of the Far East Bank Building in Chinatown. Marquez was early for his appointment, figuring his career was in the crapper anyway, no need to give the bastards any extra ammo.

He sank into the plum love seat across from his department shrink, Melanie Stein, Ph.D., a blond dyke with a girlish smile and decent legs, probably a soccer player or some damn thing. Nice enough kid, had her job to do like everybody else, but she wore that patchouli crap, which re-minded Marquez of the bandit cab and he had to ask her to open a win-dow before he blew chunks into her Cost Plus wastebasket.

"You've been here before," Stein said, holding some of his personnel file in a swollen manila on her lap. The rest of it was on her desk in a dusty cardboard box with his name and serial printed in permanent marker. Marquez smirked, held up five fingers, waggled them at her. "Five times," she said, nodding. No judgment in her voice, just getting the lay of the land here.

"Most of your contemporaries have made lieutenant, even captain," Stein said. "They've settled into a different career phase."

If Stein was baiting him, he didn't bite. He'd heard this rap before. Let the climbers bow and curtsey. He'd rather put assholes in jail. Over the years, a dozen well-meaning supervisors had pulled him aside, telling him to rein it in. Just take it easy for Christ's sake. You've got a promising career ahead of you, sky's the limit, but all these wild pursuits, uses of force, and bloody arrests make the folks in the building nervous. How about a little less ass-kicking, Miguel, and a little more baby-kissing.

He'd shunned Dale Carnegie for Doc Holliday, filling the jails with murderers, gangsters, robbers, burglars, dealers, rapists, thieves, pimps, and hustlers without regard for race, color, or creed. He'd stepped on toes, burned bridges, and never looked back. He'd known he'd be a street cop for life and had minded it not a bit. Now it was over. Part of him knew that.

"Tell me about the incident," Stein said.

"Radio call, a domestic." Marquez sighed, picked at some loose fuzz on the arm of the couch. "Some asshole's knocking the piss out of his old lady, but we can't get to her because of the fucking security gate. My partner does a Spider-Man up the front of the building and goes toe-to-toe with the guy, ends up choking him out.

"That's the job," he said. "You get the call and you've got about thirty seconds to unfuck someone's life. Probably took them thirty years to fuck it up with bad decisions, gangbanging, dope. Thirty years of 'Tomorrow, Lawd, I'm gone quit this shit an' get me a job.'"

"You blame her," Stein said mildly.

"Fucking-A right I do. Except I don't. I don't know, Doc. This shit's way above my pay grade," he said. "I'm just a street cop, right? Product of L.A. Unified, barely finished high school, but I've got eyes.

"It's like there's this big factory, a mill or something, upriver, and it's been pumping all this foul shit into the water for two hundred years.

"You live way upstream," he said. "Hell, I even live a little ways upstream from it, but I damn well know the river's poison, because I'm down there every day. And here's the thing, you can send a guy like me down there with a gun and, hey, I'll do what I can, but maybe you assholes ought to look at the fucking factory."

"The shooting," Stein said.

"Right, so by the time we get the gate open, the woman has his gun,"

Marquez said. "She's going to shoot him, so . . ." He sighed again, chest a little tight. "Could you adjust the goddamned thermostat in here?"

"I can call downstairs," she said.

"Forget it," he said.

"It's no trouble," she said. "I want you to be comfortable."

"I'm fine," he said. "Let's get this over with."

"Please, go on," she said.

"So, he's just saved her life and this broad's going to shoot him for it," Marquez said, shaking his head. "I don't know what gets into these people. I don't. I tell her to drop the gun. She doesn't." He looked out the window, squinting his eyes into the light. Sun gleamed off a river of chrome crawling up the Pasadena Freeway. "I shoot her. She dies. End of story."

"Okay," Stein said.

"That's it," Marquez said, shifting a little in his seat.

"I think there may be more we want to talk about."

"I told you everything."

"Miguel, may I call you Miguel?"

"You just did."

"Miguel," Stein said, "my information says two people were killed."

That one knocked the wind out of him.

Instead of heading back down to the underground parking, Marquez got out of the elevator at the lobby. He slipped out the front of the bank, crossed Broadway, and ducked into a little Chinese joint. He bellied up to the empty bar, ordered a shot of Herradura and a beer back. Marquez downed them and signaled for a repeat, sliding his credit card across the bar to get a tab started. He sat, letting the tequila work on him as he watched the snakeheads prowling figure eights in the big tank behind the bar.

He had a pretty good buzz going by the time the Reverend Malachi Silas clapped him on the shoulder, sliding onto the stool next to him like this was their regular watering hole. The legs of the bar stool bowed under Mal's weight. Mal had ditched his dashiki for a patterned Big & Tall golf shirt, stretched taut over a gut like a cement mixer, and black chinos. Marquez wondered hazily how Mal had found him here, but decided it didn't matter. Mal would have known all about BSS and he could have staked out the bank, but he'd more than likely just gotten Marquez's appointment time from one of his spies in the building. The thing of it was, Marquez was glad to see the guy. He hadn't realized how badly he'd needed a familiar face until Mal sat down. Mal was who he was, but he probably knew Marquez about as well as anybody and any old scores between them had been settled years ago.

"You look like shit," Mal told him, taking in Marquez's red-tinged eyes. "Let's get some food in you, *amigo*. Soak some of that poison up. I'm too old to carry your ass out of here."

"Yeah?" Marquez gestured to the bartender, forking two fingers in the air. The waiter brought them each a Tsingtao. "Me and this guy," Marquez told the bartender, hooking his thumb at Mal. "Twenty years, we go back."

"Came up together," Mal said. Mal and Marquez clicked bottles. "Hey, you remember that first time?" Mal jabbed an elbow into Marquez's ribs, his cunning smile just daring Marquez to say no, he didn't remember a thing. "*Ooooh*," Mal sang, that revival-tent voice of his taking Marquez all the way back to his probation. "Baby, I can *still* see stars."

Marquez remembered stepping into the courtyard of those same apartments with Rourke, his hardcase training officer, the two of them summoned there on some bullshit call. Miguel was fresh out of the academy, the homeboys smelling rookie a mile off. And he remembered Mal rearing like a grizzly in a blue tank top, the handle of a pick sticking up out of Mal's three-inch Afro like a blue plastic horn.

"Get your skinny ass outta my hood," Mal said and spat on Marquez's badge. "Without that badge and that gun you ain't shit." Dusting off that old chestnut for his homeboys, probably never figuring he'd have to make good on it.

"Well, Beaner." Rourke always called him Beaner or Greaser or Pancho. "You going to take that shit from this nigger buck?"

Mal heard Rourke call him a nigger, but he didn't make any noise about it. Rourke spooked the homies, and not just because they all knew he could shoot like the devil himself. Rourke had an aura, a vibe that said he'd kill you out of sheer meanness, or boredom, or on a bet. He was one of those guys who'd gone gray in his twenties, his booze-mottled nose and cheeks like raw hamburger. The ends of his mustache, teeth, and fingers were stained yellow from Marlboros. His eyes were wolfishly pale.

"Sir, would you hold this, please?" Marquez handed Rourke his Sam Browne belt. Rourke draped the belt over his shoulder and lit a smoke.

Mal swung wild, his big arms whooshing over Marquez's head. Marquez backed him up with his rapid-fire jab, his Boys Club boxing skills coming back. His right cross glanced off Mal's broad forehead, but his left hook caught Mal in the snot box, good and solid, Mal's big-ass head snapping back hard enough to send the pick spinning out of his 'fro. Poleaxed, Mal dropped like a tree, the pick thunking into the ground next to him like a mumblety-peg knife. Marquez turned to the homeboys gathered around and grinned, his fingers curling in a beckoning gesture.

" 'Who's next?' " Mal aped Marquez's wild-eyed challenge, breaking himself up with it, the wheezing baritone laughter booming out of him in the bar. "Momma, God rest her soul, drew me a bird-pepper bath and told me not to go messin' with *polices*. You know I didn't listen no how."

The television over the bar was running Fox 11 News, Big Ben Kahn giving a basso profundo press conference to announce his wrongful-death suit on behalf of the family of Connie Williams against Marquez and the LAPD. "The bottom line here is that Officer Marquez shot a pregnant woman in the back," Big Ben said, holding up what looked like a high school graduation photo of Connie Williams in happier times. "That sounds a lot like murder to me, folks, but I'm not the county or federal prosecutor. I can tell you this is a textbook case of wrongful death."

Perfect, Marquez thought. This is just perfect.

Back to the anchor, his face grave: "If you have children, you may not wish them to see the disturbing footage that follows." Cut to about four seconds of amateur video, Marquez bashing Dupriest's head in with his baton. The angle didn't let you see Patty at all. "Fox Eleven News has obtained this footage of Officer Marquez, shown here participating in what sources within the LAPD have called a questionable use of force."

Mal signaled to the bartender, who grabbed the remote and changed the channel to *Entertainment Tonight*.

"Circus comin' to town tomorrow," Mal said softly. "Gone be ugly."

"I kind of figured," Marquez said, realizing Mal had come here to warn him.

"You want to call in sick or something," Mal said. "Might not be a bad idea."

"Good lookin' out," Marquez said.

"But you're going in anyway," Mal said, shaking his head.

Marquez nodded.

"There's still a monster out there, brother," Mal said.

Marquez nodded.

They drank in silence for a while.

"Hey, how's Mal Jr. holding up in there," Marquez asked, the kid still in Chino last Marquez had heard.

"He doin' good," Mal said, briefly bowing his head in genuine penitence, like there was some serious prayer paying off here. "*Real* good. Praise the name of Jesus. Got his GED, workin' on his AA." Marquez could tell Mal wanted to say more about the boy, make a few predictions about when they'd finally let his ass out, maybe a job he had lined up for the kid. Ultimately, he thought Mal didn't want to jinx anything.

"I'm glad to hear it," Marquez said, meaning it. "You give him my best, hear?"

"I'll do that, my brother," Mal said, pushing his stool back from the bar. Marquez stood to shake Mal's hand, but Mal wrapped Marquez in an unself-conscious bear hug, the wholeness of the gesture taking Marquez by surprise.

PRESENT

Ben parked his car under a canopy of bougainvillea hanging over Seventh Street, just north of Montana Avenue. He could see the wide flagstone drive, winding up to the portico. The house looked smaller than he remembered, modest by the standards of the neighborhood, a four-thousand-square-foot Mediterranean with a pool and a Jacuzzi, but no tennis court. Never let it be said that I was born with a silver spoon in my mouth. Ben smiled bitterly to himself. I grew up without a tennis court.

He waited, wondering what Big Ben had done with his room. Storage? A gym? More than likely he'd just locked the door and avoided questions about it. That was what you did when you tragically lost a kid, wasn't it? In-line skaters, dog walkers, and nut-brown nannies pushing expensive prams passed him on their way to the boutiques on Montana. Ben reread the *Times* article about the lawsuit, gripping the California section hard enough to transfer the heavier print to his fingers. Hours later, with the sun sinking low, the same parade of strollers, skaters, and dog walkers headed back the way they'd come. It was getting dark and there was still no sign of Big Ben. He was probably working late.

Ben wiped his hands on his jeans, checked to see if the newsprint had finally come off, and saw the date reversed in his palm. "Son of a bitch," he said aloud. He started the car, took Seventh south to Santa Monica Boulevard, heading east on Santa Monica into Century City. He couldn't believe he'd actually forgotten.

Every year, Big Ben blew himself a boffo birthday bash at the Beverly Hills Room of the Century Plaza Hotel & Spa. The pitch: A Hip-hop Friars' Roast Meets a Demonic *Hollywood Squares,* a chance for Big Ben's underworld clients to rub elbows and other appendages with some of his industry pals. And behold, the lion will lie down with the lizard.

Rodney King hadn't made it to Big Ben's party that year, his absence one of the first things Ben noticed because King's sheer size and Baby Huey awkwardness would have made the big wallflower impossible to miss. The poor guy had squandered his settlement on his failed rap label and enough angel dust to wipe out the Wild Mustang, backsliding from civil rights hero to pseudo-celebrity shermhead. But Big Ben still sent King an invitation every year, a gesture of Big Ben's boundless cross-cultural goodwill, and a nifty bit of stunt casting.

His father had stocked the pond with the usual stylish bottom-feeders, B-list actors fawning over A-list drug dealers. A troop of backslapping record executives and movie producers, slouching hominids Ben would have placed a half step ahead of the feces throwers in nature's mammalian hierarchy, were getting soused on apple martinis. They reminded Ben of those leering old farts at the end of *Rosemary's Baby,* each man gripping the waist of a giggling piece of arm candy half his age and a third his weight. This being L.A., the women were all jaw-droppers, but two surgeries too many had left them with an eerie sameness, like some kid's Barbie collection left out in the sun.

The DJ—Ben recognized the guy from Serena's *quinceañera*—wearing a white silk shirt open to his navel, pressed bulky headphones to one ear with his left hand as he worked his turntables with his right. Ben saw some big-name Dodgers, Kings, and a few notable Lakers, but no Clippers— even his father had better taste than that. On the dance floor, a sweat-slick tangle of lithe bodies freaky-deaked to DJ Post-Mortem's "Poonanny Pirate." Jesus, Ben thought, how many of these previously unreleased demo tracks had Darius stockpiled over the years? It was like Darius had planned on Post-Mortem going down for an early nap.

Strange did the Dance of Shiva, whirling and gliding like a wisp of white smoke across the dance floor, the balletic liquidity of the guy's long limbs a delicate counterpoint to all the spastic rutting around him. Strange's current crop of adult-entertainment starlets formed a circle around him, swaying and clapping to the music. The DJ's strobe turned their lipstick Bride-of-Dracula black as Strange plucked them from the circle, one at a time, twirling and dipping each temptress in turn.

Ben saw Heidi Fleiss with an actor he liked, but whose name he could never remember. Heidi stood as far away from Strange as you could get without leaving the party, stealing icy glances over her date's shoulder at the dance floor. She and Strange had not been on speaking terms for years, but neither party would spill the source of their animus and Ben had long ago decided it was better not to ask.

Jaime and Ignacio fell in step with Ben, flanking him as he skirted the dance floor. Jaime slipped his hand around Ben's triceps, not making a scene, but squeezing just hard enough to let Ben know it was time to put on his listening cap. "You shouldn't be here, Benji," Jaime said, his lips almost touching Ben's ear, Ben smelling Fendi cologne and *café con leche.* "This isn't my hardass thing either. This is me to you, as a friend."

"I'm just here to say happy birthday," Ben said savagely. He'd spied Mr. Johnnie now, figuring his father wouldn't stray far from him.

"There are people here, Benji," Ignacio said. "Some of them have been drinking, smoking a little *primo.*"

"So, what else is new?" Ben snapped.

"These dudes don't sweat witnesses," Jaime said, subtly nodding across the dance floor. "Not in a roomful of friendlies. *¿Entiendes, cabrón?*"

Daddy Python, Sleepy Loc, and Poway Charlie, dressed lid-to-lifts in Boot Hill Blue, sat together at a corner table. A woman wiggled nimbly in Daddy Python's lap, idly twirling one of his gold chains around her finger. Another woman stood behind his chair, her hands kneading Daddy Python's massive shoulders.

"Duly noted," Ben said, taking his arm back.

Double-breasted and double-chinned, Mr. Johnnie held graceful court in the locus of his growing entourage. He wore Ben's annual salary and some change, resplendent in his bespoke suit with a monochromatic shirt and tie. Ben's father had always loved and loathed Mr. Johnnie. Every year, Big Ben agonized over his invitation, always terrified of being eclipsed by him, yet unable to resist the instant cachet of Mr. Johnnie's attendance. And year after year, Mr. Johnnie upstaged him. The man's fulgent charisma made the party his own, all the others his knaves and vassals.

Mr. Johnnie laughed politely at some fumbling observation from the large man at his left, letting his hand rest upon the man in a gesture at once avuncular and condescending. Ben recognized the large man as the Juice himself, sporting a tweed blazer with leather elbow patches over a Callaway golf shirt. The Juice bore the weight of Mr. Johnnie's hand like a miter upon his shoulder. Ben remembered hearing that he was coming back out west in the hopes of rehabbing his image, but nothing had come of it. He had another deeply tanned, peroxide-blonde Pilates queen on his arm. Since his acquittal, Ben had seen him out with a dozen clones, like he was courting her ghost.

And there, at the periphery of Mr. Johnnie's widening circle of favorites, hovered Big Ben himself. As always, Big Ben was late receiving the punch line, throwing his round head back to bray laughter that was too loud by half. Not a drunk's laugh, but the plaintive honking of an immigrant's son, overeager to be in on the joke. The desperate heartiness of his father's laughter still betrayed him. Beneath that tapered Armani suit beat the heart of a bitch-titted laughingstock, the one never picked for the dance.

Ben tapped him on the shoulder, and when he turned, it was like watching grandpa slap him all over again. All the color and expression drained out of Big Ben's face for a moment, but he recovered quickly, exerting court-honed control over his own paralyzed features. Big Ben summoned his deepest reserves of mock ebullience, the parenthetical lines around his mouth pulling back like old theater curtains. He actually smiled and Ben saw he'd had his teeth capped.

"Benji, my boy." Big Ben chuckled. "Welcome home. The calf is well fatted and all that jazz." Big Ben's bare forehead gleamed with thin sweat, his eyes stealing from one guest to the next. Even now, he was gauging, sizing up, scanning those empty faces for judgment or validation.

"You thought I was dead," Ben said. "I'd been thinking this suit was another sick joke, but you really had no idea, did you?" The people around them went quiet. Big Ben took his arm, gently steering him away from Mr. Johnnie's favorites, but Ben flung his hand away and heard someone gasp.

"Happy Birthday, *Pop*," Big Ben growled under his breath. "Good to see you again, *Pop*. I'm really sorry about fucking your wife there, *Pop*."

"She wasn't your wife," Ben said. "She was your car."

"Oh, but you *really* loved her," Big Ben snorted.

"I did," he said.

"Come off it. She was your dagger, man. And you know, that's what really broke her, don't you?"

"You're lying," he said.

"Oh yeah, Benji," Big Ben said. "Deep down, she always knew you didn't give a shit about her. It was always about getting back at me for driving your mommy away."

"Well, here's the final score, kid," he said. "Mommy abandoned you. I'm the one who stayed. I know I'm the son of a bitch who named you Sue and all that jazz. Never claimed to be anything else. I was improvising, you imperious little prick. I wasn't perfect, but at least I was there, god-damnit. Sure, I was a shit, but you made me a monster."

"You tried to kill me," Ben said. "I still can't believe it."

"You were always such a drama queen," Big Ben said. He was still try-ing to sound flip, but his voice had lost some of its force, like he was hav-ing trouble breathing. You could see him staggering under the weight of it. His eyes flicked to Daddy Python's table, the men still oblivious. Then he reached up, laying his palms on Ben's cheeks, pulling him close, Ben forced to bend at the waist until they were nose to nose.

"I tried to make it right," Big Ben whisper-whined to his son. He'd burned through all his bluster now, and Ben could see his father was half mad with grief. Ben thought about the man's heart attack. Jaime was right. He shouldn't have come here.

"I tried to buy him out of it, but he said he couldn't take it back," Big Ben said, biting his lip. "I begged him to let me go in your place, I did, but he said it wouldn't matter. The missiles were already flying.

"Now, listen to me," Big Ben said, chubby hands shakily smoothing Ben's hair. "I have some money stashed away. All we have to do is get you out of the country and—"

"Dad, it doesn't matter anymore. It's over. I'm a cop." He'd imagined saying those words, played out this scene in a hundred settings, but he hadn't reckoned on the man's grief. And he wondered now if his intentions here had been any nobler than his intentions with Gretchen, or had he simply forged himself into a final weapon to strike at this man?

"I don't understand," Big Ben said

"I came here to ask you to drop the suit."

"Which suit?" Big Ben slowly blinked his eyes back into focus.

"The Connie Williams suit," Ben said, "the one against Officer Marquez. He's my partner. She had *my* gun that night. That was my fault, but she really would have killed me if Marquez hadn't pulled the trigger.

"Bottom line is, you have a conflict here," Ben said. "I'm still your son. Let someone else handle this one."

Big Ben shook his head, trying to process all of it, and failing. Big Ben's fingers traced Ben's shoulders, as though brushing away lint, his hands falling heavily to dangle at his sides.

"Look, I've got to get out of here before somebody takes a shot at me," Ben said, glancing over his shoulder. "So for what it's worth, I'm sorry, okay? Okay? I'm sorry."

"Wait," Big Ben murmured, but Ben was already gone.

35

PRESENT

Coming up Broadway from the Florence Avenue exit, Ben saw the Reverend Malachi Silas's Miracle Mobile parked in front of 77th Station along with about a dozen news vans. Officers, wearing ballistic helmets and flak vests, stood in a rigid skirmish line in front of the station's lobby entrance. As Ben turned from Broadway onto Seventy-sixth Street, heading into the employee parking lot, the crowd of protesters surged after Ben's car. Piss-filled water balloons sailed across Seventy-sixth to explode against his windshield.

Ben saw Marquez in the locker room, shrugging into his uniform. Marquez slid his feet down into his well-worn boots, cranking his heels around to sit them. He swung his right foot up, the boot landing heavily on the bench, but his hands were shaking too badly for him to lace it up. Ben touched his shoulder, came around the bench, and knelt in front of him to lace Marquez's boots for him.

"Thanks," Marquez said. His eyes looked sunken, wet, and yellow. Ben hadn't talked to him since the shooting and there was so much he wanted to say, but he knew this wasn't the place.

Lieutenant Vintner charged into the locker room, striding up the row of lockers like J. Jonah Jameson, but his face softened a little when he saw the shape Marquez was in. "You two shall not leave this station, understood?" Vintner said, poking them each in the shoulder with his index finger. "Consider this an admin day. That's an order." Vintner eyed Ben. "Kid, I'm holding you responsible if he wanders out there to play footsy."

"Yes, sir," Ben said.

They skipped roll call and headed upstairs. Ben made them a fresh cup of trucker coffee. He handed Marquez a styrofoam cup, only about three-quarters full, worried Marquez would slosh a full one. They sat side by side on the edge of one of the empty desks in Homicide.

"I'm going to be okay," Marquez said quietly, sipping his coffee. "Just need to get my sea legs back."

"I know," Ben said, part of him knowing it was a lie, but wanting to believe this could still come out all right for any of them.

The big windows in front of Homicide gave them a luxury-box view of Malachi Silas's traveling circus. Mal had brilliantly fortified his front line with pregnant women. The women wore threadbare half-shirts and sports bras, lipstick bull's-eyes painted on their rounded bellies. Most of the protesters carried hand-lettered poster-board signs. A few held tall wooden crosses with black baby dolls hanging from them.

A murmuring hush fell over the crowd as Mal heaved himself onto the hood of the Miracle Mobile, the shocks groaning under his weight. Mal stood on the car, raised his face to the sky, palms lifted in supplication, gently shaking his massive head, his roguish, eyes-to-heaven grin a mark of the close working relationship Mal obviously shared with the Almighty. This was all part of his regular warm-up, Mal humbly accepting this cup if that's how the Man wanted it. *Well, here we are, riding into battle once again, my brother, and what a ride it's been.*

Mal turned his face to the crowd, deep-set eyes ablaze. Someone handed Mal's signature, gold-inlaid megaphone up to him, but Mal waved the megaphone away, so filled with the Spirit now he had no need for amplification. The crowd quieted, clearly expecting big things. He filled his lungs, nostrils flaring, and launched his first volley.

"Brothers and sisters." Mal's pumiced baritone boomed, the guy making Paul Robeson sound like Soupy Sales. "For decades, centuries, the *white* man been killin' us with his liquor, killin' us with his dope, killin' us with *his* guns, killin' us, killin' us, killin' us."

There were Eight Tray Gangsters mixing into the crowd, at least two dozen that Marquez hadn't noticed before, and more coyote-loping across Broadway. He watched Eight Trays fold in among the protesters, getting shoulder to shoulder with the news crews and some of Mal's expectant moms. No good, Marquez thought. No good at all.

"Let me ask, y'all ever seen a *brew'ry* in the ghetto?"

Noooo.

"Tell me, y'all ever seen a *gun fact'ry* down here in the ghetto?"

Noooo.

"Y'all think the black man invented crack?"

Noooo.

"Damn right, George Bush's CIA invented that mess, forged up a new chain to keep the slaves in line, yes he did," Mal said, nodding. "And when we step outta line, when we cross against the *light,* when we fuss with our women, when we play *our* music too loud, the LAPD sends over a couple of Yankee Doodle Dandies to beat us till the white meat comes on through, shove a plunger up the black rectum."

Amen, brother.

"They say they protectin' us from the gangs," Mal said, firing an accusing finger up at the skirmish line. "I say *they* the biggest gang in L.A. Look at 'em sideways an' they Diallo your black ass, shoot you a hundred and forty-tree times because you made a 'furtive movement.' Oh yes, they done *been* practicin' genocide, but now. *Now,* my brothers and sisters, they can't even wait for a black man to be *born.* They'll kill them a black Jesus sleepin' in his momma's womb!"

At this, Mal's phalanx of expectant moms wailed and sobbed, their faces twisted in anguish, shaking balled fists in the air. The chant began: *"No justice! No peace!"* And the cops on the skirmish line shifted uncomfortably. The air was still and tight, earthquake weather.

"You know, right here, in this very city, in my mem'ry," Mal said, winging it now, riffing off his own evangelical momentum. "Ol' Charlie Manson cut him a baby right out of its momma and that white judge just let him off with a warning because he was one of the *Beach Boys!*"

The crowd roared, a ballpark wave of sound that rattled the front windows of the station, reacting more to the roller-coaster cadence of Mal's sermon than its content, folks now so blood-ravenous that Mal could tell them any fool thing. The Eight Trays leaped and jostled and shoved, palsied with unfocused violence.

Constricted now by the bunching crowd, the news crews looked nervous, heads swiveling for a clear path back to their vans. They must have sensed something. Marquez sensed it too, but he doubted if Mal did. He was too far gone in a fiery loop of preach-feedback to see he had a tiger by the tail. He was like Mickey Mouse bringing those broomsticks to life, so pleased with his conjuring he couldn't see he'd lost control of his own creation.

An Eight Tray Gangster named Mookie stalked back and forth in front of the skirmish line, slamming his fist into his palm again and again, eye-fucking each cop in turn. Mookie dipped his head, left ear touching left shoulder, his big-yard eyes boring in behind those Plexiglas face shields, his soul-hating scowl daring each man to come on out and dance a little jig with him. Marquez had seen this act before. Mookie was an Eight Tray Judas goat. His object: to get one of the younger cops to break ranks, draw a lone hothead from the skirmish line, get the guy to chase him headlong into the crowd where he would be eaten alive. And after about nine minutes of wolf-pacing the skirmish line, Mookie caught his first lamb.

The *"No justice! No peace!"* chant was throbbing against the windows of the station, growing louder with each round. Mookie, evidently frustrated that all his pacing and staring had yielded no takers, unzipped his FUBU jeans, flopped out his tool, and wagged it at the skirmish line.

"Aw, fuck this!" Coomer, a young P2 with a face like a Campbell's Soup kid, charged after Mookie, baton whooshing through empty air as Mookie danced back into the crowd. Coomer's sergeant tried to call him back, but it was too late. The crowd had swallowed him whole.

Mal was shouting something unintelligible, palms out, urging calm. Marquez saw Coomer upended as though struck by heavy surf, struggling as his helmet, baton, and gun were torn away from him. Mal jumped off the Miracle Mobile, wrapping Mookie in a bear hug. Then someone broke a bottle over Mal's head and he went down.

Marquez crushed his coffee cup and ran for the stairs, taking them three at a time. Ben didn't bother trying to talk him out of it, just followed him, wishing they'd brought their helmets.

The skirmish line had broken and waded into the crowd, bulling through the line of pregnant women. An Eight Tray caught Coomer in the side of the head with his own baton, and he went down with a pack of them stomping him into the curb. Mookie snatched a heavy video camera from its tripod and before the rescue team could reach him, Mookie brought the camera down on Coomer's head.

Marquez swung his baton across Mookie's face in a backhanded stroke. Mookie did a clumsy pirouette, spitting bloody teeth against the Fox 11 News van. The rescue team formed a protective circle around Coomer, fighting back the crowd while Ben and Marquez lifted Coomer from the curb and carried him back to one of the benches in the lobby. Coomer was in bad shape, bleeding from his ears. A desk officer stuffed a jacket under his head and held his hand as Marquez and Ben headed back out.

More cops were pouring out of the lobby, batons swinging, and Marquez saw packs of gangsters running across Broadway, converging on the station. Bottles of sand and chunks of concrete flew, shattering the front windows of the station.

Just then, the county sheriff's bus, transferring arrestees from 77th Jail down to 210 West Temple for arraignment, pulled out of the loading dock and lumbered up Seventy-sixth. The sheriffs were on a different radio frequency than the LAPD, and the demo had shit-soured so quickly that no one had time to warn them.

The crowd swarmed around the bus, fists pounding against the sides. A brick spiderwebbed the windshield and the bus sagged as butcher knifes and screwdrivers punctured its tires. The bus rocked once, twice, and pitched over on its side, windows shattering on impact. The crowd clambered over the exposed side, an Eight Tray quickly working through the window grille with a pair of butter cutters. A deputy's shotgun went off somewhere inside the bus and someone screamed. The Eight Tray popped the screen. Ragged men, handcuffed together in daisy chains, wiggled out and hobble-hopped off the side of the bus to be enveloped by the boiling tangle of bodies. The bus caught fire.

Marquez rolled Mal over and his eyes fluttered, a bloody, pink flap of scalp with a patch of gray Afro hanging down over his forehead. "Come on, Mal," Marquez huffed. "Get your fat ass up." Marquez and Ben each hooked one of Mal's big arms over their shoulders, and he stood woozily.

Across Broadway, smoke and flames were boiling out of the smashed window of the *pupusería*, looters dashing out the front door, carrying electric mixers and bags of flour. A basehead staggered out the side door of the *pupusería* lugging a five-gallon bucket of fry grease.

A kind of triage had been set up in the station lobby now, mostly gauze and pressure held against the heavy bleeders. Two of the women seemed to have gone into labor. Marquez and Ben flopped Mal onto the bench next to Coomer. "Charles Manson," Marquez snorted, shaking his head. He gently swept the loose flap of scalp out of Mal's eyes and re-placed it. Then Marquez took Mal's own hand in both of his and pressed it against his head to hold the piece in place. "You asshole."

Mal blinked dazedly, taking in the lobby, probably at a loss for words for the first time since Marquez had cold-cocked him twenty years ago.

Most of the crowd had split off, surging in two directions. Airships were tracking them south on Broadway toward Manchester and west on Seventy-sixth Street toward Fig, but that wasn't the worst of it. News hel-icopters had broadcast live footage of the melee. All over the hood, bored and angry young men charged out of their homes, galvanized by the raging scene on television. Looting crews prowled the streets, setting garbage fires and tipping over cars, growing bolder as the sun dipped and their numbers swelled. There were already sketchy reports of people being hauled out of their cars and beaten to death.

The radio went nuts, frantic RTOs stepping on each other to broadcast shots-fired calls and looters hitting the Home Depot on Western. Vintner called a citywide Tac Alert. Then the first officer-needs-help calls came out. Two-man units were taking rocks and bottles as far west as Crenshaw, the other side of the world, and officers were sprinting through the station in every direction, piling four-deep into black-and-whites like they were lifeboats and the station was sinking.

Marquez and Ben headed into Vintner's office, his television tuned to live footage of the Slauson Swap Meet. It looked like Fort Apache, yellow-shirt security guards trading rounds with gangsters, half the cars in the parking lot already on fire. Looters stampeded out of the swap meet, their arms full of clothes and electronics.

Vintner was on the phone with the deputy chief. He looked up at Marquez and Ben, palm over the receiver. "Don't leave my sight," he said. "Either of you."

Ben heard weird radio calls coming in now, citizens reporting LAPD officers firing on LAPD officers. It was Risley, he thought, Marquez's *cucuy*. On the television in the Watch Commander's Office, the news anchor said they were getting uncomfirmed reports that a helicopter had been shot down with some kind of missile.

"He's calling me out," Marquez told Vintner.

"That's exactly why you're not to leave this office," Vintner said. He was shaking. "When I was a kid they lynched my cousin, did I ever tell you that? Came for him at the house. They said we had to send him out or they'd burn it down around us."

The radio squawked. Several units were trying to transmit at once, stepping on one another's broadcasts. *"Officer needs help—"* *"—ambush. Rockets. Be advised, they have—"* *"Shots fired—"* Vintner set the phone down and stared at the radio on his desk. "—*not cops*." "—*black-and-white*." "—*shoulder-fired rocket*." "*Jesus, somebody*—"

"Bill," Marquez said. "Please."

"Fine." Vintner handed him his keys. "Ride to the sound of the guns."

Marquez took the keys. Ben followed him out through the courtyard. Vintner's black-and-white was parked at the top of the parking structure, the place Marquez had taken Ben on his first day. It looked like the end of the world from up here. Even the palms were on fire.

They climbed into the black-and-white, pulled out of the parking lot, and headed west, out into the nations. Ben's eyes stung. Flurries of ash drifted across Florence, pasty black flakes landing on the car. The air tasted like burned tires and it hurt to breathe. Twisting black columns of smoke crowded the horizon, the sun setting wide and red behind them. He heard automatic-weapons fire through the unceasing dirge of sirens and alarms, but the shots seemed to be coming from everywhere at once.

Marquez drove the black-and-white through a rust-colored fog of hanging smoke, steering around obstacles. The street was choked with empty cars. Some had been overturned and set on fire. Others just abandoned, doors flung open, their occupants fled or hauled out. Ben could see shapes skulking in the brown haze, a slouching zombie towing a stackable washer-dryer on a wobbly shopping cart, a teenaged boy with a tailor's mannequin over his shoulder, and two fat women carrying a rolled-up carpet. He heard the low *fwump* of an explosion and saw a fresh pillar of smoke rising two or three blocks ahead.

Marquez drove over the curb to avoid an overturned fire truck that was engulfed in flame at the intersection of Florence and Budlong. A man in a barbecue apron charged their car with a bloody fire axe. Ben shot him in the throat. Marquez accelerated and the man melted back into the smoke.

A Buick LeSabre parked on Raymond had the tail rotor of a helicopter sticking out of its windshield. The fuselage had come down a half a block away through the roof of a ranch house, which was now on fire. A roof beam groaned and snapped and the helicopter sagged deeper into the burning house. Ben couldn't make out the markings, but he thought it was a news chopper. Neighbors to the north and south were hosing down their own homes to prevent the fire from communicating. Men with rifles and pistols stood guard in their driveways.

It was déjà vu at Florence and Normandie. A guy in a Yankees cap and blue-checked flannel used a gas-powered chain saw to cut through a telephone pole. The lines snapped and the pole fell diagonally across the intersection in front of a Honda Accord, forcing the driver to stop. Gangsters in blood-spattered clothing, their faces halved by bandannas, swarmed into the intersection. Wielding aluminum bats, tire irons, and cleavers, they overwhelmed the Accord, caved in the windows, and hauled the driver out into the street. He was a Hispanic guy in a mechanic's jumpsuit. They surrounded him, howling and gibbering.

Marquez leaned out the window of the black-and-white and fired his Smith into the air. A few of them broke and ran, but most of the mob stayed in the intersection. Now bricks rained down on the black-and-white. Ben got out of the car. A Molotov cocktail landed in the street to his right and he felt the heat of the explosion.

"Shoot the ringleader," Marquez said.

"Who's the ringleader?"

Ben heard the horn blaring "Go Tell It on the Mountain." The Miracle Mobile bounced over the curb and careened into the intersection, parting the crowd. Mal kicked his door open and waded into the mob like a man possessed, the Lion of Judah with a bloody DARE T-shirt wrapped around his head. They had the mechanic pinned to the ground. A guy straddling his chest, one hand around the mechanic's throat, the other reaching into his mouth with a pair of pliers. Going for the gold in his grille.

Mal kicked the guy with the pliers full in the face, knocking him backward off the mechanic. Mal stood over the mechanic and raised his preaching Bible over his head. The circle widened around Mal, some kind of psychic pressure wave pushing them back.

"This man is mine!" Mal bellowed at them, his eyes aflame. "You cannot have him, hear! He belongs to me!" They crouched and cowered. Some of them ran. Mal gathered the mechanic in his arms and carried him back to the Miracle Mobile. He winked at Marquez as he backed out of the intersection, the insensible mechanic lolling against Mal's shoulder like a drive-in date. That was the last Marquez ever saw of him.

Marquez and Ben got back in the car and headed west. They approached the Korean grocery on Parsifal. A kid with a Molotov cocktail burning in his hand stepped onto the sensor pad, activating the automatic doors. The kid cocked his arm as the automatic doors swung open and a middle-aged Korean inside the store opened up on the kid with a snub-nosed .38, a single wild round shattering the Molotov in the kid's hand. The sound of the explosion was oddly delicate, just the light tinkle of breaking glass, and suddenly the kid was staggering back into the parking lot, trying to beat the fire out of his own clothes until he collapsed, his entire body engulfed. His homies gathered around him, halfheartedly tamping the flames with their shoes as the boy's skin peeled and curled. Somebody tossed a goose-down parka over him, but that only fed the flames.

Two Korean men, a father and son from the looks of them, took up positions on the roof of the market, hastily assembling what looked like an antique, water-cooled .50 cal. The son mounted the thing on its tripod, swiveling the muzzle down at the crowd while the father slammed a belt of ammo into the weapon. The homies scattered, leaving the body to smolder in the parking lot.

They continued west and came across another black-and-white on Denker. It had been torn completely in half by one of Risley's antitank rockets, the bodies almost indistinguishable from the rest of the flaming wreckage.

"I'm going to eat his fucking heart," Marquez said. "I swear to God."

They crossed Western and headed north on Van Ness. A transformer had blown somewhere and killed all power to the street, nothing visible beyond their bouncing headlights. "Watch it," Ben said, pointing to a body facedown in the street, the guy wearing some kind of uniform. He wasn't a cop, but he might have been a security guard.

Ben keyed his mike. "Twelve-A-Forty-five, we're code six on a man down—" That was all he got out before he sensed something huge rushing into his peripheral vision, and turned to see the grille looming on his side of the car, the blue Ford F350 bearing down on them with it's headlights out. Ben leaned in away from the passenger door, hunching his shoulders against the impact, as the crunch of metal against metal buckled his door, throwing his body back against it. His right shoulder slammed into the grille that now filled his shattered window.

He thought they'd been T-boned by a drunk or a panic-stricken driver. Then the body in the street was suddenly up and running. Boscoe, it was Boscoe playing possum, sprinting off into the darkness because he must have known what was coming and had no stomach for it. Boscoe glanced back over his shoulder, his eyes begging Marquez's forgiveness. Now Marquez was telling Ben to put out a help call. A fucking ambush, he said, but his voice sounded far away.

Ben fumbled for the mike, but he was blinded by the high beams of another truck, this one charging out of the alley to ram them head-on. Squinting against the white light, Marquez had his gun up on target, putting rounds out through their windshield. Booming not two feet from Ben's head, his big Smith .45 sounded strangely faint, like the popping of a champagne cork. Ben watched the shells eject in slow motion, glowing silver in the swelling high beams as they flipped one by one onto the dash, little holes appearing where his rounds punched out through the windshield.

The truck's left headlight shattered and winked out, but it was still coming fast. "Brace yourself," Marquez said as the collision folded their front hood like a sheet of tinfoil. Ben didn't see his airbag deploy. It was just suddenly there, as if someone had sliced a frame out of the film. He was watching the windshield turn milky and CUT TO: something firm and white pushing hard against his face.

The black-and-white shuddered and jumped. They were still moving, the truck coming on like a bulldozer to shove them backward. Their rear wheels hopped the curb and their bumper sheared a fire hydrant from its bolts, a geyser pounding their car from below, the water somehow punching through, a tide rising to cover the floor mats and now churning up over their seats. Sizzling sparks as water fried the radio. Ben heard the truck's door opening. He sensed figures moving and circling outside, but he couldn't reach his gun. The airbag had him pinned.

Marquez groaned, head lolling back against his headrest. Ben could see the spidery bulge in the windshield where Marquez's head had almost gone through it, his nose split open, blood covering his mustache like paint on a brush and pouring down the front of him to cloud the rising water.

The water was up to Ben's chest, cold enough to put his legs to sleep. He struggled, somehow got his knife out, plunging the blade into the airbag until it sagged. The truck had backed away. Dark figures were at the doors now, wedging crowbars into the seams to get at them. No help was coming. Ben hadn't put out the broadcast. No one even knew their location. "Miguel," Ben coughed. "I can't reach my shit. Hand me your gun."

Men were on the hood now, stomping the windshield down on them. Marquez mumbled something, made almost inaudible by the blood bubbling around his lips. "Kill me," he gurgled. "Don't let them take me there."

Clawlike hands reaching hungrily through the broken windshield, tearing Ben's uniform shirt. Ben twisted away and stabbed at them until his knife was yanked from his hand. He reached for his gun, but a big hand held his wrist. He bit down hard on brown fingers, feeling knuckles crunch like drumsticks. He heard screams, probably his own. They were pulling him out by his hair.

With a yank on the crowbars, Ben's door creaked open and the sudden pull of bloody water swept him out into the street. He heard the water gurgling into a storm drain and for a wild moment Ben thought he might escape that way. Gripping the grate, he tried to lift it, but Timberland boots smashed down on his fingers. They stood over him, dark faces blotting out the night sky, howling and laughing as they stomped him. Ben's ribs buckled and a bottle exploded against the back of his head, bringing welcome darkness.

PRESENT

As long as he lived, Ben would never forget the stench of that place, the way it shouldered into his nostrils until he choked himself awake; the yeasty odor of malt liquor, marijuana, sweat, urine, and something else: this darkly thrilling musk, like the scent of an animal's den. His eyes adjusted slowly in the torchlight. Marquez and Ben lay with their hands cuffed in front of them, curled on the dirt floor of a long-abandoned Quonset warehouse.

Generations of Boot Hill Mafia Crip graffiti tattooed the corrugated steel walls, crude renderings of the Boot Hill two-fingered gang sign and a stylized scrawl of names, the gang's roll call, all the B's and H's crossed out to mark their avowed hatred for Bloods and Hoovers, most of it sprayed over so many times, the messages overlapping and absorbing each other, that the walls had become an indecipherable tangle of glyphs, cave paintings in the torchlight.

Sheets of corrugated metal curved to meet in a high, canopied ceiling, the entire structure on the verge of collapse and supported by a half-assed, asymmetrical web of sagging crossbeams, struts, and braces. Brownish water dripped from holes rusted through the steel, and charcoal-colored pigeons roosted along the rotting timber struts. Old Air Jordans, British Knights, and Adidases hung by their laces from the crossbeams, tossed up there for reasons beyond his ken. Hanging among the shoes, wispy scraps of flesh flapped like tattered parchment on lengths of fishing line. Dried scalps.

The only light in the warehouse bubbled out of bamboo tiki torches, shoved into the dirt around the rim of a large pit in the center of the floor. Uneven stacks of wooden pallets surrounded the pit. A collection of oddly shaped stones positioned on those pallets. No, Ben realized, not stones. Flyblown skulls grinning in the torchlight, some with wide holes in them where bullets had punched through cranium, each skull marked with a blue B, for "Blood." Faint sounds rose from the pit, anxious scratching and scraping. Ben took in the pagan solemnity of those torches, the skulls, the ritual care taken in their placement around the pit. He knew where they were now and Marquez had been right asking for death before this. *Kill me. Don't let them take me there.*

Dim figures milled in the darkness around Ben, thirty or more, most of them just shuffling and kicking the dirt. A few lit-up blunts, faces briefly illuminated, and then gone again. They joked and jived, chuckling with nervous anticipation, wanting to get this party started or eager to get it over with. They had to know every cop in L.A. would be looking for them by now, but were they? If the Boot Hill Mafia had a scanner, or a stolen rover, they'd know Ben never had time to put out a help call, never even broadcast their original Code Six location. By now, someone would have found their black-and-white, stripped and burned. By the time they realized their bodies weren't in the car, there would be no trail of bread crumbs to follow. No, Ben thought, the fun here was just beginning.

His head throbbed and he gently probed the inside of his mouth with his tongue, some back teeth cracked and missing. Marquez lay with his back to him, hurt bad. Ben could hear his ragged, even breathing, but he didn't risk whispering to him.

On the other side of the pit, he glimpsed a stack of a dozen olive-drab crates with a canvas tarpaulin draped haphazardly over them. The tarp was also marred by Crip graffiti, but this paint more vivid, fresher. Seeing the crates, Ben remembered what Wacc had said about Risley stockpiling the kind of ordnance Saddam wouldn't fuck with.

Someone shoved the tarp aside and set a boom box on top of the green crates. DJ Post-Mortem's "Barbequed Pork" thumped out of the boom box, the bass line rippling the corrugated walls.

Someone stepped over Ben, unzipped, and pissed on his head, hot urine spattering his face. "Rise and shine," the voice cackled. Ben twisted away, rolling, reaching for the .38 on his ankle, but it was gone. Rough hands yanked him upright and did the same to Marquez, but he was still out cold. His bloody head hung down, chin against his chest. A kid not more than fifteen, wearing a black wave cap, dashed out of the dark to tear Ben's badge off his shirt, holding the badge aloft like he'd caught a fly ball. The others whooped, snatched for it, but the kid fought them off. Another guy in cornrows and a plaid shirt ripped off Ben's nameplate, turning the trophy in his hands to catch the light. Their Sam Browne belts were already long gone. Poway Charlie, carrying a sawed-off shotgun, wore their belts across his chest like bandoliers.

Sleepy Loc shuffled toward Ben, in no particular hurry, Ben not going anywhere. He lifted his right hand, snapped his fingers, and someone tossed him an aluminum spray can. Sleepy Loc grooved to Post-Mortem, a low-key hip grind, shaking the can like a maraca. Ben struggled to turn away from him, but Sleepy gripped Ben's hair in his fist, holding Ben in place while he covered Ben's face in black spray paint. Ben gasped, blinded for a moment, blinking the caustic paint out of his eyes. "Now *you* the nigga," Sleepy Loc said with a heavy-lidded grin.

Daddy Python, the bare-chested Goliath, his hair set in foam curlers, signature Colt Python jammed in his waistband, was pushing up eight big plates on a rusty weight bench in the corner. He slammed the barbell back into the rack, stood, and beat his fists against his massive, sweat-slick chest. Ben saw the blood-soaked bandanna wrapped around the last two fingers of Daddy Python's right hand where Ben had bitten him.

"*Hell, yes!*" Daddy Python blared, working his trunklike neck around to get the kinks out, pig eyes glittering in the firelight. "I'm gone get me some," Daddy Python said, eyeing Ben, kiss-kissing and licking his lips. He reached down to give himself a squeeze. "Bust me a little pink ass." Murmurs and nervous giggles from the Boot Hill Mafia, everyone in the hood knew about Daddy Python's prison-honed predilections.

"Hold him," Daddy Python said, digging a box cutter out of his pocket, and Sleepy Loc and Poway Charlie fell on Ben. Ben rolled, bucked, and twisted. His feet lashed out, catching Poway Charlie in the gut, hearing the air huff out of him, but it wasn't enough. He was only delaying the inevitable. Daddy Python watched the three of them scrambling in the dirt, and he was clearly excited by the struggle. They had Ben pinned now, Sleepy Loc's knee pressing down on the back of his neck, grinding his face into the dirt, each labored breath a small blast of gritty dust.

"My father has money," Ben pleaded, repulsed by the sound of his own mewling as Daddy Python kneeled behind him and pulled down his pants. "Please don't do this." Ben heard Daddy Python's fly and felt him, dowel-hard, pushing against his buttocks.

"This here the God of Abraham, *bwoy*," Daddy Python said huskily, gripping Ben's hips. "He gone purge you of all your wickedness." It was rummaging against his anus now. The frenzied Boot Hill Mafia leaped and danced in the torchlight. Ben screaming, begging, bawling, as he was torn apart, wanting Marquez to wake up and then praying he wouldn't. When it was over, medallions of viscous blood speckled the dirt between Ben's legs and Daddy Python threw back his head, bellowing triumphant laughter.

Then a single shot cranked into the air and silenced them. The pigeons fluttered and swooped in a small panic, then settled back onto the crossbeams. Ben pulled up his trousers. Please let me live, he prayed. Let me live and I will kill them all.

The crowd parted for two men strutting out of the shadows to stand in the shimmering spill of firelight. Risley and Mapes wore identical black ski masks and black windbreakers over their uniforms. "Found a dance partner, mayonnaise?" Risley chuckled, nodding at Daddy Python. Then he turned to the others, his mask sucking against his mouth. "String 'em up."

Ben's handcuffs were hooked to a long chain fed through some kind of pulley on a boom high above them, the other end hooked to Marquez's cuffs. Risley motioned them forward, Sleepy Loc and Daddy Python hauling Ben to the edge of the pit. Ben struggled weakly, dug his heels in, plowing furrows in the dirt as they dragged him forward. They pulled Marquez along, his head flopping, legs trailing behind him like a paraplegic's.

They held Marquez upright next to Ben so that the two of them more or less stood at the edge. Ben peered down into darkness, at first mistaking the movement at the bottom for surging liquid. A madrigal of keening whines rose from the dark. "We've been starving 'em," Risley said. "If they don't get meat soon, they gone to turn on each other." Risley stepped between Ben and Marquez, placing his hands on both their shoulders. "Marquez here is heavier," Risley whispered to Ben. "So he gone go first and you get to watch."

Now Ben saw the dogs in the pit, faces upturned, lips drawn back over bright teeth, pig eyes glittering with inbred ferocity. Pit bulls piled and leaped over each other, scrambling and snarling. Their jaws snapped wetly on empty air. Bones littered the floor around them.

"But this boy got to be awake for it or it's just no goddamn fun." Risley slapped Marquez's face, but Marquez's head just lolled to one side, a string of bloody drool dangling from his open mouth. Then Risley leaned in close, using his fingers to pry open Marquez's right eye.

Marquez came alive all at once, head-butting Risley, Risley's head snapping backward as he dropped to his knees. Then, before Daddy Python and Sleepy Loc could fully regain control of him, Marquez quickly turned and spat a bloody gob onto Ben's right wrist.

Risley peeled off his mask, already soaked through with his own blood. His eyes watered, blood leaking from his nose. Stoned laughter burbled out of the Boot Hill Mafia. Marquez just smiled down at him, baring his missing front teeth. "Gotcha," he said.

Mapes lurched forward and drew his weapon. "I got something for your bitch ass," Mapes said, pressing the muzzle of his .45 to Marquez's forehead.

"No!" Risley shouted, holding the mask wadded up against his broken nose, his voice now comically nasal. "That's just what he wants and I'm here to tell you this border brother's not getting off that easy." He motioned to Daddy Python and Sleepy Loc.

"Officer Miguel Marquez," Risley said. "For your arrogance, your preening narcisissm, your self-righteousness, your racism, and your failure to see the big picture, namely me, I sentence you to death."

Daddy Python shoved them over the edge of the pit. They dropped, handcuffs yanked over their heads, dangling side by side for a moment, the dogs crazed at the sight of them swinging there just out of reach. A few dogs leaped at them, but fell short. Then, Ben heard the pulley above them creak, Marquez's weight pulling him down as Ben was pulled up. The Boot Hill Mafia crowded the rim of the pit, cheering, spitting, and pissing. Marquez looked up at Ben, his words soft and very clear.

"Remember our first day out," Marquez said, as he was lowered into the pack. "Better to be judged by twelve than carried by six."

A speckled bitch, with a foreshortened snout that resembled a bat's, vaulted the pack, her jaws sinking deep into the meat of Marquez's left calf. She hung there, his blood filling the crinkles in her face. Marquez twisted and kicked, but he could not shake her. The dog dangled like a gator, her short legs splaying for unseen purchase, as her weight pulled him down.

The dogs were on him then, but Marquez did not cry out. Even as they tore the meat from his legs, he did not make a sound. Marquez turned his face upward, jaw set, temples pulsing, silent, as blood-painted muzzles rooted his bowels from his belly. Then his eyes turned soft and his head slumped forward, and Ben thought of all the things he'd never told him.

Then Ben felt it, a gentle slip where Marquez had spat on his wrist, the bloody cuff riding up over the heel of Ben's palm. None of them had seen it, still fixated on the charnel spectacle of Marquez. Twisting his right hand now, Ben worked the hand through the cuff, loving those delicate hands of his, his piano player's hands, his mother's hands.

Marquez outweighed Ben by forty pounds or so, but the dogs didn't take long to rend that away from him. The pulley creaked again, Marquez rising slowly out of the pack as Ben began to sink. *Remember our first day out.* As Marquez rose past him, Ben hooked his legs around Marquez's desiccated body, stopping them both, suspended midway over the snarling dogs.

The Boot Hill Mafia shouted down at him, Poway Charlie and Sleepy Loc leaning out over the pit, trying to reach the chain and shake Ben loose. Ben's right hand slipped free of the cuff. He touched Marquez's bloody cheek and slid his hand into the Velcro slot in Marquez's torn uniform, praying they hadn't found it. His fingers closed around the smooth sandalwood grip, Ben pulling the big-bore .357 Magnum free of its holster.

He looked up and saw Poway Charlie leaning out to shake the chain. Ben fired once, catching him in the groin, and Poway Charlie pitched forward, gripping Marquez's end of the chain as he fell. Their combined weight pulled them down, simultaneously pulling Ben up out of the pit.

Ben swung back and forth, firing blindly all around him. Some of them fired back, but they were panicked now, running in all directions. Ben's feet touched the rim of the pit. Ben toppling three of the torches as he rolled free of the pit. One of the torches fell on to the canvas tarp and set it afire. Ben dove over the top of the green crates, knocking one off the stack. He crouched behind them, bullets buzzing over his head. "Don't shoot, you dumb motherfuckers," Risley screamed. "You'll hit the rockets."

Ben opened the crate in front of him, and three dark green tubes rolled out of it, each about two feet long. He uncapped the end of one of the M-72A3 Light Antitank Weapons. Sights popped up, the inner tube extending another foot or so. Ben kneeled, gripping the trigger housing, and slid his thumb over the smooth top lever that had to be the trigger. "Okay," he heard himself say. "Okay."

Daddy Python charged up to the crates with his Colt in his right fist, but he stopped when Ben stood to face him with the LAW. Daddy Python was bringing his Colt up when Ben shoved the end of the tube into his gut and pressed the trigger. *Whoosh!* Daddy Python's face went blank, clouds of acrid gray smoke boiling around them. They just stood there facing each other as the smoke cleared and Ben thought the rocket had been a dud. Then Daddy Python fell backward, mannequin-stiff, a wide blood-less tunnel burned clean through his middle, the flesh scorched hard and black.

The opposite side of the warehouse was suddenly open to the night, the blackened steel around the edges peeled away, twisted by the force of the explosion. Smoldering bodies lay on the dirt floor. More bodies landed, clothing afire, in the field outside the warehouse. Timber struts splintered and fell. The ceiling groaned and sagged.

The Boot Hill Mafia scrambled in circles, crouching in the corners and crowding the exits. Ben heard people shouting orders over each other, somebody hazarding a wild shot that banged off the steel behind him. The fire spread, flames leaping from the tarp to the crates themselves. Ben dropped the spent LAW, dashing across the warehouse out through the gaping hole, but he was too slow, his body broken and bruised. Gunfire followed him out across the vacant lot, bullets whizzing all around him. Something stung his left calf and he collapsed in the tall grass in front of the train tracks.

He lay there, gasping. Pungent smoke, carrying the odor of charred flesh, and glowing motes of ash floating over him. He heard them at the edge of the field, four of them wading cautiously into the tall grass, fanned out like beaters on a tiger hunt. "He has to be in here," one of them grumbled. "I saw his ass fall in them weeds."

"Where?" Another voice barked anxiously.

"Over there somewhere." One of them prodded a badly burned body in the grass. "Yo, man, that Frog?"

"Looks like."

"*Damn*, he all fucked up."

Dry weeds scissored and gnashed around him. Where the hell was he, somewhere west of Western Avenue, maybe down around Hyde Park? Ben snaked his hand through the grass to close around the neck of a broken beer bottle. He heard dry popping, sizzling, and snapping as the fire chewed its way through the rest of the warehouse. The smoke thickened, the air got hotter, the fire's cacophonous crackling growing more insistent. The flames leaped, spreading to adjacent structures, everything burning.

Ben lay on his side, peering through the weeds to watch them come. They were about twenty feet from each other, stepping carefully through the waist-high grass. They coughed, swatting at curtains of rolling smoke.

"Shit burns my eyes." One of them sniffled, wiping a sleeve across his face as he probed a thick cluster of weeds with his foot.

They were close enough to Ben now that he knew which one it would have to be. If they kept to their current paths through the grass, it would be the tall one with the blue bandanna tied over his face, like a kid playing cowboys and Indians. He was going to walk right into Ben.

"If a body catch a body, comin' through the rye," the kid sang softly to himself, the damp bandanna sucking against his mouth with each breath.

Hot ash landed in the lot. Fires pocked the grass, spreading into a low wall of flame behind them. Ben could hear distant sirens, rotor blades slapping the smoky air—helicopters, belonging to the department or maybe the local news, probably following the smoke. Ben gripped the neck of the bottle and waited as sneakers trampled the grass in front of him. He was shaking, but not with fear. He felt the blood clotting between his legs and he wanted to kill them so badly that he actually shook in anticipation of the act.

The tall one stepped right over him, perhaps thinking Ben was another charred body. Ben rose up, hooked his arm around the guy's neck and brought him down into the grass. Jamming his hand over the bandanna, Ben drove the teeth of the broken bottle into the exposed throat, cranking it as he did. Ben pried the kid's gun from his fingers as blood welled up the green neck of the bottle, spouting thickly from its mouth. Ben rolled off him into a prone shooting position. All three of them now perfect silhouettes against the bright flames. He squeezed the trigger until the gun was empty, watching them writhe like shadow puppets as the bullets tore through their bodies.

Still more came running in behind them, rushing through the smoke, leaping the flames with their guns up, some of them holding two guns. No fear lived in them; they lived for this. This and nothing else, because there was only ever tonight and nothing to save for, no retirement, no dreams deferred, no life beyond this hood. Smile now and cry later. You got your span of years until someone got you and never, ever let any fool say you bitched out on your homeboys.

They couldn't have seen him, didn't seem to give a shit. They fired indiscriminately, muzzles flashing like strobes in the smoke, bullets slicing through the grass over Ben's head. Then the airship swooped in like a predatory bird, its night-sun spotlight over the smoking field like a white exclamation point. They fired up at the helicopter and the chopper peeled away with smoke swirling in its prop wash.

Then they stopped firing because they were closer now, close enough to hear him breathing, and close enough to see him if he stood. The ground vibrated beneath him and he heard the horn of a Southern Pacific freight heading out to the harbor. The tracks were maybe ten yards behind him. He belly-crawled through the grass toward the tracks, feeling the vibration grow to a rumble. He could see the train's single headlight, piercing the smoke as it came down the track. Just five yards to go, all of it wide open, the gravel rising out of the edge of the field to meet the tracks. No more grass to cover him, and the train was closing. Ben stood, hobbling the final five yards. He stumbled on loose gravel, falling onto the tracks in front of the train. Shouting and more gunshots. The engineer blew the air horn. The white headlight and the blunt face of the cowcatcher filled Ben's vision. Bullets kicking up gravel around him, sparking off the cowcatcher as he rolled over the tracks, down the gravel slope, putting the train between them.

Ben staggered east along the tracks, hoping he could make it to St. Andrews Place before one of them would be able to hop onto the train and drop over onto this side. It was a long freight, moving west at a good clip. He could hear them shouting over the racket of clanking freight cars, see them squatting to peer under the moving cars, trying to pace him from the other side.

Ben limped out onto St. Andrews Place, not far from the old Hostess Bakery, and sweet merciful God, a black-and-white rolled up. They fixed the takedown lights on him and hit the light bar. He didn't blame them, his uniform unrecognizable. He must have looked like a fucking maniac wandering in the middle of the street. They stood behind their open doors, drawing down on him. The driver shouted for Ben to get his hands up and turn around. His voice sounded strange, but Ben did as he was told, figuring he might do the same in their position. The driver told Ben to drop to his knees, then to his belly in a felony prone. A knee pushed into Ben's back, handcuffs biting into his wrists, but he was safe now. He was going to live. "You don't know how glad I am to see you." Ben coughed as they hauled him to his feet.

"We're glad to see you too, mayonnaise," Risley chuckled wetly, driving his knee up into Ben's gut, doubling him over. Then Mapes popped the trunk and together they stuffed Ben inside.

PRESENT

Even before Risley and Mapes hauled Ben out of the trunk, he'd had an idea where they would be taking him. He'd started counting the winding switchbacks and now he could smell the eucalyptus, even through the scent of burning houses that drifted on the Santa Anas. When Risley yanked him to his feet, he could see the city in flame.

"You know there's no bounty, right?" Ben said. All around him ashes fell like black snow.

"What's he talking about?" Mapes said.

The gate was standing open. Risley grabbed a fistful of Ben's shirt, and Risley led them past Darius's infinity pool.

"There's nothing for you up here," Ben said. "You got shit." Flakes of ash floated in the pool, and the orange shimmer of distant fires reflected in the rippling water. "You just crossed the biggest gang in town, asshole, and when they find out you killed Marquez they're going to hunt you down like dogs. Neither of you will ever see the inside of a courtoom."

"Cabe?" Mapes sounded scared.

"Shut up." Risley drove his fist into Ben's gut, doubling him over. "Don't let him fuck with your mind," Risley told Mapes. "He learned that shit from his pops. Stay with me now, Boo." Risley pulled Ben along the edge of the pool, past the rabbit hutch. "Keep your head in the game."

"The game's over." Ben coughed. "Jesus, look around."

The grounds had run to riot. Tall weeds pushed up between the paver tiles. Ivy snaked up the walls of the house like a jungle reclaiming some ancient temple. The paint was flaking, and one of the windows had been broken and patched with particleboard. This was the House of Usher, the seat of a fallen empire.

"Where's all his paid security, huh?" Ben said. "His entourage. Where?" After all these years it was back down to Darius and Jax.

"Boy, you can jaw." Risley flipped the toggle under the planter box, and the elevator doors opened. He shoved Ben into the elevator, Ben flopping onto one of the padded benches while the motor hummed.

Mapes hauled Ben to his feet and shoved him out into Darius's master bedroom the moment the doors hissed open. Ben staggered, nearly stumbling into Darius, but kept his feet. Darius had the news on his projection TV, and the riots played across his wall. There was a suitcase open on the bed. Ben could see Risley hadn't expected this.

"Here he is, D," Risley said.

Darius ignored Risley, taking in Ben's face like he didn't recognize him at first, searching the swollen mask of spray paint and caked blood for the man he'd known. Then Darius's eyes traveled down to the back of Ben's bloody pants. Darius's nostrils flared, his eyes moist and hot.

"Nigga, this shit is *vile*," Darius hissed at Risley through clenched teeth, mouth curling around the words as the childhood rage of that alley took hold of him. "I mean, Cabe, this shit beneath even *you*."

"What?" Risley gaped at him.

"Get out of my house," Darius said.

"I-I don't understand," Risley stammered, blinking.

"Did I stutter, nigga?" Darius said. "I said get your black ass out of my house. Go on. Go put some of those motherfuckin' fires out, *Officer*."

"I'll leave when I get my one hundred fifty thousand," Risley said, coming forward across the carpet. "*Nigga*."

"Oh, it's like that?" Darius said, grille to grille with Risley now.

"It's like that," Risley said.

Jax crossed the room to intervene, but Mapes, moving with more stealth and speed than Ben would have thought the big man commanded, stepped in front of Jax. Mapes shoved his Smith .45 into Jax's abdomen, stopping Jax midstride.

"Open the safe," Risley said. His grand designs for regime change come at last to this, Ben thought, another crummy home invasion.

Darius looked at Jax, then at Ben. He turned, heading into the walk-in closet. He knelt in front of the safe, ignoring the cooler on top of it, and worked the combination. The lock popped and the door clicked open about an inch.

Risley nodded subtly to Mapes. Bent over the safe, Darius couldn't see it, but Ben did. Mapes turned to Jax, angled his .45 low, and fired two hollow-point rounds into Jax's gut. The impact threw Jax backward against the stereo, but he somehow kept on his feet. He braced his hands against his knees and sucked air, trying to catch his breath, but Ben could tell by looking at him that Jax would never get it back. Blood and translucent gray loops of his intestine poured out of a fist-sized hole in his belly.

Darius wheeled around toward Ben, probably thinking Mapes had shot him. When Darius saw Jax slumped against the stereo, his jaw slackened.

"Daddy?" Darius whispered, rushing to Jax.

Risley stepped behind Darius, dug the muzzle of his Glock into Darius's lower back, and pulled the trigger. Darius fell hard. Ben watched helplessly as Darius struggled to his hands and knees. The blood welling from his ragged entry wound was almost black. Risley had blown out Darius's liver. If he didn't pass out from the pain, Darius had maybe ten minutes left.

Risley stepped around Darius to the safe. *Wait for it.* He reached his left hand into the safe and maybe Ben imagined hearing the wet crunch of the turtle's beak on Risley's fingers, but he didn't think so. Risley screamed, his body trembling like he'd touched a live wire. He dropped the gun. When he yanked his hand out of the safe, Ben saw that his index and middle fingers had been taken off at the knuckle. He looked like he was going to hyperventilate, staring at his ruined hand like it didn't belong to him. Then he turned to Mapes with the hand spouting blood, as if Mapes might have some explanation for it.

"Don't just stand there, homie," Mapes said. "Get some direct pressure on that shit." Risley staggered drunkenly toward the bathroom, his blood spattering the plastic sheet, and Mapes moved to help him. *Now.*

Ben pivoted and slammed his shoulder into Mapes, pinning him against the wall with his body, driving his knee up at Mapes's groin, but Mapes bladed his body in the textbook judo defense and Ben's knee glanced off his hip. Ben pressed his whole body against Mapes, hoping to somehow keep him from bringing his gun up, but it was no good. The muzzle came into Ben's peripheral vision as Mapes angled the gun at Ben's head, Ben cheek to cheek with Mapes now, feeling the stubble along Mapes's clenched jaw. Ben somehow got his mouth around Mapes's nose and bit down through the gristle, tasting warm, coppery blood. Mapes screamed. Ben pushed away from him, dove over the sofa, and rolled across the bed. Bullets punched holes into the wall behind Ben as he moved. Pillows exploded, spewing a storm of white feathers into the room. Ben dropped to the opposite side of the bed and crouched against the wall, trying to make himself as small as possible. He heard Mapes's gun go to slide-lock, Mapes popping out the empty magazine as he reached for a fresh one. Ben curled his body, tucked his legs, and brought the cuffs up under his feet. His wrists were still bound, but at least his hands were in front of him. Maybe, if he could just—

"I got him," Mapes said, stepping around the bed to loom over Ben with his .45. "I got something for his ass." Mapes didn't see Darius staggering behind him, didn't see Darius twist the diamond-eyed skull and draw the sword from his cane, but Mapes had time to see the blade burst through his own chest just before it stopped his heart. He looked down at the blood-slick steel sprouting from his sternum with detached curiosity. Then his eyes rolled over and he vomited bright blood, falling sideways onto the bed. Darius dropped the sword on the carpet. He leaned against the wall, gasping. Then he slid down the wall to his knees.

Risley came out of the bathroom with a bloody hand towel tied around his left hand. He looked at Mapes, then at Ben and Darius. Risley appeared strangely calm as he pulled the Masai Simi sword off the wall and walked into the center of the room.

Darius nodded to his sword on the carpet. "Get him, G." He panted.

"Okay." Ben spoke softly, almost to himself. "Yeah, okay." He picked up Darius's sword, finding a two-handed grip that worked with the hand-cuffs.

They circled each other in front of the projection television. Looters ran across their bodies, and fire flowed over them like lava. Risley raised the Simi high over his head as he moved, Ben crouched low, his sword angled in front of him. Risley waited until Ben circled in front of the projector, squinting against the glare. He brought the Simi down, blade hissing as it descended. Ben sidestepped, parried, and swung at Risley's head. Risley ducked, driving his shoulder into Ben's chest, knocking him off his feet, the Simi stabbing down at him, sticking in the floor as Ben rolled away.

Risley pulled the sword out of the floor and lunged as Ben regained his feet, the Simi slicing into the meat of Ben's left shoulder. Ben cried out, staggering backward into the wall. He pulled the tall bookshelf over in Risley's path. Risley leaped over the fallen bookshelf, bringing his sword down as he landed. Ben raised his sword to meet him. Blue sparks as their blades clashed together, leaning into each other, almost nose to nose, shifting their footing with their swords locked. Ben shifted his weight, his elbow strike catching Risley under the eye. Risley pirouetted, the Simi coming around to slice deeply across Ben's shoulder blades. Ben's sword spun out of his grip and he stumbled forward out onto the landing. He tried to get up, slipped in his own blood, and fell again.

Risley came through the door and saw Ben on his knees with his hands in his lap, as though awaiting his execution. Ben looked exhausted, utterly defeated. Risley chuckled as he came forward across the landing and stood over Ben. He raised the Simi over his head.

"Any last words, mayonnaise?" Risley was standing on the X of blue duct tape. Behind him, the jaguar perched on the ottoman like a gargoyle. The cat lowered its head, churning its gearlike shoulders in anticipation.

"*Ulaga*," Ben said and he could have sworn the big cat smiled, emitting a low rumble, like the revving of a powerful engine. Risley's eyes widened at the sound and he whirled around, bringing the sword up too late.

The jaguar seemed to explode from the ottoman, its smooth body lengthening, vaporous musculature uncoiling, teeth and talons seeming to reach Risley even before the creature's back legs had left the ottoman. Risley's scream silenced as the impact jackknifed him, knocking the breath from his lungs, his body sickeningly folded by force undreamed. The useless sword flew from Risley's hand, clattering along the marble floor. The creature landed astride Risley's crumpled form, splayed claws playfully kneading Risley's chest.

Ben stood, back against the wall, picking his way along the landing, staying beyond the creature's reach. The jaguar growled at Ben, but the sound was jubilant, not hostile. Its jaws closed over Risley's exposed throat, curved fangs puncturing his flesh, like nails driven into soft clay. With its mouth still clamped on Risley's gullet, the jaguar backpedaled, dragging Risley to the ottoman by his neck. Risley's limbs flopped weakly, no real fight left in him. Blood gurgled from Risley's torn throat and bubbled from his nostrils. Risley's eyes rolled, finding Ben as he sidestepped back into the bedroom. Risley might have been trying to say something, but by then the cat had taken most of his windpipe.

Ben stumbled back into the bedroom, falling when he saw the two of them, his knees splashing down into their blood. Darius crawled across the room to where Jax sat slumped against the stereo. He threw his arms around Jax's neck, shoulders shaking.

"Daddy," Darius sobbed, forehead nuzzling Jax's cheek. Their blood pooled, spreading across the carpet, running under the bed.

"Don't you ever let me see you cry like a bitch, *bwoy*," Jax whispered, but his eyes were unfocused now, far away. "Get mad, *bwoy*. Get . . ." Jax's voice trailed off and his head slumped to his chest, wet curls falling over his face. Darius hugged him like that, crying into his chest, until Darius's arms fell away and he sagged into Jax and it was over.

EPILOGUE

The riots seemed to burn themselves out after news of Marquez's death hit the airwaves as though his blood sacrifice had appeased them somehow. All the liquor and electronics had been pretty well picked over by then anyway, no windows left worth smashing. A few holdout marauders were still lobbing rocks at the Five-Oh, but most folks had lost interest. Their fever broken, they wandered dazedly back to their homes to sort through their loot while the governor surveyed the damage from a helicopter.

Ben thought it should have rained for Marquez's funeral, but the L.A. gods grieve for no man, and they refused to make an exception for Marquez. Overnight, warm Santa Anas blew the lingering clouds of carbon out to the desert, clearing the entire basin by dawn. After the sprinklers stopped that morning, and the sun hit the green slopes of Forest Lawn Memorial Park, you could almost believe it was going to be all right.

The pipe band led the procession; proud retirees in feathered caps and pleated kilts coaxed somber tunes from bagpipes as they headed up the winding road to his plot. They were followed by his hearse, a limo for the family, another for the mayor and the chief, and a squadron of black-and-whites, light bars flashing. The rest of them marched in formation, a river of blue decked out in their Class-A's, long sleeves, clip-on ties, and stiff hats. Halfway up and they were already sweating, but they managed to stay in step. Every spit-shined shoe hit the asphalt in rough unison, every polished badge catching the brilliant sunlight at once.

Ben and Vintner were among his pallbearers, pulling his casket from the back of the hearse. They slid steel handles into symmetrical slots under the coffin so they could carry him without killing their fingers. He wasn't as heavy as they thought he'd be because most of him wasn't in there. They set him down on some kind of lowering device rigged over the plot, and the honor guard carefully draped the flag over him.

They stood at attention while the mourners filed into rows of white folding chairs set up on the lawn. A mariachi band stood under an oak tree behind the casket. Ben saw a seventyish couple that could only be Marquez's parents. His mother was a handsome, sturdy woman. She wore a black veil and fingered her rosary throughout the service. His father had the same Easter Island brow, the same masonry cheekbones, and the same prideful chin. He looked like a Mexican Chuck Connors. He wore black cowboy boots and a black suit with a bolo tie. His hair was the color of roadside snow with a little diesel exhaust in it, and he walked with a cane.

The department chaplain took the podium and said the way for evil to triumph is for good people to do nothing, but those words held no solace and Ben drifted. The chaplain yielded the podium to the old priest from St. Rafael's, who delivered a eulogy in Spanish. When he was finished, people crossed themselves and Marquez's mother kissed her rosary.

Then Mal was up, the mourners shifting and whispering their disapproval as he walked to the podium. Mal bowed his head, silencing them with the sight of his crusted sutures, like a breast pocket sewn into his scalp. He opened a copy of Maurice Sendak's *Where the Wild Things Are*.

Mal began to read, his voice carrying over the lawn, of Max in his wolf suit, staring down monsters. "And they were frightened," Mal read, "and called him the most wild thing of all." He stopped there, and closed the book.

"Wicked men feared Miguel," Mal said, coughing into his fist. He allowed himself a wistful smile. "Havin' been a wicked man myself, I can *attest* to that. The Lord hung some tooth and claw on this man and I reckon He was often pleased with how Miguel put those gifts to use.

"Courage is pleasin' to the Lord," Mal said. "And Miguel had more courage on him than any man I know. It's no secret we didn't always see eye to eye, but he always knew I had respect for him and I'm here to tell y'all I got love for him." Mal grimaced, touching his fist to his chest, a brotha-to-brotha salute. "*Vaya con Dios,* my brother."

Then a formation of helicopters flew overhead, one peeling away from the group to symbolize the Missing Man.

The honor guard lifted Old Glory from Marquez's casket with a series of practiced maneuvers and folded it into a precise, triangular parcel. The chief handed the folded flag to Marquez's mother.

The mariachis bowed their heads, softly playing "Misión Cumplida de Mi Padre" as the machine lowered his coffin into the moist dirt. His father got out of his chair and lurched for the sinking coffin, slipped in the grass, and went to his knees. "*Lo siento, mijo.*" The man cried. He tore up the grass and howled and cursed God as the earthmovers pushed dirt over his son's casket. The mariachis played on because silence would have only made it worse.

Ben waited while the crowd wandered back down the slope. When he thought he was alone, Ben placed a river rock on his headstone and said Kaddish.

Yis'ga'dal v'yis'kadash sh'may ra'bbo, b'olmo dee'vro chir'usay
v'yamlich malchu'say, b'chayaychon uv'yomay'chon uv'chayay
d'chol bais Yisroel, ba'agolo u'viz'man koriv; v'imru Omein.

He stammered, losing track of the words for a moment because now he could smell his father's cologne. He sighed, but did not turn around.

Y'hay shmay rabbo m'vorach l'olam ul'olmay olmayo.
Yisborach v'yishtabach v'yispoar v'yisromam v'yismasay, v'yishador
v'yis'aleh v'yisalal, shmay d'kudsho, brich hu, l'aylo min kol
birchoso v'sheeroso, tush'bechoso v'nechemoso, da,ameeran
b'olmo; v'imru Omein.

Y'hay shlomo rabbo min sh'mayo, v'chayim alaynu v'al kol Yisroel;
  v'imru Omein.
Oseh sholom bimromov, hu ya'aseh sholom olaynu, v'al kol yisroel;
  v'imru Omein.

When Ben was finished, his father stepped around from behind him and placed his own rock on the headstone next to Ben's. Still, Ben would not look at him.

"So what will you do now?" Big Ben said, keeping his voice light, as if they just were picking up an old conversation.

"I don't know," Ben said, gently toeing the freshly packed dirt.

"Because, I was thinking, if you wanted, you could come home with me," Big Ben said. "Maybe just chill at the house for a while, while you decide what's next, you know?"

"I hate you," Ben said. Then Ben turned, collapsing into him, arms tight around Big Ben's shoulders.

"Me too, son," Big Ben said, holding him, "with all my heart."

ABOUT THE AUTHOR

Will Beall is a Los Angeles police officer. He works in 77th Division.